"State your identification. And the crime to whs."

His prisoner, li_____and all in lawful su_____y—Andrej asked h_____*it would be difficult?*

Or had he, in fact, been afraid that it was going to be this easy all along?

His father had been right to send him here, and he had known from the beginning how wrong it had been for him to try to resist his father's will. He had been misguided and mistaken, and he could have had this pleasure all along, because it was all his for the taking.

He had weeks of lost time to make up for.

AN EXCHANGE OF HOSTAGES

SUSAN R. MATTHEWS

AVON BOOKS • NEW YORK

AN EXCHANGE OF HOSTAGES is an original publication of Avon Books. This work has never before appeared in book form. This work is a novel. Any similarity to actual persons or events is purely coincidental.

AVON BOOKS
A division of
The Hearst Corporation
1350 Avenue of the Americas
New York, New York 10019

Copyright © 1997 by Susan R. Matthews
Cover art by Gregory Bridges
Published by arrangement with the author
Library of Congress Catalog Card Number: 96-97092
ISBN: 0-380-78913-2

First AvoNova Special Printing: November 1996
First AvoNova Printing: April 1997

AVONOVA TRADEMARK REG. U.S. PAT. OFF. AND IN OTHER COUNTRIES, MARCA REGISTRADA, HECHO EN U.S.A.

Printed in the U.S.A.

RA 10 9 8 7 6 5 4 3 2 1

◆ Acknowledgments

During the years I've spent working on this story there were some people who just never stopped nagging me, making it their business to see that I didn't give up. There's no better time nor place than this to gratefully acknowledge the love and support of Regina Gottesman, Linda Deneroff, Sheila Willis, Security 0.5, Steve Gallacci (who coined the term "bond-involuntary"), and many others besides. This book is a product of their persistence and of the patience and forbearance of Maggie Nowakowska, who's had more to put up with than anyone else.

An Exchange of Hostages is dedicated with profound appreciation to eluki bes shahar for making it happen. Her passionate championship of my book opened the door for me to what every writer dreams of finding someday—an audience.

AN EXCHANGE
OF HOSTAGES

◆ One

Andrej Koscuisko stood at the view-port watching with dread as the ship neared the Station. There was a signal at the talkalert; sighing, he keyed it.

"Yes, Danitosh."

The Station came closer moment by moment, a bleak lifeless piece of galactic debris with a self-contained school for potential Ship's Surgeons sprawled over its surface. He didn't like it; but there was no sense in making things harder on the crew of this ship than they already were. It was simply their bad luck that the *Pride of Place* had been going in the same direction as the disgraced son of the head of the Koscuisko familial corporation, just at the time the ship had been ready to leave.

"Cleared through to offload, Your Excellency. You're to be met. A Tutor named Chonis expects to be greeting you."

"Yes, very good," Andrej murmured halfheartedly. He was late arriving. He hadn't wanted to come. He was more frightened of what awaited him than he thought he'd ever been in his life. He couldn't take his eyes off the view-port, consumed with apprehension as the ship neared for landing.

Ugly piece of rock.

Ugly Station.

Grim cold utilitarian dock-port, the ship's tugs at least eight years old, and all alike. Fleet resources. Fleet Orientation Station Medical, where potential Ship's Surgeons all had to come to learn how to Inquire.

If he'd guessed beforehand what his father would wish,

1

would he have completed his medical training?

He was here now, and there was no help for it. He would do what was needful. His father had said the word. That was all.

Gathering up his documents-case, Andrej quickly leafed through flimsies one final time. How to salute. How to speak to a Tutor. How to conduct oneself as a Student, soon to become a Chief Medical Officer. CMO was all very well, a position of significant influence and power on a cruiserkiller-class warship upholding the Judicial order in the space-lanes. Any young surgeon would jump at the opportunity.

It was only that he did not want to Inquire.

The wait-room on the loading docks was small, almost cramped, even with only two people sharing it; and one was Security. Curran hardly counted. There was the smell of too much waste fuel in the air, and more noise than could be comfortably borne for very long without ear-stops for protection. Tutor Chonis suppressed an impatient twitch of annoyance as he stood waiting for his Student to arrive. Just enough time for a final scan through the scroller, and he would be ready for the interview.

ANDREJ ULEXEIEVITCH KOSCUISKO, STANDARD SCAN ANDREW SON OF ILEX. PRONOUNCED **AHN**-DRAY YOU-**LECHS'**VICH KOE-**SHOO**-SKOE. OLDEST SON OF RANKING KOSCUISKO PRINCE ALEXIE ILMYANITCH AND PRINCE INHERITOR TO KOSCUISKO FAMILIAL CORPORATION, DOLGORUKIJ COMBINE. EIGHT YEAR COURSE OF STUDY, MAYON SURGICAL COLLEGE, MAYON MEDICAL CENTER, MAYON, GRADUATION WITH HIGHEST HONORS IN SURGERY AND HONORS IN PSYCHOPHARMACOLOGY. NO FAMILY MEMBERS ACTIVE IN FLEET. HOMEWORLD OF ORIGIN AZANRY, DOLGORUKIJ COMBINE, SANT-DASIDAR JUDICIARY.

Andrej Koscuisko.

Tutor Chonis shut his scroller down and marshaled his thoughts together. First contact, Student and Tutor. This could make or break the entire Term. It was important to get off on a good cycle. There was to be enough stress on Student Koscuisko as the Term progressed without the existence of conflict between him and his Tutor.

"Let's go, then," Chonis said. The telltales on the wall gave notice that the incoming craft had come to rest and was ready to offload. Curran keyed the exit, standing to one side for the Tutor to precede him out onto the apron of the loading dock.

Out on the apron, a maintenance team had taken custody of Koscuisko's personal effects; and there was the Student, standing alone, staring off toward the open end of the maintenance atmosphere.

"Attention to the Tutor," Curran called from behind him, to put Student Koscuisko on notice. Koscuisko looked over his shoulder at that; turning around, he started toward them, not quite hurrying but quickly enough. Once he was within a reasonable distance he stopped, saluting politely. "Student Koscuisko reports at the Fleet's invitation. Tutor Chonis?"

Student Koscuisko was blond and pale, and looked a little on the slightly built side of the Jurisdiction Standard; but Tutor Chonis wasn't taken in. Koscuisko was Dolgorukij. And Dolgorukij packed muscle. It was just that the way they packed muscle wasn't obvious to look at them.

"Good-greeting, Student Koscuisko. I trust you had good transit?"

There was the suspicion of a frown on Koscuisko's face at that, quickly smoothed over. "Thank you, Tutor Chonis." Tenor voice, and pale eyes. Polite enough, though, as was usually the case with aristocrats. "It was a quiet transit."

Koscuisko knew very well he was late. Koscuisko offered no excuses. On the other hand Chonis hadn't asked for any. "Student Koscuisko, as your briefing states, you are to be under my tutelage. You have only a few months in which to learn all that Fleet will require of you; no time like the present for us to begin. Joslire Curran. Present yourself."

Curran stepped forward from where he had posted himself two paces behind Tutor Chonis, to his left. "At the Tutor's direction." Curran was a little taller than Koscuisko, but not by much; and his face had more contour. Curran was as dark as Koscuisko was fair, even after his years here on Station away from solar browning. Right now Curran was as tense as Tutor Chonis had ever seen him—though Koscuisko might not realize that. Koscuisko was unlikely to have met

Emandisan before. Emandisan off-world were almost always
Security; and as far as Tutor Chonis knew, Joslire Curran
was the only bond-involuntary Emandisan in the Inventory.

"Curran, Student Koscuisko is your officer of assignment
for this Term. Student Koscuisko. I'm sure you've noticed
that Curran is bond-involuntary." Watching Koscuisko's
face, Tutor Chonis caught Koscuisko's quick glance at the
telltale green piping on Curran's sleeves. "Curran is tasked
by the Administration with seeing to your meals, your exercise, and whatever administrative matters may arise."

Koscuisko regarded Curran with a look of frank and good-
natured curiosity, which Tutor Chonis found rather engaging.
He hoped that Student Koscuisko and Joslire Curran would
sort well with each other. The man deserved a break; last
Term had been unusually rough on him. But they couldn't
afford to sideline one of their best while Orientation was in
session. There weren't enough bond-involuntaries assigned
for that.

"The Administration anticipates that you may not have
worked with bond-involuntaries before. It's important that
you take this opportunity to explore their resources and their
limitations."

It would be very unusual if Koscuisko had even met a
bond-involuntary, outside of Fleet. There weren't that many
of them to start out with.

"Curran will provide you every assistance; you should not
hesitate to make any of your needs or desires known to him,
howsoever personal. When you are posted to your Command, you can safely anticipate at least one Security team
of bond-involuntaries will be assigned to you." In Fleet,
bond-involuntaries could be assigned only to Chief Medical
Officers, in fact, and to no other officer on staff.

And that about covered things for their first briefing. Nodding at Curran, Tutor Chonis gave Student Koscuisko his
dismissal. "I will see you this evening in Tutor's Mess,
where I will introduce you to your fellow Student. Tutor's
Mess at sixteen, and be prepared to discuss your background
and your interest in the field of Judicial administration. That
will be all for now. Curran, you may take your Student to
quarters."

Koscuisko saluted with easy grace; Curran gestured politely toward the liftaccess corridor. "If Student Koscuisko would care to proceed?"

Tutor Chonis watched as they left, Curran giving directions as they went.

He hadn't known quite what to expect from Student Koscuisko.

He wasn't sure he knew any more about him now than he had before this interview.

It didn't matter.

There was no predicting how Students responded to the pressures the practical exercises put on them.

There were five levels between the loading docks and the administrative area where Koscuisko had quarters. Student Koscuisko hadn't spoken to him; nervous, perhaps. That was almost funny. Ship's Surgeons exercised absolute power over the bodies and lives of bond-involuntaries; why should Koscuisko be nervous?

Most of the Students Joslire had seen hadn't wanted to be here, though they'd volunteered. That was none of his business. When the liftcar arrived Joslire keyed the offload; as the doors slid away, Koscuisko straightened up a bit, alerted perhaps by the noise or the change in air pressure. Turning, Koscuisko caught Joslire's eye; and Joslire gazed hungrily at his new officer, anxious for something that might give him a clue as to what kind of Term this one was going to be.

Staring too long could be interpreted as insolence, and his governor would not tolerate insolence. Joslire broke eye contact, bowing hastily.

"Show me to my quarters, if you please, Curran," the officer said, moving past Joslire to gain the corridor outside. Pleasant and formal, and neither promise nor threat to be read in the Student's voice. Yet. Joslire hurried out of the car before the doors closed on him, hastening to his duty with resignation.

"To the officer's right." The senior member on a standard four-soul Security team led by direction, not example. One of the things that the officer was expected to learn was how to figure out where he was going by listening to the voice

of a Security post behind him. "It will be to the officer's
left at the next nexus, eight doors down."

Eight doors down the hall after the left turning. Joslire
could almost hear the officer counting to himself. There was
little to distinguish one door from another; so when the officer paused, Joslire confirmed the guess indirectly, disguising his reassurance as an explanation.

"The admit panel is to the officer's right. In the recess."
Not where the officer was accustomed to finding it, so much
was obvious. The Dolgorukij Combine Koscuisko came from
was a parochial system, very rich, very insular, rather primitive in many ways by the Jurisdiction Standard. For all Joslire knew, Koscuisko was accustomed to finding rooms
behind tall wooden doors, pivoting inward on old-fashioned
hinges.

After a moment's fumbling at the doorjamb, the officer
found the admit, and the door opened. The interior was familiar to Joslire in its functional severity: Fleet issue sleep-
racks, Fleet issue floor-covering, Fleet-issue studyset, and an
open closet full of Fleet-issue uniforms. Joslire already knew
that there was an unpleasant surprise in quarters for the officer. He wondered how Koscuisko was going to react to it.

After a moment Koscuisko stepped across the threshold;
Joslire followed on Koscuisko's heels, closing the door behind him. Posting himself near the door, Joslire watched as
Koscuisko took inventory: the washroom at the left beside
the closet, with the toilet's gray metal privacy barrier clearly
visible through the open door and the wet-shower beyond;
the sleep-rack to the right and the studyset in the middle of
the room; the inner room beyond, half-visible past the par-
tially closed slider. Koscuisko—his back stiff and his shoulders tense with understandable confusion—moved around
the studyset and stood in the doorway to the inner chamber
with his back still to Joslire, puzzling out the problem, looking for his luggage. It didn't matter that Joslire had only the
back of the officer's head to judge his reactions by. Bond-
involuntaries learned very quickly to read an officer's moods
from the other side of his face.

The officer spoke, finally. "I had brought some personal

effects with me," Koscuisko said mildly. "I do not see any of my house-master's packing here."

Nor would he. "As the officer states." Technically speaking Koscuisko was not an officer yet, but Joslire's governor would not fault him for using the formal title. It was safer to use the formal title, for the same reason that it was safer to keep to indirect address and avoid the first person whenever possible. "The officer's personal effects are to be forwarded directly to *Scylla*. To provide an agreeable sense of homecoming when the officer reports to his Command."

"Who—" There was predictable outrage in Koscuisko's voice, as well as a degree of frustration—which Joslire could certainly understand, and sympathize with. A note of savage humor there as well.

Humor?

It was a moment before Koscuisko seemed to master his reactions and trust himself to speak, after having bitten off his first response so sharply that the word hadn't so much as bled before it died. "Who sleeps on which of these boards?"

The boards . . . oh, the sleep-racks. Joslire stepped carefully into the middle of the room to post himself by the studyset. "The officer sleeps in the inner room, behind the slider-screen, which has been provided for his privacy. Assigned Security sleeps here, in order to be available to the officer at will."

"You and the mashounds," Koscuisko said, as if to himself.

Joslire didn't bother to mention that the privacy partition could not be secured from the inside. The officer would figure that out soon enough. And would doubtless realize that assigned Security slept between the officer and the door as much to prevent the officer from going out unaccompanied as to be available when wanted. "I do not suggest an equivalence, of course. How am I to call you, then?"

It was nice to be apologized to, howsoever obliquely; but the officer would learn better soon enough. "It is a matter up to the officer's discretion." Koscuisko would learn that, too. Here at Fleet Orientation Station Medical there were few conventions to define what an officer could do with assigned Security, as long as the forms of transgression and discipline were preserved. Fortunately Administrative staff was careful about things accordingly; it all balanced out in the end, more or less.

"As it pleases the officer to inquire, 'Joslire' would be preferable to 'Curran.' " Many of his fellows welcomed the psychic camouflage of the name the Fleet had given them; Joslire didn't. To be called Curran was a constant reminder of the place where Joslire ise'Ilet had died—or at least been shut away in legal suspension of animation for thirty years. Where the man that he had been had been enslaved for crimes against the Judicial order, and his honor and his five-knives with him.

"Very well, it shall be Joslire, then. Are you required to confiscate my clothing, as well as my travel-trunks?"

"And the officer's documents-case as well. An exception is to be made for one item of a religious nature." He was a little surprised at Koscuisko's obvious grasp of what was going on. There was no particular reason to be surprised; surely it was clear enough from the standpoint of basic psychology—the removal of anything that might be comforting in its familiarity, in order to render confused and disoriented Students the more receptive to the new rules and expectations of a whole new reality. Except that none of his other Students had grasped that meaning quite so quickly, if they ever had.

"What if the officer is irreligious? One item of a profane nature? Never mind it, Joslire, what am I supposed to wear to Tutor's Mess?"

On familiar ground with this, Joslire moved with confident assurance to the closet to cull the appropriate selections from the rack. "This is the officer's informal mess dress. It has been prepared from the information in the officer's medical profile, so the measurements may not be precise. There is time to arrange for alterations before the meal, but not very much time, and therefore the officer is respectfully requested to test these garments for size as soon as possible."

Koscuisko was a little different from the Students he'd seen through Orientation previously, perhaps.

But he could hardly be that different.

Which meant that the biggest problem facing Joslire in the immediate future—how to suggest that Koscuisko trim back the fine blond fringe of hair across his forehead to conform to the Jurisdiction Standard—didn't particularly worry Joslire now.

Anyone who could grasp the trick with his personal effects as quickly as Koscuisko had could surely be relied upon to submit himself sensibly to other Fleet requirements.

Mergau Noycannir was prompt in her appointment for dinner with Tutor Chonis, as she made a point to be in all her dealings with superiors. She'd been ready for an eighth, her glossy black hair neatly tied up, her uniform crisp and precise on her tall spare frame. She'd reviewed the schedule and tomorrow's ceremony several times, rehearsing the steps in quarters with her bond-involuntary's assistance until she was certain she knew exactly what was required. She wasn't particularly hungry, and she disliked wasting time over food; still, every opportunity to spend time with the Tutors was a valuable one, well worth the investment. The more she could learn about Tutor Chonis the better she would be prepared to manage him. And she would manage him, too, because she had no intention of going back to Chilleau Judiciary without her Writ, regardless of what it might take to obtain one.

Her Patron at least recognized superior ability when he saw it; Verlaine knew what was in his own best interest. For that, Mergau was exactly as grateful as she ought to be. Once she brought the Writ to Inquire back to Chilleau Judiciary, she could reasonably expect due compensation in consideration of the valuable resource she'd obtained. If it failed to come, she'd be prepared to ensure that a satisfactory adjustment was made.

She was always prepared.

She'd had her bond-involuntary escort her here to Tutor's Mess in good time. It wouldn't do to come too soon and be seen standing idly in the reception area, waiting for the Tutor to arrive; that would give the appearance of anxiety or that she was conscious of being in a subordinate position. She'd sent Hanbor back to quarters and then left Tutor's Mess, going down the corridor a few eighths around the nearest corner to wait.

Now she tapped her earlobe thoughtfully, checking the time. *Fifteen,* the little chrono whispered, its timer connected to a neuro-thread that lay beneath the surface of her inner ear. *Fifteen and seven eighths.* It was time to go. Arrival prior to seven-eighths would have been early. Arrival much past seven-eighths would be almost late.

She tugged at the unfamiliar uniform blouse to straighten the front creases, and made for the door.

The entry to Tutor's Mess was open four times a day, during each of the meal-breaks. Another Student was waiting in the small reception area just inside the door—a Student as tall as Tutor Chonis, with light-colored hair that wasn't groomed to the Standard for uniformed personnel. The Student acknowledged her arrival with a nod that deepened into a polite salute. Mergau didn't know enough about him to feel she could select the best response, so she merely returned the offered courtesy in precise measure, dismissing him from her mind. She couldn't afford to waste any energy on people who would have nothing to do with her. Peers and subordinates could be used to support her, but Tutors could place obstacles in her way: She only needed to pay attention to the Tutors. She tapped her ear again: *fifteen and sixty-two.* Just two until sixteen. Surely Tutor Chonis would come soon.

Tutor Chonis was coming through the open door into Tutor's Mess even now. Mergau turned her back to the other Student to greet the Tutor with the requisite salute, smiling in her most ingratiating manner. Chonis answered her salute with a pleased smile of his own; but, then, he seemed to be distracted by something that was behind her.

This was confusing.

Moving forward to take her place at her Tutor's side, Mergau realized that what had captured Chonis's attention was the other Student.

"Good, I'm glad to see you both in good time. Shall we go in?"

A modest smile and a diffident bow would be the most suitable response, Mergau decided. But the other Student was already bowing with a sycophantic grin on his face, so Mergau made sure to keep her expression utterly solemn.

She'd overheard Tutor Chonis complaining about a Student just yesterday as she waited outside his office. This was Student Koscuisko, then, the man who had so little respect for the Administration and his fellow Students that he had come at the last possible moment?

She would take precedence without hesitation. She had demonstrated her commitment to the program and the Administration by arriving in plenty of time to get settled in and complete in-processing. It was too bad she hadn't known who he was earlier, though. She could have used the few moments of wait-time to draw him out a bit, probing to discover his strengths and weaknesses.

Tutor Chonis had gone through to the mess without waiting for further response. Mergau hastened to take first place in following the Tutor, but the other Student made way for her quite naturally and carelessly, giving no sign of meaning to contest with her for precedence—as if he felt the issue was not important, which indicated that he did not take her as seriously as he should.

Tutor Chonis was waiting for them at a table set just short of the administrative equivalent of the Captain's Bar, the railing that divided the room and marked off the raised area at the back as privileged space for senior officers. She and her fellow Student would be sharing the bench, of necessity; protocol prohibited junior officers from turning their backs on Command Branch.

Mergau paused in the middle of the room, gazing at the Bar. Once she'd taken up her Writ, she would be entitled to turn her back to the Bar with impunity, as long as the Captain wasn't present. Ship's Inquisitor, Chief Medical Officer, Ship's Surgeon was subordinate only to the senior officer in the Command, and since it was the Writ that defined the Chief Medical Officer, she would be one of Ship's Primes.

Tutor Chonis knew well enough that Mergau would never be assigned to a cruiserkiller, since she could not serve as a medical officer of any sort. That had been part of the agreement that Secretary Verlaine had made with Fleet when she'd come here. Fleet's requirement that its Inquisitors be Bench-certified medical practitioners was appropriate for on-Line warships but hardly applicable to a Bench setting. Secretary

Verlaine didn't need a Ship's Surgeon; Chilleau Judiciary already had Medical support. All he wanted was an Inquisitor on staff, a Writ on site at Chilleau Judiciary. A Writ that he could direct as he saw fit—without having to negotiate for a loaned Inquisitor from Fleet resources to support what was, after all, a Judicial function.

They were waiting for her, her fellow Student standing politely until she took her seat. Suddenly she was annoyed at him for making her feel awkward, even clumsy, twice already in so little time. Being here was just another step in a well-mapped career for him, and from what she'd gathered about Student Koscuisko, it wouldn't destroy his life if he failed—he was a rich man, playing at doctor, playing at Inquisitor. But she represented First Secretary Verlaine and Chilleau Judiciary, Second Judge Sem Porr Har, Presiding.

The honor of her Patron depended upon her ability to survive the tests that Fleet would put her to.

". . . Senior Security, in other words the Warrant Officers"—Tutor Chonis was saying, obviously responding to a question from Koscuisko—"the Engineer's Mates, and your own shift supervisors. You'll take your meals above the Bar, of course."

He continued to talk to Koscuisko as Mergau slid into place along the bench, Koscuisko waiting until she was settled to sit down beside her. "Then there are typically four, sometimes as many as six Fleet Lieutenants, usually one to a shift. Sometimes the noise . . . but I'm getting too technical. We'll be covering this all in session, in detail." An orderly had approached their table and was waiting for instruction. "Meal three, please. And for my Students, of course."

"You seemed to be reminiscing, just now," Student Koscuisko said as the orderly went off again. "May I ask if you were posted to such a vessel yourself?"

Student Koscuisko wasn't supposed to be controlling the conversation. She was supposed to control the conversation. And if she didn't eat her meal, the Tutor would have to ask whether something was wrong with it. She'd be able to make a point about the fact that he should have consulted her preferences beforehand, rather than being distracted by Koscuisko's obvious toadying.

Tutor Chonis seemed in an expansive mood, answering Koscuisko readily—almost eagerly. "The last was the *Oxparen,* of honored memory." He slapped the table lightly with the fingers of his left hand twice in a gesture of apparent respect that Mergau had seen him use before. "Destroyed during the reduction of Karset, but that was after my time. I was called in to help activate this facility before all of that was well begun."

Koscuisko had chosen the correct approach. She had to give him points for that; maybe Koscuisko was going to take managing. Chonis clearly seemed to be enjoying himself, rather than merely tolerating the conversation. "In my father's time," Koscuisko said, "such activity—as this facility represents, I mean to say—was considered to be a Security function." Koscuisko was working it entirely too well; she could not find her way into the conversation. He must have planned it that way. People with rank and education never spoke without such hidden purposes. He would know that no Clerk of Court had ever taken a Writ to Inquire.

Until now.

"Your father's time? I suppose that's about right." Chonis was mulling Koscuisko's statement over, obviously distracted from Mergau's very existence. "Hasn't been a Security function for, oh, fifty years. Fleet Medical only gained control of the office rather recently, compared to the history of the Fleet. . . . Where was your father posted?"

"A Security assignment, the *Autocrat's Niece,* on the Desular Line. A lieutenant. When Fleet forwarded its invitation that I serve as Ship's Surgeon—" There was an abrupt break in his response, and Koscuisko looked down at the table, very briefly. "But I am being inexcusably rude. It is a family matter, of no consequence. Please accept my apologies."

On the other hand, it might prove good policy to let Koscuisko talk. He seemed to have run into quite a sensitive subject all unawares, to judge by his abrupt silence. And Tutor Chonis also apparently shared the interest that she found in whatever could seem so delicate to Koscuisko.

"I understand it is traditional in your culture for the eldest son of a great family to go into the Fleet." Chonis's remark gave notice that the subject would not be permitted to drop quite so easily. Koscuisko seemed to swallow a sigh of resignation, and his pale profile looked a bit more melancholy than it had before.

"As you say, Tutor Chonis. Once the inheriting son went to do service to the Autocrat's Household as an officer in Service. But now in some of our old families, an oldest daughter has also come to inherit, though it is not yet so in my father's House."

What was the point of all this? Was Koscuisko saying he had an older sister? How could Koscuisko possibly expect anyone to care? Why didn't Koscuisko answer the question as bidden, and be still?

"The Home Defense Fleet has no tradition to include a woman warrior, and therefore it becomes the Jurisdiction Fleet that we serve in the Autocrat's name. There is also a matter of prestige to consider, because there are no cruiser-killer-grade ships of *Scylla*'s rating in the Home Defense Fleet. My family is old, and my father is proud to send his son to Jurisdiction Fleet rather than to a post of lesser rank."

A mild and impersonal response on the face of it. Koscuisko's points about the differences between them—he was going to Fleet as Ship's Surgeon—didn't escape her notice. One way or another, however, it gave Mergau the opening she'd been waiting for to expose the irrelevance of Koscuisko's remarks.

"It is very interesting. And this activity, it accomplishes? . . . ."

Koscuisko turned his head to look at her as if he were a little startled to hear the sound of her voice. His mild frown might seem to be simple concentration, but he didn't fool her. He didn't mean to yield the ground to her. "Two things, Student . . . Noycannir? Thank you, Tutor Chonis, Student Noycannir. One, it gives one something constructive to do while one is waiting for one's father to arrive at the year of his Retirement. And also—two—it gives one's younger brothers, of which I have four, reason to live with good hope for their futures."

Chonis snorted in amusement. Mergau hadn't heard any joke. Their meals were arriving; she could channel the fury choking in her throat into politely muted but clearly visible distaste for her food. Now she wasn't sure she could afford that bit of business, though. Koscuisko had her at a disadvantage.

"You've reminded me, young man. I've been remiss. Mergau, your companion is Andrej Koscuisko; Andrej, you have the pleasure of Mergau Noycannir's acquaintance. You are expected to use the formal title of Student with each other during class hours, in token of respect for each other's . . . rank."

She understood Chonis's momentary hesitation. Other Students would respect each other's status, each other's ability, each other's shared education and background. Chonis had been told to give her every assistance, and to make sure that she got the same training and practice that any other Student might have. Tutor Chonis was not going to let anyone forget that she was just a Clerk of Court, without Bench certifications.

"But we're not quite into Term yet, and officially this is an informal meeting. How are you liking the fish?"

Be smooth, she told herself. *Feel the pavement.* It could hardly be a conspiracy. Koscuisko had no reason to go out of his way to make her feel small. Tutor Chonis's comments were innocent, if ill-advised. Keeping her focus on the goal was one thing. Going out of her way to look for opposition was a waste of energy. Revealing that she even noticed petty slights or attempts to put her down would only work against her.

She could deal with Tutor Chonis later.

She had to obtain the Writ first.

Dinner was over, finally. Joslire stood waiting for him outside Tutor's Mess, along with another bond-involuntary who would logically be the one assigned to Noycannir. He wasn't sure what to make of Noycannir. She was attractive enough in a somewhat severe fashion, and she had certainly exercised herself to be pleasing to Tutor Chonis; but something gave him the idea she didn't like him.

Andrej wasn't sure he cared one way or the other.

His feet hurt, but luckily for him they didn't have too far to go to gain sanctuary.

Safely back in quarters, Andrej sank down into the chair

at the studyset and stretched his legs out toward the middle of the room, beckoning Joslire with a wave of his hand. "Give us a hand with these boots, if you would, please. My bootjack was one of those items that you have so kindly forwarded to *Scylla* for me, to await my homecoming."

Though he couldn't be sure—having just met Joslire, and unacquainted with his expressions—Andrej thought Joslire was smiling to himself as he turned his back and straddled one leg to get the proper angle on the boot.

"The officer's footgear will be broken in within a day or two. Generally speaking, the process is completed during pre-Term Orientation."

The comment and its delivery were both aggressively neutral, even passive. But Andrej's feet hurt. He knew very well what Joslire was really saying; if he'd reported in good time his boots would have been broken in by now. The fact that Joslire was absolutely right was only annoying. He was in no mood to be nagged by anyone.

"What, are you being impertinent with me, you ruffian?" he demanded in a tone of outraged disbelief.

Joslire flinched fractionally before straightening up with Andrej's boots in hand, directing a swift sidelong glance of wary evaluation at Andrej's face.

Andrej knew almost as soon as he'd said it that he'd made a mistake. He expected to be lectured by his body-servants; and cursing at them extravagantly in affectionate response was the only protest he was allowed, whether the criticism was deserved or not.

But Joslire Curran was a bond-involuntary, not a servant in Andrej's House. He had no reason to expect this stranger to understand. How could he tell whether Joslire interpreted his joking rebuke as a serious one? And if Joslire believed he had offended an officer, Joslire's governor—responding to the specific physiological stresses created by such an apprehension—would apply corrective discipline, no matter how undeserved.

Andrej tried to clarify. "That is to say, you're right, I am quite convinced. Your point is well taken."

This was intolerable.

But souls in Joslire's category of servitude were allowed

an uncharitably narrow margin for joking. There was no indication on record that primitive behavioral modifiers like the governor were capable of developing a sense of humor.

Joslire merely bowed politely and took the boots over to the sleep-rack in the corner to touch up the polish for tomorrow's events. Arms cocked up across the arm supports, stockinged feet stretched out in front of him, Andrej glared at his tender feet with a sour mind.

Unnatural, that was what it was.

The sacred bond between master and man consisted of respect and reliance, exchanged for self-subordination; to demand Joslire's obedience without granting him privilege to speak his mind was a perversion. Was Jurisdiction. And that was what this Station was all about, wasn't it? Jurisdiction perversion?

When his father had been an officer in Security, the Bench had been less strict, and interrogation less formal. The Judicial process as his father had known it had indeed involved beatings, intimidation, even torture; ugly, sordid, but human in its scale.

Now it was different.

Now interrogation had become Inquiry, formalized into Protocols and divided into Levels. Now it required a medical officer to implement the Question, because it was too easy to kill a man too soon unless a torturer knew what to do. What had started as back-alley beatings in search of required information had evolved into systematic brutalization, forcing confessions to predetermined crimes, and all "in support of the Judicial order."

It wasn't as though torment and brutality were unheard of in Andrej's home system. Far from it. Andrej himself was Aznir Dolgorukij; any Sarvaw had stories to tell of what Dolgorukij were capable of doing when they felt that it served their best interest. It was only that the Bench increased the level of atrocity year by year, as unrest within subject worlds continued to seethe and writhe and challenge the Judicial order. The public's desire to see crimes punished in proportion to their severity could serve as a rationalization for atrocity; but only as long as such measures worked as deterrent.

And there was no way the Protocols could be described as punishment in proportion to the crime's severity.

Andrej straightened up in his chair, weary with the familiar futility of it all. It did no good to worry that old dry bone. The Station was on Standard time, and Tutor Chonis had told them that they were to be on firstshift for the duration of the Term; so it was coming up on sleepshift, which meant it was time to go to bed.

Student Koscuisko sighed and stood up. Joslire waited patiently to be noticed. It wouldn't matter if he spoke first, not so early in Term; Koscuisko wouldn't know it was a violation—but the governor would. It was best not to risk it.

"I'm sorry, Joslire," Koscuisko said. "I am brooding. There is something?"

"As it please the officer." Koscuisko's dialect seemed to include more apology than Joslire was accustomed to hearing; this was the third time, surely. It meant nothing. "The officer may wish to review the material pertaining to the Administrator's briefing?"

The information was on-screen on the studyset; Koscuisko hadn't noticed, sunk deep in thought. Now the Student leaned over the desktop, scrolling through the data, a mild frown of concentration on his broad flat face. "Presentation of the Bond, yes, Joslire. I rehearsed it in the mirror, in fact. On my way here."

Just as well. The public presentation was humiliating enough in its own right. When the Students hadn't bothered to learn their lines, Joslire felt the depth of his degradation more keenly than ever.

Student Koscuisko tagged the view off and met his eyes squarely. "There was a note in the briefing, Joslire; the option to receive the Bond now or tomorrow. Which do you prefer?"

Confused for a moment, Joslire recovered as quickly as he could. It was true. He was only required to surrender his Bond in good form. He didn't have to do it tomorrow. If Student Koscuisko would receive his Bond here in private, they'd still stand at briefing, but he'd not be forced to repeat the bitter lie of his condemnation in public this time.

"With respect. It is the officer's preference that prevails. As the Student please." He had to say it; it was his duty to try to teach Koscuisko how to use him.

"Thank you, Joslire, but I desire to consult your preference. I solicit your preference. I ask you to tell me which you would rather."

It wouldn't last.

It never did.

Koscuisko would learn soon enough to treat him as an object for use, and not as a person. But as long as Koscuisko had made the demand, he was clear to reveal it; he only hoped that his voice was professionally neutral, as it should be, and not dripping over with gratitude. It was a small thing to be asked for his preference. It was a great thing to a bond-involuntary to be asked anything, rather than told.

Koscuisko was an aristocrat; for Koscuisko asking and demanding were probably the same things. He would concentrate on that. "As it please the officer. To be permitted to present the Bond would be a privilege."

Koscuisko nodded. "We will the transfer accomplish here and now, then." Easier for Koscuisko as well, perhaps, since he need not expose himself to ridicule before the Tutor if he missed a word. "Bring me back my boots, if you would. I will just go adjust my attitude."

What did a man's boots have to do with his attitude?

Koscuisko took the boots from Joslire's hand, but he didn't want any help getting into them. Joslire had nothing to do but stand and stare at him as Koscuisko tucked in his trouser cuffs, fastening his uniform blouse smooth and straight.

Koscuisko went into the washroom with careful steps, his feet tender from wearing new footgear. He washed his hands and combed his hair—for all the world as if he were a schoolboy on his way to sit among his elders. As if he was preparing for a formal occasion. As if he felt the Bond and what it stood for was something worthy of his respect.

Then Koscuisko was ready.

"I will receive your Bond now, Joslire Curran."

Joslire opened his blouse, pulling at the fine chain around his neck to find its metal pendant. Koscuisko confused him;

he was taking as many pains as it would have cost to do this tomorrow.

"This tape is the record of my trial." Not precisely true, perhaps; it had not been Joslire Curran's trial. But it was close enough. And the formula had been established by the Bench, and could not be materially amended. Requiring that he use personal language—"my trial," "I"—was all part of the ritual, personalizing his enslavement. "Here the officer will find details of the offense for which I have been justly condemned, by the solemn adjudication of the Jurisdiction's Bench."

All of this time, and he still could hardly say "justly." He had been betrayed to Jurisdiction, condemned to this shame by the cunning and hatred of an ancestral enemy. He would survive to revenge himself. If he failed to revenge himself he would be dishonored in fact, as well as in the eyes of the Bench. He would not fail.

"According to the provisions of Fleet Penal Consideration number eighty-three, sub-heading twenty, article nine, my life belongs to the Jurisdiction's Bench, which has deeded it to the Fleet for thirty years."

Betrayed by an enemy. Bonded by the Bench, because he'd satisfied all the requirements they had for bond-involuntaries: youth, fitness, intelligence, psychological resilience . . . lucky him. He got to carry a governor for thirty years, and in return the Bench waived all charges. If he lived out his Term, they granted full retirement along with the pay that would have accrued had he been a free man; as if that could make up for it.

"The officer is respectfully requested to accept the custody of my Bond."

In two hands he offered it, the prescribed gesture of submission.

With two hands outstretched, the officer received it. With real respect, as if understanding that it was Joslire's life—and not some piece of jewelry, some dull trinket—that he was to hold for the Bench in the Fleet's name.

Koscuisko had a solemn face, a grave expression even at rest—as far as Joslire had seen of him thus far. Joslire told himself it was just weariness that made Koscuisko look so serious now. Otherwise it was too tempting to believe that Koscuisko understood; too tempting to imagine that the Bench formality could actually become the contract-of-honor that it mocked just this one time.

"I will accept your Bond, Joslire Curran. And hold it for the Day your Term is past."

It was just ritual, Joslire told himself. The words were only words, the same as those spoken by his other officers before Student Koscuisko, the same words that would be spoken by the next Student once Koscuisko was graduated and gone.

Except the promise was real this time; the hope for that distant Day was sharp and poignant, because something in Koscuisko's tone of voice utterly convinced Joslire that Koscuisko meant it.

On board a cruiserkiller, the Ship's First—the Security Officer—would husband all the Bonds for safekeeping. Here at Fleet Orientation Station Medical, the Students were required to carry the Bonds on their own person, to increase their sense of ownership and authority. Koscuisko put the chain over his neck, slipping the flat gray record-tape into his tunic.

It was over, for yet another Term.

"And now, not that it follows, Joslire, I'm tired. I should like to go to bed."

And yet he felt less enslaved—and more personally sworn—than ever he had since the terrible day that the Bench had first condemned him to the Bond.

"Attention to the Administrator," Tutor Foliate called. Chonis winced internally at the ragged shuffling sound of twenty ill-prepared Students trying their hand at Fleet drill and ceremony for the first time. Twenty bond-involuntaries and ten Tutors—the sound of their feet moving across the floor was as one sound, crisp and complete. Twenty Students, and it might as well have been two hundred from the time it took them to come to attention.

Clellelan was halfway to the Captain's Bar before the noise quieted down. Tutor Chonis could see the repressed smile of amused disgust on the Administrator's face as he passed.

Students. They ought to bring them in as cadets for the first half of Term. Really they ought.

Chonis had heard Clellelen declaim on the subject often enough. As it was, Fleet simply handed them rank and bond-involuntaries, pretending they knew how to manage both—simply because they were Bench-certified medical practitioners. But it was hard enough already to find even the marginally qualified volunteers they usually got with a Chief Medical billet and Ship's Prime status placed enticingly at the far end of the course. They couldn't afford to make recruiting more difficult than it already was.

Clellelan was posted, now, glancing briefly at the Recorder on the table at his left. Matching names to Students, perhaps. Trying to guess whether they'd all graduate this time.

"This is Fleet Orientation Station Medical. I am Administrator Rorin Clellelan, Directing. By the Bench instruction. The Term opens with the following Students in attendance, answer to your name when called. Molt. Angouleme. Yurgenhauen. V'ciha."

One by one he called out their names; one by one Students answered to him—nervous, diffident, confident, bored. Too much personal feeling by half, Chonis felt. They'd learn. Discipline was the best defense, as the bond-involuntaries demonstrated. Retreat into formality could help provide the insulation that these Students were going to need.

"Wyadd. Sansoper. Noycannir. Koscuisko."

Noycannir sounded bored and amused, above it all. Not obviously enough to give offense, no. But Noycannir was a Clerk of Court and a member of First Secretary Verlaine's personal staff. She clearly meant to give the impression that she was completely comfortable in this environment.

And Koscuisko?

There was no particular emotion of any kind in Koscuisko's voice, and Chonis wondered about that for a moment. Koscuisko had seemed clearly unhappy to be here during their meal last night. For Koscuisko to be suppressing emotional cues so absolutely meant he was more frightened than Tutor Chonis had guessed.

"Shiwaj. And Bilale." The Administrator came to the end of his list, and Chonis focused his attention to the fore. "Students, you are welcome. You represent a vital resource for the Fleet, as you know. And in these increasingly troubled times, you will be called upon to serve the Judicial order as never before in the history of the Bench.'' Because never before in the history of the Bench had civil disorder been so pervasive, so corrosive, and above all so persistent.

''Let there be no doubt in your minds, the task for which you have volunteered is a difficult one. And you will be more personally involved in the Judicial process than any of our Line officers, even those in Command Branch itself.'' Clellelan had to be careful with that one, Chonis knew. It was all to the good to encourage the Students to see themselves as uniquely valuable to the Bench. But if Clellelan put too much emphasis on their critical role, they might start thinking about why Line officers wouldn't have anything to do with it.

''Please be assured that I personally, as well as your assigned Tutors and all of our Staff, will render every assistance in ensuring successful completion of your Orientation. Each of the bond-involuntaries here assigned has been dedicated by the Bench to furthering your instruction in any way possible.''

The Bench had created bond-involuntaries specifically to support its Inquisitors. Ordinary Security, no matter how professional, sometimes recoiled from what might be required to support Inquiry. The Bench's solution had been elegance itself: create Security whose indoctrination ensured that disobedience of lawful and received instruction would be unfailingly, immediately, strictly disciplined by a ''governor'' that held the pain linkages of the brain in a merciless grip. Thus Joslire Curran and others like him, condemned for crimes against the Judicial order to a thirty-year sentence with a surgically implanted jailer in their brains.

''It is prudent and proper that you take their Bonds into your hand as Orientation commences in earnest. The troops here assigned will therefore declare their Bond.''

The signal was clearly flagged out in the orientation material. And still it always took them too long to realize where they were in the program, to turn around, to face their assigned bond-involuntaries and stand ready to receive the

Bond. Chonis could hear the shuffling sounds behind him and see the other Tutors' Students out of the corner of his eye. He heard Noycannir pivot sharply and bring her heel down emphatically, completing the move.

But there was no sound whatever from Koscuisko.

"By the Bench instruction," Clellelan said. That was his signal to turn around and bear witness to the ceremony, in order to be sure that his Students got it right.

There was a problem, though, wasn't there?

He hadn't heard Koscuisko turn around because Koscuisko hadn't moved.

"This tape is the record of my trial."

The words were spoken in unison; no problem with Security; they knew their lines. Chonis raised his eyebrow at Koscuisko's calm, waiting face, suppressing a twitch of a gesture with difficulty. Curran didn't look concerned. Had Koscuisko taken Curran's Bond already, then?

"According to the provisions of Fleet Penal Consideration number eighty-three . . ."

Student Koscuisko met Chonis's eyes with a careful, neutral expression in his own and bowed fractionally, just enough to convey the concept of the salute.

Most of the bond-involuntary troops preferred the group ceremony, because there was a measure of defensive insulation to be had from the presence of the other troops. After Curran's last two Students, Chonis would have expected the man to stay as clear as he could from anything that might involve personalizing the relationship.

"I will accept your Bond. —And hold it for the Day your Term is past."

The Students picked up quickly. Their lines were spoken in something close to synchronicity, breaking down into a babble of incoherent noise only at the point where the individual name was given. Tutor Chonis turned back to face the Administrator, dismissing Curran's anomalous behavior from his mind.

"You have accepted the Bond from your assigned troops, to be held by you in custody for the duration of the Term. It is just and judicious that it should be so. Welcome to Fleet Orientation Station Medical, Students all. We have every confidence in you, and will do our utmost to see you successfully graduated. Tutors, dismiss.''

Maybe it was a hopeful sign, and Curran's Term wouldn't be like the last ones had been for him.

With luck.

They'd all be grateful if Curran got a break that way.

◆ **Two**

The first few days of a class were the same no matter what the course material, Andrej mused, glancing around Tutor Chonis's office idly. There'd be introductions, though he'd already met Tutor Chonis and Student what-was-her-name Noycannir. There would be the review of the course schedule. And they would have a summary lecture, or else the first of several introductory lectures, depending upon the complexity of the coursework and the relative length of the Term.

The medical university on Mayon was a compound city the size of his family's estate at Rogubarachno, huge and ancient. Older than his father's House, in a sense. Mayon had already been a surgical college of considerable antiquity and status when the Aznir were still busily annexing worlds without the tedious interference of the Jurisdiction and its impressively efficient Fleet; that was well before their crucial first encounter with the Jurisdiction's Bench, and the subsequent substitution of armed conquest with aggressive market management. The classrooms he'd occupied during his student years had ranged from back rooms in drinking houses to the blindingly sterile theaters where infectious diseases were treated; but he didn't think he'd ever sat a class in someone's office until now.

"Good-greeting, Student Koscuisko, Student Noycannir. Thank you, please be seated."

Slept in teachers' offices, yes; quarreled with the Administration over the interpretation of some test results or clinical indications, perhaps. He'd never sat in class with only one fellow Student, either. Huge as Mayon complex was, it had always been packed to fullest capacity with students and staff even so, because it was the very best facility in known Jurisdiction Space for those who wished to learn the art of surgery and medicine. Only the strict planning codes that had controlled construction for over five hundred years, Standard, had prevented Mayon from becoming claustrophobic. Student housing varied naturally according to the needs and the resources of each Student; but there had been sky and air enough for everybody, even in the heart of the great Surgical College itself. Andrej had only been here at Fleet Orientation Station Medical for two days. He missed the night breeze already.

"You'll have reviewed the assigned material, of course. Rhyti, anyone? Please, help yourselves." The Tutor's gesture indicated the serving-set on the Tutor's squarish shining worktable, just between Andrej and Student Noycannir. She had declined to speak to him except to return his greeting. Andrej didn't care whether she liked him or not; there were too many other things to think about. He'd never had much use for overly compulsive Students. Aggression could cover for lack of skill for a time, that was true. Sooner or later, though, competitiveness failed before superior ability.

Andrej fixed himself a flask of rhyti in polite silence. Joslire had brought cavene for fastmeal this morning; Andrej didn't like cavene, and had said so. He would have had some now, though, if the Tutor suggested it. In Andrej's experience teachers expected everything they said to be taken as good advice or outright direction. But Noycannir just sat there—and did not move to take a flask for herself when Andrej nudged the serving-set closer to her elbow.

"You will have noted that the Term is to comprise six Standard months of instruction, twenty-four weeks. Student Noycannir, you'll not need to adjust your time-sense, since Chilleau Judiciary is of course on Standard time. Student Koscuisko, I expect you're still on Standard time from Mayon, unless going back to Azanry reset you to home-chrono. How long were you home?"

Azanry did not follow the Jurisdiction Standard, but he

hadn't been back there for long enough to have forgotten. "Two months, Tutor Chonis. Perhaps five weeks, by local reckoning." Not long at all. There had been plenty of time to embrace his old servants, to tour his fields, to visit his land-pledges. Time enough to compromise the lady Marana and quarrel with his father. Not long enough to change his father's mind or make him understand.

"Well, you'll have leave again soon enough, I'm sure. As I was saying, the Term is twenty-four weeks. Perhaps thirty, if the Administration identifies a weakness in some aspect of your professional development."

The Remedial Levels, that was what Chonis meant. An extra cushion of time to serve as catch-up for dull Students. But if the Student should fail to fulfill some element of the teaching paradigm even at the Remedial Levels, there would be nothing left to do but to recycle her to the next Term. And Noycannir would probably be recycled to the next Term because—having reviewed the lesson schedule—Andrej could not for the life of him imagine how a woman with no medical background could hope to master such a body of information in only thirty weeks. It looked challenging enough to him; and he had nearly eight years of intensive medical training to draw on.

Perhaps he was reading more into the requirements than was really to be demanded of them.

"You'll have noted also that our time divides rather neatly into two halves: one for instruction, one for practical exercise. There is a good deal of material to cover. I cannot emphasize strongly enough the need for diligent study."

Andrej sipped his rhyti, feeling a little bored. Yes, there was a lot to get through, history, philosophy, formal structure, the legal issues, the Writ. The Levels. He wasn't sure why Tutor Chonis felt good study habits needed emphasis, however. What else was there to do here but study? Well, study, exercise, and attend lecture and laboratory, of course.

"Are there any questions?"

None that had occurred to him, at least not yet. Andrej glanced over at his partner, Student Noycannir; she sat with her eyes fixed on the Tutor, not moving. So she didn't have any questions, either. Or she simply wasn't willing to raise any.

"Your personal schedules have been carefully arranged to maximize your study time accordingly. Your assigned Security will continue to provide you with your meals in your quarters. Exercise periods are scheduled before midmeal and before thirdmeal. Student Koscuisko, Curran will be your trainer. As you know, he's Emandisan, and quite good. Student Noycannir, you'll start out with Hanbor. He'll adjust your training as required to ensure that you get the level of combat drill you're accustomed to."

Interesting. The Tutor expected her to be able to fight hand-to-hand, and clearly well enough to warrant a more advanced teacher than the one provided him. She was in good physical condition, to look at her. It seemed a little unusual to Andrej for a Clerk of Court to have any background in combat drill, but what did he know?

"Let's get started, then. Andrej, you'll remember the remark you made at dinner yesterday about the role of coercive force in the interrogation process in your father's time?"

Into the lecture, then. According to schedule they would take a week to discuss why it was reasonable to use torture as an instrument of Judicial order. They would explore the communication problem, and the unquestionable truth that the single most universal language under Jurisdiction was pain, even if its dialects—fear, hatred, and fury, terror and desperation—could not be reliably interpreted.

"Yes, Tutor Chonis. I understand from the material that the Jurisdiction Bench did not shift responsibility for such functions until the tenure of First Judge Upan Istmol?"

To a certain extent it was old material. After all, much of his early medical training had focused on reading pain and how to sort it from shame or embarrassment when the Jurisdiction Standard did not satisfy. A good general practitioner needed thorough grounding in that grammar, and he had been highly praised in his evaluations for the delicacy of his exploratory touch. Eight years from entry-level general-medical to advanced certifications in neurosurgery and psychopharmacology, and all of it just so that he could go to Fleet and implement the Protocols—it hardly seemed worth it.

"Quite so, Student Koscuisko. You've started the assignment, I see. Istmol's critical reading of the implementation of Fleet Procedure Five clearly demonstrates the reasoning behind the decision. Reasoning that is, of course, still current, as received."

Andrej concentrated on the Tutor's words, doing his best not to think about why it was so important to rationalize the institutionalization of torture. Deterrent terror. Swift and strict punishment for crimes against the Judicial order. The shock value of a mutilated body on display at local Judicial centers. Living, breathing examples of what a person risked when they tried to challenge the rule of Law.

It didn't matter how he felt about it.

He would keep up and do well; it was expected. It was required. For the rest—since there could hardly be any congenial drinking-places at a stand-alone Station founded on a barren piece of rock—he would simply have to find distraction where he could.

Mergau Noycannir was prompt to class, and had been prompt each of the forty-eight Standard days that class had met since the Term had opened. Forty-eight days; six weeks, Standard. They were halfway through the initial orientation phase and still just speaking in generalities. What good could all of this background do anyone?

Did they think that they were going to lecture her to death, and be rid of her that way?

She heard the signal at the Tutor's door. It would be Koscuisko, of course, since Chonis did not signal for admittance to his own office. She threw an idle taunt at him as the door opened, pretending to be providing reassurance.

"Safe you are, Student Koscuisko, our Tutor is delayed."

Six weeks. She was bored, and getting anxious. Koscuisko was a safe target. He came into the room with too much energy, like a man who'd never been forced to watch his step, moderate his gestures, or govern his expression. People who were so egocentric, so self-defined, could only disgust her. Had he never learned to be afraid of somebody? Would he ever take any of this seriously? And yet she had to be wary of him, because he had the medical education that Fleet valued so highly.

She did not.

Secretary Verlaine had seen no reason to lose one of his best Clerks of Court to years of medical training when all he wanted was someone who had custody of a Writ to Inquire.

"Thank you, Student Noycannir. I trust you had good practice."

Koscuisko answered politely, clearly not noticing her reprimand. Koscuisko didn't notice her at all, in some fundamental fashion. That was much worse than any criticism he could have turned on her; but it was not surprising.

"Thank you, I have had good practice." Of all those here, only Security gave her a measure of the respect that she had earned, that she deserved. It wasn't hard to force them to respect her in combat drill. They were not permitted to rebuke her if she hurt them or failed to observe the rules of practice. And she could fight. "Your practice also?"

Koscuisko, on the other hand, was still learning recruit-level hand-to-hand; she knew that from things Tutor Chonis said. She was better than he was in the arena. If she could have him to herself, no interference, one-on-one, she would not even ask for a weapon. She was confident that she could make him respect her then.

Koscuisko met her eyes and laughed, small and meekly. "Not up to your standards, Student Noycannir, I am quite sure. I find it much more complex a procedure than breaking brew-jugs over peoples' heads."

He knew she was better, but he didn't believe it. She could fantasize all she liked; it wasn't the same. Nor could she afford even fantasies any longer—Tutor Chonis arrived, which meant that she had to make a good show of attention.

The Tutor set his cubes down at his viewer and began to talk without looking at either of them. It was his way to try to catch them unawares. She had learned his habits, and she could best him at his own game. "Well, as I had been saying this morning. History, philosophy, a little—shall we say—political context."

The standard Judicial Structures chart was still on the projection viewer, displayed across the length and breadth of the wall behind the Tutor's chair. Nine Judiciaries; nine Judges, with Fleet shown as subordinate to the Bench in the person of the First Judge Presiding at Toh Judiciary. There was Chilleau Judiciary, Second Judge Sem Porr Har Presiding, on a line with the other eight subordinate Benches; and even at such a global scale as the Judicial Structures chart, First Secretary Verlaine was called out by name, head of Administration.

The Sixth Judge Sat at Sant-Dasidar Judiciary. Fourth or fifth on the list of circuit Courts reporting to the Sixth Judge, one could just make out the name of Koscuisko's system of origin. Secretary Verlaine's name was easy to read on the Judicial Structures chart; the Dolgorukij Combine was all but lost in the small script. It was too bad Student Koscuisko was so clearly incapable of taking an obvious lesson from that, Mergau mused.

Tutor Chonis was still talking. "We've been through all that. The formal structure of the current organization, organizational philosophy, and so forth. I think we've worked that quite thoroughly, so unless you have any last questions? Student Koscuisko?"

She didn't have any questions, and she didn't care about Fleet's organizational structure, either. What difference did it make to her whether there were three pharmacists and a rated psychotech on staff rather than one psychopharmacist, two pharmacists, and an extra critical-care technician instead? Were the five extra staff in the complement at the Fleet Flag level ever going to matter to her? What difference did it make whether the interrogation area was within the surgical area or well removed from all other medical facilities?

Koscuisko shook his head without a word, clearly understanding he wasn't expected to raise any issues at this point. Koscuisko might well care about the pharmacists. Koscuisko might well understand what point there might be in spending two weeks and more on administrative issues like standard-skill mixes on cruiserkiller-class warships. It might be important to him in the future. For Mergau herself it was a complete waste of time, which belonged to First Secretary Verlaine, and merited more respect than that accordingly.

"Very well. You're to feel free to raise any issues that come to mind at any point, of course. Later." A formality on the Tutor's part. Koscuisko gave every indication of having studied the structure carefully. More fool Koscuisko, because once he got to where he was going, none of that would matter in the slightest. Everybody knew what Ship's Surgeons were really there for.

"Let us proceed, then. You've been introduced to the philosophy behind the Levels of Inquiry, Confirmation, and Execution, which is to say the Bench endorsement of the principle of swift and certain punishment for crimes against the Judicial order. It's time for us to begin to examine these Levels in greater detail, to prepare a foundation upon which to build when we reach the practical exercise phase of Term."

And not a moment too soon for her taste, either. This was what Mergau had come here for, after all; this was what her Patron meant for her to master. The Levels. The Levels, and the Writ itself, which they were not to consider as a separate lecture subject until nearly five more weeks had passed—just before the exercises were to start.

That would not be boring, when they got to the exercises.

"Levels One through Three, the Preliminary Levels, Inquiry. The Fourth, Fifth, and Sixth Levels, the Intermediate Levels, Inquiry and Confirmation. Levels Seven, Eight, and Nine, the Advanced Levels—Inquiry, Confirmation, and Execution. The Tenth Level of Inquiry, Command Termination. Let us first consider the Judicial foundations implicit to the process of Inquiry. Student Noycannir, if you will assist us?"

She didn't mind the sly trick in Tutor Chonis's method. She was ready for him. She was almost always ready for him; not only ready but more than willing to play the Tutor's manipulative game.

"The Preliminary Levels, Tutor Chonis. The first level at which it is permissible to invoke the use of force. Security may take measures appropriate to the Preliminary Levels, but only at risk of discipline unless the Security is under the direct guidance of a fully rated Inquisitor with custody of an active Writ.''

This was the beginning of the single most dangerous challenge she had ever undertaken, and she could not bear to stop and think of how complete her ruin would be should she fail to prevail in her Patron's name.

She let the joy of battle comfort her, instead, and concentrated on the fact that she was nearer day by day to victory.

''And with this discussion of the Writ we conclude our examination of the history, the philosophy, the formal structure, the Levels, and the Judicial mandate of an Inquisitor with a Writ to Inquire.''

Tutor Chonis addressed himself to the summary title still displayed on the wallscreen viewer behind his desk. He knew that his Students were tense. The closer they got to the crucial break between pure lecture and the first practical exercise, the tenser they became, too. ''Let's just review the block of instruction.'' Who should he call on first? He'd catch them both, of course, and off their guard if he could manage it. Much more than mere replay-knowledge was to be tested at Fleet Orientation Station Medical—and as often as could be maneuvered without becoming crushingly obvious.

He heard a shifting sound from the table behind his back. Student Koscuisko. Sliding his seat away from the study-table, probably. They'd had twelve weeks together in indoctrination and review; Chonis felt confident in predicting that young Koscuisko would be scowling, his wide, high forehead scored with irritation, his mouth pursed sourly.

Koscuisko was too easy.

So he would call out Noycannir to be first.

''Student Noycannir, will you detail the Privilege of the Writ for us, please.''

He could not hear a reaction, not even with the augmented hearing in his right ear—where he had all but lost the natural faculty years ago in an explosion. He knew what that no-sound looked like, well enough. She'd be stiff as stalloy in her seat, and glaring—an equal mix of aggression and insecurity.

"The Privilege of the Writ. Established by Judicial order 177-39-15228. The First Judge Caris Raher, Presiding." *Well?* her sullen, stony eyes always seemed to ask. *Is that good enough for you? I'll bet you thought I couldn't get it right. Well, it's high time you learned better.* She never seemed to be secure, even when she clearly knew the material very well.

"The Writ is granted by Judicial order, and cannot be voided except by Judicial order or expiration of contract of service. It is a failure to support the Judicial order to reject a grant of Writ prior to the expiration of Fleet contract."

She could be subtle, too, and politic; she rehearsed the abstract blandly, without the slightest hint that she even cared about that irony visible on her narrow, sharp cunning face. Once the Writ was granted, it was treason to attempt to lay it down before your eight years of service had been completed. Which reminded him . . .

"Thank you, Student Noycannir, it's quite a lot for one person to try to get through alone. Perhaps Student Koscuisko would explain the unique legal position granted by the Privilege of the Writ?"

He knew Koscuisko didn't like this part. As if Koscuisko could be said to care for any of it.

"Of the Judicial offenses punishable under Law, only one can override the Privilege of the Writ. That offense is challenging the Judicial order by act of treason, mutiny, or insurrectionary intent."

As represented, for instance, by failure to obey lawful and received instruction from one's superior commanding officer. Or in terms of Koscuisko's birth-culture—one's oldest brother, one's father, or the oldest brother of one's father, if there was one. In other words, precisely what Koscuisko had been trying so strenuously to accomplish before he had finally submitted to the overwhelming weight of Aznir tradition and reported to Fleet Orientation Station Medical as his father directed.

"Wrongful imprisonment cannot be cried against the Writ, because the Inquisitor does not bind into confinement but only enters into the Judicial process when a suspect has been apprehended." Koscuisko was obviously of a mind to be thorough about it, since he had been asked. "Loss of function cannot be cried against the Writ, because the Inquisitor would not be free to perform his Judicial function without fear of repercussions, and one cannot be penalized for performing one's Judicial function. For the same reasons loss of life cannot be cried against the Writ. Loss of personal or real property cannot be cried against the Writ, because the Bench does not apprehend without reason . . ."

Turning around now in his seat, Tutor Chonis regarded Koscuisko with a benevolent eye. It was always gratifying to have one's mental image confirmed. Student Koscuisko was sitting with his legs crossed and one elbow on the study-table, marking off points one by one on the fingers of his left hand; precisely as Tutor Chonis had imagined him.

". . . and the integrity of the Jurisdiction is considered to be resident in the Writ. Judicial discrimination may not be questioned in Judicial process. Loss of privacy cannot be cried against the Writ—"

Tutor Chonis held up his hand and Koscuisko fell silent, folding his itemized fingers into a pensive fist. "Thank you, Student Koscuisko. Well. You have made it quite clear that you are both thoroughly familiar with the philosophy and the crucial legalities that justify, or I should say mandate, your Writ."

Not to mention keenly aware of how useful a Writ could be to an ambitious administrator like First Secretary Verlaine. What had put the idea in Verlaine's mind at the beginning was anyone's guess; all Tutor Chonis really knew for certain about it was that Verlaine had been pulling strings, trading favors, cashing in tokens with reckless abandon over the past two years in his campaign to get Student Noycannir admitted.

Verlaine didn't want an Inquisitor on loan from Fleet who would necessarily have divided loyalties. Verlaine felt Fleet could have more Inquisitors at much less expense if it waived its requirement for Bench medical certifications. Student Noycannir was here to prove that point.

If the First Secretary had his way, there'd be Inquisitors at each Bench center, for each circuit, and for each Judicial processing center—all in support of the Judicial order, of course.

And only incidentally to the detriment of the political power of the Fleet, which had up until now maintained an unchallenged monopoly over the Writ and the lawful exercise of coercive and punitive physical force.

"I have reviewed your progress with the Administrator, who has expressed very great satisfaction with your mastery of the material to date. It has therefore been decided that the scheduled week of assurance iterations will be waived. We are permitted to move directly to the next block of instruction."

Insult 101, as Tutor Jestra had been wont to call it. The Preliminary Levels of the Question started with hearing a confession out and ran through assisted inquiry—which was the maximum degree of violence that could be invoked without a Warrant. Inquisitors were seldom disciplined for violating restrictions, though, since superior officers were generally willing to overlook such lapses as long as they didn't have to look too closely at what was happening in the first place.

To Orientation Station staff, assisted inquiry seemed so benign compared to the Intermediate or Advanced Levels that as far as Tutor Chonis was concerned it did in fact amount to little more than calling a person names.

The prospect of their first practical exercise generally affected the students somewhat more dramatically. Chonis checked the reactions to his surprise: Student Noycannir froze up in her seat whenever she felt threatened, yes, just like that. Student Koscuisko straightened up in his seat, leaning over the table and staring at the carefully replicated artificial grain of Chonis's semi-veneer wall-covering as if there was a text to be read there.

"The Administrator has asked me to declare an extra half of personal time, in token of his appreciation for your accomplishments. Please prepare the material issued for first-lecture, Segment Two, the Preliminary Levels. We will start first thing in the morning. Thank you, Student Noycannir, Student Koscuisko."

Fortunately by this time Students were accustomed to

spending their personal time alone with only their bond-involuntary Security for company. The Administration took steps with every class to ensure that Students were isolated from each other to the maximum extent possible; training was much more efficient if Students were utterly dependent on their Tutors for approval and validation.

Now, for instance, if Students were permitted to meet and compare notes, they might conceivably recognize the schedule shift for the simple psychological trick that it was. There was no time allowance for assurance iteration.

There never had been.

Every Term it appeared on the schedule, to give the Students the false sense of temporary security that a weeklong buffer between pure theory and the first messy—clumsy—practical exercise could provide.

And every Term Students were moved straight into Preliminary, to keep them off balance and insecure and so eager for reassurance—for official approbation—that they would be willing to beat some helpless stranger with their bare hands just to get a word of praise from their Tutor.

"We start tomorrow with first-lecture, usual time. And then we'll move to theater in a few days." They needed some extra nudging to get them up and out of his office. "Your first exercise is scheduled for today week. We'll review some of the previous exercises to help you prepare prior to the practicum. Enjoy your free time. Good-shift to you, Students."

Koscuisko shook his head just a fraction, as if breaking himself out of his immobility, and started to rise. The moment Koscuisko began to shift, Noycannir was out of her chair smoothly and swiftly, unwilling—as always—to see him get one step ahead of her in anything. *Tomorrow, Students,* Chonis promised them in his mind, watching them take their confusion out of his office. *Tomorrow we will begin to test your mettle.*

And in the meantime?

In the meantime reports from the assigned Security troops usually proved amusing, as each Student sought to find some psychic balance after the unexpected shock.

The door slid together behind Koscuisko's back, and Tutor Chonis leaned back in his chair and smiled.

It had been a week since the Tutor's traditional trick of moving the Students straight into preparation for their first practical exercise. Joslire had taken his officer through the evening drill; now Koscuisko was relaxing with his rubdown, quite possibly thinking of nothing more than his supper to come.

Koscuisko seemed to be relaxed enough.

Lying on his belly with his arms folded under his head, Koscuisko nuzzled his chin into his fist like a blissfully happy young animal, making undefined sounds of contentment. Joslire suppressed his involuntary grin of amused recognition: Yes, that muscle had pulled tense during today's training; and yes, it did feel good, when it surrendered up its tension to an expert hand. And if he was not an expert hand, at least Joslire was good enough by this time to tend to Koscuisko's relatively minor aches and pains to his satisfaction.

He'd had Students both more and less athletic than this one in the past, but none who accepted the requirement for exercise with so good a grace. Stiff, sore, and grumbling strictly to himself, Koscuisko never hinted at avoiding practice or suggested cutting it short, except in carefully qualified jest. That made things easier for everybody. Joslire was grateful to his Student for the grace with which Koscuisko took direction; it made living with his governor much easier. He was adequately confident of his own ability to discriminate between being sworn at in the line of duty and being sworn at because he wasn't doing his duty; but the possibility of confusion arising was an unpleasant one.

The more perplexing problem remained that Koscuisko seemed to take all of Fleet Orientation—physical exercise and soon-to-be-intensified combat drill alike—as some sort of an amusement, or a joke. Koscuisko was younger than his years, there was that. The Aznir stayed children for longer than the Emandisan did, Aznir lived longer than Emandisan, and Joslire had told himself he could have expected Koscuisko's attitude to retain some of the blithe, carefree flavor of a privileged childhood even after years of medical school.

He was finished with the strained back muscle. Koscuisko let one arm drop over the edge of the rubtable, pillowing his cheek against the flattened back of his other hand—and grinning like an infant with never a care in the world. Except Joslire could feel the base tension in Koscuisko's body had yet to yield to massage. Koscuisko kept his nerves to himself. All Joslire could tell the Tutor about Koscuisko's state of mind was what little he could gain from observation and inference. The muscles in Koscuisko's sturdy shoulders could no longer be persuaded to relax as completely as they had during the first weeks, even allowing for improved muscle tone. Koscuisko was tense; but that was hardly news, not with the practical exercise scheduled for first thing next first-shift. In the morning. There was nothing new there to tell Tutor Chonis.

Working his Student's feet, Joslire pondered his problem. Bond-involuntaries who wanted to stay out of trouble kept their mouths shut, so as to avoid giving their governors or their Students cause to discipline them. Joslire desperately wanted to stay out of trouble. But part of his job was to keep Tutor Chonis up to date on what was going on in Koscuisko's head. Bond-involuntaries learned early on that their best protection was to perfect their duty, gaining a measure of immunity from their governors' strict censorship by maintaining unchallengeably correct thought and conduct. And Tutor Chonis had gone an extra pace for him before.

"With the officer's permission . . ."

Koscuisko grunted inquiringly in response, sounding half-asleep. A good start, Joslire decided, and was encouraged to go on.

"The First Level exercise is tomorrow, as the officer will remember. In the past other Students have shared comments of one sort or another. It has often seemed to help to put things in perspective."

How do you feel? What do you feel? What are you thinking? What is on your mind?

"Hmm. Well. I feel that Jurisdiction wodac is not of the best quality, which is not surprising. And that the instructional material is badly in need of a technical update, in places."

Not precisely what Joslire had in mind, but there was no way in which he could question more directly—not and keep peace with the governor that the Bench had spliced into the pain linkages in his brain. Joslire stepped back half a pace. "If the officer would care to turn onto his back."

Koscuisko didn't mind being uncovered. Aznir Dolgorukij didn't seem to have privacy taboos about masculine nudity, at least not among men of the same age; though from what Joslire had read about Koscuisko's ethnicity, relative age made all the difference. There was a Jurisdiction Standard for personal modesty, though, as much a part of the common language as the grammar was. Koscuisko would be expected to conform to those standards once he reached *Scylla*. It was up to Joslire to instruct him by example. Joslire laid a clean towel across Koscuisko's lap and began to address the upper part of Koscuisko's right knee, where yesterday's training bruise was just beginning to mellow to a rich gold-and-purple blotch around the joint.

And after a moment Koscuisko spoke again.

"What is the manner in which an Emandisan frees himself from error, if he has sinned? Is there such a need in your birth-culture?"

It didn't seem to be related to the issue Joslire had raised, but there was no telling. Chonis had commented on Koscuisko's effective—but sometimes disconcerting—tendency to come at a question from an angle that was itself part of his answer to whatever problem.

He wasn't eager to answer all the same; such issues weren't widely discussed among free Emandisan, let alone enslaved ones. Of which latter category he was the only one he knew. He hadn't wanted to tell Student Pefisct what his crime had been, either, since it wasn't information he was required to surrender on demand; but Student Pefisct had gotten it out of him at the last, when his enforced submission had come too late to do him any good. Joslire decided that he couldn't face the memory of his last attempt at serious reticence. It would be easier to capitulate to Koscuisko's casually phrased demand.

"If it please the officer, there is only . . . disrespect. Of steel." He wasn't sure how to say it and be faithful. It didn't translate very well; he'd never tried to put it into Standard before. Perhaps he'd been lucky that his other Students hadn't been curious about his five-knives. Joslire could imagine no worse torment than to be constrained to discuss what Emandisan steel meant to an Emandisan.

Koscuisko didn't seem to be disturbed at the vagueness of Joslire's response. Koscuisko stretched, yawning, and folded his wrists behind his head, staring up at the low gray ceiling of the coolroom reflectively.

"You make it sound quite simple. Is something the matter, Joslire?"

Yes. He'd been thinking about Student Pefisct. Joslire ducked his head to obscure his confusion, following a line of muscle down the outside edge of Koscuisko's shin with the hard knuckle of his thumb. "It never is as simple as it sounds. With the officer's permission."

"There is more truth than comfort there, however." Koscuisko did not seem to suspect any hidden thought, apparently content to follow his own stream to the rock. "Where I am at home, there are three great sins, and all others relate to one or more of them in some way. But none are unforgivable except the three most grievous ones."

What three great sins were those? Joslire wondered. He had done all he could with Koscuisko's knee. Moving around to stand at the head of the rubtable, Joslire began to finish on Koscuisko's shoulders, listening to his Student talk.

"And the first, perhaps the most difficult thing, is that you must confess yourself, or never hope to be forgiven. This is very annoying, Joslire. One would think that if the whole world knew that one had spoken with disrespect about one's elder brother or one's uncle that it would be enough to have one's penance decided and made known to one, and be done with it."

This was good. This was the sort of thing that he had been hoping for when he had asked the question. There was every reason to expect that Tutor Chonis would be able to explain what Koscuisko had been getting at, when the time came to give Chonis his report.

"But one would be mistaken. There can be no reconciliation without repentance, and there can be no repentance

without acknowledgment of fault, and there can be no acknowledgment of fault without individual confession. I wonder how different it can be when all is said and sung,
Joslire.''

Maybe it wasn't all that different at that. The Jurisdiction
required punishment before setting the Record to null, and
declined to apply any of the agony that could lawfully be
invoked to force confession against the penalty to be assessed.

So Student Koscuisko saw a connection there, and seemed
to take comfort from it.

Joslire lifted Koscuisko's head between his two hands to
work the neck back to the relaxed range of supple motion
that was normal for his Student.

Somehow he could not quite believe that the two parallels
were really so simply aligned as that.

It'd been harder than mastering any of the technical material, Andrej remembered that very clearly. With the possible exception of some of the more arcane degenerative
diseases among category-four hominids, nothing had been as
difficult as learning to take a patient history; and he'd been
too grateful for his teachers' praise when he finally began to
demonstrate some skill to worry too much about what that
struggle had said about him.

All of his life he had asked whichever question he liked,
never needing to consider whether the answer would be readily forthcoming—or accurate, when it did come. All of his
life, the function of language had been to communicate his
desires for the understanding and instruction of others around
him. There were exceptions, of course; the language of holy
service was humble and petitioning enough. It was also formalized by centuries of devout practice, and no longer really
signified.

But in order to take a good and useful medical history
from a patient already ill and not in the most conciliatory
mood because of it—that required he learn to ask. To sub-
merge any hint of personal frustration beneath a sincere and,
yes, humble desire to know. To set the patient at the very
center of the Holy Mother's creation, to listen with every

combined power at his disposal, to subordinate everything he was and everything he knew absolutely to whatever unsatisfactory and imperfect responses his patient would condescend to give.

There'd been times when he had despaired of ever attaining the art. There had certainly been times when his teachers had despaired of him. He'd been counseled by the Administration on more than one occasion to consider abandoning his goal in favor of a technical certification that would require no patient contact whatever, and he'd seriously considered doing just that; but he kept on trying. Graduation with full certification from Mayon Surgical College required demonstrated ability to develop a complete and accurate patient history, one-on-one—on an equal, not autocratic, footing with each patient who came under care.

Now Andrej sat in a padded armchair in the middle of the exercise theater, thinking about these things. The theater and the chair that was provided, he'd seen before; if not this precise theater, then others much like it, as Tutor Chonis reviewed paradigmatic exercises with them during their initial study. There was a door to the right through which the prisoner would enter. There was a table at his left, sturdy enough to support the body of an adult of most of the hominid categories, high enough for him to work at without tiring. Only his rhyti stood on that table now; his rhyti, and the Recorder. They'd add things gradually as they went along—instruments of Inquiry, then Confirmation, finally instruments of Execution, and there would be a side table for the Recorder.

For now the table was still safe for him. He could take his rhyti from it without shuddering, even knowing as he did what role it would play in his further education as a torturer. Security was posted behind him even now, even though it was only the first of the Levels—a free offering of confession, unassisted. Andrej wondered if Security was as apprehensive as he was to be starting this. Surely even Security had feelings about the work ahead of them all, the blood and the torment of it?

Without shifting his posture from the position of relaxed attentiveness he had assumed when he sat down, Andrej concentrated on the movements of the two Security troops behind him. He used to try to guess exactly what faces his young nieces and nephews behind him were making at the kneelers during the long hours in chapel on one Saint's day or another; and now he found that the old pastime had the effect of giving him eyes in the back of his head, where the strictly subservient Security were concerned. The prisoner had not been brought in just yet, and Security seemed to permit themselves a bit more restlessness than they might have had they felt that someone was watching them—or watching them now as opposed to hours later on Record, where they would like as not be out of orb anyway, if the demonstration tapes were any indication. The image in his mind's eye amused him—a pleasant relief from the fretful night he'd spent.

"Gentlemen, a little concentration, if you please," Andrej said, sensing their surprise and stiffening posture. Quite probably they'd never been forced to kneel devoutly for hours at a time while Uncle Radu declaimed at length about the improbably perfect virtue of some probably hypothetical martyr.

Perhaps he should approach his task from a different angle after all, Andrej mused.

To take a medical history one had to connect with a patient, and he wanted as little connection with this place as possible. He wasn't interested in making any person-to-person contact with the prisoner; but he couldn't take a medical history without engaging his empathic self.

His final evaluations in that all-critical block of instruction had cited his "genuine and responsive empathy of a very respectable degree," and he was proud of himself to have won over his own limitations, proud of how completely his proctor had been surprised as she read the commendatory prose from his record.

It would be better for him if he could turn the empathy off, pretend he'd never fought through the icy bare-rock pass between his mind and heart. It would be better for him to observe clinically, without emotion. Except all that he was and all that he had won at Mayon depended upon his pas-

sionate empathy; how could he set that prize aside, and not
diminish himself?

He was no further toward a solution to the problem this
morning than he had been last night, talking to Joslire. What
had he been talking to Joslire about? There'd been a good
deal of wodac after supper. He wasn't quite sure.

The warning signal sounded at the door; Andrej remembered. Uncle Radu, the tiresome business of the confessional,
and the brutal simplicity of it all. Confess or be unreconciled.
Be contrite or unreconciled; accept your penance joyfully.
Or be un-Reconciled.

Reaching for the glass on the table at his elbow, Andrej
drank off half the rhyti in one draw, regretting his gesture
immediately for the uneasiness that it betrayed.

Control, he told himself.

He had to have control.

"Step through." He could hear no tremor in his voice, no
uncertainty or nervousness. He had confessed and he was
contrite, but Uncle Radu—and the whole of the Blood by
extension—could not accept that he was truly penitent while
he still resisted his father's will. He left his home for this
place un-Reconciled because he couldn't accept his father's
wishes without protest. Disgraced and unblessed, and sitting
here as though he'd been set by the Holy Mother to examine
her children for flaw or fault . . . "State your identification.
And the crime to which you wish to confess."

He looked up only as he ended the first of the listed questions. He had the series set out in text for him on the scroller
at his elbow; a Bench catechism of sorts, the litany for preserving the forms of the Judicial order. Perhaps it would be
better to approach it that way. As long as he was un-
Reconciled, he might as well be irreverent, and be damned
for it. His father had kissed him and blessed him as well as
he could under the circumstances. But the Church was pitiless.

The Church and the Bench's Protocols were well matched
for that.

"Abbas Hakun, Sampfel Sector, Dorl and Yenzing, Your
Excellency."

Familiar as the title was, it startled Andrej to hear it in

this place. On his homeworld his father was an Excellency, a prince not of the Autocrat's lineage. And since all of a prince's sons were princes—regardless of whether they would inherit, regardless of whether there was anything to inherit—Andrej had been an Excellency from his infancy. It only took him a moment to remember. Chonis had warned them that their prisoners were required to address them as if they were already commissioned.

"The crime to which I wish to confess is that of defrauding the Bench, Your Excellency."

It is my shame to be un-Reconciled, and if I cannot be relieved of fault by penance I must die nameless and unwept, never to stand in the presence of my Holy Mother beneath the Canopy.

His prisoner was Mizucash, tall, broad-shouldered, and imposing for all his bound hands and meek demeanor. The language of submission and confession sounded strangely in the Mizucash's mouth, to Andrej's ear.

"In what manner have you defrauded the Bench?"

Just like the confessional. The crime had to be quantified and categorized before the appropriate penance was assessed. And if the prisoner or child under Canopy did not have answers ready, the questions themselves would elicit sufficient information to complete the Record and define the penalty.

"My employment was in a Judicial Stores contract company, Your Excellency. Our contract lay in the provision of the nine flours Standard for fastmeal menus of hominid categories eight, ten, eleven, and nineteen."

Yes, my Mother's servant, I have challenged my father's will and my father's wisdom, and not submitted myself to instruction, as a filial child would not fail to do. I cannot accept my father's will, though I am to do it. He cannot know what he requires of me.

"Describe the actions that you took, or failed to take, that resulted in the crime of defrauding the Bench."

So easy, to pass from the neutral "crime to which you wish to confess" to the necessarily self-incriminating "crime of defrauding the Bench." One hardly noticed the all-important shift in emphasis. Was this how Uncle Radu felt when he heard confession beneath the Canopy?

"I operated the sweeper in the packaging area of my plant. My instructions specified that flour sweepings were to be collected and weighed for use as wastage statistics for the development of the billing rates."

What was the man talking about, anyway? "Explain how your actions vis-à-vis the floor sweepings defrauded the Bench." He had to concentrate on the task before him and set aside his brooding. What could be so important about flour sweepings that they would send a man all the way out to Fleet Orientation Station Medical to confess about them? Or was that the point, that it was an unimportant crime, and therefore it was no matter if a Student Interrogator botched the job?

"Wastage statistics reduce the billing rates by the value of the sweepings in flour by weight. My wife and I, we're in violation of the recommended reproduction levels, Your Excellency, and rations only allow for two children. So instead of bringing the flour to be weighed, I took as much of the sweepings home as I could manage on each shift. In violation of my published procedure."

So he was to take the confession of a man who had cheated the Bench out of a few eighths of flour. It had to be a joke. If he were in Uncle Radu's place, he would have had so pathetic a sinner turned out of sanctuary and beaten for his presumption, or for the sin of aspiring to an excess of piety. One might as well beat the gardener for having chewed on a leaf of jessamine while cultivating the plantation. Could this be some sort of an initiation prank, like throwing the class's best student into the waddler-pond for luck before final exams commenced? Andrej decided to test it, distracted from his private conflicts by the obvious absurdity of the situation.

"Describe the value of the flour sweepings you have confessed to having misappropriated." Which would in turn define the degree to which the Bench had been defrauded, so that he could form a better idea of the severity of this crime.

"We used to have a saucer-cake for the chilties' morning meal from them. A good eighth in Standard scrip, Your Excellency. Sometimes as much as four-eighths, and my Balma would eat, too."

Ridiculous.

He'd have to revise his mental comparison. To prosecute defrauding the Jurisdiction Bench at this level was like selling the gardener's children into prostitution because the gardener had inhaled too deeply of the jessamine fragrance on three consecutive warm mornings, thereby defrauding the House in concept of some minute amount and unrecoverable amount of the essential oil.

"Oh, fine," Andrej said—to the monitor as much as to the prisoner. He felt completely at ease now, his sense of the ridiculous having overpowered his self-pitying introspection. "Very good indeed. You are a very great sinner, Abbas Hakun." He couldn't tell whether Security's sudden twitchiness behind him was affront or the giggles; he didn't care. He had half a mind to walk out on this farce of a confession right now. "What impelled you to confess your crime to the authorities so that the Judicial order might be preserved?"

Or else he would continue with the questions as they were written, which had the potential for becoming really rather hilarious in the absurdity of applying them to the theft of a handful of flour.

"My wife developed an allergic reaction to one of the flours. They're not available as rations to the mill staff . . ."

It was the first trace of real emotion Andrej had heard from his prisoner; and the desperation he read underneath that neutral statement was too honest to be amusing.

Perhaps it wasn't funny.

But it was no less absurd.

"She was at risk of being accused for trade on illegal markets, so I turned myself in. It's true that she ate, but it was me who stole, Your Excellency. It is for this reason that I asked to be allowed to make this confession."

Torn as he was between his inability to take the crime seriously and his appreciation for the prisoner's obviously sincere desire to protect his wife, Andrej was unsure as to his next move. Azanry was too rich a world; no one lacked for a handful of flour, at Rogubarachno . . .

He decided to complete the forms.

Tutor Chonis would explain the joke—if joke there was—

when he and Tutor Chonis went over the tape of this session for critique.

"Very good. There was no question in your mind at any time that your violation of procedure constituted willful fraud, then."

There just had to be a joke in here someplace.

◆ Three

Tutor Chonis was not actually angry. Perhaps a little annoyed. Koscuisko's scorn had been rather sharp, and as Koscuisko's Tutor, Chonis took that personally. Annoyed, yes, but not enraged, and that meant that he had to make a conscious effort to compose his face for the desired dismaying effect as he keyed the office's admit with unnecessary force, making noticeable show of fighting with imperfectly suppressed disgust while awaiting the tiresome membrane to slide slowly apart to allow him entry.

"Can you really imagine that we're that stupid?"

Choosing the blunt unreasonable words carefully, Tutor Chonis all but spat them into Koscuisko's face before continuing past his startled pupil to take his seat behind his desk. Noycannir was startled as well, of course—but not without a subtle undershadowing of gratification in her flat, shining hazel eyes. Tutor Chonis wouldn't have had it any other way. It was his business to set Students at each others' throats and make them compete for his approval and respect. That was one of the reasons that Tutors handled two Students in the same Term, and on the same shift as well. Receiving a stern reprimand in the presence of a social and professional inferior could, with any luck at all, be counted on to set young Koscuisko's aristocratic teeth on edge.

"I've reviewed your practical exercise, Koscuisko. I am disgusted with the manner in which you conducted yourself. You seem to think that this is all some sort of a perverse amusement, an adolescent game."

And he could all but hear Koscuisko seething where he sat, with his spine locked rigid and his hand that lay on the table suddenly motionless; still, there was no hint of Koscuisko's fingertips whitening at the point of the stylus in his hand. Koscuisko had control.

Chonis didn't know if that was a good thing or not, yet.

"It is a game." Sweet and soft, Koscuisko's reply, but Chonis could hear the confusion and worry behind the response. "You explained it to us yourself, Tutor Chonis. We pretend that the crime deserves its punishment, and in return the prisoner pretends that there is hope of Judicial leniency."

It wasn't the sarcastic route Koscuisko's reasoning took that disturbed Tutor Chonis. He knew about it already, of course, from Joslire's reports; and his own experience had prepared him to expect it from a man like Koscuisko. It was not an uncommon psychological defense, especially at the beginning of the Term.

"Don't try to mock me."

He turned away from the two of them in order to emphasize his displeasure and to analyze its source at the same time. The real problem was that Koscuisko gave every evidence of possessing an unusually healthy sense of the ridiculous. He could not be permitted to leave Fleet Orientation Center Medical with that sense of the ridiculous intact.

"Capital eight-six. On the appropriate display of the accepted psychological conviction." Damn the insolent little wretch, Koscuisko was quoting his own lesson citations at him. "The Inquisitor is at all times to display clearly evident conviction that the Jurisdiction's scale of punitive measures is wise, tempered with mercy, and above all completely just. Correct moral stance on the part of the Inquisitor will greatly facilitate the creation of the appropriate attitudes of contrition and submission to the Law on the part of the prisoner."

As if he didn't know, when he had all but written the text himself. "Leaving apart for the moment the unpleasant flavor created by a Student attempting to lecture his instructor. Dare you suggest that your clownishness in the practical exercise created the appropriate sense of respect for the Judicial order in the mind of your prisoner? . . ."

He turned slowly back to face his Students again as he

spoke. Noycannir first: She seemed to be enjoying the show. If only she could learn from it. Her first exercise had been completely serious—without technical error and with every indication of utter conviction, as if her personal background—her proven skills for survival in the unspeakably sordid circumstances of her earliest years in an ungoverned Port, her demonstrated facility for carrying useful survival strategies to their logical limits—had somehow deadened her imagination. She would not make an adequate Inquisitor without an imagination. A torturer with an intensive medical background and a set of legal parameters to conform to could be considered to be a perversion of a sort, that was true. But a torturer without imagination was only a brute.

"A man," Chonis continued, "since you obviously need the reminder, who was honest enough to make a full and free confession. In order to protect his family from the consequences of his own guilty actions. Whose dignity should have been respected."

Koscuisko met his eyes squarely, and did not drop his gaze until a precise fraction of a moment before the stare would have become too insolent to be permitted to pass. Koscuisko looked rather more enraged than irritated, very much as if he was considering some internal vision of Tutor Chonis in three pieces. His glare seemed to wash the color out of his pale eyes until they almost seemed all white and no pupil—like the Nebginnis, whose vestigial eyes, no longer functional, had been replaced by sonar sensing. Chonis was gratified with the effect. It had not been easy, but it looked at last as if he had got Koscuisko's attention.

He resumed his line of discourse. "Remember well that the dignity of even the guilty must be carefully cherished. . . . And is not the painful disregard of that dignity one of the most severe marks of the Bench's regretful censure of wrong conduct?"

Except that if he didn't watch his own tone of voice he would lose all that he had gained. He sounded almost sarcastic to himself; and if he thought he sounded sarcastic—with his lifetime's worth of training in picking up linguistic subtleties—then there was the danger that Koscuisko, whose records pointed to a high level of innate empathy, might sense the same thing. Chonis pulled a weapon from Joslire Curran's daily reports to use against Koscuisko's formidable sense of center.

"You are at least nominally an adult, by the Jurisdiction Standard. I understand that in your birth-culture confessions are made only to priests, and all the rules are unwritten. It is not so here." In Koscuisko's birth-culture, no man whose father was out of cloister was an adult. The women had it easier on Azanry, in that sense at least, because women became adults with the birth of their first legitimate child—no matter how old their mothers lived to be.

Koscuisko, seemingly disinclined to be drawn out, had squared his chair to the desk and folded his hands. He appeared to be concentrating on the minuscule text printed on the index line of one of the recordsets on the library shelf, his expression one of mild, polite disinterest as Chonis lectured.

"Confession is a deadly serious legal action. And the penance voluntarily accepted by the transgressor is serious, too, Koscuisko, remember that." In order to provide the correct exemplary deterrent. "It isn't the sort of risk you ever took. That is, if you're religious."

Confession and penance. Koscuisko had nerved himself up to his ordeal by drawing the analogy himself. Koscuisko had been thoroughly scolded now, and Noycannir put on notice as to what sort of reception her first stumble would earn her. Perhaps one final pious admonition. . . .

"After all, whatever penance you might have risked could hardly be said to equate with the just outrage of the Judicial Bench."

Koscuisko stared him in the face once more, and this time his gaze was frank and honest—no trace of resentment or rebellion.

"You never had to confess to Uncle Radu after an anniversary party," Koscuisko said.

Humor.

Koscuisko's ability to find humor in the current situation only indicated that there would be more problems yet down the time-stream.

"Very well. We will speak no more about it." But the

Administration would watch and wait, record, and meditate.

"As you will have noted, the next practical exercise is scheduled for five days from now. We will be defining the Second Level of the Preliminary Levels. Please direct your attention to your screens."

Humor and a sense of proportion were both unpredictable traits, not subject to reliable manipulation. Koscuisko's unpredictability had to be explored, detailed, and controlled.

Because an unpredictable Inquisitor with a sense of the ridiculous and an imperfectly submerged sense of proportion was potentially more disruptive of the Judicial order than even the Writ in Noycannir's ignorant hand could be.

Standing in the lavatory, Andrej stared at himself in the reflector. He could hear Joslire in the outer room; it was a familiar set of sounds, easily ignored. His face did not much please Andrej this morning. It was too pale; and it had always seemed to him that some proportion or other had been neglected when the issue of his likeness had been controverted among his genes in utero. To be fair, his pallor was perhaps his own fault. He had taken a good deal of wodac with his thirdmeal, yet again, last night.

Still, a man needed more emphatic a nose if he were to go through life with such wide flat cheekbones—or at least eyebrows with dash and flair, or eyes that made some sort of an impact to draw a person's attention away from the crude materiality of his skull. Too much cheekbone and too deep a jaw; there was no help there. A plank of wood with a chip of nothing for his eyes, which were of no particular color; a splinter for a nose; and his mouth would never carry a debate against his cheek—there was too much distance there from ear to front. No color, no drama; he might as well not have a face at all. There was paint, of course, but not even the best of that had made his brother Iosev any less unpleasant to look at, so there was no help to be found in that direction.

He was only trying to put off the morning, and he knew it. Sighing to himself at his own transparent motive, Andrej dried his damp face briskly with the towel and combed his hair back from his face with the fingers of his left hand. His

brother Mikhel had all the face in the family, and all of the
beard as well. Mikhel, and perhaps Nikolij, too. But, then,
Nikolij was such an elf-faced child. There was hope for Nikolij. And even Lo—as blond and as bland of face and feature as Andrej himself—Lo had some of Mecha's height.
There was no justice in the world. Where was the benefit of
being the eldest of his father's sons if all he could hope to
inherit was all of the land, and all of the property, and all of
the authority, and all of the estate?

. Joslire would be getting nervous, and it wasn't fair of him
to make Joslire wait when none of it was Joslire's fault.
Andrej set his mind to silence, stubbornly determined to not
think of the morning's work until he was well into it.

Successfully distracted by the simple pleasures of the fastmeal table, Andrej found himself sitting in the Student Interrogator's chair once more without a very clear idea as to
how he had got there. It wasn't how he'd come back to this
room that needed his attention, though. Not really. It was
how he was to get out of it again that posed the more immediate problem. The Second Level of the Question—and
there was every chance that Tutor Chonis would take any
deviation from form as a personal insult, after his reaction
to the First Level—would be more difficult.

The First Level had been Inquiry pure and simple. The
Second was Supported Inquiry—a little pressure was to be
brought to bear. That was what Fleet called it, Supported
Inquiry. Mayon would have called it patient abuse, and sum-
marily stripped any Student who so much as threatened a
patient with physical violence of any chance for patient contact ever again in any Bench-certified facility—which also
meant, realistically speaking, losing any chance of graduating
with the prestigious Mayon certifications. But these weren't
patients in any usual sense of the word, so what did it matter?

Except that in Andrej's home dialect, the word for the
Standard "patient," someone seeking medical care, came
from the same root as the verb that signified suffering, or to
bear physical pain. Andrej did not care to mull over the double meaning. It was too unfortunately apt for his comfort.

He wouldn't have thought that he would mind simply hitting people so much, not really, and that was all today's

exercise should entail—hitting someone. Hitting them frequently, perhaps, and the fact that they were not to be permitted to hit back was certainly distasteful, but they need suffer no permanent ill effect from the blows. He certainly hadn't come all the way through his medical training without ever hitting anybody. There was a difference, of course, when it was strictly after class hours, outside the patient environment, usually in a tavern of some sort, and never without either having been hit or being immediately hit back. He had done his share of recreational brawling, with a little thin-blade dueling thrown in. Violent physical exercise could be a great reliever of stress, and as far as Andrej could remember, he'd enjoyed it—not the residual bruises, no, but the energy surge had been a tremendous mood enhancer.

Though conservative of traditional Aznir ways, in many respects Andrej's father was a progressive man who didn't think children or servants should ever be beaten for their misdeeds, and who refused to tolerate any such behavior within his Household. Therefore it had come to pass that Andrej had never struck anybody in his life who had not been in a position to retaliate, without hesitation or restriction. Andrej supposed it was a handicap, of sorts.

He heard the signal at the prisoner's door. Well, soonest started was soonest sung. "Step through." Still, there was something he'd wanted to remember. Something his teachers on Mayon had said about hurting people. What had it been? "State your identification, and the crime of which you have been accused."

This prisoner was a Bigelblu, his legs almost as long as Andrej was tall. He sauntered into the room insolently before sinking into cross-legged repose in front of Andrej where he sat.

"You c'n call me Cari." He had a deep voice, the prisoner had. Nearly as deep as Mecha's singing voice, which was so low that the saint's-windows shook in sympathetic vibration when he sang "Holy Mother." "I dunno, Soyan, s'a mystery to me."

Deep, and insolent. For a moment Andrej sat torn between reacting and thinking out his own approach to this problem.

He knew how he was expected to react. And he didn't want to have to think about it.

Much of the medical process did involve hurting people, as a necessary part of helping them heal. Surprise was as unpleasant as pain, apprehension as noxious. When one was required to do something that would hurt—remove dried-out field dressings or palpate a sprain, or any number of contacts with wounded or painful tissue—one minimized apprehension and surprise by building up to the bad part slowly. Starting with small, impersonal contact at safe body sites, always remembering species-specific or cultural taboos. When one approached the painful thing in neutral graduated steps of that sort, patient apprehension could be significantly reduced, helping to ensure that the pain involved would be kept to its lowest level.

Now Andrej was expected to strike a man who was to be restrained from striking back, and the very idea was morally repugnant on its deepest level.

He would try to sneak up on it. That was it. That was what he could do to get through, for today.

"Stand up." Andrej rose to his feet and took the prisoner by the shoulder, giving him a little push. He was horribly reluctant to so much as touch the man; and yet he would be expected to hit him, and hard enough to at least bruise. . . . "I said stand up, what are you waiting for?"

Security came to his rescue; Andrej imagined they had experience helping uncertain Students through the paces. They had the Bigelblu on his feet in short order, their efficient handling quite unimpaired by "Cari's" grumbled protests.

"Easy, you guys, where's your sense of humor? 'Vent I been standing all day, waiting for this . . . little . . ."

Andrej never got a chance to hear what Cari meant to call him; no, the Security were too efficient for that. One of them had the prisoner's arm behind his back, and apparently did something unpleasant to it; at least to judge from the expression it produced.

"One is expected to use His Excellency's dignity with appropriate respect," the Security troop said. With a straight face; truly, Andrej admired his control. Surely such a clumsy start as he'd made could only make him ridiculous in front of these people, and no "appropriate respect" about it.

"If he's tired of standing, let him kneel. But sitting on the floor gives one an unpleasant feeling that one is not being taken quite seriously . . ." No, he was better off staying away from that line of thought. Tutor Chonis would think that he was being insolent again.

". . . which is surely not what you meant to do. On your knees, then. No, here."

Working with his hands, pushing a bit, pulling a bit, moving the prisoner from side to side. Getting used to the warmth of the prisoner's body beneath his hand. Doing what he could to nerve himself to the shameful test, taking the edge off his reluctance to hit the man by pushing the prisoner around. He didn't like it, but it seemed to work. Andrej felt he could manage the next step, if only he could avoid being distracted by the fact that he meant to strike someone he wasn't even angry at.

He had a clear field now, even had a modest advantage of height as he stood before the kneeling prisoner. Andrej repeated the question in a sterner voice, trying to convince himself he was determined by speaking harshly.

"State your identification, and the crime of which you are accused."

"Now, Soyan, didn't I just tell you that? My name's Cari, and . . ."

The tension within him was not shame and reluctance, Andrej told himself, knowing he lied. The tension within him was irritation at being sworn at, and irritation could be relieved by directing it at its natural object. Andrej moved on his target with a smoothness born of thin-blade dueling, giving his prisoner a backhanded slap across the face which surprised all of them: Security, because they had to compensate for the force of the blow, and they had not apparently anticipated his movement; Andrej, because he was wearing his great-grandfather's ring on his left hand, and one test was all that was required to demonstrate the sense of using his right hand for the remainder of the exercise. He was going to have to remove the ring next time.

"Be so kind as to answer the question." He had done the

thing, now, with never a Mayon monitor to report his lapse of professional conduct to the Administration. He had successfully raised his hand against a man restrained and defenseless. He had passed the filthy test of indecency. Now all he had to worry about was the next blow; and the one after that.

"Ah, well, Cari is short for Kerrimarghdilen. My family name is Pok." Last but not least, Cari had apparently been surprised into sensibility. At least for the moment. "I was picked up for vagrancy at Merridig, but I had some timmer on me—personal use only, really, I swear—so I'm here in front of His Excellency for illegal trafficking."

At least timmer was a little less mundane than flour. There was still a problem with this, of course. Why should he himself have unlimited access to the intoxicants traditional to his culture—every bit as destructive when abused, and without sanction as a sacrament—at the same time that an otherwise honest Bigelblu could be prosecuted by the Bench for trading in a culturally traditional and sacramentally essential hallucinogen? A problem, yes, and not the less so because the answer was so obviously a matter of whether Bigelblu or Aznir had economic clout.

But the distance between what the prisoner had done and what the Bench meant to do in reprisal was not as extreme as the first had been. That was a relief.

"You have stated your personal name, but have failed to provide your identification. Full identification is required to complete the Record. State your identification, and the crime of which you have been accused."

Apart from the general problem of double standards—and the immediate ache of his knuckles beneath the weight of his great-grandfather's ring—Andrej was not as sickened at himself for having struck the man as he had expected to be. The Bigelblu was a prisoner, and for the striking. Andrej was required to strike him. And it wasn't as if this man had come to him for healing; he had been brought here to make confession.

Andrej had no false conviction that these rationalizations made it morally correct to strike a prisoner, or that he should feel no guilt for having done so. But just for the moment to

feel little enough guilt that he could fulfill the specific requirements of a Second Level interrogation was all that Andrej asked of his life.

"What a dullump, Soyan. Nobody told me that I was going
to have to put up with so much damn natter-tattering—"

Andrej hit him again, with his right hand this time.

"What'd you do that for? I've got a right to—"

Andrej responded almost easily, as if there was no barrier
of decency and shame between a man in power and one in
chains to stay his hand and moderate his temper.

"No . . ."—it was only a short stoop to glare down at this
Cari nose-to-nose, with a hand at his throat to discourage
any sudden movements—"No, you've no particular right to
anything, just at the moment, and you and I both will find
ourselves considerably less exercised at the end of our discussion if you can persuade yourself to accept that concept
now. Answer as you're bidden, I am in no mood for insolence."

The language came out of the preparatory material, with
its model interrogations and its examples from the previous
students' taped practica.

Andrej cultivated what irritation he could find to help him
forward.

"Answer the question. Or must I repeat myself?"

If yielding to irritation would get him through this—then
yield he would.

And willingly.

Tutor Chonis settled his shoulders back against the chair,
folding his hands in front of him as he spoke.

"For the Record."

Third of three Preliminary Level exercises, third of three
evaluation and observation sessions. Curran behind him, to
his right—Student Koscuisko. Hanbor behind him, to his
left—Student Noycannir. Third of three, last of three, and
life was due to become interesting for all concerned within
a matter of days. For now there was only the Record to
complete, while preparations continued to be made for
rougher exercises.

"Preliminary Levels, the Third Level, assisted inquiry. Tutor Adifer Chonis, for the Record. Students Noycannir and Koscuisko in the theater.''

Student Noycannir had taken her place with the careful stiffness that characterized her when she was more aware than usual of being watched. Straight-backed and straight-faced she sat, her gaze apparently fixed on some point of interest midway between the prisoner's door and infinity. It was an interesting meditation to try to imagine how Noycannir would characterize infinity, when her birth and upbringing had been so sordid and so crushingly constrained. There was no hope of discussing it with her, however. From all indications, Mergau still felt that everything her Tutor did or said was first and foremost something to react against; and the conversations he had with her had been a little strained accordingly.

There was no stiff artificiality to Koscuisko this morning, however. Quite the opposite. Student Koscuisko occupied space with a sort of unthinking presence, a sense of self that was as much a part of him as Noycannir's apparently inbred defensiveness. There was no disguising the quality of Koscuisko's blood, or of his upbringing, at least. Nor any getting around the fact that Koscuisko was drunk, no matter how perfect—relaxed, confident, and apparently secure—his posture might be said to be.

Chonis sighed, and set the pause interrupt on his audio string. "Curran, he's been drinking? Again?"

Curran's grave bow managed to communicate a little of the confusion he seemed to feel. "As regularly as if scheduled, with the Tutor's permission. There does not seem to be any adverse impact on the Student's health."

Yet. Koscuisko was young; his body could still take it. What should it matter to him if Koscuisko drank? Except that Koscuisko hadn't on Mayon, not like this. Not so consistently as every night, for as long as they'd been practicing on the Preliminary Levels—every night for four weeks. Students who drank like that didn't earn Koscuisko's ratings. On the other hand, Fleet didn't expect much by way of actual medicine out of its Ship's Inquisitors once they were on Line. It was sentiment on his part, pure and simple, Chonis told himself with disgust. There was no other explanation for the fact that he could not help caring about what became of Koscuisko's medical skills if Koscuisko continued to respond to the stress by self-medicating with overproof wodac.

Chonis set the string back in braid. "Student Noycannir is calm and assured in manner." The prisoner-surrogates had made their entrance, the exercise could begin. Noycannir was on the attack from the first, raising her voice, confronting her prisoner verbally and physically. "She displays no hesitation or uncertainty in enforcing the Protocols."

Koscuisko simply sat where he was with his chin in one hand, his elbow propped up on the arm of the chair. Koscuisko liked to feel his way into things. From Curran's reports, Koscuisko was still struggling with the idea that it was appropriate to hit his prisoners. "Student Koscuisko continues to display a conservative approach. Although he has fully supported the Protocols, he provides adequate intervals in which the prisoner may offer information or other responses."

Whereas Noycannir was just a shade to the wrong side of the aggressive approach to Inquiry. Noycannir waded into her Levels like a Bladerau into a street fight, and her prisoners had to work at it to get a word in edgewise. "Student Noycannir is aggressive and confident. A point of discussion is to be made on the issue of timing. She will need to prepare herself to build more slack time into her interrogations."

Not that that really mattered, either. After all, the First Secretary would expect her to get information. That would necessarily require her to stop knocking her prisoners around long enough to listen to what they had to say.

"Student Koscuisko continues to engage his prisoner on a personal level. There is a potential cause for Administrative concern . . ." Chonis heard Curran stiffen slightly at the criticism. Students who could not learn to keep their psychic distance tended to get lost more often than other Inquisitors did. There was madness along that path, and not of a sort useful to the Fleet, either. Therefore to be discouraged.

". . . which will be addressed in the Advanced Levels if necessary. Student Noycannir maintains a commendable degree of personal separation from her subject."

An excess of empathy would not be a problem with Noycannir. She took to the habit of depersonifying her prisoners quickly and well. Chonis approved of her detachment; it was a good deal easier to kick an inanimate object than a fellow being. Far better to think of them all as mere lumps of recalcitrant matter to be worked into conformity than to spend as much time getting into their heads as Koscuisko did. While it was true that Inquisitors like Koscuisko got much better information, more consistently, it was also true that less involved Inquisitors like Noycannir tended to last a good deal longer on Line.

Koscuisko had risen to his feet, standing in front of his prisoner with his arms folded across his chest. His body language was as clear a sign as any that he didn't want to be here. But the stance was also one that presented no threat, putting the prisoner off his guard. Chonis was almost as startled as the prisoner was when Koscuisko hit him. And Chonis had seen him do it before. An ability to backhand a taller man across the face—and knock him down with the force of the blow, from that awkward angle—was no small thing; and Koscuisko made it all look quite natural.

"Student Koscuisko makes effective use of limited force. In this respect he is more apt than the average Student." Praise should be read into Record when due, and might soothe Curran a little as well. Chonis took his audio out of the string, again, to talk to Hanbor about the same issue.

"She's overdoing it again, isn't she?"

On the exercise floor, in the exercise theater, whether training or Inquiring, Noycannir did not seem to possess much of a sense of proportion. He and Hanbor had talked about the problem more than once during their daily status meetings.

"The Student did not receive the Tutor's prior comments on the issue as the Tutor would wish, with the Tutor's permission." Hanbor had his work cut out for him this Term: Noycannir was not responding well to shaping. Curran had the easier Student of the pair. "She did make a comment that may be pertinent, as the Tutor please. In reviewing the instructional paradigms, Student Noycannir called this troop's attention to the fact that when she hit people they stayed hit.''

There was no hint of tension in Hanbor's voice; he was a consummate professional, like Curran. And Hanbor wouldn't bother to mention it if she did beat him, unless he felt it pertained to information that Tutor Chonis would find useful. On the other hand, if Hanbor hadn't been superlatively qualified for Security work, he wouldn't have been Bonded in the first place.

Safety for bond-involuntaries lay in exceeding the Bench requirements for professionalism. Tutor Chonis was just glad he had a good caliber of support staff to work with. Out on Line in the Lanes, only Ship's Inquisitors were privileged to receive support from bond-involuntaries.

"Makes sense," Chonis nodded his thanks, and his agreement. "We'll need to work on that, before we get much further. Thank you, Hanbor."

Back into braid. Noycannir had knocked her prisoner-surrogate into a corner, and Security were taking their time dragging him back to the middle of the room—giving him a little space to catch his breath, and not being too obvious about it, either. Koscuisko's Security had stood away from him, leaving Koscuisko alone in the middle of the theater with his prisoner. Koscuisko didn't seem to need any help managing; he had a good hold on the prisoner's arm, twisted up behind the man's back. Chonis frowned, very slightly. It would be a shame if Koscuisko broke a bone at this point; he'd be forced to call the exercise for violation of the Protocols, and Koscuisko didn't deserve that kind of embarrassment.

"Student Noycannir puts her issues forward well and strongly." He had to be careful of what he said on Record. Anyone could review these tapes; anyone with the proper levels of clearance, of course. First Secretary Verlaine, as an example. "Student Koscuisko is relatively quick to gain the advantage but continues to display a certain degree of reluctance to press the advantage once gained."

As now, for instance, when Koscuisko released the prisoner's arm with a rough push that sent the prisoner staggering to his knees. He needn't have worried about the arm,

Chonis realized. Koscuisko's fault lay in reluctance to use as much force as was necessary; Noycannir's, in a consistent use of more force than was necessary.

"These issues will be discussed individually with the Students after completion of the exercise. Neither Student presents cause for any serious concern at this time."

Well, not as far as the exercises went, at least.

And that was as far as Tutor Chonis was expected to go.

" . . . very commendable progress."

Tutor Chonis's voice was fat and hateful in Mergau's ears, self-satisfied and oily. She didn't mind the powerful reverberation of authority that she could hear there. It was the hint of gloating that turned her stomach.

"There is always room for improvement, of course. As an example—very quickly—Student Koscuisko, you still don't appear to be taking this quite seriously; Student Noycannir, you need to relax, the prisoner cannot strike back at you. These minor details aside, however, the Administrator is very pleased. And he's empowered me to make a tangible gesture of that appreciation."

It was a trick, she knew it, her belly was tense and cold with it. A trick like the last one had been, to push them out into unknown territory before they'd really had a chance to master the material. A cheap manipulative trick.

"There will therefore be an extra study-day in which to prepare for the beginning instruction for the Intermediate Levels. After your apt handling of the first three exercises, it is anticipated that you'll not need extensive preparation . . ."

Mergau glanced to her left across the table, surreptitiously. Koscuisko was frowning. So he was suspicious, too.

" . . . therefore there's no lesson plan for this extra day. Student Koscuisko, you might enjoy a tour of the Infirmary; Curran has been instructed to obtain a copy of the pharmaceutical library for your use."

Koscuisko's scowl deepened. For herself she knew better than to display such a reaction in front of her betters—but Koscuisko didn't seem to think he had any. "We didn't do much with the Jurisdiction's Controlled List on Mayon, Tutor Chonis. Few of the drugs have positive medical applications.''

The "pharmaceutical library" confused her, but "the Jurisdiction's Controlled List" made all plain. Tutor Chonis was talking about the speaksera, the enforcers, the pain-maintenance drugs. She couldn't blame Koscuisko for disliking the idea. Where she'd come from, people feared the Controlled List even more than even the Ship's Inquisitor.

"But your skill, dare I say flair, with psychoactive applications is well documented as your subspecialty, Andrej. Perhaps the Controlled List will be made richer by your investigations.''

Yes, it was gloating in Tutor Chonis's voice. Very small and very subtle, but none of his mockery and taunts escaped her. Tutor Chonis was almost too pleased with the potential he felt he had identified to conceal his pleasure. Koscuisko glared down at his left hand, which he had closed into the fist he hadn't dared clench upon the table. For no particular reason, Mergau found herself noticing that there was an odd crease in the skin at the base of his middle finger. "I will browse the library, Tutor, at your instruction. Permit me to observe that I would prefer not to add to a resource that has such potential for being misused, and which is of so little positive benefit to anybody.''

Koscuisko would be damned before he had anything to do with the Controlled List, was what he meant. Noycannir shot a glance of shocked amusement at Tutor Chonis to make it clear that she disapproved of Koscuisko's near-insolence and disrespect as much as Chonis himself surely did. Tutor Chonis's face revealed no secrets, though.

"And, Student Noycannir . . .''

She blinked at Tutor Chonis's beard, demurely.

"The First Secretary has requested periodic reports from us to be forwarded every three Levels. You and I both understand how much he has invested in your training here.''

She knew how to behave in front of people who outranked her, even if Koscuisko did not. Koscuisko would learn. She'd love to have the opportunity to teach him. For now she would be content to benefit from the contrast between his attitude and hers.

"Am I to be present during review, Tutor Chonis, or shall I merely assist in preparing the report?"

Making her voice meek and submissive, Noycannir projected her understanding of her subordinate position, her earnest desire to please. It wasn't easy to fawn and cringe before Tutor Chonis, though it had to be done. Tutor Chonis didn't like her. His charge to Koscuisko had been double-edged, she realized—on the one hand giving her fellow Student his orders but, on the other hand, providing yet another reminder that she had no special medical education. She was ignorant of all but the practical basics of field medicine, and her fellow Student was a neurosurgeon qualified across eighteen of the thirty-seven hominid species and the obligatory exemplar from each of the non-hominid classes of intelligent species—with a secondary qualification in the biochemical applications of psychopharmacology, which she wasn't prepared to swear she could so much as spell correctly. She had no right to be here, as far as Tutor Chonis was concerned. No one would be there to intercede if she should fail, to stand between her and the humiliated wrath of her Patron.

Tutor Chonis's little smile, half-hid beneath his neatly trimmed mustache, was as hateful to her as his tone of voice had been. "That's up to you, Student Noycannir, of course." Tutor Chonis would just as soon leave her out of it. That was the principal reason she would insist on participation, just to be sure that no negative comment went unchallenged. "Report tomorrow morning, and we'll review your progress to date. All right?"

Fleet wanted her to fail because Fleet's vested interest was in retaining sole control over the Writ. Fleet was waiting for her to fail. Fleet would be happy to throw her to one of her own fellow Students for the Tenth-Level Command Termination just to express its resentment of First Secretary Verlaine's power play.

Half-sensing Koscuisko's sympathetic gaze, she stood, determined to exit with what dignity she had. Koscuisko's sympathy was intolerably patronizing. He disgusted her, him from his privileged background, money, rank, everything. She was ten times as good as Andrej Koscuisko, Bench medical certifications or no. She had worked for everything she had attained. Nobody had ever dropped an appointment in her lap.

"Very good, Tutor Chonis. Are we dismissed?"

The Tutor waved his hand, still smiling. Mergau bowed stiffly and left the room, struggling to contain the frustration, the fury, the fear that seethed within her.

She would be damned before she would give up her purpose.

Because she would unquestionably be damned if she should fail in it.

The serious concerns in life, Andrej felt, could best be pondered in one place and one place alone. One could think in one of the pathetically generic chapels that Jurisdiction Fleet provided for the spiritual welfare of its members under arms; but in chapel, one was expected to be silent, if not reverent, and Andrej had always done what he considered to be his very best thinking out loud.

Sitting on the slatted bench in the sauna that Joslire had located for him, Andrej took a deep breath of the hot, wet air and sighed with the satisfaction of it, coughing slightly as the thick heat caught in his throat. The heavy warmth was relaxing from the inside out. *Just what the doctor ordered,* he told himself dreamily *And I am the doctor, so I know.*

Joslire had posted himself by the door, but whether it was to control access or simply to be closer to a patch of cooler air, Andrej couldn't tell. The man's posture was as correct as ever it was, regardless of the fact that he was half-naked; there was something a little unusual about Joslire's state of undress, what was it?

"Joslire, will you come here for a moment, please?"

Joslire had folded his uniform for him and stowed his clothing carefully away before Joslire had even started to undress, and Andrej had been halfway into the sauna by that time. Obedient to his word, now, Joslire came to stand at attention on the wooden grating that covered the heated floor. Leather straps, that was what it was. Leather straps across Joslire's narrow slanted shoulders, binding his forearms, tight across his barrel-ribbed torso—leather straps, to anchor the sheathing Joslire wore.

Understanding came with a shock of recognition. Andrej turned his head away, waving Joslire off. He was ashamed of himself for not having considered what he was requiring when he'd decided to have a sauna. Joslire was Emandisan, and wore five-knives. And Emandisan were reputedly so private about their five-knives that you had to be married to one to even know which one went where.

"Go and dress yourself, Joslire, you look cold." He was the one who'd insisted Joslire strip to his towel; he was the one who'd assumed that Joslire would be uncomfortable in the unaccustomed heat if he tried to accompany Andrej into the sauna fully clothed. "Or will it be a violation, if I am alone for eight minutes?"

A violation. Joslire would not violate his discipline, and part of that clearly meant giving no hint as to his personal preferences one way or the other. As if personal preferences were a privilege of free men, and officers had to be discouraged from considering their bond-involuntaries' comfort as if it mattered. His insistence that Joslire take off his clothing in order to bear the sauna's heat more easily had probably generated twice as much discomfort between them as had he simply permitted Joslire to fall flat on his face of heat exhaustion in the lawful pursuit of his duty, and be done with it.

"The officer should not exercise himself." That was a joke; he hadn't voluntarily exercised anything except for his drinking arm since he'd got here. Participation in the combat drills that Joslire demonstrated for him so patiently twice a day was certainly not voluntary, or he would happily have done without. "There is no reason for the officer to be concerned on this troop's behalf."

It was disgusting. He was supposed to pay more attention than that. He was accountable for what belonged to him. "I don't believe you, Joslire. But I'll take your word for it." Because he was liable to create even more awkwardness if he didn't. Andrej settled himself against the paneled wall of the sauna, and closed his eyes. "Tell me, if you can, then. To how many Students have you been assigned, prior to this particularly thickheaded one?"

He wasn't aware of any prohibition against gossiping

about former Students. If there was such a prohibition, Joslire would find some way to observe it without letting on, in which case Andrej would learn nothing, in which case he would know.

"There have been five, previous to the officer." From the sound of Joslire's voice he was back at his original post by the door. "The first of the Intermediate Levels has been a critical point for each one of them."

He might as well have said "each one of you," "all six of you." "Am I really so obvious? You may neglect to answer that question, Joslire. I actively encourage you to neglect to answer that question."

Three levels in the Preliminary set, suitable for persons accused or suspected in regards to whom there was not yet enough evidence to make an arrest. Almost they could be said to correspond to basic physical examination, and the taking of patient histories. The invasive techniques came next, here as they had at Mayon; but the focus was all wrong. Andrej could not shake a feeling of unreality, the stubborn suspicion that there had to be something that they weren't telling him. He was certain of it. They could not—they *could* not—expect any thinking being to take such Levels seriously, and go forth to beat a shopkeeper on suspicion of having shortchanged a Jurisdiction clerk by an octe's weight of sallets on a slow day five weeks gone.

That kind of a joke was not so bad, as long as it remained a joke. His thin-blade duels had all been jokes, in the end, a recreation comprised of the hazard of lethal force against the flimsiest pretexts imaginable. It was precisely that tension that had made it so exhilarating—not that their student duels had been lethal; no one had been seriously injured in a duel in all his years of schooling. But there was always the chance. It was for that reason that he treasured the thin white scar underneath his right eye and had steadfastly refused to have it smoothed away. He had earned it fairly in contest against his friend Sourit, who had suddenly decided in the midst of their fifth-year finals that a man who sweetened his cortac brandy could not be permitted to live.

"The Administration expects a crisis. No fault is to be found with the officer on that account. The Administration simply requires that the officer continue with his orientation. Not that the officer find it agreeable.''

No, of course no fault would be found, not as long as he continued to perform as expected. And it was no longer to be enough to simply hurt people; according to the exhaustively defined Protocols of the Intermediate Levels he must proceed to harm them as well.

There was no possibility of a joke of any kind in that.

''Speaking of Administrative requirements, Joslire, I am to take myself to Infirmary to meet the Resident, I understand. Have I mentioned that the Controlled List is an abomination beneath the Canopy?''

Three turnings, and he'd have to face the test and find out if he could bear to do what had to be done and stomach the passing of it. A little distraction in the meantime would not be unwelcome.

''After the officer's sauna. Laboratory facilities have also been reserved for the officer's use, during the remainder of the Term.''

Had they indeed? He had no intention of doing any Controlled List research. But it would do no good to tell Joslire that. Joslire would only have to report it.

''Sing out when I am finished in the sauna, then.'' Since the appointment had obviously been prearranged, Joslire would obviously not let him miss it. There was something to be said for Curran's constant shepherding; he couldn't be misplaced nearly as easily as Andrej usually misplaced his other time-keepers.

''As the officer requires.''

Enough thinking for the moment.

He could feel the sweat run down his face, down his ribs, along his feet.

If he really worked at it, perhaps he could convince himself that he was actually relaxing after all.

 **Four**

Frowning to himself, Tutor Chonis put another mark down on his record, still not quite satisfied with his report. The signal at his office door was expected, if a little early; he keyed the admit without speaking, unwilling to interrupt his thought. The Administrator was satisfied with his report. He himself knew that each point he had made was solidly, independently defensible. And yet there was a problem.

He looked up.

"Student Noycannir reports, Tutor. As the Tutor instructed."

Yes, Student Noycannir. "Good-greeting, Student Noycannir. You may be seated."

She moved stiffly, as terrified of a misstep as ever. She had pride, and she was not stupid—not in the conventional sense. In ways she was clearly as intelligent, perhaps even as creative, as any of his Students had ever been, Koscuisko not excepted.

"The first thing that you should know, Noycannir, is that the channels are down. We will not be able to have our scheduled conference with Secretary Verlaine until several days from now."

Her self-control was formidable, but he had trained Inquisitors. And he could see the effect of his news—surprise, relief, joy, resentment, suspicion. Always ending up with resentment and suspicion. Tutor Chonis swallowed a sigh of resignation and continued.

"I have here the report that the Administrator has released

73

for transmit to the First Secretary. If you like we can discuss
this before it's forwarded.''

What crippled her intelligence was her defensiveness and
the mean-spirited narrow scope of her reason. She was too
sensitive; reactionary and suspicious. Her resentment of anything that she interpreted as a personal reproach cut her off
from any real support that he could offer; and her self-
absorption brought her to see everything as personally directed against her.

''As the Tutor thinks best,'' she said tonelessly, her eyes
fixed on the Recorder in front of her. ''I know I only want
to know what I can do better.''

She had convinced herself that the report was negative, so
much was clear. Chonis cloned the draft to her screen.

''Take a moment to scan the text, Mergau, if you please.''
The translator would provide a Standard version, the only
language Noycannir could read. She was like the creche-bred
in that, although he doubted that she would have appreciated
his pointing that out.

Tense and silent, she stared at the screen in front of her.
Chonis decided to take the opportunity to read it through for
one last time himself.

*Student Noycannir has successfully completed the basic
orientation portion of this Term. She displays a better than
average ability to recall Judicial precedent and supports her
interpretations of the discussion cases with pertinent citations. Her grasp of the theoretical basis of the Writ is above
average in complexity and thoroughness.*

He didn't think she was breathing. It would only make her
even colder if he noticed that, though. He read the next section over to himself instead.

*She has successfully completed the practical exercises at
the First, Second, and Third Levels. There is no abnormality
in her implementation of the Protocols. There has been no
inappropriate use of force.*

That was pushing it a bit, granted. She had not violated
the Protocols by going further in the interrogation than was
called for. She did have a tendency to hit twice, when once
would have been enough; still, she was hardly unique in that.
Students expressed their internal conflict over the things they

found themselves doing here in different ways. Noycannir
hit frequently, desperate to prove that she could hit as well
or better than Students with Fleet-approved qualifications.
Koscuisko simply hit, and then went off to take a drink or
six.

*In summary, the Student is performing at or above ac-
ceptable levels and has been passed to the next stage of
instruction. By order of the Administrator.*

She was rereading it, he could tell, her eyes jumping from
the foot to the top of the text as she scanned the lines, frowning slightly in her concentration. Chonis waited for her to
look up at him before asking the customary question —a little
ironic, under these particular circumstances.

"Do you have any comments to add, Student Noycannir?"

She seemed at a loss for words. And—regrettably, but
predictably—resentful of that fact. "I am . . . very satisfied
. . . with this evaluation." Her voice sounded curiously dead.
"Is there some deficiency not mentioned that requires my
attention?"

What, apart from the obvious?

"I need hardly point out that you are at somewhat of a
disadvantage here, Noycannir. The practical exercises will
become increasingly difficult for you." They would become
increasingly difficult for Koscuisko, too, obviously. But for
entirely different reasons. "As your Tutor, I feel that an in-
depth review of additional records on top of those chosen
for class exemplars would benefit you. This requires more
of an investment of time on your part, however."

She was an apt pupil. She could learn from observation.
As long as she spent sufficient energy actually observing and
not seething with resentment over perceived slights, as she
seemed to do in class.

"I will gratefully comply with the Tutor's suggestion,"
she said stiffly. Her breathing was a little ragged, as the tension she had been under when she'd come in began to wear
off a bit; and Chonis couldn't tell—for once—if she was
uncomfortable because her gratitude was genuine or uncomfortable because she felt compelled to use the submissive

phrase. "Has the Tutor a suggestion as to an appropriate starting point?"

Indeed he had. "I took the liberty of scheduling some tapes into a reserved screen in the library." Basic exercises, carefully selected to be as similar as possible to the situation she would face during her next practical exercise. "Hanbor will escort you there. And then I'll be needing him for an hour or two, but he'll be back to wait for you before your afternoon exercise period." So she would be safely out of the way, as well as Koscuisko. "If you haven't made other plans, of course."

She stood up. "I am at the Tutor's disposal. Thank you, Tutor Chonis."

"And you, Student Noycannir. Dismissed."

Secretary Verlaine might be right, that Noycannir's lack of medical background could be surmounted.

About her attitude—the more serious obstacle, at present—he was rather less than optimistic.

The officer was in the capable hands of Station Pharmacy staff for the moment, and would remain their responsibility for the next few eights. It was the first time that Joslire had been on his own since Koscuisko had arrived—except for the class sessions, of course, and that hardly counted, since that time was usually taken up in review with the Tutor. All he had to do for the next while was listen to the same lecture he'd heard six times before; and then spend a few eighths being introduced to Robert St. Clare, providing him with some background on the officer's habits of thought and tendencies in lines of questioning.

This was one of the worst parts of the entire Term for Joslire.

He knew where he was going, he'd been this way before. A long hallway well removed from the administrative areas where the Students lived and worked led to a featureless door among eight and sixteen others as innocuous, which led to a short corridor, which lead to an assembly room. There would be an exercise room, he remembered; a mess area, and a sleeping-bay beyond. Right now the assembly room—small as it was—was full; five Tutors at the foot of the room, ten prisoner-surrogates on the far side of the room. Day-new bond-involuntaries, just graduated from their long months of orientation, carefully selected for their superb physical health and their psychological resilience. There were only ten of them here, but there were only twenty Students on Station, and this was the briefing for the firstshift cycle. There would be another such briefing half a day from now to cover the other five Tutors, the other ten prisoner-surrogates, the other ten bond involuntaries assigned.

Finding his place among his fellows, Joslire took comfort in the company of other Bonds, waiting for the briefing to begin.

"Stand to attention for Administrator Clellelan!"

It required no thought to shift from command-wait to salute in response by learned reflex. The Administrator returned the required courtesy with a quick gesture, coming briskly through the ranks of Staff Security to stand on the platform at the head of the room.

"Listen and attend. You all know why you are here."

Joslire remembered when it had been him on the other side of the room, only five years ago. Listening to the Administrator, curious about the Tutors and the Staff Security, and too ignorant to be fearful . . . he didn't like remembering. Which of these naive children would it be, to test his officer's hand?

Which of these fresh zombies was Robert St. Clare?

"You have each received your individual briefings, and executed the required statements of expectation and compliance. For the sake of the Record, we will review these a final time now, before the exercise begins."

Not children any more than he had been, not really. Young, so that they could absorb the shock to body and to spirit and still recover to be useful to the Fleet, but all of them adults by Jurisdiction Standard. It was only the contrast between what he'd known then and what he knew now that made him think of them as children. Blessed in their ignorance. Soon to receive instruction.

"You have been carefully selected to play a critical role in the training of senior staff officers for the Jurisdiction's

Fleet. The importance of your part in the training process cannot be overemphasized.''

They had to be reminded that Fleet was unforgiving. He would never have made it through on the strength of his own will; in the end it had only been his keen awareness that failure would bring suffering far in excess of what he had already endured that had carried him safely through until the exercise was over. He'd never liked knowing that about himself. But it was true.

''If you do not complete your assignment, you will have compromised the training of an extremely significant Fleet resource, a candidate for Ship's Surgeon. There has been failure to complete the course in five out of the six regrettable cases in which one of you has proved unequal to your task. A continuing resupply of qualified Ship's Surgeons is an absolutely vital Fleet requirement. We do not suffer the loss of any Student lightly.''

They were likely enough to lose their Students to despair and the ultimate escape of suicide. The Writ could not be laid aside before an officer's eight years of service had expired, except as an act of treason.

''It is therefore critical that you keep the following requirements firmly in your mind. One. You are not to confess to your offense until midway through the Fifth Level.''

He'd been too confused to tell when the midpoint had been reached, since there'd been no chronometer he could see. He'd forced himself to hold out till the end, because that had been the only way he could be sure he was complying with instructions. And by the end of the Fifth Level, he'd suffered from a dangerous lack of focus, so that sorting out what he was encouraged and expected to confess from what he was forbidden in the strictest terms to even hint at had taken more of an effort than he'd ever dreamed possible.

''Two. Your officer must be given no hint or intimation of your status as a prisoner-surrogate. You can expect your officer to realize you're hiding something . . .''

Not if they were lucky. If they were lucky the officer would be only too happy with the information supplied, and would gladly ignore any but the most blatant hints of anything more. He had been lucky.

"... but you are expressly warned, on pain of a Class-Two violation, against revealing any more information than you have been instructed to provide."

It was only that Koscuisko was too responsive by half to subtle clues and cues. Koscuisko had startled Joslire more than once with his odd insight; and things that Koscuisko said about jokes and playacting hinted unnervingly at some subconscious understanding on Koscuisko's part that the "prisoners" he had seen in the Preliminary Levels were not prisoners at all. St. Clare would have a harder task to hide his truth than Joslire liked to imagine.

"The Security assisting the Student will ensure that the Intermediate Levels are respected." As well as they could, when they were forbidden to intervene without direct orders from the Tutor. "Succeed in this mission, and you will have proved yourself a valuable Fleet resource in your own right."

An educated resource. A more sophisticated resource. One with firsthand knowledge of how much a man could be hurt, confused, humiliated, humbled—all within the relatively benign restrictions of the Intermediate Levels, where no major soft tissue damage could be done, where none of the senses could be seriously compromised, where only half of the body's major joints and long bones could be broken and severe burns had to be confined to a strictly limited proportion of the total surface area of the skin.

A resource that understood about fear.

"Fleet will show its gratitude and appreciation accordingly. You will receive automatic deferment from Line Fleet duty for an eight-year period of time, and four years will be stricken from your Bond. These are only tokens of the importance that we place on your successful completion of your mission."

Would it be worth the price?

Could it be worth the price?

The same event that had stricken four years off his Bond had taken six years off his life. Or so he felt.

He could only hope that for St. Clare it would be different.

He'd been born Rabin with the Ice Traverse, but Robert St. Clare was what Fleet had decided to label him. Robert

St. Clare was the name to which he had learned to answer, this year and a half gone past. He wouldn't be Rabin again until the Day came.

He was Robert St. Clare, and he was as close to bored as he could remember ever being. It wasn't that he was looking forward to the exercise; no, not at all. But he was looking forward to something different; and as early as tomorrow, firstshift, it would begin.

"This man is Joslire Curran, Robert." The Tutor he had met when he'd first got here; Chonis had interviewed him briefly but thoroughly at the time. He wasn't allowed to stare at Chonis anyway, prior acquaintance aside, but he could stare at Joslire Curran all he wanted, full of wonder. Emandisan, the Tutor had told him. He hardly even knew what Emandisan meant, apart from the rumors. One thing was clear enough: Emandisan didn't look anything like any Nurail that he'd ever met.

"You're to have a few words with him, in final preparation. You may ask him anything that you feel may help you in the exercise. Joslire, I'll see you before thirdmeal."

A brisk salute from Curran echoed rather clumsily—he thought—by his own, and the Tutor went away. It was only Bonded Security and prisoner-surrogates here now.

"The Day will come," the Emandisan said, laying his hand on Robert's shoulder in formal greeting. Oh, yes. Right.

"The Day, after tomorrow." Yes, that was the response, and the Emandisan—apparently satisfied—let his hand drop to St. Clare's elbow, guiding him over to sit on the bench against the wall. Joslire Curran was very dark, compared to the people St. Clare had grown up with. The Black Mackeles weave had hair as dark as that, but even so their skin was lighter, and their eyes certainly nowhere near the intense black of this Curran's. Dark, not tall, and solid as stone by the look of his shoulders. Curran had already been through the exercise. St. Clare was impressed with him already.

He let himself be sat down meekly, watching Curran for his next move. Curran had a flat face, and did not look happy. Not as if he should be surprised at that, St. Clare told himself; none of these people lacked for reason to find fault with the world, and why should they?

"Your Student—you already know this—is Andrej Koscuisko. He's Dolgorukij, and he drinks."

It was a funny way to pronounce the name. "Aandrai." *Why didn't he just say Anders and be done with it*? St. Clare wondered. Of course Anders was a Nurail name, and Koscuisko wasn't likely Nurail. That would explain it, right enough.

"What should I expect from him, friend Curran?" St. Clare felt a little awkward using the term of familiarity; it sounded almost unnatural to him in Standard. Fortunately Curran did not seem to have taken it amiss.

"Oh, there's no predicting. It's too early in Term for that." Leaning his head back up against the wall, Curran stared up at the lights. St. Clare didn't think that Curran looked particularly comfortable. "There is a consistent trend, and it may be helpful to you, I don't know. He's pretty good at putting the procedure on. The thing to remember is that no matter how much it hurts, he's only going to hurt you enough. No more than that."

What could "enough" signify? Enough to get the answers, when they both knew that wasn't at issue? "I don't understand you, friend, what are you saying?" He only had a year and a half of Standard. Well, a year and a half of intensive Standard apart from the language he had learned for trade when he'd been much younger. There was a good chance that Curran was making very sound sense, and that he was simply too thickheaded to grasp it.

But Curran sighed, with a squinting of his eyes and a dropping of his head. "I think what I mean is that it's to be a fair test. He doesn't try to get around the Levels. You may find it useful to hang on to that while you're with him. I think that he's an honest man. Fair-minded."

Maybe he did understand what was going on in Curran's head after all. Curran had been here before. "What was of help to you, when it was your turn? Or it could be that you don't care to speak of it." Curran was uncomfortable, St. Clare was sure of that much. For all he knew, it was in as bad taste to ask about Curran's duty as prisoner-surrogate as it was to press your fellows for the details of their Bonds.

Shifting his weight a little, Curran leaned up against the

wall once more. "My Student wasn't very good. It was a hard exercise, because he kept on making mistakes and had to do things over again to satisfy his need for a good demonstration."

Still, it didn't seem to be thinking about his own experience that was making Curran itchy. Something else, maybe. Maybe Curran was just an itchy sort of a man in general.

Itchy or not, Curran was still talking. "With Koscuisko you aren't going to have that problem. He pays attention to getting things right once through. That's an advantage. Just . . . try to remember . . . you can't afford to let down your guard. Not for an instant."

St. Clare thought he understood now. Curran was worried. And Curran didn't want for it to show, since he'd know that St. Clare was worried enough already, and it was bad luck.

"We've had a bit of training," he reminded the Emandisan by way of reassurance. "They try to teach us concentration. It may help out, did it you?" As long as Curran was willing to talk St. Clare was eager to enrich his flock as aggressively as possible.

"Was all I had to go on, in the end. There's a lot of emphasis on . . . focused concentration, among my homefolk." Well, and what little St. Clare had heard about Emandisan focused on fanatic devotion to martial arts. Religious veneration of their five-knives, with litanies and rites and oracles. Maybe Curran had just snagged himself on the fact that Nurail were characterized by weaves and drinkable, instead of strength of will.

Drinkable could create a state of intense concentration, that was true.

But concentration on getting more drinkable—or knocking one's neighbor's head in, or crawling into a corner to die of the bodywrack—was probably not what Curran had in mind.

The room had begun to clear out a bit; it was getting to be time for Curran to leave, then. St. Clare stood up, to allow for a graceful departure. "Thanks for your help," he said, as Curran rose in turn. "I'm sure to be grateful to you for it in the morning." Such as it was. What did he know now about Andrej Koscuisko that he hadn't known before? He didn't see where honesty and fair-mindedness came into it at all.

"It'll be rough." Curran acknowledged St. Clare's thanks with a nod of acceptance. "But you'll make it through just fine. I'm confident of that."

Possibly the rumors about Emandisan self-discipline were true, and Curran was a stalloy-strong rock of unshakable will. Unfortunately he was not a very good liar.

"Until the Day, Joslire Curran."

Giving St. Clare's shoulder a reassuring shake, Curran completed the formula.

"The Day will come. Good luck." He smiled, once—it was rather alarming—and went out of the room, leaving St. Clare to sit back down and digest the whole thing.

A fair test, Curran had said. By clear inference, Curran's had not been, and that was why Curran was a little anxious. Doing a little projecting, it could be, reliving his own exercise in his mind as St. Clare prepared himself to meet the challenge.

But what if Curran was right, to be concerned?

Did Curran think there was a chance that he might fail in his duty?

Out of the question. Curran himself clearly had not wanted to make any such suggestion. And they'd know soon enough how it was going to go, either way.

He could not afford to begin to think about his sister.

Andrej Koscuisko had been up all night, and was beginning to feel the effects of the liquor that had kept him company. The easy availability of seemingly endless quantities of alcohol still surprised him, though he was grateful for the apparently limitless access to his drug of choice that was provided. As long as he was capable of asking questions and hitting people who couldn't hit back, it seemed the Administration didn't really care if he did so staggering drunk.

Staggering he was, if no longer quite incapacitated. The fragrance of the rhyti in the jug was not acceptable to his stomach just at the moment. The Security troop handed him his glass with a respectful bow, so Andrej accepted it to be polite; but he found he could only manage a deep inhalation of the steam before handing it back unsipped. No, it simply was not a good time for rhyti.

Out of an all-night drunk came clarity of a sort. He was here; there was nothing he hadn't tried to avoid it—with the exception of a pretense at suicidal depression, and he was not inclined to be such a coward as that. As long as he was here, there was little profit in agonizing over it, because agonizing wouldn't get him out any more quickly than making up his mind to get it over with.

The instruments appropriate to the Fourth Level had been laid out for his use and consideration, and he let his eyes rest on the instrument table while he beckoned for his rhyti to come back. Surely instruments were simply instruments, and not evil in and of themselves? A thin supple stick covered with leather, something rather like the riding crops he'd carried while riding out to hunt—more for tradition's sake than anything else, the hunters in his father's stable being notoriously bloodthirsty themselves and needing no urging to the chase. A coiled whip with a weighted butt; a handful of screws and clamps; some knives as thin as needles; and a stouter stick almost like a cudgel: These were instruments of Inquiry and Confirmation, and whether or not he could imagine himself actually picking one of them up and using it, the fact remained that he would not be permitted to leave the theater until he had at least made a beginning.

The rhyti settled rather more successfully in his stomach this time. His prisoner was ready for him, he heard the signal; with a casual gesture that he expected would fool no one, Andrej waved the Security to their posts.

Very well; let it begin.

"Step through."

Tall, again, the prisoner was rather tall. That wasn't unusual from Andrej's point of view, since he himself was to the short side of the Jurisdiction Standard. Tall and younger than the other prisoners had been—Andrej had expected as much from the Prisoner's Brief Joslire brought him last night. Joslire had seemed distracted. Andrej hadn't paid much attention at the time—he'd been concentrating on getting drunk—but now he wondered what had been on Joslire's mind.

"State your name. Your identification." He sounded decidedly cross to himself; it startled him to realize how drunk he still was. Just as well. The last thing he wanted to be right now was fully aware of his surroundings.

He did have to pay some attention to what he was doing, that went without saying. Just now, for example, he was almost certain that he'd asked a question, but as far as he could remember, he'd heard no response.

He frowned.

"State your identification, and the crime of which you have been accused. For which you have been arrested," he amended hastily. At the Preliminary Levels it was the crime of which one had been accused. At the Intermediate Levels it was the crime for which one had been arrested, and never without good and convincing reason, which was why the confession was so important. To validate the Judicial order. Because they never would have arrested this sullen young Nurail hominid if they hadn't had excellent reason—eyewitness testimony or a preponderance of circumstantial evidence.

No answer?

Andrej focused his attention on the prisoner's face. He had to look up to do it, and the lights in the ceiling seemed bright for whatever reason; so he gestured with his hand, and the Security behind his prisoner brought the man down to a more reasonable kneeling level. Where Andrej didn't have to squint at him. Where the mixture of amusement, contempt, and defiance on his clean-shaven face could be analyzed in detail. Clean-shaven: so he wasn't married. For what that was worth.

"Do you know how to speak Standard, or are you just being coy with me?" Andrej asked, watching the man's eyes for his answer. Yes, the prisoner understood well enough. "Then we have a tiresome problem to resolve, here, just as we are getting started."

If he turned his head, he could examine his instruments once again. He didn't like to brood on them; but he'd learned the use of other tools on Mayon, and there was no sense in blaming the tumor on the knife, surely. He knew precisely what each one was for. Their use and application had been demonstrated during the preparatory briefings. He just couldn't imagine himself touching any of them of his own free will.

"You know why you are here, and I know why you are here. We both know that the Bench requires a confession." Because the Bench prohibited itself from adjudging deterrent punishment unless guilt had been freely admitted, and would concede only so far as to accept a confession that had been somewhat assisted—but no further. "I could sit here and talk to myself, but that would only waste your time and make me look ridiculous in front of these amiable gentlemen. And nobody likes to be made a fool of. Be so kind as to state your identification and the crime for which you have been arrested."

To which you must confess. That was the first requirement; Tutor Chonis had been very clear. *We don't mind hearing what else the prisoner may wish to tell us, Student Koscuisko. But we never lose sight of our objective, and that is the confession as accused.*

But the prisoner only stared at him, smirking. Andrej wondered where he found the nerve; on the other hand—he reminded himself—being confronted by a half-drunk Student Inquisitor still only learning his craft was perhaps not the most intimidating experience to be imagined.

Andrej stood up.

"Have it your own way, then." He knew perfectly well what the prisoner's name was. That wasn't the point. The point was that it was in poor taste to take information as granted before the prisoner had confessed to it. And also that included among other pertinent details in the Prisoner's Brief was the identification of gene pool and subspecies ethnicity, and there was something about Nurail he'd been curious about in school. "Gentlemen, will you undress this mute for me, please? . . . To the waist will be sufficient. For now."

The walleyed alarm on the man's face was almost funny in light of how Andrej felt about what he was expected to do. There was no sense in getting alarmed just yet, although the prisoner could not know it. For all his resolve, Andrej still did not have the first idea how he was going manage to apply one of those ugly implements forcefully enough to draw blood, and not just nervous giggles.

There was some scuffling involved in the stripping process, it seemed. But it was brief enough; and when it was done, the Security had returned his subject to the kneeling position, the only discernible differences being anger and frustration as well as contempt on the prisoner's face and rather less clothing on the prisoner's body. Andrej stood up and beckoned for more rhyti. He was beginning to get hungry. That was bad news; it meant he was sobering up.

"Let's talk about the crozer-hinge." If the prisoner didn't want to make conversation he'd have to try and interest the Security. "Peculiar to the Nurail, usually confined to the male of the race; vital to the deployment of the famous crozer-lances. Specifically, a sort of a biological fulcrum, and a little more wicked than most." Or, rather, an odd arrangement in the shoulder joint, beneath the shoulder cap. Andrej had found it a fascinating study in anatomy, but he'd not been able to convince the lone Nurail in his class at Mayon to let him do any hands-on exploration. Not surprising, really, because the crozer-hinge was vulnerable to dislocation from one specific angle, and joints when out of joint were almost always intensely painful—no matter what the class of hominid, no matter what the species of animal.

He was expected to hurt the Nurail. He was required to. If he made a test of the crozer-hinge it would hurt the Nurail badly, and still not harm him to any permanent degree. If he could persuade the prisoner to cooperate in that way, it might smooth the course of the exercise for him. Andrej took half a glass of rhyti and handed the remainder back. It was handy having the extra Security present. It was supposed to be intimidating. Andrej stepped closer to the Nurail, choosing a shoulder.

"It's one of those structural oddities that complicate our lives. You can put eight and eighty units of pressure against the joint from this angle, and it has no effect whatever." At least the prisoner had the basic decency to begin to look worried. It was about time. Andrej didn't care how drunk he seemed to be, he knew his anatomy.

"And on the other hand the wrong degree of torque from

the back angle can tear the whole thing out of alignment.''

It needed two fingers at the inside joint, a little help from Security to rotate the elbow in the right direction. Or the wrong direction: The crozer-hinge popped out of the protective hollow of the shoulder, a large white lump of cartilage and bone deforming the skin of the upper arm like a very large and exquisitely unpleasant bird's-egg bruise on one's head.

The Nurail's body jerked with the shock of the pain, his face gone white with it. Andrej stared at the Nurail, frowning. There was something peculiar about the unwilling contortion of the prisoner's body, his muscles tensed in pain; what was going on? ''Abstract knowledge is never wasted, my friend. One has so few opportunities to examine such a complex jointure. Feel free to speak up if you should find yourself with anything to say.''

No answer; only a stifled sort of gasping as the Nurail's body convulsed with pain. Skeletal pain in itself was usually a referred phenomenon, but there was no brighter or more brilliant sort of pain than that associated with the joints, especially the smaller ones. Watching his prisoner writhe against the constraining hands of the Security, Andrej found himself keenly apprehensive of the pain the Nurail suffered from his shoulder. Suffering was noxious stimulus. He had spent long years in school on Mayon learning how best suffering could be relieved. But the prisoner did have to talk to him. Any of the instruments that the Administration expected he employ would cause more gross physical damage, so this was a conservative approach—although the prisoner could not be expected to appreciate that. And he could put it right in a moment, once the prisoner had surrendered up his name.

The prisoner wasn't talking.

Andrej backed up to the chair that stood ready for him. Motioning for the Security to bring his prisoner forward to kneel close in front of him, Andrej sat down, fascinated by the struggle on the Nurail's face. The choking sound of the Nurail's breathing and the clear cold sweat of pain running down his cheeks was giving Andrej a very peculiar feeling in his stomach.

''Your name.''

He was supposed to be after information, not so interested in his prisoner's evident agony. Andrej took the Nurail by the jaw to angle his face up to the bright lights in the ceiling. The Nurail's lips had gone white, and there was a stuttering sound as though his teeth were chattering; but the jaw was clenched so tightly Andrej could not imagine any teeth chattering. Intense. Yes. That was what it was. Intense.

"Tell to me your name."

No answer.

Andrej couldn't have that.

What could this miserable Nurail mean by defying him in this manner?

He was tempted to make the prisoner suffer for his stubbornness.

Loosening his grip on the Nurail's jaw, Andrej struggled with an unnamed temptation for a bitter eternity during the time it took to draw a breath and let it out once more. He felt his irritation as a physical sensation, a flush of humiliation and resentment that reddened his face and prickled his skin from head to toe.

"You, there, be so good as to take his head. How are you called, Mister . . . ?"

He wanted to be able to watch the Nurail's face carefully for his reactions, and for that he would need help. The troop at the Nurail's right bowed as best he could while holding to the shivering body of the prisoner.

"Curran, if the officer please—Sorlie Curran," the Security troop added quickly, in evident response to the confusion Andrej felt. Curran? But yes. The Curran Detention Facility was where Joslire had been condemned to the Bond. Any bond-involuntary similarly processed through the Curran Detention Facility would bear the name.

Andrej was reluctant to call him Curran, though.

"Sorlie, then. Keep his face well lifted; I want to be able to look at him." Oddly enough the flush of irritation he'd experienced had not faded away but settled on him somehow, making his extremities tingle not unpleasantly. His hands. His lips. His . . .

The Nurail's eyes were tightly shut, his body trembling. Andrej reached out to touch the taut skin across the displaced hinge, delicately. The instant his fingertips made contact, though, the prisoner cried out closemouthed with a high keening note that seemed to find a sympathetic echo of some sort in Andrej's belly. Or perhaps not his belly, perhaps it was his fish that was responding to that cry, thickening with involuntary interest . . .

Oh, what was it, what was happening to him?

He wanted more.

Laying his hand over the Nurail's shoulder with deliberate pressure, Andrej cupped the deformation of the hinge beneath his palm. The Nurail's whimpers of reluctant pain felt like the caress of a lover's hand to Andrej, arousing him with lust for more of the same music.

He moved his fingers delicately, warming his palm on the heat of the skin, testing the boundaries of that heat with a mild disinterested pressure of his hand.

It almost seemed too soon before the Nurail found words and spoke at last.

"My—name—is—Rab. Luss—man." Rabirt Lussman, yes. Meant something like Rab-the-small-herbivore-snarer, if Andrej remembered anything of Ingles Chapnier's dialect aright. "—I—am—accused—of—"

Almost abstractedly, almost dispassionately, Andrej stroked the Nurail's shoulder as he waited for the man to finish his statement, massaging the inflamed skin over the joint between his thumb and forefinger.

" . . . —of—will. Of. Willful. Destruc. Tion. Juris—dict—ion prop. Erty. Pl. Pl. Please."

Then in a sickening instant of insight Andrej realized what was happening to his body.

Quite suddenly Andrej understood that the Nurail's suffering had aroused him; and the uncertain sensation in his belly twisted into a spasm of ferocious nausea. Spurning his prisoner's body to one side with a savage gesture of rejection, Andrej pushed himself out of the chair and turned his back, unable to find his balance in time to avoid falling to his knees on the hard cold decking.

Sick to his stomach.

He tasted the fluid in his mouth and knew that he was going to vomit in revulsion; but the sensation could not be denied. His fish strained eagerly against the fabric of his trousers as though the Nurail's pain were the most enticing ocean his fish had ever dreamed of in which to disport itself. Eager to get out. Passionate for more pain.

"The officer is unwell?"

Security, careful and reserved, beside him. He could not spew what little he had in his stomach out onto the floor. Such a thing would be disgraceful. Drunk. Yes. Drunk, that was it, he would pretend that he was only drunk, and not so horrified at what he thought he felt that his very vitals rose in protest against the sinful desire that had come on him so suddenly, so strongly. Drunk. Yes. That would do the trick, very well.

He had to set the Nurail's shoulder straight.

"Your pardon, gentlemen, a surfeit of wodac merely." He could hardly choke the words out, and the strained high pitch of his own voice was nothing he would have recognized as his. They would know he lied. One of them helped him up onto his feet, and for a moment Andrej stood where he was and eyed the door at the far end of the theater longingly. He could just leave . . .

Yes, and go where?

He could just leave, but if he did, he would only have to do this over again, and in the meantime the prisoner suffered from a dislocated shoulder, and for no good or necessary reason.

Reluctantly Andrej turned back to his task.

The trick with the crozer-hinge was working all too well. Rab Lussman knelt constrained and suffering, waiting for painease. Swallowing hard, Andrej approached his prisoner; it had to be done soon, or the Nurail was going to lose consciousness. Could he touch Lussman's body, and not be disgraced by his own? Two hands on Lussman's shoulder, the dislocated joint hot and swollen beneath his hands. Andrej readied himself for what was to come, half-breathless with the conflict between abject horror and frank shameless lust.

Soon; and cleanly—

With his fingers tight against the shoulder and his two thumbs pressed against the ball of the joint, Andrej forced the crozer-hinge back under the cap of the shoulder blade

into the shoulder-joint, where it belonged. The Nurail
shouted aloud with the ferocious shock of it, his body con-
vulsing against the Security who restrained him, his feet
kicking out from underneath him in spasms of uncoordinated
protest at the pain.

Andrej fell back heavily into his chair in turn, staring hungrily at his prisoner, savoring the tense drawn lines of agony
on Lussman's face.

Oh, yes, his body said to him, as clearly as if flesh could
speak high Aznir.

Oh, yes, indeed.

His prisoner, living flesh, subject to his will, and all in
lawful support of the Judicial order. Why—Andrej asked
himself—had he been afraid that it would be difficult?

Or had he in fact been afraid that it was going to be this
easy, all along?

His father had been right to send him here, and he had
known from the beginning how wrong it had been for him
to try to resist his father's will. He had been misguided and
mistaken, and he could have had this pleasure all along, because it was all his for the taking. Lussman had to confess.
It was up to him to see that Lussman confessed, and in good
form, and convincingly.

He had weeks of lost time to make up for.

Saints, Saints, Saints under Canopy, what was he thinking
of? How could he even imagine he was to torture an unarmed
man, naked and in the presence of his enemies, and find joy
in such savagery?

Andrej swallowed back the bitterness in his mouth, almost
scornful of his own weakness—his pity, and his shame—
under the influence of the passion that overwhelmed him.

There was no need to appeal to the imagination.

As real as Lussman's pain, as real as agony, as real as
blood—that was as real and sharp and quick as the delight
that he felt in it.

Wasted time.

And no time like the present to claim his native right and
enter into his ancestral place. The Church had tried to teach
him: Sin merited suffering in atonement. His teachers on Mayon had taught him differently, that suffering was to be

avoided and alleviated by every possible means a man could find at his disposal; and he had believed them. He had swallowed the alien philosophy as though it could nourish him throughout all his long years in school.

He was sick to his stomach with the poison of the alien creed.

He was thirsty, hungry, starved for the sweet sound of pain in Lussman's voice, famished for the pleasure that he had in Lussman's fear of him, desperate with ferocious need for Lussman's helpless pain to feed upon and pleasure him.

All of those years.

How could he have been so blind to the simple truth?

And what could be more true than honest pain, and the brilliant scintillating sweetness of strict torment?

Rab Lussman half-lay against the Security troops behind him, with his face turned up to the light and his mouth trembling. Andrej rejoiced to see the signs of awareness returning to the man; because he had plans. And each new concept of atrocity was more beguiling than the last had been.

"Lussman," Andrej said.

The Nurail's head rolled restlessly against Sorlie Curran's steadfast grip, but he said nothing.

Rising unsteadily to his feet, Andrej took a whip up from the array that lay ready on the table for his use. A short, stout black-oiled whip with a heavy butt, the weight of it was welcome to his hand, and every fiber of his being seemed to strain to the utmost in anticipation, eager to be gratified.

"Come now, we were discussing." He was not going to vomit and flee. He was going to complete his exercise. And he was going to enjoy it. "Truly I must insist you pay attention, Lussman, answer as I bid you, or I will suspect that you are not listening to me. Yes?"

No answer.

Andrej wrapped the striking length of the whip around his fist so that the weighted butt swung free at a short drop. He took the measure of his distance and gauged the angle of approach, eager to test his grasp of the Judicial process against the shaking body of his prisoner.

"Your name. And the crime for which you were arrested.

Answer to me 'yes, Your Excellency,' else we will have to talk about your manners. Yes?''

Perhaps Lussman was simply a little dazed.

The best thing for that would be a sudden shock, to bring him out of it. Andrej swung the cudgel-butt of the whip in a wide, high arc and down across the Nurail's injured shoulder. He liked the sharp and stifled sound of the Nurail's cry of pain, the certain knowledge of his own absolute control over the next few measures of his prisoner's life. There was no sense in lying to himself, not now, not since he finally understood what he had been trying to hide from himself for all those wasted years.

"N-no, if it p-p-pl—''

Lussman started to speak but stopped himself, swallowing his words before Andrej could guess where he had been going with them. Andrej waited. He could afford to allow Lussman a few moments in which to collect himself.

"That is . . . I mean . . . Your Excellency. Rab Lussman. Falsely accused. Your Excellency. S-sir.''

Had he asked for an evaluation of the Charges? He had not. He had only asked what the Charges were.

He was all but compelled by this cogent fact to strike Lussman in order that the Nurail would gain from instruction, learning how a man would be well advised to conduct himself in the presence of an Inquiring officer.

He unwrapped the cruel thin length of the whip's lash from around his fist and took the cudgel-butt into his hand instead, striking Lussman across the face with the doubled lash so hard that the blood came in the furrow of the welt it raised in passage.

He was Andrej Koscuisko, before the Holy Mother, before all Saints under Canopy.

He was Andrej Koscuisko, Surgeon and Inquisitor, and when he left this place he would carry the Writ to Inquire, and uphold the Judicial order by its lawful exercise.

He was Andrej Ulexeievitch Koscuisko.

And he was come into his dominion now at last.

◆ Five

Joslire Curran stood in his place behind Tutor Chonis's chair, dividing his dismayed attention between listening to the Tutor and watching Student Koscuisko. The Record was off-line; Tutor Chonis had apparently made all the official comments he felt might be appropriate. Now there was only Chonis's musing, half to himself, half for their benefit, watching the two exercises.

"I think I like that hook for the present," Student Koscuisko was saying. "Gentlemen, if you please. Yes, both arms, and perhaps you could contrive to see his left shoulder is to bear the most part of his weight."

He'd told Robert St. Clare that Koscuisko was a fair-minded man, and would only hurt him enough. Something had gone wrong from the beginning of this exercise, however. Because the pressure that Koscuisko brought to bear on his prisoner-surrogate had been more intense than any Fourth Level Student exercise Joslire had ever seen.

"Willful destruction of Bench property is a species of treason, friend Rab, we must have details in order to measure out the penalty. I cannot say that you have been very forthcoming. One would almost think you did not feel remorse for what you have done."

Koscuisko had not exceeded the Protocols, so in that specifically limited sense Koscuisko had in fact hurt Robert only "enough." But there was no trace of fair-mindedness in his Student's behavior. Koscuisko was clearly enjoying the brutal tricks he had contrived to play on his prisoner. There was

95

a confusing dislocation between the officer Joslire had believed Koscuisko to be and the mocking torturer that he'd
been watching for these few hours past. Something was happening to Student Koscuisko, and Joslire did not quite understand what it was; but he was certain that he didn't like
it.

"Once again, from the beginning. I am heartily sick of
your refusal to acknowledge your whip-worthiness, there is
Evidence enough to convict you a liar. You are not doing
yourself any favors by withholding."

There had been Students who had liked pain, his pain,
their prisoner's pain, any pain they could get, always ex-
cluding their own. There had been Students who had simply
been indifferent to pain, or who had actively deplored the
use of it. Koscuisko was not a man to be unmoved, from
what little Joslire had learned of him. He reacted with genuine and innate compassion to the sufferings of the accused
in the paradigm tapes. It made no sense for that resistance
to have been superficial; Joslire had been completely convinced of the honesty of Koscuisko's empathic sympathy.
But if Koscuisko's horror had been real—and this, this
sharpening skill with whips and mockery was also convincing—it did not augur well for Student Koscuisko's future.
For his sanity.

"Noycannir seems to have run out of options, Hanbor,
wouldn't you say?"

Tutor Chonis's voice interrupted Joslire's brooding and
brought him back into real time. The Tutor was being charitable, in Joslire's view; it seemed to him that Noycannir had
lost control of her interrogation early on, when her "prisoner" had declined to even start to cooperate. Chonis had
wanted to see how she'd handle it. Koscuisko had found a
way to encourage Robert to surrender at least his false identification, as a start. Noycannir had asked once or twice and
then gone directly into beating her partner with the black-
stick, apparently content to reproduce the paradigm tapes that
she and Student Koscuisko alike had studied blow for blow.

Joslire knew which index-Level tape that particular beating was on, having seen it with each of his previous Students.

It was a Fifth Level tape, preparation for the next exercise. She'd gotten her Protocols confused.

"Student Noycannir is apparently trying to pretend that her prisoner has not lost consciousness. She's unlikely to get anything more out of him today. Sir."

There was a perverse sort of professional pride on Orientation staff, a black-humored brand of "my Student is more efficiently cruel than your Student" running joke. Lop Hanbor sounded genuinely disgusted with Noycannir's overzealous approach, since she'd put her prisoner-surrogate out of the arena for a few hours. Joslire had felt that way before. Given that their Judicial function involved the methodical application of pain, bond-involuntaries tended to evaluate Students based on their ability to use enough to satisfy the requirements and accomplish the task, but no more than that. It was precisely that prejudice that gave their function what little meaning it could be said to have: They were here to support the least-wasted-pain approach to Inquiry.

"Well, we'll give her a minute to call the exercise. Wouldn't want to interrupt young Koscuisko. Speaking of whom—shall we have the sound, Curran?" Tutor Chonis asked, and it was not really a question, needless to say. Joslire didn't much care for the prospect, but perhaps Chonis only wanted to get a flavor of what Koscuisko was saying.

Lop did the honors, bringing up the sound from one exercise theater even as he muted the sound from the other.

Robert had been stretched from the ceiling, and since Student Koscuisko had specified it, Security had given his bad arm less slack so that most of Robert's weight was on it. Robert kept trying to stretch his other arm up to the anchorbolt to grasp the hook and take some of the weight off of the injured joint. Koscuisko, however, wasn't having any of it; and Joslire suffered for the young Nurail.

"I can tell that this is going to take some practice," Koscuisko was saying. "For now I can only trust that my lack of craft does not offend you."

Robert was already off balance because of the unequal length of the chains that bound him. The impact of the whip was throwing his whole weight upon his injured shoulder, and Robert—it seemed—couldn't help but cry out against it.

"Your feedback will, of course, be critical to the success of this training exercise, although I fear I cannot promise you that it will remain confidential. Unless you would prefer to discuss some of the more interesting details of your crime. What was it, again? Willful destruction of Jurisdiction property?"

For all his disclaimers, Koscuisko had a natural talent of some sort; his eye-to-hand coordination was obviously more than adequate. Nor did he seem to be afraid to put a bit of muscle into the blows. Whether it was weals or blood, there was no question but that Andrej Koscuisko was making his mark on Robert St. Clare.

Who could not catch his breath, tormented by the whip even as he was distracted by the pain in his shoulder. "I . . . won't."

They weren't picking up Robert's voice very well. Chonis frowned, gesturing for Lop to increase the directional on the plait. Even then it wasn't easy to figure out what Robert was saying. His breath came in fits and starts, his sentences chopped up into disjointed, fragmentary phrases almost devoid of meaning. "Can't. Won't. Risk. Not long enough for . . ."

Long enough? It didn't have to mean anything. But he should not have said "not long enough." Would Koscuisko pick up on the phrase?

"With respect, Tutor Chonis—"

Koscuisko had demonstrated his ability to take an appropriate tool and use it on his prisoner; and that was all that the Administration really required, at this juncture. Whatever else he might be demonstrating was beside the point.

Lop apparently had a more immediate problem. Student Noycannir had kicked her prisoner as he lay on the decking, in an apparent paroxysm of frustration at his failure to respond.

"With respect, sir, Student Noycannir has violated the restriction at the Fourth Level, request the Tutor call the exercise?"

Student Noycannir kicked her prisoner again, at the point of his jaw this time. Joslire recognized that maneuver from the index-Level tapes as well. On the index tape, the Student

Inquisitor had indeed kicked a prisoner while he was down, and hard enough to bring blood to the victim's cheek.

Joslire knew that Tutor Chonis had temporarily forgotten about Noycannir, absorbed in watching Koscuisko. He'd been absorbed in watching Koscuisko, too, but he had a better excuse—not that he was going to hint that to Tutor Chonis, who took one look at the companion screen and smashed his fist against the emergency-call toggle.

"Administrative orders. All exercises to cease."

The signal went to both theaters, and Joslire watched his officer lift his head toward the talkalert with a look of confused apprehension on his face.

"This is Tutor Chonis. I repeat. Administrative orders, all exercises to cease. Students will disengage at once." Toggling off-braid, Tutor Chonis pushed himself angrily out of his chair, swearing at himself and moving so quickly that he was halfway to the door before he'd finished his directions.

"Son of a cuckoo, useless excuse for a . . . Hanbor, come with me. Curran, shut down the monitors before you go and collect Koscuisko. Perdition take . . ."

There was a world of difference between kicking a prisoner's face and kicking him at the back of his head or up from underneath the point of his jaw. From the unnatural angle of the prisoner-surrogate's head as he lay, Student Noycannir's blow had compromised Idarec's spine— perhaps fatally so.

Alone in Observation, now, Joslire closed down the monitors and secured the tapes. Koscuisko would be expecting him.

Koscuisko was all he had to worry about.

Student Noycannir crouched down beside the prisoner where he lay, desperate to discover whether he was only trying to put a joke on her by feigned unconsciousness. The bastard couldn't be unconscious. She hadn't hit him that hard, didn't she know as well as anyone how hard you really had to hit before some thickheaded gravelstamper finally lay down to be quiet?

The prisoner didn't move.

She could have shrieked in frustrated rage, but strangled

the curses in her throat so fiercely she was sure only she had
even heard the sound. He couldn't do this to her. He was
pretending. She could deal with pretense, she knew how.
Snatching the man's limp arm out to the farthest extent of
its length on the floor she hammered the elbow joint with
the heavy cudgel, once, two times, three times. Pain never
failed to get a man's attention, it had never failed her before,
but the prisoner did not respond. She could hit again, but she
couldn't be sure that she was clear to damage the joint more
severely at this Level. She didn't dare. If she should splinter
bone, they would hold it against her as proof of her lack of
fitness for the Writ.

Mergau stood up.

A man who lay silent and unmoving through such blows
as she had given his elbow was not pretending.

If he was unconscious, how could she gain confession?

Sudden mindless fury swamped her heart and mind and
soul. This was unfair. They had no right. They had given her
a weakling for a prisoner, a man so fragile he escaped to
silence before he had so much as said his name. They would
blame her for it. It wasn't her fault, it was their fault, their
fault and his fault, the fault of the prisoner who mocked her
where he lay in unresponsive stillness.

Be damned to all of them, she decided. *All of them be
damned. Their tricks. Their superiority.*

"Get up." Snarling at the prisoner, Mergau did not bother
trying to disguise her disgust, her contempt. Let them make
of it what they liked. "I said get up, you pathetic coward."
He didn't move, and by now she knew he wasn't going to.
It made kicking him all the more satisfying, a good solid
blow striking sharp against his ribs. When he woke up again,
he would know she had meant to punish him. "Don't think
I don't know exactly what you're trying to pull."

She kicked again, and at his head this time, to see if she
could take a few of his teeth for souvenirs. She was beginning to feel better. As long as he was unconscious anyway,
why shouldn't she?

There was a sharp click at the talkalert, and suddenly Mergau wondered if she had overstepped somehow.

"All exercises to cease. Students will disengage at once."

Tutor Chonis's voice, and sounding very intent. What, there was a problem?

What had Koscuisko done?

Was it her imagination or were the prisoner's lips turning blue?

A mistake. She had made a mistake. Terror seized her bowels and bones, but Mergau dampened it sternly. She'd made a mistake, but the last thing she could afford to do was show it. Show weakness and there would be no mercy.

She knew what to do when she'd been caught doing something wrong. Her ability to project innocent nonchalance was part of her survival. Turning her back on the prisoner on the floor, Mergau set the truncheon back with the other instruments on the table, arranging them neatly. She would not have long to wait, she was sure.

Tutor Chonis's signal was almost welcome.

"Student Noycannir. You will return to quarters, instruction to be forthcoming." He was excited about something, but she—quite naturally—could have no idea what it was. Mergau schooled her face to a bland mask of mild, concerned confusion to overlay the turmoil in her heart. It didn't have to fool anybody. All it had to do was get her safely out of here.

Mergau bowed to her Tutor and left the theater, standing aside to let the medical team through as she passed.

She was glad to go to quarters.

She had to understand what had gone wrong.

But more than that, she had to decide how she was going to cover up for it.

"Administrative orders. All exercises to cease."

The sudden announcement startled Andrej. He lost his focus on the lash, stumbling clumsily to one side as he missed his prisoner entirely.

"This is Tutor Chonis. I repeat, administrative orders, all exercises to cease. Students will disengage at once."

Staring at the wall-monitor, he tried to understand Tutor Chonis. Disengage? How could they ask him to disengage when that meant he would have to leave his prisoner? Had he made an error in procedure? They'd been given instructions about command disengage, true. Under emergency circumstances the Tutor would call the exercise. No hints about what emergency it might be were forthcoming from the now silent wall-monitor; and after a moment, Andrej shook himself out of his paralysis of arrested movement.

He didn't want to disengage.

If he didn't disengage at the Tutor's instruction, they might make him wait before they gave him another prisoner, though. It wasn't worth the risk, regardless of how little he liked the idea.

What had Lussman been trying to say about risk?

"Very well, friend Rab." Folding the whip back upon itself, Andrej handed it off to one of the Security. The lash was heavy and dark with the prisoner's suffering; it had stained his hands with blood. He couldn't afford to stop and think about it. He wanted more. It would only make it more difficult for him to accept postponement of his pleasure. "Since I have failed to make myself understood thus far, perhaps we could revisit these issues in the morning." According to the Prisoner's Brief, the prisoner's offense was severe enough to warrant sequential invocation of the Fifth Level if he couldn't gain confession in the Fourth. He and Noycannir had been warned about such a possibility.

Was this an administrative trick of some sort?

Or had something gone wrong with Noycannir's exercise?

"Take him down, yes. No. One moment . . ."

The prisoner seemed scarcely conscious. Security would handle him roughly, if efficiently; and Andrej did not like the idea, somehow. He moved to stand in front of Lussman where he was bound, nodding his signal to Sorlie Curran. "If you will. Now."

Lussman cried out when his wrists were loosed from the anchor-bolt in the ceiling, falling heavily forward to his knees. Andrej braced himself against Lussman's weight with one hand at Lussman's side beneath the uninjured arm, catching the prisoner at the side of his neck with his other hand in an embrace which did the trick, howsoever awkwardly. Lussman did not fall over, and Lussman did not pass out, and Andrej stood and steadied the man for a moment so that he could regain his balance. He wasn't sure why he cared one way or the other. All Andrej could do was to hold Rab Lussman for now and hope to sort out his precise feelings about it all later.

"With respect, the officer need not concern himself, there is a requirement to return the prisoner to holding—"

"A moment," Andrej insisted, his thumb tucked across the base of the Nurail's throat. Joslire had arrived; Security would be wondering why he didn't leave. He'd been anxious enough to leave after the other exercises. "Give us a moment, he will return to himself, and he will be able to walk with you."

The pulse beneath his thumb was steadying and strengthening, but Security's evident confusion made Andrej apprehensive. They would probably be within their rights to insist on dragging Lussman off immediately. Andrej didn't want that. He wanted Lussman to find his center before they thought to suggest such a thing. If he moved his other hand to the base of the man's neck, he could perhaps find the right nerve bundle as it entered the spine.

There was an uneasiness and a shuffling of feet in the room as Lussman stiffened suddenly. What, did they think that he was hurting the man, still? The exercise had been called. Andrej wasn't sure he even wanted to hurt Lussman now.

What had happened to him, that had fired him body and soul with pleasure in response to Lussman's pain?

It was the right nerve bundle, that was a plus; Lussman shook his head several times—as if to drain his ears of water—and started to rise clumsily to his feet.

"There, now. That is better." He continued to apply a steady pressure against the Nurail's spine as Lussman stood, dampening the noxious messages of pain from Lussman's shoulder. "If you care to go slowly with him, he can walk. Be careful with the shoulder, gentlemen, we are done for the moment."

High time he was out of here, because he had probably reached the limits of the interference he would be permitted. Since he was to be able to do nothing with or for Rab Lussman, it was best for his own peace of mind if he were to get away before something unfortunate should happen. "Thank you for your effort, gentlemen, and I will see you all in the morning, I suppose. Joslire, let's go.''

All that he could do for his prisoner, he had done.

And now there was nothing left for him but to consider what he had done to Lussman, as well.

He left the exercise theater like a man walking in his sleep, responding to Joslire's polite directions without thinking about where Joslire was taking him. What had he done? How could he have enjoyed it? And, oh, how long would he be forced to wait until he could do it all again?

Quarters. That was where Joslire was taking him. That was a surprise. Swallowing hard, Andrej frowned at the time-mark on the screen of his studyset. Surely it was some eights yet to thirdmeal?

"What is this, Joslire, we are not to practice today? Not that I object." The idea of going to exercise was suddenly more attractive than it had ever been before. Andrej felt that he could profit from mindless and repetitive activity, something to distract his body and numb his mind with purely physical demands—something uncomplicated. Unambiguous. Safe.

"The Administration excuses the officer at the end of the practical exercises, now that the Preliminary Levels have been passed. If the officer please."

Joslire stood well away from him, eyes carefully lowered. Joslire watched his exercises—Joslire and Tutor Chonis alike. His shameful behavior was on Record.

Gradually the red haze of his passionate pleasure in Lussman's pain began to clear from the foreground of Andrej's mind to reveal the gaping chasm of horror that lay beneath it.

"Let me have a look at the next Level, then."

If he looked into the fathomless pit of his own heart, he would lose his balance and fall in. Andrej shuddered at the thought. He had to find something to hang on to, something he could use to steady himself. Review was unnecessary; they'd studied the protocol before this. But it would excuse his staring at the screen. He could take his supper early, go shut himself behind the thin barrier between his sleep-rack and Joslire before time. He was strangely exhausted, but the discomfort of his body would not permit him to wash and change into his sleep-shirt. Not just yet. Bad enough that they had watched him in exercise. That the residual signs of his flagging desire should betray him so obviously to Joslire was more than Andrej could accept.

It would take Joslire a moment to call up the correct packages. Andrej went into the washroom to clean the blood from his hands, struggling to understand. He couldn't begin to feel clean until he had changed his uniform. Catching a glimpse of his face in the reflector, Andrej stared at himself for a long measure, confused for a long moment about whose face that was, staring back at him with so much shock and distress. He would never be able to wash the stain of this away, no matter how he tried. Rab Lussman's blood had soaked clear through his flesh into his soul, and he was filthy with it. A prisoner, and he had tortured the man, and before the Canopy he had had such pleasure in it. . . .

This was different in kind as well as in degree from the previous Levels. His challenge and his shame had been to simply do the distasteful thing. And today he had done the distasteful thing, and he had not minded it. He had accepted it, embraced it, submitted himself to it, and taken pleasure from pain as his reward. The message of his body was unequivocal. There was no mistaking the source of his new-found ability to strike a helpless prisoner, or the effect that it had. What had happened to him?

What door had he opened to what ancestral demon, in his desperation to find his way through this place?

Joslire had gone away from the studyset, probably seeing to some domestic chore. Andrej remembered at last to rinse his hands and shut the waterstream off. The instruction tape was loaded on-screen; Andrej found his way to his place and sat himself down heavily. The Fifth Level of the Question. A paradigmatic exercise, a prisoner naked and bloodied. A vise, a cudgel, the restraints at the wall and the pulley in the floor to stretch a man's joints from one another. The ragged sound of the Nurail's panting breath still sounded in Andrej's ear; he shivered with the memory, and knew that the source of the shudder was not horror or pity but something unacceptable. Something unthinkable, shameful, sinful.

Something powerful and passionate, basic and fundamental to his being, more intense than any explicitly sexual experiences had ever been . . .

Half-unwilling and half-greedy for renewed pleasure, Andrej watched the tape scroll forward. The image in the cube-viewer was as it had always been to him—horrible and pitiful. As long as he did not indulge in imagining trying these pleasures for himself—on the chained body of Rab Lussman, and tomorrow, a scant few hours from now—he felt no differently about those images than he had when he'd first seen them. It was an abomination under the Canopy of Heaven to do such things to sentient creatures, whether or not the Church agreed with him. Therefore, necessarily, he was an abomination, regardless of any pretensions he had cherished in his life to decency or morality. Andrej's moral conviction was unchanged by the epiphany he had experienced, as profound and absolute as anything in his life.

The rule of Law was no excuse for torture.

He could not do these things.

How could he hope to live with the shame, now that he knew he had an appetite for pain?

He would make a stand. He would refuse the duty; he would take vows and go to cloister. The Church would deny him if his father turned his back, but the Church would have to take him in if he repudiated his name and elected the Malcontent. The Church could not deny a man who chose to elect the Malcontent. He could forget that he had ever been Koscuisko, and take sanctuary. Then at least no one would ask him to strike a prisoner, or tempt him with the seductive promise of the sound of agony.

Nor would he have a chance to help, to heal; no chance at all to try to right the balance and atone for what he was to do. And prisoners would still suffer torture, and they would still die, whether or not he was there to delight in their anguish. So what good would it do him to seek sanctuary, when he took the longer view? He would be able to escape self-censure for crimes committed against feeling creatures, whether or not Church and Bench and Fleet pretended to believe that Judicial torture was no crime.

But he could never put himself behind him. Nothing he

could do would ever change what had passed with him today. He had sucked the pain from Lussman's captive body and feasted greedily upon a man's torment. All that he could gain from running away, now that he knew this about himself, would be the thinnest veneer of self-respect; and in return, he would have to forswear forever any potential chance he might have in the future to do a bit of good within the work to which he was to be condemned.

He could never hope to run away from himself.

Hadn't the Holy Mother known from the beginning what she had done, when she had shaped him?

What was he to make of himself?

If he closed his eyes and summoned up the image of the Nurail, his prisoner, with an elbow locked in the vise or a hand bloodied with the fingernails split . . .

Andrej searched the confused landscape of his inner state with anxious care. He had to know. He could not afford to deceive himself, to conceal his own truth from himself. Forcing himself to dwell on details both remembered and imagined, he sought to grasp what it might be within him that had felt so differently about it all during the exercise; and he took a measure of bleak comfort from the fact that it did not delight him now to muse on what had beguiled him so keenly less than two measures gone.

There was no question that he had taken intense pleasure in the work.

But now that he was away from it, his body only remembered its pleasure with a dim, muffled echo of that same delight. He found he took no new satisfaction either from memory or in anticipation of the morning.

"What am I, to have done such a thing?"

He asked the question of the air in a hoarse despairing whisper, his eyes closed in anguished concentration and wonder. To take sexual pleasure from the pain of others had surely never been hinted at in his psychological profiles, else he would have heard of it by now. There was an urgent clinical need for people who were capable of such a response, people whose own psychology enabled them to support the treatment of those whose pain was so extreme and so intransigent that no others could so much as abide in its presence. Some of his trauma studies had left him with horrific nightmares. . . . On Mayon there had been no pleasure associated with pain for him. If there had been, he would have noticed.

And had he not noticed, his teachers would have done.

"The Student has successfully completed an entirely adequate Fourth Level exercise," Joslire said.

Rapt in his own horrified thoughts as he was, it took Andrej a moment to grasp Curran's meaning, and a moment longer yet to understand why Joslire had spoken at all. He'd asked a question, yes, that was right. He simply hadn't expected any answers.

"Oh, not just that. Surely not. I was on fire with my lust to make him suffer, Joslire, and I never knew that I could take any pleasure in rank cruelty, never mind such potent pleasure as I had in him. . . ."

Of course he had been cruel to the Mizucash and the Bigelblu and the Onymsho, in the Preliminary Levels. But he'd had to force himself to execute the Protocols. And he had not enjoyed any of it.

"The officer is respectfully requested to remember that the exercise was technically well performed. There was no violation."

And everything he said would be Recorded, here in quarters as in exercise theater.

"The Levels are profoundly flawed, Joslire, but that is not your fault." He didn't stop to wonder at the phrase until it was out of him and could not be called back. What did that mean, it wasn't Joslire's fault? Surely there was no reason to imply that the point could ever even be in question. It did no good to try to talk to Joslire. It was unfair of him to impose on the man. Andrej reached for something he could safely say to Joslire, something that might communicate his dread in terms that the Administration could not fault him for.

"I mean that he has already had enough pain for the Level, and a beating on top of that. By rights we should accept the man's denial, and send him off." Still, what did rights mean, for a prisoner? He knew the answer to that one well enough. He didn't like it any better for that.

"Respectfully request permission. To offer a comment, at the officer's pleasure." Joslire was standing at command-wait by his sleep-rack, looking straight ahead. He would have assumed the required position of respectful attention as soon as Andrej had spoken; but Andrej only noticed it now.

"Please. You don't speak to me often, Joslire, and I am grateful for your assistance." In fact Andrej could not remember Joslire ever asking to be allowed to make a comment. Joslire had been watching him, Joslire knew . . .

"Sir. The Student will know from his education that thinking creatures are capable of responding to a wide variety of stimuli. With all due respect, the Student is encouraged to consult his own knowledge concerning accommodations reached by the intelligent or sentient mind under high-stress conditions. Sir."

For a moment the absurdity of the situation overrode the confused welter in Andrej's mind with a sharp sense of how ridiculous it all was. "Joslire, are you trying to teach me psychology?"

No. Wrong. It was not a good thing to say to a bond-involuntary; Andrej knew it immediately from the subtle but perceptible stiffening of Joslire's body at the implicit rebuke.

"If the officer permit. The orientation of Staff Security includes exposure to a range of concepts that may be of assistance to Students of assignment during apparent crisis. Any misapplication is to be set against the troop's own failure to judge the officer's meaning correctly. If there has been a mistake, the troop in question may profit from correction."

Joslire's voice was clear and strong and utterly devoid of any emotion. Andrej pushed himself away from the studyset, burying his face in his hands in a convulsion of distress. Correction meant discipline, and discipline was punishment. Andrej tried to put Joslire in the Nurail's place in his mind's eye, bitterly fearful of the test. Joslire, with a livid whip-stroke full across his dark intense face. Joslire, breathing in great gasping sobs between clenched teeth, his body wracked beneath the impact of the whip. Joslire, screaming, that hoarse high sound that had so moved Andrej when he'd first heard it from Rab Lussman.

He could see the image clearly enough, and it did not please him.

As much as he had wanted to hear his Nurail cry, that much and more he did not want to torment Joslire Curran.

"Holy Mother. I would to all Saints you could ever be at ease with me, Joslire. Only error is to be corrected. Not a mistake. Still less the truth, no matter how ill-received it may be."

The accommodation of a sentient mind to unreasonable stress, a psychological trick played by himself on himself to make it possible for him to perform his task? No, what he remembered had been much too intense and immediate for that, and he dreaded the possibility that it might happen again next time. The body learned more quickly than the mind, and in direct proportion to the intensity of the sensation. It would be difficult not to become addicted.

Surely it would be easier for him to allow himself to become addicted, and let the perverted appetite of his mind and heart work to help him through. . . .

Andrej had not bidden Joslire to stand down or released him from his position; and yet Joslire stepped up close to Andrej, kneeling down with a species of formal grace to rest with one knee flat to the floor just to one side of where Andrej was sitting on the edge of the seat. He was so close to Andrej that Andrej could feel his body's heat, and Emandisan were usually on the lower side of the Jurisdiction Standard for normal temperature. Andrej wondered at the man's intimacy.

"The officer is under a great deal of pressure," Joslire murmured, his voice low, his eyes on Andrej's boots. "There has been no exercise, no release for physical tension. Perhaps the officer would care for an alternate means of relaxation."

Sweet Saints.

Joslire was propositioning him.

Not only that, but something in his belly looked on Joslire where he knelt and saw a prisoner, and joyfully embraced the concept of abusing him.

Andrej fought with an instinct to strike Curran, to punish him for even suggesting that he was so depraved as that. There was no reason for Joslire to know that his offer presupposed two kinds of sin, two out of the three most deeply damning sins in the entire Book. This was just another one of the things that Joslire was required to do, to say, when the situation presented itself. That was all.

"Yes, Joslire, I would like somewhat by way of relaxation. You're quite right." A man was forbidden to accept such courtesies. It was an affront to the Holy Mother. And quite apart from that, the last thing he wanted to do, here and now, was misuse the man, regardless of the things the Tutors made Joslire say, regardless of the treachery of his own body. "Wodac, in fact. I think I'll have my supper early."

A man was not to take pleasure from the flesh of children, either. Children were sacred to the Mother of all Aznir; and by extension, servants were not to be exploited for personal satisfaction, since—like children—they were not in a position to refuse to grant their compliance. Andrej carried Joslire's Bond. He was responsible to the Bench for Joslire's best interest. To serve Joslire's "best interest" by gratifying the undiscriminating appetites of his own body at Joslire's expense would be betrayal of a trust that was sacred to Andrej, no matter how little protection the Bench extended to its bondslaves.

Joslire hadn't moved. "The officer will of course be provided with the wodac, but wodac inhibits rather than releases." Joslire's voice communicated only promise, no argument. If he sat here for a single breath the more, he was going to take the implied offer greedily. He could not bear the thought of such a thing. Andrej pushed himself out of the chair with an effort and put several paces of safe distance between himself and Joslire before trusting himself to speak.

"Wodac." His voice sounded harsh and angry to Andrej, but he wasn't angry at Joslire. How could he pretend to experience moral outrage after what he had found out about himself today? "Thank you, Joslire, your offer is most charitably presented. But what I want is wodac. Nothing more. I do not wish to hear any such proposal from you again, please mark my will in this."

The passion he had learned today was his problem.

Andrej had no intention of burdening anyone else with it.

*   *   *

She was careful to keep her pace measured and deliberate as she returned to quarters with her slave. Nothing was wrong, after all. She had done nothing.

And she held carefully and grimly to that pretense until she was safely arrived, and the door closed behind her; then she could control her rage no longer.

"Face to the wall, slave!"

Pivoting on her heel, she shouted up into Hanbor's startled face, furious with him for being where he was, furious with him for having witnessed her lapse in Observation, furious with the entire Administration for making her feel the way she did.

Hanbor's expression of surprise iced over almost immediately into a safe and inoffensive blank. Bowing, he turned to the wall crisply, standing to attention with his nose scant fractions from the featureless surface. Fine. He could face the wall. She was sick of being watched, all the time watched, every moment under observation.

There, that was better.

"Command-wait. Until I call for you."

Hanbor was Security. Let him demonstrate his discipline. She had to think.

Mergau undressed with short, sharp irritated gestures, tearing at the Fleet's Student uniform impatiently. She despised Fleet, she despised Fleet Orientation Station Medical, she despised the uniform.

She had to swallow it and manage this somehow.

Washing herself with grim determination with the water-stream turned to icy cold, Mergau began to reconstruct the events that had led up to Chonis's intervention.

What had happened?

What would they say she had done?

She had done nothing she had not seen on instructional tape.

Belting the sleep-tunic from her closet around her waist, Mergau sat down at the studyset. She knew what she'd seen. She would find proof that she had made no errors.

She would be ready for them when Tutor Chonis came to

blame her for whatever pretended error they could find in her conduct of the exercise.

"I ought to be sent back to Orientation processing for this one, Ligrose," Tutor Chonis commented grimly, watching the diagnostics. "Damned if that little Aznir didn't distract me." Not as if that was any excuse. On the one hand Koscuisko was interesting to watch from a professional point of view. The usual tension and uncertainties seemed to have a way of coming out in unexpected ways that surprised Tutor Chonis, even after so many years. And on the other hand, he should have terminated Noycannir's exercise at the point at which it had become obvious that Idarec was unconscious and liable to remain so.

No excuse.

A ruined exercise, and a ruined bond-involuntary, and Fleet didn't like losing bond-involuntaries. They were more and more difficult to come by these days. Fleet was not going to be impressed by the First Secretary's protégée, or by Chonis's handling of her, either.

"You're allowed." Ligrose Chaymalt was the Chief Medical Officer on Station, and the task of running an infirmary for a constant stream of practical exercises seemed to have hardened her over the years. Most of her patients were bond-involuntaries; Fleet valued their pain at somewhat less than the price of expensive medication. Perhaps it was natural that she'd come to value their lives somewhat less than Tutor Chonis felt she should. "You haven't had a suicide for, what, four Terms now? Nobody here can match that record. Security troops are still easier to find than Ship's Surgeons, after all. No offense, Harper."

The man's name was Hanbor. But he just bowed politely, no trace of having noticed the careless error on his face. It wasn't as if her accommodation was an unusual one; there was one Tutor who never bothered to learn their names at all, addressing all Security alike by an obscure ethnic term for "slave." Chonis had never quite decided if Tutor Heson cared that everybody knew very well what the word meant.

"Gross neurological. Hmm." Chonis was too far from the medical training of his youth to be confident that his interpretation of the statistics on Idarec was correct. "Your prognosis, Ligrose?"

She shut off the imager with a gesture of profound boredom. "Not worth the upkeep. You're not going to wake him up now, not after—how many times did she kick him? You?"

Hanbor probably did know, but Chonis felt that it was in poor taste to ask him. "Too many times," Chonis answered for Hanbor, accordingly. "We could expel her right now, for gross violation of the Levels. Except that she's too ignorant to understand exactly what she did wrong."

Koscuisko could probably braid a man's bones into his own muscles and not step one half of a pace out of Protocol. Koscuisko probably knew how to kick a man in the head a dozen times and have him wake up with no worse than a headache. But Koscuisko had education, on top of what seemed to be revealing itself as a native, if latent, talent.

"Charge the loss back to her patron," Ligrose suggested. "What's another few hundred thousand Standard, after all the money he spent getting her here in the first place?"

Andrej Koscuisko.

The presence of a Student with genuinely respectable medical qualifications was unusual at Fleet Orientation Station Medical, where most of the Students had been drawn from the ranks of the mediocre. Graduates with good qualifications got jobs in clinics, hospitals, private practice; some went into Fleet as rated practitioners. Fleet Orientation Station Medical generally got what was left once the decent jobs had been filled by decently qualified candidates.

"You've met my other Student?" And then there was Koscuisko, who had graduated at the top of his rated field from the single most competitive surgical college under Jurisdiction.

"Koscuisko. Yes, you parked him here yesterday in the lab. Too bad he's not on staff, isn't it? Bet he could fix Idarec almost as good as new."

Ligrose wasn't totally brutalized by her demanding environment; she sounded almost wistful. But she was right, though he hadn't realized it in the first flush of his wonderful idea. Koscuisko could not be asked to treat Idarec. Koscuisko would know that the man was bond-involuntary the moment he scanned the nervous system and found the governor.

Koscuisko would wonder why a bond-involuntary had been injured severely in a way that would surely remind him of the paradigm tapes he and Noycannir had studied. And the use of bond-involuntaries as prisoner-surrogates for training exercises from the First through Fifth Levels was one of the single most sensitive secrets in all of Fleet Orientation Station Medical.

Well, it had been an idea.

"Maybe next time," Chonis offered, rising from his seat in Ligrose's office. "Hang on to Idarec for now, will you? No sense in terminating until we need the bed." He'd talk to the Administrator about it. The First Secretary might want to send a medical specialist of his own, to avoid paying the replacement costs.

But it wasn't very likely.

"No sense in keeping the bed on hold, either." But Ligrose clearly didn't care one way or the other. "As you like, Adifer. Keep us informed, of course."

"Of course."

He'd talk to the Administrator tomorrow, when he would have a successful report on Koscuisko to balance it all out. And the Administrator would probably side with Doctor Chaymalt.

Then it would be out of his hands.

It was better to leave Hanbor with the impression that Tutor Chonis was at least trying to protect the interest—the life—of the comatose bond-involuntary.

Mergau Noycannir had gone to bed without her supper, unwilling to expose herself to the aggravation of speaking to the patient slave in quarters in order to get a meal. Now as she rose—refreshed and confident—from her night's rest, she was hungry—but still satisfied enough with what she had found out that she could speak to Hanbor with genial good humor as she opened the slider of her sleepcloset to come out.

"What, still staring at the wall? Release."

And had he not been, there would have been penalties

assessed; she had very particularly told him to wait to be released. He was to get off easily enough for his fault. She need feel no shame for having let him stare at the wall all night.

He staggered very slightly as he turned and saluted, shifting his weight to keep his balance. Technically speaking a violation, failure to complete salute in proper form; but she could afford to let the lapse pass. This time at least.

"I'll have my fastmeal, Hanbor. But first there's something we need to get straight between us."

Hanbor knew better than to speak before spoken to, and kept his mouth shut. Just as well. She wasn't interested in anything Hanbor might have to say.

"I expect to be able to rely on you, Hanbor, to provide the correct training material, according to the Tutor's plan. There's a problem with your performance in this area, I'm afraid."

It hardly mattered if he knew that she was lying. She was glad she'd found the way out. "There are instructional tapes logged here for my Fourth Level exercise, but somehow—and I don't mean this as a personal criticism, necessarily, anyone can make a mistake—there are tapes logged for the Fifth Level exercise as well."

Of course there were. They typically studied several days ahead, and the Tutor had put them on notice that if confession could not be obtained at the Fourth Level, they would be expected to move straight to the Fifth Level the following day. That was probably where Koscuisko was right now—unless he'd got confession at the Fourth Level, of course.

"That wouldn't be a problem, Hanbor, ordinarily. But you haven't made an adequately clear distinction between these tapes. I went Fifth Level on that prisoner yesterday because of that. Tutor Chonis is going to be very angry with you."

The tapes were marked as clearly as ever, but that wasn't the point. The point was that she could claim to have been confused, could claim Hanbor was at fault for not making more of a point about it. It hadn't been her mistake. It had been Hanbor's fault. Nobody even had to believe it was true for her stratagem to work.

"If we're lucky, there will be no notice taken, Hanbor.

Tutor Chonis may toggle the whole thing as my mistake. I'll take the hit for you if I have to, man, but I hope you understand the position you've placed me in.''

Quarters were under surveillance. Everybody knew that. Tutor Chonis knew she knew that. They all knew exactly what she was saying. . . .

"If it comes to an issue, I'll be forced to discipline you. So let's just both hope it doesn't get that far, shall we? That'll be all. Fastmeal, Hanbor.''

Her claim that she had been misled by inadequately labeled instructional tapes was fabricated, but she could insist upon it no less firmly for that.

So if they meant to speak to her about her mistake, she'd be forced to admit Hanbor had made an error; and once that happened, she'd be forced to discipline him—or else her claim would lose credibility. If Hanbor's error had resulted in her making a mistake, naturally, Hanbor would have to be punished for it. So she'd punish him, if Tutor Chonis said two words to her about it, simply in order to validate her claim.

"As the Student please," Hanbor replied, his voice flat and neutral—if a little rusty and strained from disuse. Nodding, Mergau dismissed him to go for her fastmeal, wondering whether she should overlook the wilted condition of his uniform just because he had been up all night, or whether she should rather say a word or two to him about it.

She was protected against Tutor Chonis now.

The Administration had been put on notice that if they accused her of a violation of Protocols, she'd take the next possible opportunity to beat her slave bloody for the fault he had committed.

This cheerful meditation whet her appetite.

Whistling to herself, Mergau went into the washroom to put her hair in order, waiting for her breakfast.

Andrej approached the exercise theater with a different species of dread than during previous trials, when he had doubted his ability to support the Levels and do his duty. Then he had suffered from the unnatural demands of the exercise, fearful that he would fail in the test. And now, today, this morning, he was free from the fear that he would fail the test, certain of his ability to carry the Levels forward.

His certainty itself troubled him grievously.

What if it happened again?

What if he could not do the thing unless he surrendered to the pleasure that he dreaded, and gave himself over to the passion that had made it all so easy yesterday?

They were allowed to use no drugs, in these exercises. The Administration wanted to be sure its graduates would be able to run a field-expedient Inquiry when required. No drugs; but fewer restrictions than at the Fourth Level were in force. He could break an arm or a leg, if he liked, perhaps knock out some teeth, do some real—if still restricted—damage.

None of which was particularly helpful.

His prisoner—Rab Lussman—knelt waiting on the floor, waiting for him. Lussman didn't seem to be particularly alert, and he was favoring his swollen shoulder as best he could with his arms shackled behind his back; but that was no more than expected.

Lussman's presence did give Andrej rather less time than he might have wanted to think about how he was going to go about this.

Lussman looked up at him as he came through the door, meeting his eyes briefly before he lowered his head out of evident weariness. Andrej wasn't quite sure how to read the expression—there seemed to be an element of relief there somehow.

Andrej stopped close to Lussman's side and touched his hand to a whip-welt he'd left across the man's face, testing. Wondering how he was to take command of the situation and not soil himself with the sinful sensations he had so enjoyed the last time. Considering how to approach his problem. The weal had purpled with bruising, the skin still red and angry where the lash had scraped up blood; tender, Andrej imagined. Lussman recoiled from him with a disgusted gesture, contempt and anger in his eyes; one of the Security cuffed Lussman across the back of the head with casual brutality, but Andrej wasn't affronted by Lussman's instinctive

gesture. Only natural, Andrej supposed. He would very likely
have done the same in Lussman's place.

"What are these things on his feet?" he asked Security,
gesturing with his hand. Lussman was still half-dressed from
yesterday, but he'd been shod when he'd come in here, and
Andrej was beginning to have a thought. Maybe he could do
it. Maybe it would not be so bad. At this point he was almost
willing to give Rab Lussman pain, if only he could manage
to avoid enjoying it.

"Ah, Nurail leg-wraps, if the officer please. Native footgear." Vely—Andrej thought that was his name—sounded
a bit confused. It was an odd phrase to use, wasn't it? Native
footgear. As if the uniform were the norm, rather than the
exception.

"Have him out of them, if you please, gentlemen."

His table was here, but the complement of tools provided
had increased. Andrej found what he wanted, trying not to
listen. He could sense the first vague hints of an unnatural
interest in the sounds the scuffling generated, stifled groans,
grunts of pain. He did the best he could to concentrate on
planning his procedure.

When all was settled and quiet once more, he took the
shockrod in his hand and turned back to confront his problem. Yesterday he had certainly exceeded the spirit of the
Levels, if not its code. Today he wanted to get the exercise
over and done with, but he did not want to violate the spirit
of the Levels, he wanted to be fair—as far as possible, under
the requirements of practice. He would see if he could make
it work without a nasty trick played with Nurail physiology.
He would use the shockrod. He was only required to do so
much.

"A rope, Mister Curran." Which meant that he would
need to restrain Lussman somehow, and he wanted to keep
Security out of it if possible. Too many hands confused the
issue and muddied the waters. Nor could he imagine that the
Security would enjoy the requirement they were under to
participate in these exercises, as a rule. "I want twelve
eighths of rope, to bind him. And a pair of gloves." Twelve
eighths would be somewhat more than sufficient merely to
bind a prisoner's arms, and there were shackles, after all. But

Sorlie Curran wouldn't argue. And Andrej had something specific in mind for the rope. He meant to approach Lussman man-to-man and contest with him without the interference of Security. The least he owed the man after his savagery from yesterday was to engage him one-on-one in recognition of Lussman's existence as a feeling creature like himself.

Sorlie Curran was back within half a cup of rhyti's time, with the rope and the gloves and a respectfully confused expression on his face. Andrej tried on the gloves; supple and well-fitting, they would do very nicely. "I'm impressed," he told Sorlie Curran truthfully. He hadn't counted on getting a good fit, not on such short notice. "I'll take the rope now, if you please."

His idea hadn't been to unshackle the prisoner. His idea was to loop the rope through the shackles and around Rab Lussman's throat. It would have the effect of drawing his arms up behind his back at rather an awkward angle, and that would stress the vulnerable shoulder, but there was nothing to be done about that. Andrej needed to have a handle on the man.

"Very well, stand away."

"Excellency, with respect . . ." Vely was looking a little confused, a little worried. "This man, he's a dangerous . . ."

Criminal. Andrej didn't hear the last of Vely's protest, because Lussman chose the moment to kick out at him from behind. One instant in which to successfully regain his footing, or lose his balance and fall to the floor. One instant between an unexpected thinblade-thrust and a successful parry. . . .

One instant was time enough for Andrej Koscuisko. He levered himself against the rope in his hands, the rope that he had wound around Rab Lussman's throat, and it was Lussman who lost his balance and went sprawling to the floor.

Square onto the wrong shoulder.

Lussman would learn.

Andrej crouched down slowly, reluctant to look at Lussman's face. Lussman had set his teeth against the pain, his breath coming in muted sobs of agony. Andrej spoke to Security to separate himself, to shield himself from the keen temptation he felt to admire Lussman's distress. "Thank you, Mister Vely." It was wonderful, how much of an impression a little sprain could make. "A man must be involved in his work, don't you think? Else it is just an empty exercise. Instead of a contest. Now, Rab, what had we agreed on, yesterday?" He hardly dared to look at Lussman. He wouldn't look at Lussman. "Your identification?"

Twisting the rope up snugly in his fist Andrej rotated his wrist, putting an additional half-twist in the taut loop around Lussman's throat and pulling in the direction he meant Lussman to go. Half-strangled, choking on the noose, Lussman struggled to his knees painfully. Andrej knelt in turn across Lussman's lower legs to hold the man in place. He could do what he would be required to do behind Lussman's back, and be safe from himself. He could maintain control with one hand on the rope at Lussman's throat. He didn't have to look at him. He gave the rope a quick, sharp quarter turn to assure himself of Lussman's full attention.

"Well?"

"Rab Lussman. 'Your Excellency.' " The sneer was predictable, even through the man's pain. Andrej had begun to develop a great deal of respect for Rab Lussman; he was obviously no coward. On the other hand, he clearly could not be permitted to be so contemptuous in his phrasing, even out of respect for his discomfort. Andrej laid the shockrod across the naked sole of Lussman's foot, riding his prisoner's convulsion of agony as if it had been a bit of turbulence encountered while skikiting.

When Lussman found his voice, it bore clear witness to the strain, but was stubborn and determined all the same.

". . . Arrested on a charge of willful destruction of Jurisdiction property. Of which I am innocent. Your Excellency."

Andrej tried the shockrod against Lussman's heel, considering. Lussman snorted like a riding-ram through stubbornly clenched teeth, his back and shoulders arching involuntarily in response to the pain. "Did I ask you, Lussman?"

"No. Your Excellency."

Yesterday Lussman had his shoulder put out of joint and forced back into place without revealing more than the most innocuous information. Non-actionable information; because unless he had been condemned in absentia, there was no law against being Rab Lussman, and there was no law against being arrested by accident, either. Nor had being flogged with his weight on his injured shoulder made enough of an impression on Lussman to matter.

It was only a problem if he sought mastery. He didn't need to win. He only needed to get through. This approach might be boring and predictable, but it had to be safer than what had betrayed him to himself yesterday, and there was no objecting to the strategy for that. Shockrods were fairly common instruments of oppression; Lussman had quite probably experienced their effects prior to this. It could not be said that the punishment was unimaginable, or even out of the ordinary. And still it was an approved and effective tool.

"Listen, I will tell to you my thought." He almost thought he could hear sharp hunger in his voice, and swallowed hard before he dared continue. "We are going to be done with this, I am very bored. I am going to ask you some very simple questions, easily understood, even for a Nurail."

He let the shockrod trail across Lussman's instep, tightening his grip on the rope at Lussman's throat as the body jerked in uncoordinated protest. He sensed the danger that lay in wait for him, but he could not decline to put the exercise forward simply because he was afraid of what might happen to him. Nor could it be said that he feared failure; when he was apprehensive of success instead—or of the thing that had helped him to succeed in their last meeting. "You are going to answer my questions. And if your answer is not satisfactory I am going to strike it from the Judicial record . . ."

Full contact, prolonged for perhaps so long as an eighth, mercilessly. Doing all he could to close his ears to the seductive music of Lussman's reluctant cries. ". . . in this manner. Well? Is that clear?"

Oh, Holy Mother.

It was going to happen to him again.

He couldn't even see the Nurail's face, and still he noted all the signs of pain with something too clearly different from compassion to be taken for reluctance to inflict the pain he had it in his power to promise Lussman.

"You are to answer me politely, Rab." His own voice sounded rough and harsh, but Andrej knew what passion roughened it, and lifted his face to the cold white ceiling in despair. *Keep talking,* he told himself. Maybe if he could only just keep talking, he could put the appetite away. If he could not curb it or control it, perhaps he could pretend that he ignored it, and get through this after all. "You are to answer me 'yes, Your Excellency' and 'no, Your Excellency.' Lack of good manners offends me, Lussman. Do you understand?"

Lussman didn't answer. *You have undone yourself, Andrej,* he thought. *Since you have asked, you must enforce an answer. And when you force his answer, you are going to enjoy it. You are lost. And since you have defied your father, you cannot so much as hope that your Holy Mother will raise Her divine hand to succor you.* He set the shockrod to the bottom of Lussman's foot once more, seeking the nerve that would respond best to the noxious stimulus almost despite himself. Touching the naked soles of Lussman's feet, first one, then the other, rolling the impulse end of the torture tool against the small bones, hesitatingly at first, then with increasing assurance and deliberation. The sound of Lussman's pain was more than he could find it in himself to resist. It was lovely. It was sweet. He wanted more.

"Yes. Your Excellency."

"Your name is?"

"Rab Lussman. Your Excellency."

Andrej felt his face warm with a flush of gratification, his pleasure redoubled because he took it against Lussman's will. "And you are accused of willful destruction of Jurisdiction property, yes? Have you committed this crime?"

This was the second day of Lussman's interrogation. Cumulative pain and stress should have begun to seriously cloud Lussman's judgment. Andrej could almost sense Lussman's confusion of mind as he struggled with the deliberately incriminating phrasing of Andrej's demand.

"Yes, Your Excellency. No—"

He couldn't let Lussman finish, not if his plan was to work. He set the shockrod against his prisoner's foot and smiled as he heard Lussman's cry of agony.

"Very good. You have confessed to having committed the crime for which you have been arrested." Not really, no. But the Writ did not require that he play fair, as long as he got something out of it that could be considered close to a confession. Shifting his weight and rising, Andrej gave the rope a savage jerk, and Lussman struggled to his feet with his breath rattling painfully in his throat. "There remain only the details to be determined. How many of your family were involved, then? All?"

He shouldn't be asking Lussman questions like that. He wanted Lussman to submit to him, to answer his questions and make his confession. He wasn't going to get very far with the line he was taking. Wasn't such an accusation all but guaranteed to evoke the utmost resistance from his client?

He had to be clear in his own mind or he would surely only confuse the issue in the mind of the prisoner. It was reasonable to expect Lussman to become increasingly anxious to understand what Andrej wanted, increasingly eager to supply whatever was required. Lussman wasn't going to be able to do that unless Andrej gave him a clearer idea of what the requirement actually was. Andrej knew what the requirement was. He required Lussman's pain, and then Lussman's submission. But he wanted Lussman's pain more than Lussman's answers. "Talk to me, Rab. Tell me about your crime."

"Excellency, I am not guilty of . . . the crime. . . ."

Andrej twisted the rope savagely yet again, and Lussman's protest rattled into strangled incoherence.

It wasn't fair to Lussman to approach him in this manner; he wasn't being candid. Why should he hurry Lussman to confessing when all that meant was that punishment would follow? Because since punishment was to follow, it could not be decent, fair, nor just to seek ways in which he could prolong the punishment that Lussman was to have before confession. One way or the other, Lussman had little chance of understanding what he was expected to confess as long as Andrej continued to communicate such mixed and contradictory signals to the man.

"No, I won't have it," he warned, and let some slack out

at Lussman's throat. "You are accused of willful destruction of Jurisdiction property, and I mean to have details, I tell you."

He would be master here, whether it meant he soil himself or not.

He had no choice.

"I don't believe I find that answer acceptable, Lussman." The shockrod had gotten dirty during the past hours, and there was blood on his uniform where he'd brushed it against his trouser leg in passing. "Let's try it again. I'm getting tired of your childish stubbornness."

The prisoner lay on his belly on the floor, moving one foot in little irregular spasms—as if there was some corner of Lussman's mind that thought that he could get away, if he could only manage to move. As if he couldn't stop himself from hoping that there was some place to which he would be permitted to escape. Andrej knelt at Lussman's side, quite close, and let his knee rest casually against the swollen mess that yesterday's trauma and today's punishment had made of the young man's shoulder. "You are to tell me why you chose the site—who helped you? Who was it that decided your target?"

Lussman was afraid, Andrej could hear it in his voice. "Excellency. Innocent. Of the crimes . . . accused . . ." It was only reasonable to be afraid, but Andrej wasn't going to put his weight against so obvious a target. Yet.

"You have already confessed to the crime, it is only a question of the details. What sense is there in further resistance?"

With a surprisingly determined effort Lussman moved, shifting away from Andrej where he knelt. Andrej knew how much it had to hurt Lussman to move; all in all, Lussman was clearly courageous, of strong will and determined temperament. It was really a shame that such a man should be sacrificed to the Judicial order; but—since so much was pre-ordained—the least he could do was see that Lussman completed his confession before too much more blood was spilled. Or deeper blood was spilled, at any rate. Perhaps he would be offered a contract as bond-involuntary, a strong young man, physically fit, of such admirable strength of character. . . .

"Not true. Innocent. Have not. Committed, any. Such crime. . . ."

Lussman's voice dried up in his throat as Andrej leaned over him. Steadying himself with one hand pressed against Lussman's back, now, Andrej reached across his body to take a jugular pulse, wondering where that thought had come from. The Bond was only offered to Accused prior to Intermediate Level Inquiry, and then only when Judicial staff had evaluated the candidate and found him suitable. If Lussman had been qualified for the Bond, he would have been offered one before now, and then been subjected to the implant of a governor whether he had agreed to it or not. Rab Lussman was not going to be offered any Bond.

"This has gone on quite long enough. Really, I am becoming bored." Perhaps eight hours, perhaps longer, and he had confused his prisoner and tormented him, troubled him with half-true accusations and tortured him with a rope and a shockrod and a keen sense of where it hurt—and Lussman would not surrender. Oh, the appearance of a confession had been approximated, by trickery—the doubled question that could not be answered without incrimination. It was a dirty technique, and Andrej had never forgotten his fury at the confessor who had tried it on him. But it worked—or at least it worked here, where the prisoner could not storm out of the confessional in righteous outrage. Here, where Andrej would be encouraged by his Tutor in his duplicity instead of disciplined by his ecclesiastical superiors for trying to manipulate a Koscuisko prince so crudely—instead of in the more traditional, time-honored ways.

So the forms could be completed.

But Lussman had not given in.

His throat was scraped bloody from the pressure of the coarse rope, the trauma of yesterday's beating renewed and doubled by the shockrod, his shoulder red and furious with the insult, and his face white and glistening with the sweat of his pain—but Lussman would not give in. And Andrej wanted his surrender, wanted it, quite apart from the forms and the requirements, quite apart from his respect for his prisoner's courage and strength of will.

He was Koscuisko, and he would have dominion.

He set his knee firmly against Lussman's injured shoulder and put his weight full on the crippled joint, leaning over to speak close to Lussman's ear. "Aren't you ready for a break, from this?—Because you shall have none, till you confess." He said it half in charity, half with intent to deceive. "You've managed to defy me for quite some time, but there are limits to how much you can be expected to endure." Which Lussman seemed both ready and willing to challenge, but that was beside the point. It was only a difference of degree, after all. "Be a little easier on yourself. Haven't you suffered long enough? And for what? For whom?"

"Excellency. . . . Long enough?"

Lussman had begun to repeat what had been said to him in random fragments, without any indication that he understood what he was saying—as if he were drugged by shock, or by his pain. Lussman's dazed repetition of disjointed phrases could be useful in constructing a "confession." But this sounded like a real question, with real feeling behind it.

"Long enough to break for midmeal, at the very earliest." He had indulged himself to the fullest with the halter and the shockrod. He was going to have to graduate Lussman to some sharper torment if he was to keep the man's attention focused where he wanted it. "I'll have to send out for a box, I suppose. Perhaps Mister Sorlie Curran will be kind enough to go for me."

The knot he'd set in the halter had pulled very tight over the past few hours. It took Andrej a moment to work it free. Lussman was too exhausted after half a day's struggle against the rope to need too much managing, at least until Andrej decided what new treat he should go after. It was an interesting problem, given his options, his opportunities. Unless Lussman disappointed him by capitulating too soon, of course.

"Midmeal. Halfway. Through the Fifth." Lussman sounded relieved, even through his evident suffering. Grateful. What in the name of the Holy Mother's mirror could he be talking about? "Safe, then. All right—"

Not only that, but Sorlie Curran was interrupting, and if Andrej hadn't known better he could have sworn that Sorlie Curran was anxious about something.

"His Excellency prefers for his midmeal the bread and cheese, or perhaps the greens with protein?"

There were undercurrents here that Andrej did not understand.

Sorlie Curran had not only interrupted him but had interrupted the prisoner as well, and Sorlie Curran, as a professional Security troop, surely knew better than that.

And while Lussman clearly seemed to have something on his mind, it didn't sound to Andrej as though it was about anything that they'd shared throughout the long morning. Sorlie Curran was anxious—not obviously so, but Andrej had a lifetime's experience reading the voices and body-language of Household servants in order to find out what was wrong when he had offended. Andrej realized immediately that Sorlie Curran was afraid that Lussman was going to say something—or that Andrej was going to pay attention to something that Lussman had already said.

"Perhaps not quite yet, Mister Sorlie Curran. Return to the other side of the room, if you please. Immediately." He wanted to be alone with Lussman. What had the man said? *Midmeal. Halfway through the Fifth. Safe, then. All right.* This was almost as intriguing as Lussman's agony, and Andrej had fed long and drunk deep of Lussman's agony throughout the morning, and was not so avid for it now that he could not be distracted by this new development. Easing Lussman onto his back, Andrej carried his nerveless arms with the hands swollen from their bonds carefully to the front of Lussman's body. Granted that Lussman's back was bruised and bloodied; a little additional distraction might not be unproductive, at this point.

"That's right, Rab. It's halfway through the Fifth Level. It's all right now. You can tell me." He could only guess at what was going on, but with any luck Lussman would oblige him—

"Excellency." It was a sigh of relief, almost of gratitude. Gratitude, again. "Begs leave to confess. To you. I have committed. The crime."

And suddenly Lussman was willing to confess, was eager to confess. "Of willful destruction. Of. Jurisdiction . . ."

"Why now?" Andrej could make no sense of it. "What do you mean by telling me this now, when I've been asking you about it all day long?"

"Begs leave to confess," Lussman groaned, and his agony was clear and genuine. "Halfway—for Megh. Halfway, halfway through . . ."

Understanding came to Andrej like a basin full of icy water in his face. Suddenly Andrej knew exactly what was going on; and the horror of it banished all the delight Lussman had provided him away, body and soul, and left him cold with certainty and outrage.

He knew what was tormenting Rab Lussman, or whatever the man's name was.

He knew what was troubling Sorlie Curran.

He even realized why it had occurred to him that Lussman might be offered the Bond.

"Yes, halfway through." He lied without remorse, without compunction. They had been lying to him all along. "You're free to make confession now; it's time. It cannot have been easy for you, Lussman. Do you remember what you are supposed to say to me?"

He meant to have verification before Tutor Chonis called the exercise. And Tutor Chonis would call the exercise the moment Tutor Chonis—watching, as Andrej knew he watched, from whatever review room or vantage area—realized what he was up to. Sorlie Curran's attempted intervention had made that very clear. So he had to act quickly.

"Yes, Your Excellency."

Clearly disoriented, Lussman obviously had no idea that he had revealed the secret.

"Tell to me your truth, then, what you are instructed to do. I want to hear it from you. The truth, Lussman."

Lussman had closed his eyes tightly as if he wanted to shut out the unpleasant memory of the past few hours. Andrej couldn't blame him for that. He knew exactly how unpleasant it had been for Lussman. "Halfway. Fifth Level. Not before. Class-Two violation . . ."

Andrej heard the subtle shift in the background noise from

the ventilators, and knew that the Tutor's intercommunication channel had finally been engaged. "Administrative orders!"

He'd heard it yesterday, he knew what it was. But they were too late. Had Noycannir found hers out, yesterday?

"All exercises to cease, repeat, all exercises to cease. Disengage at once."

And here was Sorlie Curran now, again. "Respectfully request His Excellency stand up and move away from the prisoner."

The prisoner. A bond-involuntary Security troop playing a role, forbidden to reveal the deception on pain of a Class-Two violation—even at the Fifth Level of Inquiry. Even through the stern and savage punishment that "Lussman" had been suffering, forbidden to say the word that would make it stop.

Andrej rose to his feet, sickened, dazed. He had taught Chonis a lesson, then, hadn't he? They had lied to him, and he had demonstrated the futility of trying to lie to him. He had desired mastery, and he had attained mastery, but it did not feel the way he had expected. How could they play such games with men in Joslire's position—men without recourse—as pawns?

More Security were entering the theater now, and he had been expecting a medical team for the "prisoner" now that the farce was over. They were not Security that he had seen before, and he did not mind snarling at them when two of the four began to drag "Rab Lussman" off by the arms.

"You, what do you think you're doing?" He heard the horror in his own voice and suppressed it sternly. So much depended upon the correct attitude. Security might obey an irritated officer. An overemotional Student could be safely ignored. "Set that man down at once. He requires medical attention, not additional injury."

They did as they were told, right enough, even though they looked a little puzzled about why they were complying. They really didn't have any choice, did they?

Had the Administration given "Rab Lussman" any choice?

"Excellency." Sorlie Curran, once again, and it was unusual to hear the direct form of address from a bond-involuntary. Sorlie Curran sounded upset. "They are required to take him into custody. No medical intervention is permitted unless there is a life-threatening injury. By the Bench instruction."

By the Bench instruction. He should have guessed. The logic of it all was blinding in its inhuman rigidity. He should have taken one of Joslire's five-knives and slit the man's belly open, forcing "medical intervention"—except that they would only have treated the knife wound, not the welts, not the weals, not the joint. They would not treat the pain.

"Very well."

He should have hurt the man so much that they would have to treat the pain to save his life. And he had not. And therefore the man would suffer, locked up in a cell somewhere, and that was where his conservative approach to injuring his "prisoner" had got him.

"You may carry out your orders."

He had forced the issue. He was responsible.

He needed to have a word with Tutor Chonis.

◆ Six

The situation was about as bad as any Tutor Chonis had ever faced. Joslire Curran had been dispatched to bring Koscuisko to his office directly. He had an idea that Koscuisko would be coming whether bidden or not, and he had to maintain as much control of the situation as he could. If he could.

He stood up from his desk as Koscuisko entered, nodding to Curran to leave them alone and seal the entry, pulling one of the chairs at the conference table around for Koscuisko as he did so. It was no less important to maintain his momentum, his control, than if he was performing an Inquiry again, after all these years. It was more important. He guided Koscuisko to the seat by his elbow as the door sealed behind Curran's back; seating himself beside Koscuisko—like a co-conspirator, two Students together—Tutor Chonis began to try to find out how far the damage went.

"Student Koscuisko, do you know what you have done?"

Koscuisko had been still during Chonis's arranging; and it was a dangerous stillness, a waiting stillness. It was not good. Koscuisko should be too angry to think twice, not cold enough to watch and wait and see what was going to happen.

"I await your instruction, Tutor Chonis. Tell me what it is, exactly, that I have done."

For the first time in his long career Tutor Chonis wondered what his tutelage had wrought, what manner of Inquisitor he had created. How had Koscuisko caught on? He had been watching every move; Noycannir had not yet been matched with a replacement, so there'd been nothing to distract him.

St. Clare's lapse should have meant nothing to one not already in the know. How could Koscuisko be so calm now, in the face of this disgraceful secret?

"Only carefully selected Security are trusted with this portion of your training. And they volunteer for it on Safe, with a Class-Two violation as the price for any failure. Do you recall what a Class-Two violation means, for a bond-involuntary like St. Clare?"

Shock value. He had to shake Koscuisko's arctic calm. He had seemed emotional enough when the Security had come to take St. Clare away; he should not have been able to freeze his feelings over, not so quickly, not so well. It was unnatural.

"And that is why you were so disappointed with Student Noycannir's, ah, study partner, I imagine. After all, the Tutor had to call that exercise at the Fourth Level."

Chonis stared, genuinely confused for a moment. "What are you talking about? She lost her head, we lost the man. Our selection techniques for prisoner-surrogates have a failure rate of less than three in two eighties, Koscuisko. This isn't supposed to happen."

Wrong choice, wrong approach. Koscuisko smiled, and Chonis found that he did not like the color that Koscuisko's eyes seemed to have turned; they were too cold by half. "Then either he—St. Clare?—is very stupid, or I am very good. Is that what I am meant to conclude, from this dishonorable charade? But I don't think St. Clare is stupid at all. I've been rather admiring his backbone. I should therefore conclude that I am better at this filthy business than one hundred and fifty-seven out of every hundred-and-sixty of your other Students. Did I get that right, Tutor Chonis?"

Koscuisko should not be taking that tone of voice with him. And it was up to him to convince Koscuisko to mind his manners.

"That is one conclusion to be drawn." Not that he would suggest that Koscuisko should be ashamed of a success of this nature; Koscuisko's own reluctance to be here in the first place would take care of that for him. "The other conclusion may be as important, in the long run. You said that you 'rather admired' St. Clare, I believe?"

"Indeed. Knowing what I know now, my respect for him only increases. I could never have managed so fine an effort. I am certain of it."

"Then I should like you to consider what you have done to him by expanding the scope of your Inquiry."

Koscuisko frowned. "My brief called for his confession, I obtained two, he answered as he was bidden. What is the problem?"

Finally, a line, a handle, a weapon with which to regain control of this too-successful Student. "Your brief called for a confession to willful destruction of Jurisdiction property. Had you been content with the confession you obtained—"

"With the Tutor's permission, no confession was obtained; the appearance of a confession merely."

Good, he had found a way in. "If, as I was saying, you had been content as you should have been with the confession that you had been directed to obtain, Robert St. Clare would not be condemned to the equivalent of three days of Inquiry at the Seventh Level. He would have earned the remission of four years off his Bond, and the Fleet would have rejoiced in the service of a strong and dedicated Security troop. As it is . . ."

At least he had Koscuisko's attention, and there was visible emotion on Koscuisko's face. That it was fury and hatred was beside the point. Where there was passion there was weakness. Koscuisko could not be allowed to escape Tutor Chonis's strict control; and Tutor Chonis could not obtain control without some weakness on Koscuisko's part—that much seemed suddenly all too clear.

"There will be execution of discipline for a Class-Two violation, and then we'll have to decide whether St. Clare can return to service at all. There is rather a high failure rate after a Class-Two violation has been adjudged, not surprisingly. We will probably have to terminate."

There was evident shock in Koscuisko's eyes now, and obvious pain. If it hadn't been for the steely front Koscuisko had presented scant eighths ago, Tutor Chonis felt he might have been fooled into feeling sorry for his Student. But Tutor Chonis had seen the temper of Koscuisko's will, and he knew better than to believe that he could afford to give a sixteenth if he was to hope to retain the upper hand.

"It makes no sense to risk the resource when failure means a loss of four hundred thousand, Standard. It is wasteful. Fleet cannot afford it."

Still Chonis was tempted, so tempted. Koscuisko's conflict was honest and clearly painful, even if he expressed it in such neutral language. All the same, Chonis knew the line he had to take for the sake of the Fleet. For the sake of Koscuisko's own survival as well, in a world where the only authority would be a hardened Command Branch officer whose word would be law and who would not take kindly to Koscuisko's autocratic defiance. For Koscuisko's own sake, Chonis had to break Koscuisko's spirit, his pride, his will.

"Fleet expects its Inquisitors to confine themselves to their stated duty. And not go off chasing hints and suspicions, that's Security's business." Of course once he got out there he would be sent hunting, from time to time, not so much to gain confession as to see what else he could uncover; but that would keep for now. For now the point was that Robert St. Clare would be disciplined then probably killed as an unrecoverable resource, and all because Andrej Koscuisko had stepped out of bounds. "Are there any questions?"

"There is one thing."

He knew he'd made his point, but Koscuisko's face held none of the conflict he'd seen there moments before. It was the face Koscuisko had come in with, all over again. Chonis knew by that token that there was hope for Koscuisko's survival after all.

"Yes?"

"If, what is his name, St. Clare is a bond-involuntary and under orders, then he cannot be convicted of a Class-Two violation. The administrative instruction states that a bond-involuntary cannot be put in jeopardy by the issuance of contradictory, equally binding legal orders."

It was a weakness in the system, and Koscuisko had found it out. He had hunted it out as quickly and as surely as he had hunted St. Clare's secret out. He was too good for his own good: but as long as he could be convinced to conform, it would be all right.

"Ordinarily you would be correct."

"What is out of the ordinary about this situation? A man has been placed in artificial jeopardy through the issuance of contradictory orders. The Administrator—I presume—has ordered him to confess to one thing, but never to the other. I have ordered him to confess to me his truth, and tell me what it was that he had been directed to do."

And probably—Chonis mused—if he were to review the training record, he'd find that Koscuisko had in fact used that language, at one time or another. It was an ingenious defense. Too bad it could not be allowed to work.

"I'm afraid the Administration cannot accept your reasoning. In this instance the order you issued was not binding or lawful, inasmuch as you did not know your prisoner-surrogate to be under orders at the time that you gave your instruction. And your surrogate in turn had prior lawful clearance to disregard orders from you, for the sake of the exercise."

"And for this point of Law, the Administration would rather destroy the resource than salvage the man?"

Failure to obey lawful and received instruction was a Class-Two violation either way. What difference did it make? "Explain yourself."

"My order negates the previous one. St. Clare has disobeyed me by attempting to withhold the confession I demanded of him. I have the option of disciplining him myself or referring him for the Class-Two violation. And if I discipline him, Fleet need not lose the resource, since my options are restricted to the Class-One level."

"You have a point, Student Koscuisko." Should he give false hope or quash any hope right now? "What reason would the Administration have for endorsing such an unorthodox resolution to the problem?"

It seemed that Koscuisko hesitated, as if searching for the right words. "I could swear very solemnly to abuse my Security whenever possible, and never forget myself so far as to let the truth get in the way of the confession that I have been instructed to obtain. Would that not conform to the Fleet requirement?''

There was the sound of genuine petition in Koscuisko's voice, regardless of the form of his offer.

But it was no good.

"Thank you, Student Koscuisko. That will be all." No, they could not afford to let Koscuisko have his way.

Koscuisko could never be permitted to doubt that he had brought an essentially guiltless man to torment and to death because he had stepped outside of his boundaries.

The door to Tutor Chonis's office opened and Koscuisko came out with a look on his face that was desperate and analytical at once. Joslire made his salute, but Koscuisko ignored it, and Koscuisko had always been careful to acknowledge, as a courtesy, that which was demanded of Joslire in respect for the officer's rank.

"I will go to Infirmary, Mister Curran," Koscuisko said. "Be so kind as to show me the way."

There was no arguing with it, of course, but he was responsible for reporting on Koscuisko's state of mind, and therefore a little probing was in order. "According to the officer's good pleasure. But the officer has not eaten, and it is well past midmeal."

Koscuisko had turned his back, starting down the hall as if he didn't really care where he was going as long as he was going away from Tutor Chonis. Pivoting suddenly on his heel now, Koscuisko glared at Joslire, who had to step back hastily to avoid running into him.

" 'The officer' does not have time. I'll eat in the lab. Let's go."

Koscuisko had to know that St. Clare was not in Infirmary. Why was he in such a hurry to get there? Joslire couldn't understand the tension that he sensed. He had to hurry to catch up with Koscuisko. The one thing he did know was that he had better stay with his officer, at all costs.

He had watched with sickened fear as Koscuisko caught the minute crack in St. Clare's discipline: "begs leave," because "this troop begs leave," rather than "I beg leave" as a man would in the first person—and forced it wide open.

He thought he knew how his officer had felt when Koscuisko had realized that not only was his "prisoner" no such thing, but that the man was to be brutally disciplined for having permitted any shadow of the truth to escape him.

Why was Koscuisko going to Infirmary?

Koscuisko had full access to dedicated lab space. Tutor Chonis would not revoke it because of this incident. Was he really concerned that Koscuisko meant to take some medication to relieve himself of his guilt, and his life with it? No. He didn't read that kind of desperation in the set of Koscuisko's shoulders, or in the angle at which Koscuisko held his head. But the desperation was real and immediate.

So what was going on?

Koscuisko was silent on the way and stood mute in the security clearing area once they arrived, letting Joslire do all the talking. He wasn't looking at anything that Joslire could identify, his eyes apparently fixed on some target several eighths down the corridor on the other side of the wall.

"Student Koscuisko, with Tutor Chonis. Laboratory space to be provided ad lib at the Student's pleasure."

The Security responsible for Infirmary were Station Security rather than teaching staff. Joslire had acquaintances among the troops, but they needed a Chief Warrant to clear Koscuisko through to his laboratory space—it was procedure. It took a moment for the Security post to find the Warrant on duty and log the release in due form, but Koscuisko never stirred from where he stood. Koscuisko might have been asleep with his eyes open, for all Joslire could tell. Except that he did react immediately once Security had received the clearance they required.

"Logged and listed, very good, Curran. The officer has been assigned four-one-H-one. Travis can show the officer the way. Will the officer be requiring Curran's attendance?"

Because otherwise Joslire had no business in the Infirmary area, and good little bond-involuntaries simply didn't go where they had no business being. If Koscuisko didn't want him, he'd have to go to Tutor Chonis and let the Tutor know that Koscuisko was surrounded by every chemical substance a man could want for any purpose, and unsupervised as well; and Tutor Chonis would have to authorize surveillance inside

Infirmary, and Koscuisko would notice sooner or later, and it would not sweeten his temper by much.

Koscuisko turned his head and looked over his shoulder at Joslire with cold empty eyes. Empty on the surface, because the mind was far away, working furiously to solve a problem whose identity Joslire could not begin to guess.

"I'll want to send him for my supper when the time comes," Koscuisko said. "And in the meantime, he could bring my rhyti."

It was good enough for Joslire, and good enough for the shift supervisor as well apparently. "There is no impediment. If the officer will please follow Travis."

The laboratory space assigned to Koscuisko was deep within the Infirmary complex. Joslire had to keep a sharp eye on the turnings to be sure that he was going to be able to get in here and out again for Koscuisko's meal. It turned out to be a smallish room, not much larger than Koscuisko's quarters; their guide bowed Koscuisko through, meeting Joslire's eyes with mild curiosity, and then prepared to leave Koscuisko to his work. Whatever it was.

"If the officer requires anything further, I'll send an orderly," Travis said. She had a pleasant voice, neutral and professional, that showed no hint of curiosity as to what was going on.

"I want three-eighths to think." Koscuisko's statement in response was startling after his contemplative, absorbed silence. At least Joslire was startled. "Send an orderly after three-eighths. Or show Joslire where to fetch one. From the pharmacy, of course."

And then he sat down at the documents-bench and stared at the blank screen as if the rest of the world had abruptly lapsed back into the state of nonexistence that had been its position since he had left Tutor Chonis's office.

Travis shrugged from where she stood out in the corridor, safely shielded now from Koscuisko's line of sight by the intervening wall. "I'll send the orderly," she repeated, speaking directly to Joslire now that Koscuisko had effectively dismissed her. "Are you going for rhyti, or shall I?"

"Thanks." The option was appreciated, but Travis had no way of knowing how Koscuisko liked his rhyti. Koscuisko was particular. "What if he needs you in a hurry?"

What if Joslire needed help with him, in other words. Travis grinned and answered the question he hadn't asked. "Security call, your basic black button, both sides of the door. Guaranteed response time, two skips of a 'cruit's heart. Anything else?"

"If there is he hasn't let on yet."

She winked and went away, and he retreated into the lab, closing the door.

To stand and watch, and wait Koscuisko's bidding.

After a while Koscuisko bestirred himself to activate the documents-review screen, apparently finding several entries of interest. When the orderly came, Koscuisko discussed some drugs with her, names that meant nothing to Joslire and apparently little enough to the orderly. Koscuisko sent her away to prepare an analysis cart for him, sending Joslire away at the same time; but Joslire wasn't worried any longer by then. If the chemicals, the drugs, that Koscuisko had ordered could be used against himself, surely the orderly would at least have recognized them. The memory of the exercise aside, Koscuisko did not feel like a man at risk, to Joslire's mind. He seemed too completely absorbed in an abstract issue of some sort to be thinking about anything as messy and mundane as suicide.

Joslire was surprised to find out how late it had gotten to be—Koscuisko's thirdmeal shift already. He took a meal as well as the rhyti back to the lab, but Koscuisko didn't react to his return—apart from reaching for his rhyti just as Joslire got it stirred and set out for him. Too deep in his analysis, whatever it was. Joslire sighed and once more covered the meal tray, waiting for Koscuisko to remember that he hadn't eaten anything since his fastmeal in the "morning."

Except that Koscuisko didn't seem to notice.

The hours wore on, and Koscuisko did not seem to be paying attention. Joslire stood on watch, since that was what he was expected to do, wondering how long it would be before the officer's lack of sleep and lack of food caught up with him.

Not any time soon, obviously.

Computer analyses and reaction models, more chemical

profiles, time out to scan a long text article, then back to the imager to tweak a holo-model of some chemical formulation or another.

Hours . . .

"Joslire."

What was Koscuisko up to, anyway?

Had he decided to lose himself in his work?

He'd had a very trying day; most Students found themselves exhausted beyond belief by the unexpected demands of the Intermediate Levels. A man couldn't really expect himself to work all day on a jug of rhyti. It wasn't that effective a stimulant.

"Mister Curran, I have been remiss. Are you with me?"

What?

"I want to see Tutor Chonis, Joslire. I regret that I must insist upon it immediately."

Joslire blinked rapidly, trying to focus. Koscuisko was standing in front of him, eating a piece of cold egg-pie taken up from the meal tray Joslire had brought him, how long ago?

Asleep.

He'd fallen asleep.

A fine Security troop he made.

"The officer's pardon is—"

But Koscuisko wouldn't let him finish. "I know, I know, 'respectfully solicited.' Yes? It does not import. I want to see Tutor Chonis, do you know where he sleeps?"

Well, if Koscuisko wasn't interested in being apologized to, there was nothing in particular he could do about it. "That information is not available. An emergency call can be made at the officer's discretion."

"You needn't be cross with me, Joslire, although I am at fault. I should have sent you to bed."

It wasn't that, even if he couldn't explain it very well. It was only that he was asleep, and reverting to the safety of absolute formality accordingly for his own protection. Koscuisko was still talking—

"Do please make the call, then. I don't know how much time I may have left. In fact I am afraid to ask."

Afraid to ask about what "time left"?

He'd never known an officer to break the secret. He had no idea any more what was on Koscuisko's mind. But he did have an idea of his own, something that had just occurred to him—as if it had taken an unscheduled nap to remind him of the unaccustomed freedom available here.

"Laboratory facilities are not under surveillance," he said. "Chief Belyss told me so. There is no one listening to whatever it might please the officer to say, should the officer wish to take the opportunity to swear."

In fact Infirmary and the Administrator's Staff areas were the only places in the entire facility that were not monitored, as a matter of principle. He could see understanding come up slowly into his officer's eyes; and then all the self-composure seemed to spark out of Koscuisko at once. Koscuisko reached out for him and grabbed his overblouse—alarming; but, as Joslire realized, only for emphasis. And perhaps to keep his balance. Koscuisko didn't raise his voice, but the fiercely controlled desperation that Joslire heard was more affecting to his carefully guarded heart than howls of outrage could have been.

"How can they have done such a thing?"

Then, as if he only then noticed what he was doing, Koscuisko seemed to master himself once more. He loosened his iron grip at Joslire's collar, taking care to brush away a stray crumb from his egg-pie as he did so, and collected his energies back into himself to continue more calmly. No less desperately, however.

"The obscenity of it cannot be described. I admire that man, Joslire, that man St. Clare, and it cannot be said that he lacks discipline."

Only now, as Koscuisko fought for self-control, did Joslire realize how passionate Koscuisko actually was about this; perhaps about other things, as well. He had done such a thorough job of wearing his calm, neutral Student's mask that Joslire had not dreamed there was such passion in him, apart from the passion Student Koscuisko seemed to be developing for pain. It was like meeting a stranger in place of the man whose meals he had been preparing all this time.

"It cannot even be said that he disobeyed his orders. How could it? He revealed nothing. Oh, perhaps one little mistake was made, but no violation. And they will murder him for it."

Joslire searched for something he could say that Koscuisko could use to bring himself back under control. "Participation in the exercise is voluntary, as it please the officer. And solicited on Safe, to ensure that he was genuinely free to decline without repercussions. He knew the risks and accepted the penalty. All of us did."

"All of you . . ."

Koscuisko was pale to begin with, and now the shock had whitened his countenance until he looked almost blue with it. "Oh, Joslire. It is beyond shameful. That man is to be tortured and probably killed, for no good or necessary reason. I can make no sense of it, and yet I am to be a part of it. How can I hope to function within such a dichotomy? There is a clinical term for this conflict, Joslire. . . ."

He knew what Koscuisko was getting at. "It is a useful thing to focus on—for those tasked with the officer's responsibilities."

Koscuisko was still talking, as if he hadn't heard. "But it is a false refuge, grotesque cowardice. One has need of all one's wits to survive in such an environment. One cannot afford any separation of personality."

A surprising turn, Joslire thought. His standing orders were to encourage the doubling, if possible; to support the formation of a "not-me" persona that would be able to fulfill an Inquisitor's duties, while the more morally acceptable "me" persona remained safe from taint, removed and remote, deploring the cruelty of it all. So successful had the psychological trick proven over time that the Administration was considering teaching some rudimentary techniques, to try to reduce the steady loss of functional Ship's Surgeons.

"I need not ask if you made any mistakes," Koscuisko said after a moment's silence.

The unaccustomed freedom to speak without being recorded betrayed Joslire to his own honesty, and he answered truthfully rather than in soothing words such as the Administration might have preferred he use.

"If the officer had been my Interrogator, it might easily have been different."

It was a painful idea for Koscuisko. Joslire could see that. He could not find it in him to regret his honesty in spite of it.

"Then I would have been responsible for your agony, as I am responsible for his. I must try this, Joslire; I have something that Tutor Chonis wants. Perhaps I can bargain with the man. With the system."

How could he say it? He could not but honor the officer's intention. How could he convince Koscuisko to set aside every better instinct yet undulled by Fleet's Orientation?

"The officer can do nothing for his prisoner-surrogate now. The Administrator will Record the assessment of penalty firstshift." And Koscuisko, in his determination to take things personally, had already done more for St. Clare than any of the other Students Joslire had served would have done. Anyone else would have written it off as a terrible conflict: *Oh, but the rules are larger than any one officer, and I cannot take on all of Jurisdiction Fleet. What must be, must be.* "Excellency, you play into the Administration's hands. The Tutor means to use the officer's pain to discipline him. Young Inquisitors must be trained to strict conformity. Do not edge the blade that rests in the hand of your opponent."

Facing the closed door, Koscuisko was apparently eager to go to confrontation. But he glanced up to meet Joslire's eyes, quickly, and he smiled.

"You are good to comfort me," Koscuisko said. "I will keep your charity in my heart. But I must try it, Joslire. I could not sleep if I did not try to stop this monstrous cruelty. This waste."

Joslire could think of nothing more to say after that.

Therefore he merely bowed and keyed the communication net to make Koscuisko's emergency appointment with Tutor Chonis.

He had been drunk the night before last. He had not been drunk last night, but he had not slept well, and it was halfway to morning now. Andrej felt his weariness like a pricklefruit in his throat, but he could not afford to think about sleep-syrup to soothe the aching of it, not just yet.

The Administrator would Record the assessment of penalty firstshift, Joslire had said. It was already six eights into fourthshift. He had only two eights in which to stop whatever judicial farce was customary and bind the man who had been Rab Lussman to himself, since that was the only way he could be sure of the bond-involuntary's continued safety. It was an emergency, as Joslire had explained to Tutor Chonis. Perhaps he would able to make a better case of it if he waited until after fastmeal, but he was afraid that if he put it off by so long he would be too late.

Tutor Chonis met him in his office. It was unsettling to see him out of uniform; he was waiting when Andrej got there, sitting at the table instead of behind his desk. The rhyti jug and two glasses were set out at his elbow, one of them half-filled. Like one of Uncle Radu's Counselors, Andrej thought. *Come in, make yourself comfortable, relax. What is troubling you, my nephew?*

"Come in, come in," Tutor Chonis waved him to the facing chair, rubbing one side of his face as he did so. Whatever he was wearing looked a good deal like a bed-coat to Andrej. Had the Tutor come in his bed-dress and slippers? Perhaps he wasn't out of uniform after all. Perhaps he was wearing Tutor's Rest Dress. Andrej took the proffered glass of rhyti and drank it down for concentration. He was getting punch-drunk.

"You needed to talk, Andrej?"

He couldn't think how to begin; all he could do was sit, staring stupidly at the clear vial in his hand. He'd put all of his energy into his idea—his single hope for a chance to change the Tutor's mind. He couldn't quite remember why he'd thought it was going to work.

"Maybe another glass of rhyti, then?" Tutor Chonis suggested.

Why not? He had no idea where to begin. How could he have imagined that this would work? He might as well give up, he might as well go back to quarters and accept defeat like the powerless slave that he was in this place.

Except . . .

Except that there was a chance.

And a man could not be managed without his permission—unless he was a bond-involuntary. No other could be excused for submitting to coercive management.

He was Koscuisko.

He was responsible for the work of his hand, and for the work done at his direction, and for the people who carried out his bidding.

"I want that man for my Security." The rhyti was helping; reaching out a tentative hand, he poured a third glass, remembering almost too late to top off the Tutor's glass politely—like the submissive little Student that they wanted him to be. "You know the one, St. Clare. And after our last meeting I had a thought."

Tutor Chonis's skeptical raised eyebrow was no less effective for the disorder of his hair. Granted, he looked like a sleepy scurryhunter, but a sleepy scurryhunter was a scurryhunter none the less.

"I believe that if the Tutor reviewed the exercise, it would demonstrate that St. Clare did not in fact at any time give up the restricted information—until he was convinced that he was clear of the environment in which it was restricted, as indicated by the question he was asked, a question which clearly presupposed full knowledge of the entire situation." Not as if he was as confident as he would have liked to be of that, but he had to relate it as he remembered it.

"The Tutor has also expressed a concern over my inappropriate expansion of the Writ. I have meditated on the Tutor's comments . . ." —to find a way around them, a way to use them to get what he needed to have. No matter what it took—"and have determined that the Tutor is correct. There is no way in which St. Clare can be bound over to me after his unfortunate lapse. And also that the Tutor's reservations about my . . . attitude . . . must be accepted as valid criticism."

How was he going to approach this?

Tutor Chonis made no move, showed no reaction. Perhaps Tutor Chonis was asleep. He was on his own either way.

"The only uncertainty in my mind concerns whether one of these circumstances might in fact change. Because if one could change, it would be an indication that change was possible in other areas as well."

Now at last Tutor Chonis bestirred himself to drink his rhyti. "One might ask oneself if Student Koscuisko believes that the rule of Law is to be amended with no more substantial or significant a cause than one Student's vanity."

All right. They both knew what he was trying to say. It was time for his last-chance offer, the desperate gamble that had kept him at work in the lab until he'd found what he'd been looking for.

"It is the vanity of a good Student, Tutor Chonis. Whether or not I was remiss in chasing down the secret—and I will sup the sin-cake freely, if I must—the fact remains that it is not a thing often done. You told me as much yourself. With respect. Sir."

At least he thought so. He was almost certain that he remembered Tutor Chonis telling him that.

Or had it been Joslire?

He was so tired that his hand shook as he reached the clear vial that he held out across the table to where Tutor Chonis's hand rested, holding the rhyti glass. "And there is something that the Student has to offer to the Bench in consideration. Apart from any claim to skill or efficiency, at the Question."

Tutor Chonis plucked the vial away from Andrej's nerveless fingers, frowning at it as though there should be some explanatory text within. "And you are referring to?"

"The Tutor had expressed the hope that the Student would enrich the Controlled List." The Controlled List was an abomination under Heaven. So was he. He was a man who had learned to take ecstatic pleasure from torturing a bound man.

"That which you hold may well prove worthwhile from that point of view." And even with so much at stake, it was almost too difficult to promise such a thing. Andrej was surprised at how hard it was to say it.

Especially in the face of Tutor Chonis's sudden eagerness, his greedy interest too plain by half on his no-longer-sleepy face as he held the damning vial to the light and rolled it in his fingers to make the liquid sparkle. "What have you brought me, young Andrej?"

My honor. My honor and my decency, which I will give

to you as sacrifice in exchange for the life of that hapless bond-involuntary. I will trade. Give me his life, and I will do as you have asked me.

"It should be a speakserum." He was no longer quite sure what it was, in the specific sense. He was too keenly aware of what it was in the general sense, for his own peace of mind. "For Mizucash, since you gave me one of those. Or was he actually Security as well? Species-specific. But I think it can safely be deployed against a broader spectrum. Something about a handful of the protein clusters looked quite familiar, except I didn't have the time to run it all down before firstshift."

"Your duty to the Fleet requires you—"

Andrej was ready for that obvious objection. "My duty to the Fleet requires that I perform according to my Writ and according to my rated field. Which is not pharmacology. That lies outside—apart—"

"You've got it all worked out, haven't you?" Tutor Chonis sounded either sarcastic or curious, Andrej could not tell which. "Let me see if I understand you, Student Koscuisko. At the heart of the matter, you are saying that if I oblige you, then you will oblige me. The Fleet. The Bench."

No, surely not, wasn't there some problem in suggesting he "oblige" the Bench? "I think so, Tutor Chonis. I may not have expressed myself correctly, I am not thinking very well." He reached for the rhyti jug, surely near empty by now. But by the time he had it in hand, he'd forgotten why he'd wanted it, and stared at it stupidly, trying to focus his thought.

"Only give me the life of that man, I will administer discipline at the Class-One level, and I will undertake to provide speaksera . . ."

". . . And the sensory factors. And the nerve agents."

Andrej shuddered in profound horror at the thought. Or was it just fatigue? It didn't matter. All he wanted was the life of Robert St. Clare. He would do anything they wanted. "I will satisfy the Bench for it, Tutor Chonis. If only this man can be not guilty of fault, since it was none of his."

There was a silence, as Tutor Chonis mused over the vial in his hand.

"Very well." Finally Tutor Chonis tucked the vial into a pocket of his bed-dress and stood up. "I will bring this to the attention of the Administrator when the case is heard. Perhaps an exchange of hostages would not be inappropriate, when all is written and read in."

Did that mean yes?

"Thank you, Tutor."

It didn't matter any more what Tutor Chonis meant. He had done his utmost. There was nothing else he could do except wait and see whether they would take the trade or not. "May I be excused? I think it may be time. For fastmeal. And I think I may be hungry."

Tired, too tired to think straight.

"Go to your quarters, Andrej. Get some sleep."

What was Chonis talking about? He didn't have time to get any sleep. He had class in less than three eights, class with Tutor Chonis.

"You're excused from training until further notice. I have to discuss this matter with my superiors. But—in the time intervening . . ."

Between now, and what?

". . . since you already know, there is something you can do for us, quite apart from the matter of St. Clare. The man who served your fellow Student as prisoner-surrogate needs surgery within your rating. We're not rated an assigned specialist on site, so there's no one else here qualified for the job."

Between now and the decision, obviously. Andrej stood up, and nearly fell over, hanging against the back of the chair for balance. Didn't he know better than to run the time-string out like this? "Noycannir. Is he stable? I couldn't do anybody any good, not right now." Except that Tutor Chonis had told him to get some rest. So obviously the man was stable.

"I'll inform Infirmary, they'll be ready for you. Once you're rested. Curran."

He hadn't heard the door open behind him. Tutor Chonis must have signaled for Joslire, because Joslire was here, and Andrej was fairly certain that Joslire had not been privy to the entire conversation.

"The Tutor requires?"

And shame on him, too, for keeping Joslire up so late, when Joslire could hardly beg off his assigned duties—whatever they were—just because a Student had been having a long night of it.

"Curran, take Student Koscuisko back to quarters. He is to be excused from training until further notice. Once he's rested, he'll be wanted in Infirmary. We think that he may be able to salvage Student Noycannir's prisoner-surrogate Idarec."

"Heard and understood, Tutor. With respect, the officer should come to quarters now."

There was an arm at his back, steadying him. A hand at his elbow, turning him gently. It was time for him to go to bed.

Had he remembered his prayers?

"Good rest, Andrej. Try to get some sleep."

It was a voice from far away, speaking a language Andrej no longer understood.

He was asleep before he could decide whether it was important to reply.

Administrator Clellelan pushed the relish-pickle dish across the table, frowning past Tutor Chonis's head at the front end of Tutor's Mess as he did so. "No, it won't do, Adifer. It won't do at all."

Clellelan was a good man for detail, it being so important in Fleet Medical to know which details one was assiduously to ignore for the sake of one's own peace of mind. Because Clellelan was so good at minutiae, Tutor Chonis was confident that the pickles were to be taken as a sign, and not absentminded hospitality; nothing that Clellelan did was really absentminded, no matter how casual it seemed. The gesture was meant to offset a categorical rejection of Chonis's proposal with an unselfish offer of a mutually favorite—and rather scarce—breakfast salt-pickle. Chonis appreciated the balance, crunching loudly on a nice chunk of imtell to show his gratitude. Just because he was going to make the Administrator reverse his position didn't mean he wasn't happy to hog as much of the salt-pickle as he could during the process.

"Now, Rorin, you aren't paying attention. I'm offering a real benefit for us all." Intangible, perhaps, but no less valuable for that, and the Administrator had to know what he was thinking as well as Chonis himself did. "The last six Consultations all proved it. The less these officers have to get their hands dirty, the likelier they are to live out their assignments. Judicial Concern MC-double-two-sixteen, sub five, and all the rest."

The orderly came to refill the steaming-jug, and the Administrator took advantage of the moment to spear a piece of salt-pickle for himself on the end of his pronged knife. It was a positive sign. Say absolutely not, offer salt-pickles; say maybe, take some back.

Chonis gave his superior a moment to chew on his thoughts, and his pickle, before he continued. "Maximizing our resources is the thing to do these days, what with Fleet bleeding us dry out in the Lanes. Get Koscuisko's cooperation, get him busy, and we'll start seeing benefit immediately. One Inquisitor is worth any number of bond-involuntaries, as far as the Bench is concerned. You know that better than I do."

Both Inquisitors and bond-involuntaries were getting harder to come up with, that was true. But it was still significantly easier to find qualified Security material under Judicial order than it was to find Inquisitors who were capable of performing their Judicial function for even as many as eight years without letting themselves succumb to paranoia, psychosis, or other dysfunctionalities along the way.

"You really want me to do it, don't you? Adifer. Only last night you were telling me that your Koscuisko could turn into a battery with a random detonation sequence, if we weren't careful with him."

"Did I say that?" No, actually, Chonis didn't think he had. Clellelan had put in too much time in Engineering in his youth, and still tended to think of uncontrolled aggression in young Inquisitors as if it were a simple matter of reinstalling a worn-down safety circuit. "That was before he came to my office, this morning."

The conversation was beginning to get serious. Chonis paused for a moment to savor the memory of his early morning interview with that spirited little Aznir autocrat-to-be. The intensity. The desperation. The self-conscious pledge to accept being managed in return for an annulment of the consequences of what he had done, as if he had actually been at fault.

"It's usually not an issue, you know that. Most of our Students are too depressed by being here in the first place to question authority. Controlling Koscuisko could be a real problem for the Fleet. He doesn't like being told what to do—has got no practice in being told what to do—and he seems capable of putting a real sapper in the works, making a mockery of Inquisition. Remember Poneran?"

Clellelan winced. "Please, Adifer, not at the fastmeal table. Four years of deliberate obstructionism, just short of insubordination. Just short. And then she disappears, and into the Free Government, from all indications. We don't need any more like her."

"So we give Koscuisko what he wants, we leave him with a reminder of why he should behave, and out of it we get to keep the troop. And we get a rope around Koscuisko's neck, to avoid any more embarrassments like Poneran. And we extend the working life of every Inquisitor in Fleet by giving them more and more ways to do their jobs with nice clean drugs instead of the instruments of Inquiry and Confirmation. We even make the First Secretary happy, and that makes the Second Judge happy, and that means we might even get funded for better quarters next year."

Chonis could tell that the Administrator was tempted by the glazed look in his eyes. After a moment, however, he shook his head, reaching for a piece of brod-toast.

"It would be nice. But I can't authorize an exception, not without a Judicial hearing. You know that. And then they'd want to know how it got so far out of hand in the first place. Unacceptable."

It was as close to a criticism as the Administrator had come yet; but in the warm glow left by Koscuisko's submissive petition, Chonis felt he could easily accept so mild an implied rebuke without wincing. "That's not the least of the things that impresses me about my Andrej, you know. I still don't understand what tipped him off." Joslire Curran had said that the prisoner-surrogate had started to call Koscuisko "the officer," once, during the Fourth Level. That was true enough. But then Curran was apparently convinced that Koscuisko saw people's thoughts, and smelled what they were thinking.

"And?"

"And you can do it without having to authorize an exception. Take Koscuisko's offer of speaksera. The regulation allows bond-involuntaries sentenced at this Level to serve as experimental subjects."

The Administrator snorted in disbelief, as Chonis had anticipated he would. "And how am I going to manage all of this? There's a Class-Two violation on Record against St. Clare, we can't just lose it as if it was a Student Exception."

It was understood that Students tended to overreact to their first taste of absolute power. There was an administrative pressure valve in place to prevent the assigned bond-involuntaries from being egregiously abused. Complaints against bond-involuntaries could be set aside as "Student Exceptions," on advice from the assigned Tutor—when the bond-involuntary involved could get to a Tutor in time, that was. But that wasn't what Chonis had in mind.

"Think about the Controlled List for a moment," he urged his superior. "It is permissible for research work on the Controlled List to be carried out at this Station, isn't it? Research and testing. Valid Fleet enrichment functions."

Now Clellelan had got it; Chonis could tell by the way he chewed on his pickle. "Research and testing," he repeated slowly. "You're right, of course. Koscuisko is young, untried, we don't know for certain what he is capable of."

Just so. "There isn't any qualification on statute about what kind of Controlled List drug it has to be. Simply that the condemned can be offered the choice, at Administrative discretion."

As a matter of fact, there were only nine places in all of Jurisdiction Space where the exception could be applied. Eight research stations; and Fleet Orientation Station Medical. Naturally the provision had been made with other drugs less innocuous than mere speaksera in mind, if even speak-sera could be called harmless when an entire community could be condemned through the action of the drug.

Most often there was very little to choose between suffer-ing discipline for a Class-Two violation and serving as a Controlled List volunteer. Since many of the drugs on the Controlled List were lethal in ultimate effect, any bond-involuntary with an eighth of self-preservation would natu-rally elect the purely physical—predictable, dependable—punishment.

The fact remained that on any one of nine stations a bond-involuntary who had committed a Class-Two violation could be offered research duty as a substitute for discipline. And Koscuisko had developed a speakserum. Given Koscuisko's scholastic record, it was unlikely that anything that he de-veloped along the lines of his psychopharmacological Second Branch would turn unexpectedly terminal on Robert St. Clare.

"I like it." Clellelan took a moment longer, clearly en-joying his meditations on what Chonis's proposal could get for him. "It satisfies on a number of counts. Koscuisko gets what he seems to be so anxious for, by your report. We manage without having our embarrassing lapse show up on the replacement request." And no matter whether they had been in fact negligent, or Koscuisko was just damn good. As far as Fleet Procurement would be concerned, the request for a replacement body for St. Clare would signal a careless waste of the resource, pure and simple. "All right, Adifer, answer me two questions and I'll agree to it."

"Two questions?" He was mildly surprised; he could only think of the one, at a guess.

"Making Verlaine happy. And how do you mean to keep it all from going to Koscuisko's head, bending the regula-tions to get what he wants, and so forth."

Oh, well, *that.*

Chonis smiled.

"Verlaine is happy because we graduate his very own pet Inquisitor. Think about it, Rorin. She doesn't need to go through the same course as the others; she'll never be in a field environment anyway. Isn't that what the Fleet Exception specifies? We're to prepare her to assist the Bench in routine inquiry, to be exercised by direct Bench warrant instead of Fleet's Command directive?''

Clellelan was nodding, but Chonis couldn't tell if it was because he remembered or because he wanted the server who had come up to take away his hot-dish to bring him his aftersweet.

"So all she needs to know is how to press the doses through with an osmo-stylus. Koscuisko can show her that. Practically anybody could show her that, the osmos have gotten so sophisticated these days." Leaning back in his chair, Chonis paused while the server put the fruit dish down in front of him. "She'll take her Levels, all right, but just this once it's going to be drug-assisted all the way. And that's the only way to guarantee that she'll get through, with her background."

At least Clellelan was thinking about it. Chonis could practically hear the microgates clicking. "And, coincidentally, a neat trick on the First Secretary," the Administrator said slowly, as if tasting the idea in his mouth as he spoke. "Sending him an orderly when he thought he was going to get, well, someone like Koscuisko, for instance. Access to the Controlled List—she'll do more harm than good for him, not knowing the interaction tables. It's ingenious.''

And Chonis didn't mind accepting that bit of flattery, either. It was one of his better jokes, if he said so himself. Noycannir would have access to the Controlled List without the first real notion of how to use it, which meant—even taking her native intelligence into consideration—that there simply wasn't a great deal she was going to be able to do.

There were too many intangible considerations affecting use of drugs on the Controlled List. The Administrative criteria had yet to be reduced to any expert system under Jurisdiction; use of Controlled List drugs remained a judgment call, one which Noycannir could not hope to make without killing the First Secretary's victims on too regular a basis.

The First Secretary didn't want his enemies killed.

He wanted them intimidated into submission by his proprietary access to an Inquisitor capable of plumbing their most damning secrets, who was just waiting for the word to

go to work on them. Once it became obvious that their deaths
were the worst they had to fear from Noycannir, Verlaine
would find that all his influence and manipulation had got
him precisely nowhere. Fleet would have made its point. The
only truly effective Inquisitors were medical officers. That
was the way it had to stay.

"Come on, man, the other thing."

He'd let his mind wander, savoring the pleasing complete-
ness of Verlaine's future frustration. "Sorry. Yes. Koscuisko.
Needs to be firmly kept down. And he was the one who
proposed it. . . ."

Granted, that it wasn't playing quite fair. But St. Clare
still was getting off easy, no matter which way the blows
fell.

"When Koscuisko came to my office yesterday midsec-
ond, he suggested that St. Clare be considered insubordinate
to him, and disciplined by him at the Class-One level accordingly. I propose to keep my young Andrej in hand by
requiring he administer the punishment per his suggestion.
And bind St. Clare over to him for the duration, to serve as
a constant reminder of what almost happened when he decided to express a little temperament. Student Koscuisko suf-
fers his pangs of conscience very deeply, from all
indications. I think it will work out very nicely."

There was a problem, of course, with suffering any pangs
of conscience too deeply in this line of work. But that was
not the immediate problem. The immediate problem was that
the Administrator was frowning.

"You want to hazard him with the new drug, and then
arrange a flogging on top of it?"

Chonis had had foreseen the problem, and Chonis could answer for it. "It's only a speakserum, Administrator." A little
more formality couldn't hurt, at this crucial point. "St. Clare
will lose his deferment, but you'll have the option of granting
the reduction in his Bond. That's well worth a whipping,
surely. And Koscuisko knows what he's doing in that lab, at
least to judge from his scholastics. If the speakserum itself
is going to cause a problem, he'll let us know. We can negotiate."

Clellelan chewed on his lower lip for a long moment.

But when he spoke again Chonis knew that he had won. "Thought of everything, haven't you?"

"It's an important opportunity." There was no room for false pride. It was a judgment call in the end; Clellelan's judgment call. "I had to be sure that it was justifiable." And neither of them were under any illusions concerning precisely what was at stake for Koscuisko's unfortunate prisoner-surrogate.

The Administrator nodded, acknowledging several layers of meaning at once. "How do you propose to execute?"

Clellelan would have to be present to adjudicate St. Clare's discipline; it was a requirement. Chonis had checked the scheduler already.

"Koscuisko is sleeping things off, and I want him in surgery once he wakes up. Idarec." No further explanation was required. The potential loss of a bond-involuntary would reflect badly on the Administrator's cost management, let alone the potential loss of two—and within a single week, at that. So he could be confident that Idarec's case had been on the Administrator's mind.

"Worth a try," Clellelan said. "This evening?"

"You've got the third quarter free, this secondshift. I don't know how long Koscuisko will take in surgery. I rather thought that making an appointment for the third quarter would be safest, if it suits the Administrator's convenience."

Clellelan nodded. "Let the scheduler know what you want blocked. You've outdone yourself this time, Adifer. Not one, but two cost savings, both at the First Judge's favorite 'tactical significance' level. Give yourself an extra commendation or two."

His words were casual as he rose to leave, his hand on Chonis's shoulder to prevent the otherwise obligatory courtesy of standing as one's superior left the table. Chonis accepted the token with a bowed head. It was a lot of money. And two lives. Three lives, if you counted bringing Koscuisko into line, and making a productive resource out of all that talent and passion.

He hadn't been certain that the Administrator would agree to go along with his plan.

And only now was it safe to see St. Clare.

◆ Seven

Robert St. Clare was hungry and hurt, cold and despairing, but he knew enough to find his way to his feet when his guards came to sharp, heel-clicking attention. There were two of them posted on either side of his open-fronted cell—stationed there as much for their benefit as for his own—to take education from the bad example that he presented. The sudden movement alerted him: someone was there, someone with rank. He knew what to do in the presence of people with rank. It had been drilled into him to the point of reflex, and not even the hopelessness of his situation could stifle the insistent voice of his conditioning or stay the governor's inevitable response to any attempts to resist it. *Stand up:* but they're going to murder me. *Stand up:* but they're going to torture me again. *Stand up:* but there's nothing they can do to punish me if I don't, not more than what they're going to do to me already.

The Jurisdiction's Fleet had trained him all too well.

You will stand to attention in the presence of a superior officer.

Stumbling in his dizziness, he rose from the unpadded block that served as the cell's one piece of furniture—too shallow to lie flat upon, too short to lie at length upon. He stood up and straightened his spine as best he could, trying to ignore the throbbing agony in his shoulder. Perhaps it was just as well, after all. His family were dead. His mother was dead, and his father was dead; his brothers were dead; his uncles—most of his cousins—his kin-group were all gone.

158

Perhaps it was just as well for him to join them.

But his sister . . .

Pain that was deeper than physical seized him, writhing in his gut like a nest of adders. His sister. Because of his failure, his flaw, his betrayal, he'd never be able to find her, to buy her back from Jurisdiction, to take her away from the life that the Bench had mandated.

Because he had not been able to keep his mouth shut.

Because he had—vaingloriously hazarded the offered chance to reduce his term, and reduce her term with his, she was condemned to a full thirty years—if she could survive that long, in shame and suffering. Never to know what had happened to him until the day when her Bond was past, and her body would be hers to call her own again.

His sister . . .

"Robert St. Clare. Do you remember me?"

It would have been better never to have tried. But those four years . . . what four years in a Jurisdiction service facility could mean to Megh—

"Sir. The officer is Tutor Chonis. Sir."

Eight years, with hers and his together. Eight years he could have won, and Security was honest service compared to what Megh was to be put to. Instead there would be nothing for her, nothing, because he had not been able to do his duty by his sister.

"Relax, man, you're not at Mast, not yet. Stand at ease. Better yet, go and sit down."

The words were meaningless. He stood numbly at attention as the guards opened the power grid, carrying a chair through for the Tutor's use. Chonis himself came right up to him, pushing him gently back until his legs struck up against the edge of the restblock, and he sat.

"Clearly you don't need to be told what an unpleasant situation we have here."

The Tutor's words were beginning to come clear through the heavy pounding of his pulse. They might have been funny; but he wasn't sure why he thought so. "Sir."

"It may—I must emphasize that word, may—not be quite as impossible as it seems. There is no question about the offense, of course."

Of course. Despair and shame flooded his mind; but anger swamped those sapping emotions, fury at being spoken to as if his imminent torture—not to speak of poor Megh's prostitution—were inconveniences, in the greater scheme of things.

"There is no question about the offense." That Tutor Chonis gave him. That the Jurisdiction had committed. "Sir."

"Rabin, have you ever heard of the Jurisdiction's Controlled List?"

"In Orientation. Yes. Sir." And they used his name so casually, his private name, the name that none but his deprived sister had any right to speak without permission . . .

"On an experimental station a bond-involuntary who has committed a Class-Two violation may elect to serve as a sentient subject for Controlled List purposes, rather than undergo other discipline. Now. Here we have . . . a problem."

Except that this was not an experimental station but a teaching station. And only a man more desperate than even he would risk the Controlled List by choice: They didn't need condemned men for the speaking drugs, after all, it was only the other sorts that would be involved. "Yes, sir. The officer states the existence of a problem."

It wasn't quite coming out the way it should. He sounded rather thick-tongued to himself, not to say disrespectful. Why should he care about disrespectful? He was going to die.

Because his governor didn't care whether or not he was going to die, and to his governor disrespect was much more serious than mere termination.

"The officer—Student Koscuisko, your Interrogator. You remember him? Of course you do."

Of course he did. Repulsive, short, pale, colorless man, his voice the only live thing about him. Oh, and his hands, his pitiless strength, his mocking eyes. "Sir."

"Koscuisko is determined that there was no Class-Two violation, but that a Class-One offense has been offered to him by you. For which he wishes you to be disciplined. Student Koscuisko has a gift, St. Clare."

Oh, was that what it was called, here in this place? "A gift, sir. Yes, sir."

"He has a gift for drugs. For psychoactive drugs, specifically. Student Koscuisko is willing to trade his skill for your life, Rabin. And his skill may be worth far more to us, in the end, than you could ever hope to be, alive or dead."

And, oh, but that was precisely the thing to tell him, wasn't it? This man, you see, he's a poisoner, and we need good poisoners. We don't particularly care what happens to you one way or the other. One must keep one's poisoners happy. "Sir."

"Good, I'm glad you're following me. Now. Koscuisko has presented us with a speakserum, and we want someone to test it. Volunteer to test this speakserum, Rabin, and the Administrator will accept it in lieu of Class-Two discipline, as long as there is no question about the Class-One violation."

Something was not adding up, and Robert shook his head to clear it. "Class One? Two? Experimental station? Sir—"

"Although this is not an experimental station we are permitted to carry out research for the Controlled List. Therefore the exception applies." The Tutor rose to his feet now, pacing the few measures of the cell with deliberation. As if he was not quite sure on his pronouncements and wanted to convince himself as he laid the argument out.

"You have committed a Class Two violation. Therefore you may elect to test a Controlled List candidate drug in lieu of other Class-Two discipline, if you are offered the alternative by the Administrator. Koscuisko is determined that you have committed a Class-One violation. Therefore we will let the Class Two pass with the token ordeal—a talking-drug . . ."

Stopped in front of where he sat, now, the Tutor fixed his eyes on Robert's face. For emphasis?

"And you will accept Class-One discipline from Student Koscuisko. Your officer."

He couldn't be sure, there was too much to think about. He almost thought that he was being offered a way out, a chance, his life; but that was too dangerous to dream on. Hope had confused his mind, making him hear things that never had been implied. That had to be the explanation.

In his confusion he said the first thing that came to his

mind, in response to the last thing he'd heard the Tutor say. "The greater fault overrides the lesser fault. Sir. The more severe discipline replaces all the lesser."

As if he would object on that head, if he could believe that there was any hope at all. As if that would make a difference, between a chance for life and death by torture.

The Tutor smiled. "Yes, of course you're right," he said. "At least under normal circumstances. But in this case, the greater punishment is being waived on a technicality, because Koscuisko has got stubborn about it. Do you really mean to challenge the Bench on this issue?"

Mindless panic flooded Robert's mind at the mere phrase. Challenge the Bench? Challenge the Bench? Of course he could not, dare not, challenge the Class-One discipline. To challenge the Bench would be . . . it would be—

"Be at ease." Tutor Chonis was quite near to him now, speaking low and confidentially in his ear. "It's just your governor, Robert, running a little hyperactive, probably should be adjusted for stress. Of course no one suggested such a thing. I—regret—my thoughtless use of the phrase."

There was the strangest note of strained unbelief in Tutor Chonis's voice, almost as if he did not understand why he was saying the words that he heard himself speak. Believable or not, the words restored Robert's psychic equilibrium—to a degree—almost as quickly as it had been upset in the first place.

"Sir." The Tutor moved away, quickly. "No disrespect was intended, if the Tutor please. Spoken for clarification only. Sir." In fact he was unsure why he had made so ill-advised a remark; but the Tutor, nodding, merely continued in his explanation, as if he had decided to treat it as unobjectionable.

"It is already a rather extreme appeal to Administrative privilege to substitute the trial of such an innocuous drug where the other less benign ones were clearly intended. The Administrator must demonstrate that his decision was based on reason and sound Judicial practice, and the best interest of Fleet. And this has nothing to do with you, St. Clare, we aren't doing you any favors. It has everything to do with Andrej Koscuisko."

Now it began to be real, to Robert. He finally started to grasp the actual meaning of what the Tutor was saying to him. That they would offer him reprieve was not within the realm of even the wildest fantasy for a bond-involuntary with a Class-Two violation. That they would reprieve him by the way, as a casual gesture designed to ingratiate them with their young torturer, made much more sense.

He remembered Koscuisko's fingers in his shoulder, the officer's cold amused tone of voice, commenting on the beating that he was administering. He couldn't suppress a shudder.

"It might be quicker," he whispered. "With the Tutor's permission. To take it all at once, and die of it. Instead of . . . what?" The conflict of emotions warring in his mind unmanned him, leaving him vulnerable to nameless imagined horrors. "What is this Koscuisko, that he wants so much to see me bleed? Again?"

Talking to himself, he did not at first realize that the Tutor was answering his question.

"If he wanted merely to see you bleed, we'd have given you to him for your Class-Two violation, and see what he would make of his Advanced Levels. No, I think he's trading something he very much doesn't want to do, simply in order to get you off the charge. But it doesn't matter what either of us thinks."

The Tutor signaled at the gate, continuing to talk with his back turned as he stepped out into the corridor.

"You're to be assigned to him, as it happens. Permanently. Get used to the idea."

Assigned?

To Koscuisko?

To be responsible for the life of the man who had shamed him, to die in defense of the man who had put him to torture?

"And he's the one who wanted it that way." The Tutor stood on the other side of the gate now, with his hands clasped behind his back and an odd look of amusement and self-satisfaction on his face. "So you'll have plenty of time to decide how you feel. And twenty-six years is a long time, isn't it, Rabin? But not so long as thirty."

Then Chonis nodded—in the face of Robert's speechless stare—and was gone from his line of sight.

Twenty-six years?

Instead of thirty?

Then Megh would not need to suffer the extra term, after all. . . .

For the freedom to ransom his sister he could do anything.

He could even submit to Koscuisko, and wait for the Day.

Near the second quarter of secondshift, Joslire woke to the sounds of Koscuisko starting to stir. Slipping out into the corridor, he ordered the officer's meal—a little on the heavy side, Koscuisko hadn't eaten for nearly five shifts now. Koscuisko was in the wet-shower when Joslire got back, leaning up against the back wall with the water full in his face—trying to clear his head? To wake up? Under other circumstances, Joslire might have grinned, Koscuisko was so obviously struggling with his sleep. But officers were not to be smiled at, no matter how indulgently, not even in the privacy of one's own thoughts.

Joslire contented himself with setting up the meal tray instead.

Koscuisko took his time in the wet-shower. Joslire got the uniform of the day hung neatly on the rack in the inner room, without hurrying, and was just about to check the depth of steep in the rhyti brewer when the shower shut off. Koscuisko came out of the lavatory dripping and half-naked, toweling his hair; he was beginning to look a little less asleep, but only just, and Joslire stood to attention to greet him without any sort of trepidation about what sort of mood his Student might be in.

"The officer slept well?"

Which only made the shock, and his confusion, the more abrupt and disorienting. He hadn't been expecting Koscuisko to do or say anything in particular, certainly nothing like this . . .

"I imagine. What time is it? Good morning, Joslire, would you be so good as to remove your clothing."

It was a moment before Joslire quite understood what Koscuisko had said, the order coming directly on the heels of

Koscuisko's rather disconnected response. But Koscuisko was clearly waking even as he spoke, and by the time Joslire absorbed the fact that he'd been told to undress Koscuisko had already become a little impatient with the delay. ''If you please, Joslire.''

In fact he sounded almost angry, angry at Joslire. Bowing quickly, Joslire moved his hand to the secures at his blouse's collar almost before he'd well completed his salute. ''The officer's pardon is—''

''To be used for an improbable anatomical experiment. Did you wear your five-knives, when you were . . . when you played the game?''

The game . . . when he served as prisoner-surrogate, perhaps. There was only one probable reason for Koscuisko's order, Joslire knew; not as if it would be the first time, no. Bond-involuntaries were expected to accommodate their officers in any manner their officers might choose to specify. But what difference would his five-knives make to Koscuisko, if that was what the officer intended? Why would it matter?

''It was necessary to perform the exercise without, by the officer's leave.'' A bond-involuntary might be permitted his five-knives. They could be considered to fall under religious exception; and served also as a constant reminder of his shame, to have dishonored his five-knives by wearing them as an enslaved man. But a prisoner would naturally have been stripped of them immediately. For security purposes, quite apart from all the rest.

''Then you will oblige me by taking them off. Now.''

Joslire dropped his head in submission, glad of the opportunity to hide his conflict. ''According to the officer's good pleasure.'' Koscuisko's meal would be getting cold, the rhyti oversteeped. It wouldn't do to mention that, though he was just as likely to suffer for the fact. No, that wasn't so— Joslire scowled at himself, stripping off his underblouse hurriedly. The officer hadn't seemed the type to make use of a compliant body in quite this way. What had happened to Koscuisko in the Tutor's office? The Tutor had seemed pleased about something, that was true.

Koscuisko had gone back to the washroom to leave the

towel and frown at the mirror. Joslire couldn't afford to steal more than a glance, he'd been told twice now, he didn't dare keep the officer waiting. Fumbling with the catches, he loosed the sheathing that bound his five-knives to him, so close—so much a part of him—that the simple requirement to remove them had been almost as much of the torment of the game, as Koscuisko had termed it, as any of the rest. Did Koscuisko know that? Did Koscuisko care? Why should Koscuisko care, except that Joslire had imagined that Koscuisko had been serious about his Bond, except that Koscuisko had seemed genuinely distraught to think that St. Clare would have to stand discipline for a Class-Two violation, and likely die of it. . . .

Koscuisko stood in the washroom's doorway, watching him. Joslire laid his five-knives down on his sleep-rack as reverently as he dared, and pulled his boots off clumsily. Moving into the center of the room Koscuisko contemplated his meal tray, and for one moment Joslire cherished a forlorn hope that the officer would permit himself to be distracted. Would change his mind and decide that the satisfaction of one appetite would serve as well as that of another.

He should have known better, he told himself, and laid his trousers neatly to one side of his folded blouse and his five-knives. It was better not to indulge in such fantasies. The more quickly the officer's appetite could be satisfied, the more quickly he could get on with the rest of his job, and the Tutor would receive the report on Koscuisko's sexual activity as a positive sign of a healthy libido functioning in more or less traditional ways. Joslire reached for the drawstring of his hipwrap, anxious—if not eager—to be on the other side of the next few eighths; but Koscuisko's cold voice stopped him a scant sixteenths short of total nudity.

"That's quite all right, Joslire. I should like you to turn to the wall, if you would. I understand that the posture is a familiar one?"

Familiar, perhaps, but not because of frequent and fond practice. Joslire turned to the wall and set his hands flat against the unforgiving steel, his arms stretched well out, turning his face to the floor. "At the officer's discretion." At least his voice was neutral, level, betraying no hint of his inner turmoil. It was a little unusual, still. He had been more frequently flogged against the wall like this than . . . than what the officer would seem to have in mind.

He could sense Koscuisko behind him, his skin prickling unpleasantly from the heat of Koscuisko's own newly showered nakedness. Koscuisko was reaching his hands out, touching his back, touching his shoulders—perhaps it would be over quickly.

Koscuisko's touch was light and clinical, considering, touching with the tips of his fingers, not his whole hand. Settling gently against Joslire's skin before stroking his back, as if he was being careful not to startle him—as if Koscuisko could startle him, Joslire thought, and knew the bitterness of the betrayal that he felt in the helplessness of that necessarily passive resentment. He should have known better than to have imagined that Koscuisko was different than any of the others. He should have known better than to have thirsted after the respect Koscuisko had seemed to show him, as grateful as a starving man for any casual gesture Koscuisko made that could be taken as an acknowledgment of Joslire's personal dignity. He was a bond-involuntary. He had no dignity. No title to his name, no title to his person, no title to his body. Nothing.

Koscuisko hadn't said anything, still touching Joslire's back, lingering for a moment from time to time over a particular spot, always moving his hands slowly enough to keep the skin from crawling in reflex trepidation. What was going on in his mind? There did seem to be a pattern, perhaps . . . Koscuisko seemed to be working his way from Joslire's spine toward his sides, from the small of his back up to the back of his neck and across his shoulders. Almost Joslire had an idea, but no, it couldn't be. It was too far-fetched. Just more wishful thinking, and why wouldn't Koscuisko have just asked?

Koscuisko put his left hand out to Joslire's hand, splayed as it was stubbornly against the wall. "I'm sorry, Joslire," Koscuisko said. "But I require a more extreme angle. Move your arms out a bit, if you would please."

What was Koscuisko after?

And why was waiting so much harder than being put to it, as brutal as that could be?

Koscuisko had both hands at the back of Joslire's shoulder, and Joslire could feel those questing fingers traveling along the line of the muscle stretched taut by Joslire's constrained posture, lingering—briefly but perceptibly—over a knot that Joslire knew was there.

No, it couldn't be . . .

Down along Joslire's flank, now, tracing the thin line of unresponsive skin—the scar tissue that shielded the insulted flesh from pain by refusing to admit all further sensation. Joslire caught his breath in a sudden sobbing gasp, startled out of all his discipline by the shock of his realization—and the paradoxical shame he felt. His scars. That was what Koscuisko wanted, his scars, Koscuisko was reading his body with his hands, feeling and finding the scars that did not show on the surface: the little dead knots where the uttermost tip of the lash had bitten deeply, the long lines down his side where the Student Interrogator had tested his silence with hot metal. The cry escaped his tightly clenched teeth in something like a cough, and Koscuisko flattened his damned hands against Joslire's back and stilled them there, waiting.

"It is very difficult?"

Koscuisko spoke gently, quietly, leaving plenty of space for Joslire to respond.

"Would it be easier for you if I consulted the record, instead? Is there a record that will tell me what I want to know?"

How could he respond? He could be honest, or he could do his duty. And his governor would not permit him to commit a violation, not if it noticed one coming.

"The officer holds the Bond." He sounded half-strangled, even to himself. "The officer is to be provided whatever the officer wishes. The information is on Record." Usually restricted, because of the secrecy of the program, but Tutor Chonis would surely release it to Koscuisko if Koscuisko asked, now that there was no further sense in trying to keep anything from him. "The instructional tape. Is on file. To be viewed at the officer's pleasure, in the Tutor's library." As if he wanted to even think about that, when it was all he could do to keep his voice from breaking . . .

"I should not have asked it of you," Koscuisko murmured, as if to himself. "You will forgive me, Joslire, please. I hope."

Joslire could sense Koscuisko turning away, stepping away, moving toward the inner room.

"On the other hand . . ."

It was forlorn, that note in Koscuisko's voice; forlorn, and utterly desolate.

"On the other hand, after all, you are obliged to."

He did not trust himself to move; nor had he been given leave to, come to that.

"Dress yourself, Joslire. I do not wish to examine your medical records, or your . . . the tapes. There is word from Tutor Chonis for me? Never mind, I will be out in a moment; tell me then."

There was the sound of the privacy barrier sliding to, and Joslire was alone in the outer room, alone and shaken all out of proportion with what little had actually happened to him.

Koscuisko had been so careful, in his touch. . . .

Pushing himself away from the wall, he willed the rock-hard tension that ran through his body to subside. There had been no threat. There had been no assault, no intent to assail. And he would not have been permitted to do other than submit, had there been any.

He wiped his face and dressed himself as quickly as he could, and hoped that the officer's meal might still be judged acceptable.

It was humiliating to be so grateful to Koscuisko for the simple fact that Koscuisko hadn't used him.

But well-brewed rhyti was the only way he had to show that he was grateful, humiliating or not.

Oh, Mother of this man, Mother of us all, look upon his suffering, and may it be enough. May honor be satisfied, may you find it full punishment, and condescend to shield him from his sins in your sweet favor. Mother, so we pray, accept his suffering in atonement, and grant it be sufficient; frown no longer upon him. . . .

But the Holy Mother cared only for the Aznir, her children, and Joslire was Emandisan. What could the litanies of his childhood avail him here? When he sought to do his duty, there was suffering. If he sought to relieve suffering, he made it worse. There was no getting away from it; it had been torture for Joslire to suffer his touch, and so much more torture was attested to by the mute but damning evidence of all of that subdermal scar tissue. He had no right to reach for Joslire's private heart, and expose him to his own shame. There was victim guilt to consider, Andrej reminded himself. The more one's servants were beaten, the more completely they became convinced that they deserved even stricter discipline yet—a folk truism authenticated by the common psychology of sentient species, a defensive trick played by the order-greedy mind to make sense of an arbitrary world.

Oh, he wanted a drink. Or . . . No, he corrected himself, he didn't want a drink; what he wanted was to be drunk, and not thinking about anything. Not about what he had done to that bond-involuntary, either earlier or later. Not about what he had done to Joslire's fragile sense of self-determination just now. Certainly not about how pleasant it had been to torment St. Clare, up to the moment when he'd realized that there was something that they were keeping from him. Yes, that was it, he wanted to be drunk; and still he couldn't shake a persistent feeling that there were reasons why he couldn't be, not yet.

Joslire had surely had time to dress and to regain his composure by now. Andrej stood up from his sleep-rack, sighing, pushing his hair up out of his face with the spread fingers of his right hand. He supposed he should get dressed, since he'd been staring at his uniform so intently. He couldn't hide in this tiny closet of a bedroom forever.

When he slid the partition open, feeling embarrassed and abashed, he noted to his relief that Joslire had his back to the room, standing at the door. He was spared the awkwardness of initial eye contact, at least. There was someone in the corridor beyond, and that was unusual. Andrej didn't think he'd seen anyone else in this corridor since he'd got here—part of the Administration's scheme to isolate them all and make them vulnerable to the Tutors for approval and validation, it went without saying.

Perhaps if he concentrated on what was going on, he could salvage some self-respect for himself and for Joslire alike. Standing by the studyset, Andrej poured himself a flask of rhyti and waited for Joslire to finish with whatever transaction it was that occupied his time.

"Student Koscuisko has just awakened. He'll be ready once he's had a bite to eat. I'd give it an eight or so."

Nor did Andrej believe that he'd ever heard Joslire refer to himself in the first person. His thoughtless demands had upset Joslire, breached Joslire's careful defensive formality. What must Joslire have thought he meant to do? Andrej shuddered at the enormity of it.

And still Joslire did not sound as though his nerves were on edge.

"Patient prep can start whenever." He thought he recognized the voice of whomever was in the hall. Female voice. His guide in Infirmary yesterday? Travis, her name had been. He thought. What had he been doing in Infirmary yesterday? "Just give the word."

Joslire closed the door and turned back toward the studyset, giving an almost imperceptible start at the sight of Andrej standing there beside his fastmeal. There was a documents-cube in Joslire's hand; Andrej reached his hand out to take it, realizing—now that he remembered—what they had probably been talking about. "Who was at the door, then, Joslire?"

And yet Joslire didn't surrender the cube when Andrej grasped it. Startled, Andrej looked more directly at Joslire than he really wanted to, meeting Joslire's dark, sharp, glittering eyes, trying to decipher what he thought he read there.

After a moment Joslire lowered his eyes and bowed in respectful salute, releasing the cube into Andrej's outstretched hand.

"Travis, from Infirmary, by the officer's leave." Joslire sounded a little subdued but otherwise much the same as ever. "The officer may wish to review the surgical record?"

It had been meant deliberately, as a substitute for some light quip, to show Andrej that he'd been forgiven. Andrej felt his face reddening with gratitude and relief. Wordless gestures were all a bond-involuntary had to communicate interpersonal issues to superior officers. Andrej didn't feel superior. Just now he felt—not for the first time this Term— that Joslire was very much the better man than he, governor or no governor.

Worrying the issue would only keep the memory fresh. Andrej slid the cube into the viewer, sitting down to his fastmeal as he did so. It was rather a full tray for a fastmeal, now that he had a look at it. That was a good thing, Andrej decided. He was ravenously hungry, now that he was awake.

Two keys, and the medical workup appeared on his screen. A man in early adulthood, second-class hominid, subspecies Ovallse. Traumatic injury to the central nervous system, torn fiber in the brainstem, several ugly lacunae along the spinal column, two days old—perhaps three—but not too old yet. The nerves could be persuaded to forget that they'd been bruised and frayed apart, if they could be reconnected with minimal surgical trauma before the fluid of that trauma it- self—currently holding the damaged tissue static, waiting for the light—ebbed away again, and let the tenuous connections lapse.

It could be done.

What was the patient's current status?

What therapies—if any—had been engaged up until now?

How old was the Station's surgical machine?

His left hand was full of brod-toast. It was a little clumsy, keying from the right, but the information was there, right enough. Core metabolism had been submerged to the deepest level that could be sustained outside the cryogenic environ- ment. The surgical machine was apparently two or three years old, but with luck it had not been overused during that time. He should be able to achieve primary alignment, if the apparatus had been maintained properly and not allowed to deteriorate.

He had to eat; and then he had to wait after he had eaten, to maximize the extent to which his own physical apparatus would achieve optimal recovery from the abuse it had sus- tained from stress and alcohol over the past few days. He could use the time to review the species-specific peculiarities of the average adult Ovallse. He had better get into it right away. It had been—what—as much as two days since the injury had occurred?

There was no time to waste.

"Did I hear Travis saying something about patient prep?"

Joslire had posted himself at Andrej's shoulder instead of seeing to whatever other chores he might have had. Still trying to provide reassurance, of a sort? When it was surely Joslire who had been abused, Andrej who should provide comfort . . . Andrej appreciated the gesture, even though he was uncertain of its meaning. At the moment he felt willing to take all the supportive comfort he could get, whether or not he could feel that he deserved it.

"As the officer says. The Infirmary has a theater on standby, at the officer's disposal."

And what about St. Clare?

What about the contract he had tried to make with Tutor Chonis, the contract he still shuddered, even now, to so much as contemplate?

"What time is it? Tell them to give me an eight and four. We can be ready to start by then, I'm sure."

He couldn't afford to start thinking about St. Clare.

He was going to need all of the concentration he could muster if he was to succeed in walking through this man Idarec's brain, and leave no damage in his wake.

Doctor Ligrose Chaymalt had been curious about Koscuisko since Term had started, although her brief introduction to him had not impressed her overmuch. Alerted by Security's signal that Chonis's Student was on his way, she made it her business to be at the main entry-station when Koscuisko and his Security escort arrived. A man's life in the balance—even a bond-involuntary's life—surely called for a little formality.

Koscuisko's Security troop stepped up to the barrier at the receiving station, bowing sharply in Chaymalt's direction. "Student Koscuisko reports on Tutor Chonis's instruction to provide possible assistance within his rated field, on bed eleven. As Her Excellency please."

Her usual practice was to let the Ward supervisors deal

with the Students during their required referral on Wards. Signing off on her subordinates' assessments of the actual medical qualifications of the soon-to-be-Ship's Surgeons as assessed in clinical practice was as close to Ship's Surgeon as she wanted to get. This appeared to be rather a special case, however—to judge from Chonis's interest in him, at any rate. And she had to admit that his academic record was impressive.

"Stand away, Curran. Student Koscuisko and I have already been introduced." A day or three gone by, as a matter of fact. "When you came for your tour, Koscuisko, if you remember."

"It is a distinct pleasure to renew the privilege of your acquaintance." Koscuisko's response was polite, if as formal as his salute. "Am I to have the benefit of Doctor Chaymalt's consultation with the scheduled surgery?"

Almost too polite. Ligrose eyed him skeptically. He hadn't done any practicals since he'd got here. What made Chonis think that this youth—this pale and apparently underrested child, so recently graduated—was up to pulling the complex procedure off? It wasn't for her to say, of course. None of her staff were going to be stupid enough to try it without the rated specialty. Bed eleven was a dead man any way one looked at it, unless Koscuisko managed to get through the surgery without letting the mechanical probe slip by a single fraction of a sixty-fourth in the wrong direction.

Student Koscuisko was regarding her with a look of courteously muted expectation. She shook her head. "Sorry, not my specialty. Or we'd have done it sooner, of course. But I'll be watching you." More out of boredom than anything else, and it was a useful opportunity to see what kind of surgical practitioners Mayon was turning out these days. She hadn't seen a Mayon graduate through Orientation Station Medical in all the years of her tenure here. Mayon's graduates could name their price, and students who could pay off their schooling in other environments could be relied upon to stand well clear of Inquiry, as a rule.

It was hard to stay abreast of technical innovations, isolated on this tiny station—not as if bed eleven's case called for anything new or innovative. The procedures were actually fairly basic. It was only the fact that they had to be performed perfectly that presented complications.

"In that case I would like to get started, by your leave, Doctor Chaymalt. Is there an orderly assigned?"

Not really. Shiuka had done the patient prep, but Shiuka wasn't rated for the actual procedure—he'd never been properly checked out on the monitors. Chaymalt checked the status board quickly. "Looks like Beeler is coming off shift, you can have Beeler. I'll have him meet you. You, Curran. Take your Student to theater one. Do you know where to find it? Never mind, one of the orderlies can escort you both."

For a moment she thought that Koscuisko was going to protest, to hold out for an orderly who was fresh and rested and at the beginning of his shift, instead of one who would probably not be either. Not as if it made any difference, as far as Chaymalt was concerned. Either Koscuisko had what it took or he didn't, and no orderly of hers was going to make a mistake on the monitors, no matter how tired or hungry he might be.

"Is there a problem?"

Direct challenge was a useful tool. He could hardly question her assignment to her face; it was her Infirmary, after all. Koscuisko merely bowed.

"Very well, then. I'll be observing from my office."

Or sleeping, one of the two.

But maybe it would be interesting to see Koscuisko perform.

For now there was nothing in the world but the surgical machine—the operating chair—and the patient who was waiting for him.

The orderly assigned was tired and bored, obviously frustrated at being held over shift; but he did get the setup completed quickly, without incident. Andrej strapped himself into the chair to perform the calibration exercises. Each chair was different within the standardized range, because the level of detail was so specific and exact. While a deviation of the smallest imaginable fraction of a sixty-fourth in the path of the surgical beam could be easily tolerated in most cases, there was no room for error whatever where the nervous system was concerned. There was no problem with the power reserves, no focus degradation to speak of; still, the tolerances had slipped noticeably off scale. It took Andrej several attempts with the beam and the block of pseudoflesh before he could get the instruments to respond as he liked. There was a simple test of whether or not he was in control of the apparatus, his own variation on the standard measures he'd been taught in his student surgeries. When he could sign his name precisely midway through the block of pseudoflesh— when he could sign his name with the surgical beam, and have it all of one distance from the mark-point, and have the lines all no more than three particles in thickness—then he was ready to carve within a brain.

He was ready now.

Patient preparation had been completed, the body lay anesthetized—to ensure stability, not because there would be any pain—and selectively exposed within the sterile field. Fastening the goggles over his eyes, Andrej reviewed the operant grids one last time, to be sure that he knew what he was going to do and how he was going to come at it. Spinal first, where the nerves were fatter and the consequences of less than absolute surgical perfection were less severe. Subcortical function was the critical area. There was a lot of work to do, and no time like the present to be started.

He sent the machine forward into the sterile field with a quick press at a foot control, activating the enclosure. The mask was already in place. As the webbing smoothed around his body to support his weight, Andrej surrendered to the familiar comfort of the operating environment. Focusing on his first site, he saw nothing but the scanner registration, heard nothing but the subtle pinging signal that the laser made at rest. From now until he was finished with his task, he was no more than the mind of the machine, the operating chair translating his every gesture to the scale of the cellular environment. One wrong gesture could sever a nerve for good and all. One twitch at the wrong time could bisect a muscle or engrave the bone.

There could be no room in his mind for anything other than his patient—and that was relief from his other concerns.

This simplification of his life, howsoever temporary, was a present that the patient had provided for him. Obviously the only polite response was to return the favor if he could.

Secure in the serene calm of pure technical expertise, Andrej began to work.

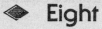 **Eight**

Mergau Noycannir had welcomed the call to the Tutor's office when it finally came. She knew her ground and field; she was confident. She could do nothing more until she found out how the Administration meant to respond to the incident.

"Tutor Chonis?"

He looked up from the stylus-pad on his desk as she spoke from the open doorway, diffidently. His scowl of concentration seemed to lift as if he was actually pleased to see her.

"Student Noycannir. Yes. Come in." Well, it could be that he was glad to see her, and that his smile was in anticipation of dismissing her from Term for her mistake. But somehow it didn't quite smell that way to her. This was confusing.

"I am concerned, Tutor Chonis. It has been a day and the next day, now, since I was to continue the Intermediate Levels, and I have not had the benefit of instruction."

Abstractly speaking, yes, she had made an error. Abstractly speaking, yes, she had violated the Protocols, although Hanbor was at fault—not her—for his failure to correctly emphasize the difference between the tapes that she'd been studying. It didn't take a qualified surgeon to figure that out.

But what was the Tutor going to do about it?

"Mergau, in the past two days we've come to understand that we have not been supporting your needs. In fact we feel that we may be at risk of failing you in a significant sense."

As if he was going to pretend it was the Station's problem. As if he was really concerned about her.

"I've spoken to the Administrator about it. It's not reasonable of us to put you into situations where you can't really be expected to perform. And we think we may have come up with a solution."

Something was not scanning here. There was no reason to revisit these issues yet another time. It couldn't be just that she'd made a mistake. Other Students made mistakes; that was why there were Remedial Levels. "The Tutor is suggesting?"

Rising from his desk, Tutor Chonis went to pull a jug and two cups out of his side closet. "Let me start at the beginning."

Yes, we must always start at the beginning, Mergau jeered at him in her mind. *Start at the beginning, so that you can hold the ultimate point in suspense for as long as possible.*

Setting his cups and the jug down, he poured for both of them. Warmer. Maybe the Tutor actually preferred warmer; or maybe he was trying to trick her into letting down her guard.

"You're here because the First Secretary sees a need for a qualified Writ at the Bench level, in order to pursue the Judicial function. We must stop and ask ourselves—what does the Judicial function at the Bench level entail?"

Whether he was laying a trap or not, he served good warmer. That only made her more suspicious, of course. He'd been keeping notes on her preferences.

"Our station must produce officers who can carry the Writ in the field, down to the cruiserkiller class. That's the working level; that's where the appropriate blend of authority and necessity lies. Now, there is a point to be made from all this, Student Noycannir, with your indulgence."

As if he needed her "indulgence." Oh, she hated them. Hated them all. Would she never be permitted to forget. . . .

"I am at my Tutor's disposal entirely," she assured him meekly, sipping her warmer. What if there were treason to be discovered here, in the heart of Fleet Orientation Center Medical, and an Inquisitor was required to sift the sour from the sweet? An Inquisitor without a Fleet assignment, without a primary loyalty to the Fleet. . . .

"At the Bench level the functions of Inquiry and Confirmation are most essential. It will always be possible to refer to a regional detention center, if a penalty is to be assessed. What I'm trying to get at, Student Noycannir, is that there's no real need for you to take the same full course of study as that for officers who must Inquire, Confirm, and Execute as well. We can best serve the First Secretary's needs by modifying the course of instruction to a slight extent."

He could not be suggesting that they compromise the Writ. Verlaine had paid so much to get her this far . . . and there was no precedent, no special category under Jurisdiction. The Writ was absolute. Either she would hold it or she would not. "I am confused." Genuinely confused, at the turn that the conversation seemed to be taking. "How can I serve Chilleau Judiciary as Inquisitor if my training is to be modified, as you say?"

The Tutor took a moment before answering her. He glanced idly at the cup of warmer in his hand with the benevolent expression of a man who had a surprise gift for a child, hidden behind his back. It made no sense.

"You know the material, Mergau." But how could he tell her that when she had violated the Protocols? Hanbor's fault, yes, but her deed; on Record, and the Record was permanent. . . . "There isn't any question that you understand the theory and the rules of practice. Anyone can make a mistake. But unless we can do a little fine-tuning, as it were, you are simply going to keep on making mistakes, because your broader education is deficient."

The other Students could make mistakes without repercussions, as long as they were within medically acceptable parameters? Was that what he was saying? "I have studied the cases that the Tutor selected. There is more that I should study, Tutor Chonis?"

What was he getting at?

"The further we get, the worse the mistakes will be. The Administrator and I have been working on a way around it. And we think we have a solution. There need be no preparation in field techniques if you will never be required to perform in the field environment.''

She did know the material. She did understand the Levels, and their restrictions, and the Protocols for Inquiry and Confirmation and Execution. Field techniques meant blood and striking people, and it was hard for her to restrain her hand when everything she had ever learned of hurting people was to hurt them for once and all, so that they would not trouble her again. The streets of Lathiken had not been holding cells. And from the first that she had ingratiated herself with the man who had started her in Bench Administration, she had understood that in politics as in street-fighting, prudence took no prisoners.

''The Jurisdiction's Controlled List is among the most significant resources available under the Writ. And while the employment of the appropriate drugs does not under usual circumstances satisfy the punitive scales, they are fully satisfactory as instruments of Inquiry and Confirmation.''

He was talking about drugs.

This was a new thing, a novel idea, unanticipated input. It rather stunned her, but panic was not far behind.

Panic was never far enough behind.

''But, with the Tutor's indulgence—'' she began, and then shut her mouth abruptly when she realized that she didn't know what to say.

''I know what you're thinking, I imagine.'' Tutor Chonis put up his hand to quiet her protest. ''The practical exercises are required for graduation. And you will do your practical exercises, but there is something more important that we must teach you about them. You must learn the Controlled List.''

How could she hope to learn the Controlled List when it relied upon more arcane knowledge of the body's function than any field-expedient physical medicine she had ever learned? Was this in the end just another step toward failing her? Had she in truth done well enough, to date, in the scheduled course of instruction, that the Administrator feared that she might successfully complete the course after all?

''Adjudicated Levels and standard interrogation techniques are not, after all, infallible instruments. Why, in a field environment, even the best Inquisitor may lose up to half the prisoners referred at the top end of the Intermediate Levels, not to speak of expected mortality rates at the Advanced. It wouldn't do for the First Secretary to have to trust such imprecise methods for information.''

Yes, prisoners died. They were expected to die. It was deemed preferable that they die after they surrendered their secrets, rather than before. But Mergau was beginning to see Tutor Chonis's point.

"You are telling me that my Patron is not well served, if I am just to know the Protocols.'' The First Secretary wanted the Writ; the power to take the secrets. In Fleet it was not so important to get the secrets. There were always others with the same secrets available to Fleet. For Verlaine's purpose, the secrets were much more individual and private. There could be no waste of prisoners in dying before surrendering their information.

"Precisely so.'' Tutor Chonis agreed, sounding a little surprised. "When you are graduated and sent back to Secretary Verlaine with the Fleet's compliments, you must be able to get to the information more reliably than Fleet practice dictates.'' Where the whole point of Inquisition lay as much— if not more—in its use as a weapon primed with deterrent horror as in any actual need for information. "The Administrator proposes to refocus your course of instruction toward that end, and provide you with the basics regarding the Controlled List. We don't usually study the Controlled List in depth here, as you know.''

They were not questioning her ability.

They were offering her additional information, and knowledge that she would need to satisfy First Secretary Verlaine's ambition.

It didn't make any sense.

"I am eager for this knowledge,'' she lied glibly. "How does the Tutor wish me to begin?'' Would she be taking extra classwork, was that what Chonis was getting at? More individual study? How could there be any time for her to learn the Controlled List, when the length of the Term was already filled with the standard course of instruction?

"We will revisit the Fourth Level, tomorrow or the next

day. Student Koscuisko will assist you in an advisory role. With his help, we mean to build a catalog for you from the Controlled List. When you return to Secretary Verlaine you will have a complete arsenal at your disposal, and—more important—you will know how to demonstrate your mastery. How to use it."

Every Student, every commissioned Ship's Inquisitor, had the Controlled List at their disposal. If she could learn how to use it, though . . . And still something was not right. She remembered Koscuisko's emphatically negative reaction to the Tutor's suggestion that he enrich the Controlled List for the Fleet. And now she was to believe that Koscuisko was going to customize the Controlled List? For her use? When Koscuisko would just as soon walk on her as acknowledge her existence?

"For the Tutor's care, I am me grateful." The stress was too great, and her dialect was slipping. She had to maintain better control over her emotions. If Koscuisko was involved, didn't that mean it was still just a plot against her? And if it wasn't, how had they got Koscuisko to go along? "How shall I prepare for this?"

The possibilities were intriguing.

"There are some details yet to be worked out with the Administrator. We'll meet here tomorrow midshift; I'll send the exact time later on today. We can talk with Koscuisko, discuss the prisoner, see if he knows of something suitable on the List, and schedule your Fourth Level retrial accordingly. In the mean time, you should acquaint yourself with the architecture of the Controlled List, and how it relates to the Levels."

It was clearly the end of the interview. Mergau stood up. "I obey my Tutor gladly. Shall I go now?"

Chonis nodded, with a gesture of release or dismissal. "Hanbor has some introductory material logged to your studyset, waiting for you. You're doing good work, Mergau. With your best effort—and Student Koscuisko's help—we can turn out a really first-rate resource for Secretary Verlaine."

And where had Student Koscuisko been these past two days?

She bowed in salute and took her parting, content to let her Tutor have the last word.

She wasn't sure how she felt about this new development, or whether or not there was a trap in it somewhere.

She would study and consider. And see what came out in the days to come.

Joslire Curran stood at the authorized position of command-wait, trying not to think too much about anything. Koscuisko was in surgery. Tutor Chonis had called him to Disciplinary Mast, and there was only one real possible reason, which was—of course—Robert St. Clare. Lop Hanbor was here; he'd seen it happen from the Tutor's viewing room, even as Joslire had. Sorlie Curran was here, with the rest of his team; they'd actually been present when it had happened. The Security team that had removed Robert from the exercise theater was here, and a few of Station Security, all waiting to hear what they already knew, required by Administrative policy to witness the inexorable decree of the Jurisdiction Bench. The Administrator didn't like to publicize mistakes like the one Robert had made, but when it happened, the Administrator liked to be sure everyone who knew that there had been a problem also knew exactly what the penalty was. Certain and swift punishment was the very cornerstone of Fleet discipline.

The signal came, and Joslire stood to attention as Administrator Clellelan and Tutor Chonis made their formal entrance from the back of the room. They would occupy the raised platform at the front, above the Bar: the Administrator sitting; Chonis on his feet, in the presence of his superior officer. Robert would stand there, too. There would be no difficulty in seeing everything that went on, whether or not any of them were eager to do so.

"Attention to orders." An innocuous opening, and Tutor Chonis made it sound so routine, as if there was not a life to be savaged here. "Disciplinary hearing concerning Class-Two violation, disobeying lawful and received instruction, Robert St. Clare. Administrator Clellelan, Presiding. By the Bench instruction."

Not as if he'd never been at Disciplinary Mast before.

There had been one this Term already, as one of Tutor Po-ho's Students cried an offense of disrespect against assigned Security. Two-and-twenty, then and there, and the Student had made an absolute botch of things. There was no two-and-twenty to be anticipated here. The Administrator had come to condemn a bond-involuntary to death by torture, and all because Andrej Koscuisko had heard the wrong thing at the wrong time, and seen through to the heart of the deception.

"Robert St. Clare, step through."

Since all the Security assembled stood at attention for the duration of the hearing there was no turning to look at the man as they brought him in through the ranks and up onto the Command platform above the Captain's Bar. Two Station Security escorted him, standing to either side as Robert turned to face the room. Medical had been at him, needless to say, dosing him with sufficient stimulants to ensure that he'd be able to walk and answer the Administrator's questions just as well as if he understood them. Joslire eyed St. Clare skeptically while the Administrator waited for Security to bring him up to the proper mark. Drugs or no drugs, the man looked half-dead already. It hadn't been two days . . . but the exercise had started three days ago, and that meant three days with an injured shoulder and a fresh whipping, and no medical support authorized. Robert was going to collapse as soon as the drugs wore off, so much was clear.

It was the Administrator's turn to speak, his responsibility to complete the Record.

"Your name is Robert St. Clare?"

"Yes, Your Excellency."

It was a voice from the back end of beyond, as if Robert's brain had to travel so far past his pain to find the words that half of their meaning had got lost again on the return trip.

"You stand before the Bench for disobeying lawful and received instruction; to wit, revealing your true status to the Student Interrogator during the critically important Intermediate Level exercise. Do you understand the charge?"

Robert staggered a bit, swaying where he stood. Station Security reached out to steady him. *No,* Joslire thought. *Not that arm. That's the wrong arm.*

"Yes. Your Excellency. I understand the charge."

"The Administration has reviewed the Record." It was always a little odd hearing Clellelan referring to himself as if he were the institution, rather than the man. But it was necessary. It helped reduce a sense of personal responsibility for what had to be done. "There is no question that Student Koscuisko knew your exact status prior to the end of the exercise. Nor is there any other possible source for this information. We must necessarily conclude that Koscuisko knew because you told him. If not explicitly, then implicitly in some way."

It was wrong and it was unfair, but it was unavoidable, even if Koscuisko himself couldn't accept that fact. If Koscuisko knew, then Robert must have told him. Somehow. There were no allowances in Fleet Administrative Procedure for guessing, or for having the bad luck to draw an unusually perceptive officer, one who would catch one word—one word, out of thousands—and build a damning case out of so small a thing.

"However."

A nervous shock ran through the room, and Joslire felt himself stiffen against an involuntary twitch of surprise. However? Some consideration of degree? Some amelioration of the offense?

Some hope, where none could possibly hope?

"The Administration in review of the Record with the assistance of the assigned Tutor and neutral evaluators has been unable to determine the precise manner in which the information was transmitted. To the best of the Administration's professional judgment, there was no explicit statement on your part that could be construed as release of unauthorized information, prior to a direct question from the Student Interrogator."

The air was heavy with a sharp smell of confusion mixed with fear. There was no precedent for reading such allowances into the Record—not unless discipline was to be adjusted. And Class-Two violations were never adjusted. Never.

"Since you cannot in all fairness be faulted for answering a question posed with a clear presupposition of the restricted information, it is difficult to justify the determination of the penalty. The Administration does not feel that an error was made on your part as a result of misunderstanding the question.''

Fear, because Clellelan seemed to be leading up to a commutation of penalty, and that was unheard of. Fear that what seemed to be happening would turn again at the last minute to almost-certain death by torture for Robert St. Clare—who, as Joslire noted, was having a harder time of it keeping to his feet with every moment that passed.

"You understand the severity of the offense, St. Clare, and you understand what you are accused of having done. Now think for a moment, and answer on your Bond. Did you— at any time—release the restricted information to the Student Interrogator?''

Biting his lip in an evident effort to concentrate, Robert closed his eyes in a spasm of pain. That had been a mistake. Joslire could tell by the way his knees buckled beneath him. It was better not to close your eyes. It deprived you of a focus that helped to keep the dizziness and the disorientation at bay.

Station Security helped him back up to his feet—leaning decidedly to one side, Joslire noted—and Robert found his voice once more. "By my Bond, as I hope for the Day. I cannot remember what I might have said. Your Excellency.''

It had to be true, because his governor would not permit him to swear by his Bond otherwise. The governor could sense internal conflict, read the physiological signs of stress specific to prevarication or lying. And what the governor sensed it punished.

"It goes without saying that there was no intent on your part to compromise the exercise. But there are statements on Record that support an alternative secret to the one you were to release. We cannot set aside the fact of Student Koscuisko's realization. Student Koscuisko himself has an interest in this matter as well.''

They couldn't condemn St. Clare for ambiguity, not when the exercise had terminated in the middle of the Fifth Level, whether or not the Fourth-Level exercise had been prematurely called. That trick of Koscuisko's with Robert's shoul-

der had been as good as an augmented Fourth under any
Protocol, the actual time it had taken aside. Most of the Security here had firsthand knowledge of how hard it was to
concentrate with so much pain. The Administration had always been sensitive to that, overlooking sometimes major
mistakes if only the Student Interrogator had not followed
up on them. But this time, although the mistakes had been
negligible, the Student Interrogator had pulled the horrible
truth out of the concatenation of confused misstarts, and
Robert would necessarily suffer for it.

Koscuisko had gone to the Tutor to beg for remission of
Robert's punishment; and the Tutor had been smiling when
he had released Koscuisko to Joslire's keeping. Chonis
wasn't one of the Tutors who would think enforcing a Class-
Two violation was anything to smile about.

The implications—even as well prepared as Joslire was,
much more so than any of the others—were almost too much
for him to handle.

Discipline was absolute and inevitable.

The tension held them all braced to a knife-edged sharp-
ness of attention.

"Student Koscuisko has in fact brought a separate com-
plaint against you. He has stated his desire to discipline your
lapse by his own hand. We will be unable to comply with
Student Koscuisko's lawful request if this Class-Two decision goes forward." Because Robert would probably be
dead, for one thing. And perhaps it was an exaggeration to
describe Koscuisko's demand as a lawful request. But nobody was going to argue with Clellelan.

"Do you understand me, St. Clare?"

They were going to have to call a medical team at any
moment. Robert had clearly reached the last few measures
of his reserved and drug-enabled strength. "Yes, Your Excellency. . . . No."

"Student Koscuisko has also proposed a speakserum for
addition to the Controlled List. As a training station, we are
empowered to offer a choice between the standard Class-Two
discipline and voluntary service for evaluation of drugs being
considered for Fleet Interrogatory purposes. Are you with
me?"

One of the Station Security reached out for Robert from behind him, and laid a firm hand on the injured shoulder, the swelling of which was visible even from where Joslire stood. It was a brutal trick, and Robert cried out against it, in a strangled protest against the pain. Joslire knew it had been well meant, all the same—even well done. Because the sharp agony clearly helped him regain some degree of concentration. "Yes, Your Excellency. The Controlled List. Student Koscuisko. Sir."

"Answer me on your Bond, then. Do you elect to serve as the experimental subject for the evaluation of Koscuisko's new speakserum, in lieu of other Class-Two discipline?"

Of all the things Joslire had imagined having gone between Koscuisko and Tutor Chonis, none of them had touched on such a potential escape. Koscuisko had gone to Chonis to bargain with him, Joslire had known that all along. But for the bargain to have been made, and in this format. . . .

"Yes, Your Excellency. Experimental duty, new drug for the Classified List. On my Bond, as I hope for the Day, I so elect. Sir."

This was too far beyond the realm of possibility to be happening. It made no sense. Why did Clellelan think that it made a difference? The drugs on the Controlled List were every bit as brutal as discipline administered at the Seventh Level for a Class-Two violation.

"You have elected to test Student Koscuisko's new speakserum, in order to provide additional resources for the Jurisdiction's Controlled List. There is now the issue of Student Koscuisko's Class-Two claim."

Except that the Administrator consistently specified Koscuisko's new drug, and had read the complete description into the Record. Not just a new drug for the Controlled List. Student Koscuisko's new speakserum for the Controlled List. Speaksera were not nerve factors, were not wakekeepers, were not pain-maintenance drugs. Speaksera were only speaksera, even though they were on the Controlled List. And many of them weren't even fatal.

"Student Koscuisko has requested the adjudication of discipline at the aggrieved officer's level. The Administration finds his request reasonable and responsible. The Class-Two violation cried against you by Student Koscuisko will therefore be struck from the Record, and Student Koscuisko will exercise the Judicial function at the Class-One violation level.''

What could it mean?

"Your Excellency. By my Bond. It is just and judicious that he do so. As I hope for the Day."

Robert hadn't committed any Class-Two violations. And even had he done Koscuisko would not have referred it to punishment, at least not in his current state of mind. But Tutor Chonis wouldn't have made that up.

"Very well. Appropriate punishment for the Class-Two violation failure to obey lawful and received instruction has been Adjudicated and accepted. Appropriate punishment for the Class-Two violation brought against you by Student Koscuisko will be administered by Student Koscuisko and the violation stricken from the Record. Under these circumstances your Fleet deferment is refused. The reduction of your Bond will be permitted to stand. It is prudent and proper by the Bench instruction, just and judicious in the eyes of the offending party. The Record is complete."

It was official, then.

It was done.

The Administrator had declared the Record complete; no alteration would be permitted, now that the critical point was passed.

"You will be taken to Infirmary, there to receive appropriate medical care. The Controlled List trial will be scheduled later, depending upon your recovery. The Administration will decide the timing of other discipline after the Controlled List trial has been completed. You are remanded into custody. Dismissed."

Robert St. Clare bowed in salute, a bow that betrayed him to his dizziness. He seemed to lose his balance and consciousness at one and the same time, crumpling slowly to fall forward across the Captain's Bar. Tutor Chonis stepped up smartly, coming to attention in front of the table where Clellelan had the Record.

"This session of Administrator's Disciplinary Hearing is concluded."

Clellelan rose and left the room, and there was silence for as long as it took him to step down from the Command platform and clear the doorway at the back of Tutor's Mess.

Then discipline dissolved into a chaotic mass of murmurs and moving feet, the immense unparalleled wonder of it all too much for any of them. Tutor Chonis raised his voice so that he could make himself heard over the noise, signaling with his hand for the litter to be brought forward. Joslire hadn't seen the medical team before. Clellelan must have brought them, and left them to wait outside until it was all over.

"Sorlie Curran, take the prisoner to Infirmary. Joslire Curran, stand by. I want a word with you."

Robert would test a new speakserum, and he would not die of it—Koscuisko would see to that. That was what Koscuisko had been working on, that was what Koscuisko had offered to Tutor Chonis in exchange for Robert's life. And Tutor Chonis would force Koscuisko to administer a beating, just to be sure that Koscuisko didn't get any ideas into his head about getting his own way. St. Clare would not die of that either, and Koscuisko had done this impossible thing. Koscuisko who could read bodies with his hands and stop the grim wheel of Jurisdiction Fleet discipline and force it back on its unforgiving track. Koscuisko had done this. Robert was not to be tortured and killed.

Koscuisko was a sorcerer, and Joslire was afraid of him now, afraid as he had never been of any man on either end of a whip.

"As for the rest of you," Chonis declared, stepping out of the way of the litter bearing the unconscious body of the salvaged man. "You will return to your duty stations not later than two eighths from now. That will be all. Joslire Curran."

He needed two eighths, four eighths, six eighths to recover himself. He had to look after this Student, this sorcerer. How could he hope to conduct himself correctly in the presence of such a man?

Refuge could be taken in the forms of courtesy and discipline, regardless of the turmoil in his mind. "The Tutor requires, sir?"

Now more than ever the Tutor would need him, to report on Koscuisko's mood and attitude.

Now more than ever he had to protect himself.

She'd planned on keeping an eye on the theater in order to be able to update Chonis if he called. She found instead that she was interested. The screen gave her a close-up on the body: she could see the gray spidery needles walking over the seminude body of the unconscious man, carrying the microlasers to the sites beneath the skin where the fault lay. Where the damage had been done. She'd done some microsurgery herself, although most of what they treated here was gross tissue damage; and she was fascinated by the speed, the skill, the confidence that Koscuisko—even enclosed in the operating chair—expressed with every motion of those thin gray wirelike probes. He never hesitated at the dermis level; he never seemed to reposition a probe; he never seemed to probe too deeply by accident, and have to come back out and try again. He knew the angles of approach he wanted, and he hit each and every one of them flawlessly, without a single misstep.

He hardly seemed to be working at all, it went so fast.

And when the laser fingers had traveled up the spine to nestle beneath the brain box at the base of the skull—the site of the most critical damage, where Noycannir had kicked her unconscious prisoner-surrogate in an apparent spasm of frustration—Koscuisko only slowed his pace a bit. The most delicate of all the surgical interventions, repair of critical connections at the cellular level, and Koscuisko only slowed down, as sure—as certain—as he'd been before, only more deliberate in respect to the more dangerous environment.

Then the surgical machine was moving away from the table, backing up against the wall. Chaymalt shot a startled glance at the chronometer on the wall—had it been that long? Already? She'd hardly been aware of the passage of time, Koscuisko's absolute self-confidence had mesmerized her.

But it was done.

The scanner descended from the ceiling as the operating chair retreated, and tracked slowly up the torpid body on the table. Chaymalt coded the display abruptly, suddenly anxious that she know the criterms now, when she could just as well have waited for them. The scanner report began to scroll across the desk surface: residual bruises, torn muscle fiber, edema—but the neurological damage had been masked by surgical repair.

With the astonishing speed characteristic of successful microsurgery, the normal electrical activity of the nerves was already beginning to recover—for all the world, as if the damaged tissue had not been functionally nerve-dead with shock and trauma three scant eights ago.

It was incredible.

Healing was neither instant or absolute, of course. All Koscuisko had really done had been to restore the system's integrity in the places where it had been compromised by Noycannir's assault. And he had done it with minimal surgical trauma, although the conventional standards recognized that the surgery could do as much damage as it undid, even in the most skilled of hands.

Ligrose Chaymalt knew as well as anyone how natural it was for newly graduated medical practitioners to overrate their own abilities, relative to more objective assessments.

This was the first time she could think of where the performance of a Student actually exceeded expectation.

Tracking complete, the scanner returned to its place in the ceiling, its statistical report processing into Standard language phrases as it did so. She could read the same information Koscuisko saw from within the operating chair: substantial restoration of neurological function. Baseline activity returning to normal, adjusting for effect of anesthesia. No significant operational trauma. Consciousness may safely be invoked within three days, physical therapy to be scheduled after completion of waking tests.

Prognosis excellent.

Her orderly was preparing the patient to return to the recovery room. Koscuisko had switched the surgical machine off; it unfolded from around him, the webbed restraints that had supported the weight of his body in suspension loosening gradually to ease his body to the floor. Chaymalt could not help staring at Koscuisko as the chair backed off and left him standing alone, the white of his underblouse stark against the dark gray walls.

He looked completely centered in his life, a master of his craft, a surgeon of significant potential.

It was an obscene waste to abandon such skill to Inquisition.

Andrej stood alone in the operating theater fastening up his dutyblouse, drinking in the solitude, relishing the relative privacy of the now-empty surgery. Oh, there were monitors in place, he knew that—had this been an ordinary operating theater, there would necessarily have been monitors. It wasn't that. From the time he'd arrived at Fleet Orientation Station Medical, he'd hardly been alone for a single moment; either because Joslire was in the next room or because he was in class. And he was alone now, alone to bask in the satisfaction of a surgical procedure well completed. Alone, to cradle the comfort of having helped to heal an injured man to himself, and to cherish the blessing in his heart.

He could not hold the pleasure long.

So sensitive had he become to the expectations and regulations that being alone began to worry him. Where was Joslire? Or where was Travis, for instance, in Joslire's absence? What was going on out there, out in the working areas of the station, outside this sanctuary space?

He covered his face with his hands for a moment, then finger-combed his hair with a decisive gesture. Enough was enough. There would be sufficient with which to concern himself, he could be certain of that. It was time to return to the real world, harsh though it was. This surgery had been a brief respite of sorts, but there was still as much to be done, and as little to his liking, as there had been before.

Turning toward the sterile-lock door, Andrej saw Joslire Curran standing beyond the near-transparent membrane. At least it looked like Joslire to Andrej, and whomever it was bowed politely in salute, which rather strengthened the supposition.

Andrej went through.

"Well met, Mister Curran." There was another Security post in the corridor, but she was nothing to do with Andrej, so he ignored her, beyond using a more formal address for Joslire in token of her presence. "Is it too early for thirdmeal?" Because he was hungry again. A little full of himself, just now perhaps, but surely he could be permitted a little egotistic self-congratulation under the circumstances?

Joslire looked as if he'd not been fed for a few days, though. Pale and drawn, with a glazed look in his eyes that seemed to speak to Andrej of a stunning shock of some sort. Oh, what now, what now?

What next?

But he knew better than to ask the question, at least in so many words.

"The officer's thirdmeal shift is two hours old, the officer's meal can be made available at any time. With respect, Your Excellency. . . ."

That was odd. He wasn't an Excellency outside of practical exercise theater, not yet, not to Fleet. Not to Joslire. "Yes?"

"Tutor Chonis has suggested that the officer may wish to provide an additional service in Infirmary, if the officer pleases. It was suggested that the officer might consent to take a moment, once the scheduled surgery was completed."

Nor did Joslire use a direct form of address when he was paying attention to himself, no matter how many extra words there were to separate "Your Excellency" from "if the officer pleases." Surely he wasn't still shaken by what had passed between them earlier?

"That which my Tutor has suggested, I must me receive as instruction." It was actually a quote from Mergau Noycannir, not as if Joslire would know that. Andrej found Noycannir's dialect rather engaging. It was her bullying, manipulative personality he found objectionable. "Let's go, Mister Curran, lead on. Is this our guide?"

The Security post simply bowed, and took off, with Andrej and Joslire following up the rear. Through mazes of corridors and doors she led them, until Andrej felt a little dizzy. It wasn't as if they needed to keep the location secret from him. He didn't know where he was in the first place. How would he even know the difference, if they'd led him around the spiral steps for some obscure Security joke?

No matter.

Except that it kept him from his supper, and he wanted to go see Tutor Chonis, just to test once more whether there was to be any hope at all for his unfortunate prisoner-surrogate.

If they refused his offer, he would not be in honor bound to support the Controlled List, which was an abomination beneath the Canopy. He could hold himself stainless, in at least that one piece of his larger degradation; and it would be good to have some little thing in which he could comfort himself that he was not utterly disgraced. But if they refused his offer—an innocent man would suffer horribly, and probably die, and Andrej could not make himself believe that it was worth it that a man should die if only he could avoid the Controlled List.

Finally a long corridor with a clearly visible door at the far end—the way out. Oddly enough, the same Security team that he had had with him for that fateful exercise—two days ago? Just yesterday?—was waiting in the hallway as they came around the corner. Sorlie Curran and the rest, Andrej was sure of it. They were too busy saluting him to allow him any time to question them, however, because Sorlie Curran had apparently signaled at the door, and Joslire behind him was still moving at too brisk a pace for Andrej to feel confident of his ability to put a brake on the man's momentum before he ran Andrej down.

All right.

Into the room, then.

A minor surgery facility, clearly enough, with a body on the levels and a technician standing by with a pharmacy unit while two orderlies worked at cleaning the wounds of a man who had been beaten. It all looked quite commonplace to Andrej. What was the point behind all this?

"Attention to the officer," Sorlie Curran called sharply, from behind him. The two orderlies backed away from the levels quickly, almost as if they were timid about something. Andrej acknowledged their salutes quickly, waving them off.

He was beginning to have an idea.

"What is this man's status? . . . Best close the door." He advanced on the body that lay on the levels, unsure of how interested he really was in looking at the evidence. Swollen flesh and fiery inflammation two and three days old, bruises upon bruises, welts upon welts. A shoulder swollen and livid with insult, striped and bloodied with blows from a whip that had struck just exactly where it would hurt the most. An ugly beating all 'round, and Andrej recognized his handiwork, although he shuddered to see it. They had brought him to St. Clare. Why?

One of the orderlies, turning the record-monitor at the head of the levels so that he could see the display more clearly, gestured nervously and saluted once again. What in the name of all Saints were they so jumpy about? The medical record was clear enough. But the status block had a continuation code; frowning, Andrej keyed the scroller to see what it was that was causing such consternation.

ROBERT ST. CLARE, the Status Block said. BOND-INVOLUNTARY, CURRENT OFFICER OF ASSIGNMENT STUDENT ANDREJ KOSCUISKO. LAST RECORDED ACTION, ADJUDICATION OF PUNISHMENT FOR A CLASS-TWO VIOLATION, EVALUATION DUTY FOR CONTROLLED LIST SPEAKSERUM. TO BE RETURNED TO DUTY STATUS AT ASSIGNED OFFICER'S DISCRETION TO STAND EVALUATION DUTY, OUTSTANDING CLASS-ONE VIOLATION PENDING, TO BE STRICKEN FROM THE RECORD. BY THE BENCH INSTRUCTION.

St. Clare was his?

"Joslire, what does this mean?" he asked in a hushed whisper. "I cannot trust myself to understand." Or to face the bargain he had made without cringing away from what he had sworn to do. What he would do.

"With respect. Sir." Not that Joslire sounded much better, at the moment. "The Administrator has permitted St. Clare to test his . . . the officer's new speakserum, in lieu of other Class-Two discipline. It is on Record."

And there could be no hidden trick or reversal if it was on Record. They meant to have what he had offered them, and how could he grudge it when they had delivered St. Clare from the sin that Andrej had committed against him?

He was numb with the accumulated shocks his spirit had sustained over the past two days.

He could find it in him neither to rejoice nor weep.

He checked that the sterile field was up and active instead, and started to unfasten his dutyblouse once more. "Very well. Give me the medical report, I'll want to check on this. You, there, technician, what are my clearances for practice?" As opposed to research. Obviously no decently run Infirmary would permit just anyone to gain access to proprietary stores, whether physician or no; and there was no particular reason for the Fleet to allow him to do so. Hadn't there been a nasty comment of some sort in the administrative material about different levels of treatment support for bond-involuntary troops in need of medication?

Joslire took his blouse, and the technician blushed and bowed. "The officer is cleared to order at the officer's discretion and best judgment. A credit ceiling of four hundred thousand, Standard, has been imposed to cover the cost of medication only. Doctor Chaymalt's personal instruction."

"I am deeply obliged to Doctor Chaymalt, and hope I will have the opportunity to tell her so. Joslire. Is there rhyti?" Supper would wait. Four hundred thousand, Standard, was it? The official replacement cost levied against a Fleet command whose loss of a bond-involuntary was judged to have resulted from criminal negligence. Even then it was the Command's administrative budget, and not the Commander, who paid. But if Chaymalt was willing to recompense him in this manner for the surgery that he had performed under her authority, Andrej was more than willing to accept the grant as given, crude though it was.

He could hear the door open behind him; Joslire going for rhyti, he supposed. He hoped. The orderlies looked confused; he wanted them handy, he might be needing them later on. "Who is senior of the two of you? What are your orders?"

The shorter one was senior, a Binbin woman with her head half-shaved after the fashion of her kind. "With respect. We were tasked to provide primary support in the officer's absence, and to assist the officer at his discretion. We are at the officer's disposal."

And if he didn't feel like troubling himself? There would be no secondary support. Or there would be treatment of the injuries, and it would stop well short of soothing for the pain. They would have been quite sure that he would do what was needful, though, having already paid such coin for the man. "Very good. Prepare me a double dose of hanerdoi, and I'll want a good vasodilator as well. What have you got on hand for Nurail besides extract of sandspreader?"

The shoulder first, and hit it with a deep neural block straight off, so he wouldn't have any problems if St. Clare began to wake up. Not that he expected that to happen any time soon, not with what the metabolic blood report had to tell him about protein starvation and too much jacherul for common sense and reason. They'd wanted St. Clare conscious to stand his hearing, well, that made a certain amount of sense.

Andrej wondered what St. Clare was going to think of all this.

There was a good deal to be done. The shoulder sprain, complicated as it had been by neglect and abuse and left untreated for so long, was just short of sustaining a permanent injury. It wouldn't have mattered to Fleet, since crozerlances were not Standard issue. But St. Clare wouldn't have appreciated the chronic pain. Then there was a significant dehydration issue to be addressed, and it seemed that St. Clare had been fasting; but whether that had been because of lack of appetite—or because Fleet didn't waste rations on dead men—Andrej neither knew nor cared to speculate.

Fluid and nourishment provided in solution, the shoulder numbed, the swelling seen to, there were still the bruises and the blood all down St. Clare's back, all down his sides, his arms, his legs, the welts across his face. Tutor Chonis would require him to scourge St. Clare all over again, and he *had* promised. He was going to have to study how it could be done, to do the least amount of damage—hopefully without anybody catching on.

By the time that Andrej was ready for the orderlies to help him turn St. Clare over onto his newly bandaged back, the man was thinking about regaining consciousness, from all indications. It was true that St. Clare was in absolutely superb physical condition, recent events aside. And also true, as Andrej had some personal reason for knowing, that the right ointment applied with a careful enough touch could really make a difference when a man was hurting from head to foot. Andrej kept an eye on St. Clare's face, watching for the movement of the eyes behind closed lids. He didn't want to use any more soporific than he had to; it could interfere with the action of the painkiller he was using. He didn't quite catch it in time even so. Cleaning fragments of rope fiber away from the torn flesh at his patient's throat, he was distracted, and when St. Clare spoke to him he started in surprise.

"What are . . . Why did . . ."

Andrej snapped his fingers for the dose he'd had the technician hold in reserve, and she pressed it through with commendable efficiency. "Shut up," he advised St. Clare, watching the muscles of his patient's face fall slack as St. Clare sank into deep unconsciousness once more. "Go to sleep. We'll talk about it later." He was certainly not going to address any of those issues now, with all this work on his hands. And he wasn't sure he had the first idea of what he was going to say when the time came.

"Is there a bed reserved?" he asked the senior orderly. They were almost done, except of course that rehydration and nourishment did have to continue, and there should be someone to see to pain reduction medication should St. Clare wake again during the night.

"Full supportive, if it please the officer." Andrej let his hand rest against the least bruised skin that he could find on St. Clare's naked chest, considering his progress on the tracks the rope had left. He'd known when he had started with the rope that it was liable to shed a myriad of irritating fragments of stiff fiber, wearing away at St. Clare's throat like spun glass ground into a wound. At the time it had struck him as an interesting concept, one that would contribute to a certain degree of erosion in the prisoner's self-control. Now he wanted to know what kind of a pervert had ideas like that, when they involved making such a mess out of a perfectly good physical machine, the body of the prisoner.

Clearly there was a conflict of some sort, here.

As if he hadn't known.

"All right, then." Beckoning to Joslire for his rhyti, Andrej wondered suddenly what time it had gotten to be, and how late he'd kept his poor Joslire up again. "There's stasis on the bed, of course? Well, one must be sure, no offense was meant. You may remove the patient to his bed. I have logged four units of amart to be delivered every two hours, and seven of storliva to be administered if his temperature should chance to rise. If there are any other developments, I should like to be notified, immediately. I trust there will be no problem with that?''

Not that he expected any unforeseen developments, because St. Clare really was rather a splendid young animal, and there was nothing wrong with him that rest and food and drink and painease could not mend. It was a good thing for them both that he was so new at his craft, Andrej decided. St. Clare would carry no scars. Joslire wore too many, even if most of the evidence had been cosmetically concealed— to render him more aesthetically pleasing in the eyes of his Students? To remove the checking influence it might be said to have if one should chance to notice that the man one was preparing to strike was already scarred, to face brutally vivid evidence of past punishment as one worked oneself up to deliver punishment? The Administration did not want young Students to think twice about beating people. The Administration did not want them to think about it at all.

And there was another problem.

Andrej knew how hard he'd struck St. Clare, and how much pain it had created, quite apart from the nasty trick he'd played with the crozer-hinge.

How much more pain had Joslire suffered, to have given him such scars? And—had it been some other physician— there might have been no grant of medication, not even for worse welts—

Two-and-twenty could be decided and delivered without Charges brought, without hope for appeal or moderating influence. Two-and-twenty was Standard issue for bond-involuntaries.

He could not bear to think about it. He had been through too much today. And he had come out ahead of it all, at least in one thing, and that was an important thing—the life of the man who lay unconscious beneath his hand. St. Clare belonged to him, and he was responsible for St. Clare. It was a bit of comforting familiarity in this alien place that persisted in Andrej's mind even as the orderlies removed his patient to his bed.

Alone in the room now with only Joslire for company, Andrej drank his rhyti and remembered that he was hungry. "Joslire, am I to see Tutor Chonis, or am I to go to bed?" His rhyti was still hot, and that was odd. How many times had Joslire had to go for rhyti, to have it hot and ready for him now?

"Tutor Chonis has requested that the officer meet with him after fastmeal, in the morning. For the remainder of this dutyshift, there is no training scheduled."

No, Joslire was sitting on something, Andrej was certain that he could hear it in his voice. He glanced behind him sharply, but Joslire gave no hint of an expression on his somber, guarded face.

Maybe he didn't want to know.

"Let's have my blouse, then, if you please." Well, they'd go back to quarters and be done with the day. He did want to see Doctor Chaymalt, but a formal appointment would probably take a day or two to set up through the proper channels. He'd have to read up on his Sixth Level, and he wasn't looking forward to that any more than he had to any of the preliminary exercises, but he didn't have the energy to waste in indulging himself in conflict of that sort. "Can you call ahead for my supper, I wonder? Or perhaps a midmeal and a thirdmeal at once, if it is possible, unless there are rules against permitting Students to make gluttons of themselves?"

Joslire helped him into his blouse, stone-faced and silent. Joslire keyed the door and bowed, silent and stone-faced, for Andrej to precede him from the room. Andrej could see Sorlie Curran and the rest of the security team in the corridor beyond, two on each side, standing to attention. Had they really been there all this time? If they were St. Clare's jailers, why hadn't they followed the orderlies when the orderlies had taken St. Clare off to Ward?

Andrej went out into the corridor thinking about his supper, and came to an abrupt halt.

It wasn't only Sorlie Curran, and the team who had been with him for the exercise.

There was a Bigelblu, and a Mizucash, and the Holy Mother only knew how many others besides. All bond-involuntaries. And the corridor was absolutely solid with them, standing to attention against the walls on either side to wait his passing.

Staring about him in wonder, Andrej started down the hall toward the door at the far end. How had all these people gotten in here? And he recognized the Mizucash and the Bigelblu from his Preliminary Level exercises, both saluting him with precise and respectful bows as he went past. He could hear Joslire behind him, but he could also hear the troops turning to close ranks across the corridor just behind the two of them, forming row upon row of Security troops that deepened the closer he got to the door at the end of the corridor. And when he got to the door, it was worse, because there were more of them on the other side, and most of those were Station Security and Infirmary staff, and not bond-involuntaries at all.

What was a man to do in such a circumstance?

Andrej paced the distance with grave deliberation, keenly aware of the silent formation that surrounded him. Reaching the end of the gauntlet at last, he turned to face back the way he had come, Joslire moving quickly to stand behind him.

There could be only one response truly appropriate, truly adequate to express his confused appreciation for this astonishing tribute.

He looked through the ranks for a long moment, trying to make eye contact with everyone there, trying not to wonder why they weren't at their duty stations.

And he bowed.

With every bit as much heartfelt gratitude and respect as a filial child bowing to his father, or before the Canopy.

"You do me very great honor. And I thank you for it." It was a poor return, but it was the best he had to offer. "Good night, gentles, all. I will. Never. Forget this."

Now he should leave the area quickly, so that they could disperse with all deliberate speed; but not so quickly that they would feel he was slighting their profound gesture by discarding its importance with his haste. Forcing himself to take unhurried steps, Andrej walked out of the area, with

Joslire following. He could only just hear Joslire behind him, close to his shoulder, speaking soft and low, his voice pitched to Andrej's ear alone.

"Neither will we. Your Excellency."

He didn't believe that he deserved this accolade, strangely as it had been given. But there was no arguing with one's Household. When they decided that one had done well, the only thing that one could do was to accept in all humility and submit with as good grace as one could muster.

He only hoped that no one would come to grief for it.

 **Nine**

There had been a disturbance of sorts in Infirmary during thirdshift, and although Tutor Chonis hadn't heard many details, he considered it almost certain that Koscuisko had been involved somehow. Koscuisko was expected after fastmeal, but—Chonis realized, frowning at his time-strip—he hadn't specified a time when he'd given Curran his instructions yesterday mid-second. He'd not been quite sure how much Curran would be able to retain of what Chonis had wanted to tell him. The whole roomful of Security had been in shock, Bonded and un-Bonded alike, after witnessing the actualization of the impossible.

He need not have worried. It was the mark after the start of the normal training period, precisely as close to "after fastmeal" as a man could get; and here was Student Koscuisko, signaling at the door.

"Student Koscuisko respectfully reports at the Tutor's convenience."

And, oh, but didn't he sound polite this morning. Pale, and there were dark stains beneath his eyes, like those that signaled incomplete restfulness in some of the races of category-six hominids. He always had used polite language, that was true. It was all the more interesting how different it sounded when Koscuisko appeared to actually mean it.

"Step through. Thank you, Curran, stand by. Good-greeting, Andrej, have you slept well?"

Koscuisko took his seat a little heavily. "Thank you, Tutor, I believe so. But I have a good deal on my mind, if perhaps we could discuss it.''

Yes, he'd just bet Koscuisko had a lot to talk about. ''All right. Where shall we start?'' That should be an interesting choice, given the range from which Koscuisko could choose.

Koscuisko lay his hand out on the table flat, palm uppermost, studying his fingers. ''Well, there is St. Clare's status, and I would like to be permitted to follow up. I understand there is to be an evaluation of the speakserum, and I wonder if I am permitted to adjust the formulation to include the Nurail lineages. Also there were some gentles to see me to my quarters last night, and I can't help but worry that the Administration might misinterpret their courtesy. I have promised to enrich the Controlled List; I would know how the Administration wishes to define my contribution, a schedule, or whatever. Also, finally, my Sixth Level. I have some anxiety on all of these points, Tutor Chonis.''

He had just about hit all the marks, that was true. ''I'll see if I can't set your mind at rest. You'll prompt me if I leave anything out.'' Because there was a good deal of ground to cover. ''Let's start with the unusual occurrence last night, since I've just found out about it. The Administrator's morning report describes it as a not-unlawful assembly, not outside the range of customary and acceptable procedure. Though it seems to have pushed the limit? Hmmm?''

Koscuisko blushed and bit his lip. It was an unfair question, Chonis supposed. ''No matter. There don't seem to be any problems, at least not at this time. A natural expression of concern for two fellow Security troops and bond-involuntaries, that is all.''

Perhaps not all. Perhaps very much more than that, and all to do with Andrej Koscuisko, marked for the rest of his Fleet career as a man who could command personal loyalty from bond-involuntary troops.

''As to St. Clare. You will assume the responsibilities of attending physician until he can be returned to duty to stand evaluation of the speakserum. You will administer appropriate punishment for the violation you mentioned to me. . . . Do you remember?''

Koscuisko was uncomfortable with this part. Chonis intended that Koscuisko be uncomfortable with this part. That was the whole point of the exercise—or of what was left of the exercise, at any rate.

"I remember, Tutor Chonis. And I have not yet thanked you for taking my petition forward. I . . . cannot say . . ."

His knuckles tight against the tabletop, his mouth pursed white, Koscuisko fought to contain his emotion, while Chonis watched, fascinated. Passion was not usually seen in Students, either because they had learned neutrality in their medical schooling or because they had drawn a layer of callousness over themselves for self-protection. Koscuisko was a passionate man, and it was instructive to see how he handled it in himself; though it was surely not necessary—Chonis reminded himself, a little guiltily—to let him suffer, in this manner.

"You are quite welcome, Student Koscuisko. No one on this Station but welcomed your suggestion."

There, that was better. Koscuisko took a deep breath, and his shoulders seemed to smooth out a bit as he relaxed. "Even so, I will not forget, Tutor Chonis. I understand that I must discipline St. Clare, as I have sworn to do. Naturally I would prefer to restrict myself to two-and-twenty, but that might not satisfy the requirement. I therefore must ask . . ."

Chonis already knew that Koscuisko would just as soon go two-and-twenty and forget it. He was tempted to let it rest at that. The idea had been to ensure that Koscuisko suffered for his lapse of taste in embarrassing the Administration, and that he would continue to shudder for his sins every time he laid eyes on Robert St. Clare. It was clear enough to Chonis that Koscuisko was suffering rather flamboyantly over the risked Class Two itself. There was the question of the Administrator, however; Clellelan would not understand letting it go so lightly. Given the leniency Administrator Clellelan had granted in the matter, Chonis felt it was better not to push things.

"The Administration will accept four-and-forty as a good-faith demonstration, Andrej. Yes, it is a bit stricter than you would have liked, I know." Perhaps Koscuisko had hoped three-and-thirty would do. Koscuisko had too much respect

for pain, that was his problem. Bond-involuntaries were expected to stand two-and-twenty as a matter of course, six-
and-sixty being considered merely adequate to get their
attention.

"The choice of instruments is to be made from among
those provided at the Intermediate Levels?" Koscuisko
sounded a trifle choked, but obedient and submissive still.
"Am I to schedule this, or is it for the Administrator to do
so?"

Nodding, Chonis remembered a question he had been
wanting to ask. "Yes and yes. That is, the Administrator will
schedule the discipline once St. Clare is returned to duty. It
goes on Record. I'd like to know, now that you've rested, if
you could tell me what revealed the secret to you. —Oh, no
further penalty will be assessed," he added quickly, in the
face of Koscuisko's evident alarm.

It was alarm shading into a subtle sort of confusion as
Koscuisko searched his mind. "I'm not . . . exactly . . . sure.
I had been thinking about how stubborn he was, which meant
that he had courage, moral strength. Because I could tell how
much he had pain. I started to wonder whether such a man
would be offered a Bond, and then I wondered why I had
thought that; and what it could have been that Sorlie Curran
hadn't wanted me to notice. I'm not sure. With your permission, Tutor Chonis."

No, Koscuisko had grabbed it out of thin air and St.
Clare's admittedly ambiguous mutterings. But if the secret
could be caught out of things of the sort St. Clare had said,
then no single bond-involuntary in the program would have
been safe. Koscuisko had an empathic sort of truth-sense. He
would be good at his work, if only he could be persuaded
to relax and enjoy it.

Figuratively speaking, of course.

Leading naturally up to the next subject, one that Student
Koscuisko had asked him about—as good an opening as any,
Chonis congratulated himself. "Sometimes understanding
comes without understanding how it's come by. I should like
you to concentrate on that aspect of Inquiry and Confirmation
during your next exercise. Shall I schedule you for, say, three

days from now? What do you think? Will you be rested enough?''

The Sixth Level was as bad as it got—before it got truly unreasonable. Preliminary Levels concentrated on Inquiry; the Intermediate Levels, on Inquiry and Confirmation. By the time the Advanced Levels were reached, the fine line dividing Inquiry and Confirmation was necessarily smeared over with an overriding requirement to Execute. Prisoners weren't even referred to the Advanced Levels without confession—if not theirs, then somebody else's. And the Protocols more or less ensured that if the prisoner was referred at the Advanced Levels, the prisoner would die. Then skill became an issue: Die sooner? Die later?

Chonis brought himself out of his meditation abruptly. He was getting ahead of himself, and Koscuisko hadn't answered him. ''Andrej?''

''In three days' time, yes, Tutor. I will be ready. And what is the Tutor's pleasure for the meantime?''

No argument, no neutral insistence on the tiresome fact that the Sixth Level had been originally scheduled for five days' distance. Not three. Chonis decided that he liked this meek demeanor: Koscuisko, as good as his word, was trying to behave.

''You're to give us half-days in the lab and spend the rest of the time preparing for your practical exercise. You're welcome to tinker with that speakserum, if you like, but we do have a rather more specific need for your talents just at present.''

''Yes, Tutor Chonis?''

''Student Koscuisko. I know how much you dislike the idea of the Controlled List. And it is not the Administrator's intent to demand disproportionate return for St. Clare. We will be content with a finite set of new drugs''—although he hadn't discussed it with the Administrator in so many words. It didn't matter. What he had decided to ask Koscuisko for would keep his Student busy enough.

''I do not regret. I will not renounce. The bargain that I made. What did you call it? The exchange, as of hostages.''

Chonis smiled at how apt his Student was. ''We have a special need at this time for a library of sorts. I would like you to build for me three each of the four classes of Controlled List drugs, and I must specify that the three preparations taken together cover as broad a range as possible." So that Mergau could be taught to use them for as many purposes, as many prisoners as possible, without requiring her to actually learn much of anything more than a list. "Your fellow Student will test these drugs in her practical exercises"—*that* startled him, even if he was too subdued to say anything—"and it goes without saying that all prisoners will be bona fide prisoners. Upon my word of honor, neither you nor Student Noycannir will be exposed to a prisoner-surrogate for the remainder of the Term."

It was just lucky they'd got a fresh batch in, what with the Term gearing up for the Advanced Levels. Mergau's Fourth and Fifth could be recycled for someone else's Seventh, if all went well.

"You are content to sacrifice effectiveness for applicability, then. I think that I understand."

Not the whole tape, no. Not quite yet. But soon. As soon as Noycannir's repeat on the Fourth Level, which he had better schedule for before Koscuisko's Sixth if they were not to fall too far behind. "How soon do you feel you can have something ready for me?"

Koscuisko shrugged, apparently distracted by the technical aspects of the problem. "It will not take long to update the first speakserum for Nurail. If you have a Nurail"—for Noycannir's Fourth Level?—"we could be ready perhaps tomorrow."

There should be no problem there; the Bench was blessed with a multitude of Nurail on Charges. They'd pick one out of the manifest for Noycannir's Fourth Level. Then, of course, the formal trial of the speakserum against St. Clare would be a redundancy; but that part of the program had never been intended as a serious test, so it made little difference either way.

Chonis nodded his approval, smiling. "Tomorrow, then. Give me your status first thing in the morning. Please don't neglect your physical exercise, Andrej, I know how easy it is to become distracted, but really we must keep you in the very best of health. And Curran is responsible to the Administrator for you."

Rising from the table, Koscuisko bowed formally—as always—but there was something different, all the same. "As you wish it, Tutor. If I am to be excused now, I will begin in the lab immediately."

Then Chonis understood.

There was no mockery in Koscuisko's salute, this time.

"Good day, Student Koscuisko." Oh, this was getting better and better by the moment.

St. Clare might be worth more to the Administration in the long run than Chonis had imagined.

Rabin was afloat in a cushiony sea of pleasant music, the air full of the sweet smell of the springbrake that bloomed for two short weeks through the late snow in the high windy. The disconnected drowsiness that addled his brains he understood; he'd been drunk before. There was no explanation that sprung to mind for the pictures he was seeing, but they were too pretty to object to. His primary concern was whether he would be able to remember what kind of liquor it had been once he woke up.

"May I have status, please."

He heard the voice carrying through the breezy strains of the sheepshank pipes and wondered what it meant. A clear voice, a quiet voice, with a funny little accent—of course they all had accents. He'd never met anyone who could speak proper Standard, not since he'd left home. Since he'd been taken from home. But under the influence of whatever it was he was drunk on not even that nightmare of blood and screaming could move him to distress.

"His temperature is fluctuating a bit, but well within the range the officer had specified as expected. Swelling doesn't appear to be going down as well as the officer would wish, if the officer would care to examine?"

Some other voice. They were all his friends, he was certain. And because he felt so good that there wasn't any room in his limited consciousness for any other possibility. A cooling breeze had come up from somewhere, and he shifted against its soft luxurious caress, reveling in the pleasure of it. Warm and happy, and a lovely breeze. Could life possibly get any better than this?

Did he care about the multitude of ways in which it could get worse?

"I think I'd like to follow up on these with more of the bmilc ointment. You're quite right, though, this still looks ugly. I am inclined to hit it with another few sixteenths of ofdahl to get the swelling down."

Oddly enough, he could sense a sort of a pressure against his body, a pressure that made him nervous in an unfocused sort of way. There didn't seem to be any pain associated with the pressure as it shifted from place to place; nor was the pressure itself very hard or very widespread. Why was he nervous? The touch was against his shoulder, that was why he was nervous. Why it should be so, he was unsure. He cleared his throat to complain about it; he could hear some whimpering, very close by, but the pressure lifted.

"Let me have six eighths of the neural block. Immediately, if you please."

He held his breath, trying to understand who was crying. And he felt pressure, again, but only for a moment, and there was no more crying. The pressure that he felt was like a caress, now, soothing and comforting.

"There, now, that's better, isn't it? Thank you, technician, I will apply the ointment, if I may. You may be dismissed, if you like."

There was nothing to worry about, forever. Or until he was sober again, which amounted to the same thing.

He smiled and drifted off, content.

"I am not sure we should be unconcerned about this," Clellelan said, thoughtfully tapping his stylus against the stack of report-cubes. "I'm not rejecting your reasoning, Adifer. But there must have been half the Security on Station down in Infirmary last night."

"Perhaps an augmented third," Chonis demurred politely. The chairs in the Administrator's office were too comfortable for him to bother with becoming exercised over his superior's displeasure. "There've been no reports of duty stations left unattended, after all. —Have there been?"

Chaymalt snorted from her position of repose at Chonis's right. "Only because there wasn't anyone left at duty stations to report anybody. What I'd like to know is how the word got out so quickly. What is it with these Bonds—do the governors lock into serial transmit when there are too many of them in one place? What? It was unnerving, is all I've got to say."

Clellelan set his stylus down, sighing in resignation. "Can't say that I blame them. 'The one is the many and the many are as one,' I've heard them say. Infirmary staff would have appreciated his surgery on Idarec, so I can understand them joining in, but I'm not sure why Station Security decided to open the clinic area to the Bonds the way they did."

Nor did Chonis, come to that. But nobody had expected anything like a mass demonstration, or they'd have taken steps, so much went without saying. Bond-involuntary troops were easily managed as long as they were surrounded by the un-Bonded, but when there were too many of them in one place and emotion started to run high—as high as it had run on this Station last night—conditioning could fail. Unpredictable things had been known to happen.

"It'll get out, of course." He was thinking out loud, since neither Clellelan nor Chaymalt seemed to have much to say. "Wrap a reputation around that boy before he so much as clears Orientation. Could be good for his old age, in the long run." Could be helpful in ensuring that Koscuisko would live to see his old age. Fleet Medical Officers could be very unpopular people under Jurisdiction. If there was going to be an attempt made on the life of any given Ship's Prime officer, it was good odds that it would be the Ship's Surgeon who would be targeted.

"Good for more than that." Chaymalt had been relatively subdued all through the late morning's informal staff review. Hadn't made a single insensitive comment about bond-involuntaries for, oh, eighths now. Chonis wondered what had set her off angle. "Good for that man Idarec's old age. Did I mention the diagnostic is calling for consciousness in three days? He was dead meat, Rorin, this time yesterday, I'd have told you to cancel his Bond and forget about it."

She more or less had told *him* that, Chonis remembered.

More than a day ago. Was that what was on her mind? She certainly sounded emphatic enough.

"Compared to the talent we've seen come through here the past eight Terms, Student Koscuisko is all the way out to Gissen, all by himself. All right, we already know he's not your usual run of volunteer. I hate to think of him wasting his time with the Protocols, Rorin, I really do."

She sounded as if she meant it, which was unusual. Ligrose didn't get excited about much of anything, not that he had ever noticed. Color in her cheeks, fire in her eye—he was going to have to review the surgical record, he decided, just to see if he could figure out what had gotten through to her like this.

Clellelan was scowling at her in evident consternation. "What bit your elbow? He's a good surgeon, he's going to *Scylla*, he's got eight years to mark. Eight years isn't even all that long for Aznir. You know you can't have him."

In the general, rather than the specific sense, of course. Yes, of course. Chaymalt looked a little sulky, all the same.

"I just don't like to see the waste, that's all. You wouldn't send a Tutor to teach the tweeners, would you?"

"No, and I wouldn't release restricted narcotics for a bond-involuntary on a Fifth Level, either. Let alone ad lib. And what kind of a limit is that? Four hundred thousand, Standard? Do you know what we could do with an extra four hundred thousand, Standard?"

Chaymalt actually blushed. Whether in embarrassment or vexation, however, Chonis did not care to guess. "I don't have to justify it. Any basic cost-benefit analysis would endorse the action."

Clellelan was clearly more up to date on what was happening in Ligrose's area than Chonis had realized. Chaymalt didn't seem inclined to let the issue rest, however.

"I'm having a hard time understanding why I can't have this one, while we're on the subject. It isn't as if he'd be likely to object—"

"If you declined to pass him?" Clellelan sat back in his chair. "Doctor Chaymalt. If you have any reservations to express about Student Koscuisko's medical qualifications, we should restrict them to a more formal hearing. It would seem to contradict your earlier statements, however."

This was ridiculous. Chaymalt had never seriously challenged graduation on the grounds of insufficient qualifications, no matter how sarcastic she got; and the whole point was that Koscuisko was good. There was no precedent . . . but that was what the last two days had been like, wasn't it?

"I cannot object to the Student's medical qualifications." Chaymalt sounded subdued, but still resisting. "Quite the contrary. I simply cannot understand how a qualified neurosurgeon with his ratings could be adequately utilized at the Ship's Surgeon level. There would seem to be an unusually extreme degree of difference between the two required roles."

Whereas indifferent surgeons made adequate Inquisitors, superlative surgeons made inadequate Inquisitors? Was that her point? Because if it was, all he would have to do would be to show her Koscuisko's Fourth and Fifth Levels. Koscuisko clearly had the makings of a superlative Inquisitor, whether or not Koscuisko was interested in hearing about it.

"How does the schedule look, Adifer?" Clellelan turned his attention toward Chonis, clearly determined to turn away from the potentially sticky hole that Chaymalt seemed bent on wedging herself into. Chonis put his glass down, clearing his throat. If he'd realized that Chaymalt was going to get emotionally involved, he'd have approached Clellelan privately; yet there was no help for it, he supposed, but to go forward bravely.

"It depends on Doctor Chaymalt, to an extent." He hadn't anticipated any problem, but it was always the unexpected issues that really fouled things up for one. "I've told him to take half-days in the lab, pending the speakserum trial and his Sixth Level. I had assumed that Doctor Chaymalt would not object to waiving the clinical evaluation phase."

They usually sent Students to Infirmary for a week or so between Intermediate and Advanced Levels. The Fleet requirement for on-site evaluation of Students' medical qualifications was a little outdated, perhaps, since their ability to perform as Ship's Inquisitor was what counted. Nobody expected leadership from Chief Medical Officers anymore, and they had staff to support them. Koscuisko might well prove a throwback of sorts; Chonis wondered how *Scylla* was going to react to the anomalous presence of a Chief Medical Officer who was clearly capable of growing into the job. For once.

Chaymalt was frowning, but Clellelan beat her to the mark. "I dare say our good Doctor has already done as much, even just this morning. What do you say, Ligrose? Any reservations signing his sheet?"

They would ignore the potential threat that she had half-made, then. Well, that was one way to handle it.

"I'll sign the sheet on instruction either way, Administrator. And no, there's no doubt in my mind about his fitness, not his technical qualifications, at any rate. I'd been looking forward to having him on Wards for a week. What's the problem?"

"We need him in his lab, Doctor." Chonis figured he'd better pick up the argument, since he hadn't filled the Administrator in quite yet. "As good as he may be on the floor, he's possibly even better in the lab. I told him he could be responsible for his St. Clare, but if we're to keep his course on schedule and make good use of his second rating at the same time, we need you to free up that referral block."

She chewed on her lip for a moment, drumming her fingers against the arm of the chair. She could insist on the week's referral; it would be within her rights to do so. They could—hypothetically—hold Koscuisko over, pretend he needed to be recycled for the next Term, use him that way. There were potential political problems with that approach, of course. Koscuisko was the Prince Inheritor of a very old, rather influential family in the Dolgorukij Combine, one that had family ties to the Autocrat's family itself—in the illegitimate female line, but they were there. The Autocrat's Proxy might well take an interest in why Koscuisko had been kept back, and no one was going to want to try to tell the Autocrat's Proxy that Andrej Ulexeievitch Koscuisko was a dunce.

Chaymalt shrugged, and Chonis knew he could relax. "To hell with Koscuisko. Who cares, anyway? I mean, really. Take all the lab time you want, Rorin. I won't bother the boy."

"Thank you, Ligrose." Chonis knew that Clellelan was

genuinely relieved, from the tone of his voice. "It's a prudent decision, and I appreciate your flexibility. Adifer, what about Noycannir, where do we stand?"

Noycannir would still be a challenge.

But with Koscuisko's help they'd get her through with flying colors. Then Verlaine would find out for himself why it was a mistake to send a Clerk of Court without Bench medical certification to try to learn an Inquisitor's craft.

There were four classes of drugs comprising the Controlled List, and Mergau felt as if she had tried to read them all in the past day. Four classes, each with three basic subdivisions, and a bewildering array of suggested uses and contraindications associated with each individual preparation. How did they expect her to keep them all in mind?

How could she ever hope to keep them all in mind?

Summoned to Tutor Chonis's office toward the middle of second, Mergau paused to compose herself carefully as Hanbor signaled for admittance. Koscuisko's slave was here, she noted with interest. Perhaps she'd find out what Koscuisko's role in this new paradigm was to be, since Koscuisko was obviously also with Tutor Chonis.

"Step through."

Koscuisko sat at the far side of the Tutor's long study-table, half-rising from his place to nod a polite bow in acknowledgment of her presence. There was something in his face, at the back of his pale eyes, that she found strangely familiar. What? But she had to concentrate on Tutor Chonis. Koscuisko was to be subordinate to the Tutor's course of instruction for her, according to Chonis's proposal. So Koscuisko could wait.

"I present myself in obedience to my Tutor's instruction. I hope the day has found my Tutor well." She took her place beside the beverage-set that had been arranged on her side of the table. Warmer, again, by the smell. All right, she didn't mind taking a nice drink of warmer. If Tutor Chonis felt he needed to woo her so obviously to his plan, it could only mean that she had him at a disadvantage, and she liked that.

"You'll recall the conversation we had yesterday,"

Chonis replied. "For Student Koscuisko's benefit, let me just recap briefly. You are to learn a specially tailored group of Controlled List drugs with which Student Koscuisko is to provide us. This will ensure that you can successfully carry out the functions most necessary for Secretary Verlaine— those of Inquiry and Confirmation."

She wāved the warmer jug in Koscuisko's direction to catch his eye. He looked at her only briefly, then shook his head in a gesture that declined the unspoken offer. She already knew he didn't drink warmer. Chonis always set out rhyti. She would drink rhyti when she felt there was a political point to be made by doing so. The provision of warmer, however, was a very intriguing development in terms of the balance of power.

"You have been hard at work since yesterday, studying the Controlled List. What do you remember, offhand, about a primary series drug from the speaksera class?"

She'd only skimmed the speaksera, more anxious about drugs her Patron would be most interested in—wakekeepers, pain-maintenance drugs, psychogens. Enforcers. There were many names for them, but one transcendent reality. We can keep you from sleep, we can keep you from unconsciousness, we can keep the pain from fading off its first bright agony, we can turn the unknown horrors of your own mind against you until you tell us what we want to know. A man at Verlaine's level of responsibility wouldn't want to be bothered with speaksera, surely. Why restrict oneself to such single-purpose medications when the others were so much more terrible?

"A primary series speakserum is authorized at the Preliminary Levels. And higher, of course." Still, the rationale behind the three subdivisions in each class was constant across the entire Controlled List. She could fake it. "To be employed at the Inquisitor's discretion as substitute for, or in addition to, the established Protocols. Therefore also restricted to disabling the internal editor somewhat, rather than depriving the prisoner of any freedom of choice in the matter of confession." It got easier as she continued, although she wasn't really certain whether she was remembering what she'd read or was making it up as she went along. "At the secondary level, speaksera are employed that deny any conscious selection of response, although the prisoner may still decline to speak if determined enough. At the tertiary level there is an additional element of compulsion.''

Koscuisko straightened in his seat. ''It becomes of importance to note—with the Tutor's permission,'' he said, lowering his eyes politely in Chonis's direction, ''—that the same drug may fall in primary, secondary, and tertiary levels, depending upon the species. Care must be taken to match the drug against the Level, else a mistake may potentially occur.'' A tertiary speaksera might be ''accidentally'' used in the Preliminary Levels, in other words. Mergau could tell exactly what he was getting at. If she learned the species for which a primary level speakserum was tertiary in effect, she would be clear to cheat the prisoner.

''Such errors must of course be carefully avoided.'' She didn't bother with whether or not she sounded as if she was making an effort to be sincere. Koscuisko simply lowered his eyes again and made an irritated expression with his mouth. She knew what it was that she recognized about Koscuisko, now. He had been whipped. His face was the face of a beaten man, in the presence of the one who had punished him. She felt a flush of pleasure, of gratitude toward Tutor Chonis for sharing the humbling of Andrej Koscuisko with her in this manner. And she thirsted to know how Chonis had done it, what Chonis had used for a belt. Whatever it was, she wanted one just like it for her own use.

''I am glad that we understand each other so well.'' Tutor Chonis's rather dry comment recalled her to herself; he did not sound entirely approving. She had to watch herself more carefully to avoid alienating the Tutor. But it was sweet to see her fellow Student bend his neck—his proud neck, his rich neck—to do her service in submission to the Tutor. To be below her, at her bidding, even if only in a limited sense.

Her Patron would give her people like Koscuisko, and they would kiss the ground at her feet if she bade them—and thank her for it.

''Student Koscuisko, will you brief Student Noycannir on this speakserum, please. We've scheduled a retrial at the

Fourth Level tomorrow morning after fastmeal, Student Noycannir. Proceed.''

And, oh, but she was eager for the work, for the dominion.
She was beginning to have a sense of how it really felt to
hold the knout.

Having slept less poorly than in recent days, Andrej Koscuisko woke a few eighths before time, feeling better than
he had since he'd gotten here. Yes, there would be Noycannir's Fourth Level today, and Tutor Chonis wanted him to
observe and note the effect of the drug. Yes, he was to start
work after midmeal on developing a pain-maintenance drug
benign enough in its effect to be cleared at the Intermediate
Levels. He would not be asked for nerve agents, psychogens,
or wakekeepers until Mergau had completed her Intermediate
Levels; and the wakekeepers would present interesting problems whose application to Inquiry might not be obvious
enough to be too depressing—as long as he could maintain
his concentration. There was a day yet before he had to go
to the Sixth Level; and he'd decided he had a positive use
even for that, since he needed to learn his whip. And which
whip. All in all there were to be no difficult demands today,
apart from the fact that he had combat drill scheduled before
his supper. Joslire was an excellent instructor, fearlessly in-
flexible in his demands on the exercise floor. And yet even
the workout that he faced had its pleasant aspects, because
Joslire would give him a rubdown after Joslire was finished
demonstrating his inadequacies in close-order drill—and Joslire was quite good at massage.

Life was perhaps not good, exactly.

But he felt less morose about it than he could remember,
without thinking about it too hard.

The chimer went off and Andrej reset it with a casual wave
of his hand. St. Clare would be free enough from pain to
wake sometime today. Andrej was not sure what their first
interview would be like. He could not imagine that St. Clare
would be happy to have been bound over to the man who
had tortured him, let alone so clumsily. And still he took
comfort from the simple fact that St. Clare healed aggressively and adequately, and was content.

"The officer is respectfully invited to rise at this time."
The sound of Joslire's calm, admonitory tone from the other
side of the partition made Andrej smile. It was an improvement over his old nurse, her scolding so imbedded in his
mind that he could almost hear dear Gelsa even now—*Lazy
little lords who aren't washed in time for prayers never come
to a good end,* or *If you aren't out of bed in two Sacred-art-
thous may the Holy Mother help me if your feet don't fall
right off.* Yes, it was time to get up and wash, even though
he hadn't said morning prayers—let alone evening ones—
since he'd left home. Andrej sat up, putting the cover aside,
aware of Joslire's anxious waiting presence in the room beyond.

"Thank you, Joslire. I am coming." Joslire had gotten a
little shy of him in recent days—since he had shamed the
man by looking at his scars. There seemed to be an extra
layer of distance there somewhere, though as far as Andrej
could tell, Joslire had forgiven him for his lapse. Nodding to
Joslire as he passed on the way to the washroom, Andrej
pondered the change, wondering whether there was a problem. As if there would be anything that he could hope to do
about it if there was a problem. On the other hand, Joslire
was the one who had told him that his lab space was not
monitored. Should he wait until he was in his lab to try to
tickle Joslire out of his reservation of spirit?

Andrej shut the shower stream off with an exasperated
snap. There must have been something in his supper that had
made him abnormally thickheaded about things. Of course
he couldn't tickle Joslire. He'd only humiliate the man by
trying. It would be asking too much of life—Andrej concluded, in his morning's meditations, rinsing out his
mouth—to expect to feel content about all aspects of it.

He ate his fastmeal and read his briefings, his mood of
slightly manic gaiety still on him. He was even pleased with
his uniform this morning, and his boots fit with very little
difficulty. A psychological pressure valve of sorts? he asked
himself. Some kind of an adjustment to the stresses of the
Term?

Joslire was to see him to the exercise observation area,
where he would meet Tutor Chonis. As they left quarters,

Joslire asked the same question he asked nearly every morning, in exactly the same tone as usual, at exactly the same moment as usual, as soon as the door had closed behind them in the corridor—but before Andrej had taken three steps forward.

"What suits the officer's preference for the midmeal, if the officer please?"

He simply couldn't concentrate, and he was too busy enjoying his feeling of euphoria to care. "Whichever has the darkest eyes, I think." Hearing Joslire miss a pace behind him, he slowed his step so as not to lose his guide. He'd never been to the exercise observation area. He had no idea where he was going.

"If the officer would care to elaborate, at the officer's pleasure?"

"I said dark eyes, Joslire. Dark hair, dark eyes, very exotic. Twins, perhaps." Marana had dark eyes, nearly as dark as a good cup of rhyti, with the same bronzed cast to them. He hadn't thought much about Marana since he'd been here, and it suddenly occurred to him to wonder how she was making out. Marana could take care of herself; he had always admired that about Marana. The problem being, of course, that he was not supposed to have admired anything in particular about Marana, no matter how long they had been friends, no matter that they had played together as children. Once he was married, he would be able to return to admiring Marana without fear of disapproval. Once he had bred children to his sacred wife, he could ride his favorite mare from saints to sinners; and no one would fault him except perhaps the woman he was married to, who should know better. Lise Semyonevna Ichogetrisa—the bride to whom his father had pledged him, when he'd reached the age—was no good at toleration from what Andrej had seen of her so far. He hoped she wasn't making herself unpleasant.

"Among the Emandisan, it is the officer's coloring that is exotic. If the officer permits."

Joslire sounded amused, and had clearly caught the way in which Andrej's mind was running this morning. A gratuitously offered comment. There was hope in the world.

"And tall, yes, you know? Aznir women are not tall. Nor

do they tend to assert themselves, not in an obvious manner. I tell you, Joslire, there is a peculiar fascination to women as unlike those in and of my father's Household as possible."

He was telling secrets on himself, but what harm could it do? Perhaps it would even the balance out in some obscure way. He had taken Joslire's secrets, the secrets of Joslire's scarred body, and he hadn't even asked.

If the Holy Mother was gracious, Joslire would accept this confidence as a grant of intimacy, and be healed of the shame to which Andrej had put him.

Collecting his thoughts with an effort, Andrej stepped through to the exercise observation area to subordinate his attention to his Tutor.

"You had better make up your mind to it; the Bench requires your response. What is your name?"

Student Noycannir's voice was a little muted in the observation area, and Joslire knew without looking that Lop Hanbor would click the sound levels up a notch. There was only one screen to watch today, and no real reason for him to have to watch at all, since he would not be needed to relay special insight on his Student's performance.

His Student sat with the Tutor, watching Noycannir bully her prisoner. The prisoner wasn't anybody Joslire recognized. Either a new arrival—and generally there were circumstances unusual enough to call attention to themselves when new Security were assigned mid-Term—or an actual criminal. Well, an actual un-Bonded criminal.

"M-my name?" Nurail, by the accent: the flattened vowels. He'd noticed an accent of the same sort in Robert St. Clare's speech, at any rate. "A'don't understand, you know my name, it's in the detention order—"

Noycannir struck the man across the face with the ribbed stick; not because she needed to, but because that was what the paradigm tape had shown. Joslire sensed Koscuisko shifting uneasily in his seat; and Tutor Chonis must have sensed the same thing, because Tutor Chonis followed up on it.

"Something the matter?"

"She . . ." Koscuisko gestured at the screen, at an apparent loss for the words he wanted. "It would seem the drug's working, Tutor Chonis. The prisoner speaks his mind without engaging in self-censorship. She is only delaying the process if she won't let him speak.''

"None of your insolence," Noycannir was saying smugly, with a knowing glance at the screen. Almost as if she'd heard Koscuisko's criticism. "You're to answer the question that I asked, no more, no less, no argument. Understood?"

Chonis pointed his finger at the screen, tilting his head toward Koscuisko conspiratorially. "That technique can be effectively used at the lower Levels especially. Consider that the usual strategy is to hit the man until he's ready to answer the question.''

Koscuisko nodded. "It would seem to be the point of the exercise. By your leave, Tutor Chonis.''

There were Students who simply refused to play the game; Joslire had had one. Her attitude had been that there was no sense in making any more of a mess out of a confession than strictly necessary, because there would certainly be enough of a mess as soon as confession had been Recorded. Such Students made perfectly adequate Inquisitors; but Joslire wasn't sure Koscuisko was oriented on precisely that track.

"Yes, of course, Student Koscuisko." In the exercise theater Noycannir was continuing to play through a paradigmatic exercise, but neither the Tutor nor Koscuisko was paying very much attention to her now. "Noycannir's approach is one that has demonstrated effectiveness. Not all Students can be expected to be capable of improvising." Unlike Koscuisko, whose Fourth and Fifth Levels had been clear improvisations made up of bits of several paradigms, and at least one invention of his own.

Joslire rather wished Tutor Chonis would pay more attention to Student Noycannir. She was having a great deal of fun with her prisoner, if in a different way than Koscuisko enjoyed himself. They all knew there was a speakserum in effect—one that certainly appeared to be functioning perfectly. Students who had too much fun with their prisoners frequently ruined them before time.

"She selects too hard a course, Tutor Chonis," Koscuisko protested. "Listen to him, he is quite willing to answer the right question. She could have her Evidence and be done by now.''

Tutor Chonis turned in his chair, clicking the viewer to grayscreen. ''Yes, it could be better done. Do you resent the fact that it's not your prisoner? Because there are enough to go around.''

As obvious as the question seemed to Joslire, it appeared to be the furthest thing from Koscuisko's mind. Half-rising in his seat, Koscuisko stared at Tutor Chonis with astonishment and horror. ''Tutor Chonis. I do not know what to say. Surely I have not . . . I'm not . . .''

Tutor Chonis raised an eyebrow at the vehemence of Koscuisko's response, and Koscuisko mastered himself with a fierce effort whose stern intensity was clearly communicated in his voice. ''That is to say, I ask for pardon . . . to have spoken unadvisedly. I have not been troubled by such a thing as that, Tutor Chonis. And still I cannot say I like to see the thing ill-done.''

It bothered Joslire in some obscure fashion to see his Student so anxious to conform, when he knew how ruthlessly Fleet would use that meek submissiveness. Tutor Chonis restored the visuals on-screen. Student Noycannir was crouched over her prisoner, and appeared to be taking a statement. At last. ''Your performance is all you're responsible for, Student Koscuisko.''

Robert St. Clare would be sent to *Scylla* with Koscuisko, but Robert was virgin Security yet. First assignment was usually brutal for newly commissioned Inquisitors. What Koscuisko really needed was a seasoned hand to help him over the rough spots. Robert didn't have the experience to do it.

His eyes on the viewer, assessing Noycannir's performance, Tutor Chonis almost sounded as though he was talking to himself. ''We'll let her run with this one; she's not violated the Protocols, and she is taking confession now— so you need have no further cause for concern on that head. I'll talk to her about it during debriefing.''

As a compromise it wasn't half bad. Joslire was afraid for Koscuisko's sake that he might not recognize extraordinary Administrative flexibility when he saw it—not after having taken Robert back from the whip, the irons, the twister.

"You know best, Tutor Chonis. I don't mean to overstep my bounds."

Tutor Chonis seemed pleased with the exercise, but whether it was with Noycannir's performance or Koscuisko's, Joslire couldn't tell. Chonis laid his hand on Koscuisko's shoulder to give it a friendly avuncular shake, fond and forgiving at once.

"Oh, it's nothing to worry about, Andrej. You're very much involved in the use of your formulations, we understand that. On your way to the lab now, I gather?"

Dismissed to the lab, that was to say. Koscuisko rose to his feet, a little diffidently. "I had hoped to check on St. Clare on the way to the lab. Unless the Tutor would prefer—"

Chonis waved him off. "No, no, you know best how to deal with your time, Student Koscuisko. Let me know when you're ready to return him to duty. We can have a better look at your speakserum then. You'll feel better."

Koscuisko bowed, his face empty of emotion.

What were they going to do with Robert after the speakserum trial?

Robert had been assigned to Koscuisko; Joslire was assigned to Koscuisko.

Did Chonis mean to reassign him in mid-Term?

Did Chonis mean to relieve him of his duty?

Koscuisko was waiting for him in the corridor to lead the way to Infirmary. His Student quirked an eyebrow at him, but said nothing; hastily, Joslire blanked his face of his confusion.

A man would have to be crazy to be given a chance at light duty and not jump at it.

And there was no reason under Jurisdiction why he should be jealous of Robert St. Clare.

◆ Ten

He had been waking from time to time for a while now, although he couldn't really judge how long the while had been. Someone would come in to reset a monitor, someone would test the transdermal patch that lay along his arm, someone would leave, and he would go back to sleep again.

This time it seemed a little different.

There was someone with him in the room. He guessed that simply because he was waking up. It seemed he couldn't set his wakefulness aside this time, not as as easily as he had done before. That didn't bother him; it was probably past time to get out of bed.

He lay and waited for his body to cooperate.

There didn't seem to be a great deal of pain, which was unusual, since all he could remember—since before the start of the exercise—was pain. Not a lot of pain, not a lot of pressure; and he wasn't hungry, and he wasn't cold. It was probably a mistake to want to sit up, because the odds were good that the waking world was going to be considerably less comfortable for him than this half-dreaming one. It would feel good to stretch, though, and his mouth tasted foul with an excess of sleep and a rotten taint of old blood.

Whomever it was came nearer to him now, exposing his arm to adjust the transdermal patch. No, to remove the transdermal patch, and he guessed that there had been a drug in whatever they'd been feeding him—because his mind started to sharpen almost immediately. A drug? That was right, a speakserum. The Student Interrogator—Koscuisko—had taken his secret, somehow, some way, but there was to be only a speakserum to test instead of the penalty he had incurred. The Tutor had said . . . What? Twenty-six years? And how long had he been lying in this bed to have his wounds healed to the point that he felt little discomfort from them?

Closing his eyes tightly, he nerved himself to the effort of sitting up, turning to his side to give himself some leverage. Sitting up. Yes. Sitting up, with whoever's help—and there might actually turn out to be two whoevers, from what he could gather from the count of helping hands—sitting up, and his brain fogged in immediately, and he had to give himself a moment to let his blood pressure catch up with his posture. It didn't do to try to sit up too quickly. Careful. He would be careful.

After a moment the supportive hands fell away, and he could steady himself on the bed's surface by leaning on his hands. Oddly enough, it seemed to be a stasis field, like the ones rich men slept on—or children with burns. Or people who had been whipped, he supposed, as long as they weren't bond-involuntaries. So what was he doing here?

His shoulder didn't hurt.

Setting his weight carefully over his rubbery legs he stood up very slowly, using the bed and the wall for support. His shoulder should hurt, shouldn't it? He rotated the shoulder gingerly, using his other hand for support in case he should hit a sore spot while he wasn't looking. No, it didn't hurt, and that meant that, to the very best of what little analytical ability he had, there was only one possible conclusion to be drawn.

To wit: He only thought he was Rabin with the Ice Traverse, Robert St. Clare.

There was a reflector in the room, hung above the sanitary basin in one corner. Stumbling a bit, but otherwise steady on his feet, he took himself over to look in the mirror and see whom it would turn out to be that he was. Who would have such an odd sort of delusion?

It wasn't as if being him was any fun at all. Surely it was preferable by far to be some rich man who could afford to sleep in the pressure-neutral embrace of a stasis field, who had clearly not been beaten to within an inch of his life by an up-and-coming young poisoner with a whip, who had not failed in his mission to deliver his sister from her shame.

Some kind of a pervert: that had to be it.

In his home valley, a pervert had generally been taken to be a man who preferred women to drinking, but allowances were to be made for the more subtle derangements of an alien species. Maybe he wasn't even a Nurail at all. It might be nice not to be Nurail; so many terrible things would not have had to have happened.

For a moment he didn't quite know his own face, staring into the reflector. He looked very white, and needed to scrape the hair off his chin. He was sorry to realize that he did recognize himself, though, once he'd had a chance to think about it. He was still unmistakably who he thought he was.

And the people in the room with him, the people he'd not been paying proper attention to, the people wearing darker colors than Infirmary staff?

Ducking his head as if to catch his wits, he stole a sidewise glance. Dark uniform, Security, no telling whether it was bond-involuntary or Station Security from the leg portion. Light-colored uniform, not light like Infirmary, light like Administrator Clellelan, like Tutor Chonis, like . . .

Best faced at once, if faced it must be, he reminded himself grimly. Straightening his back as best he could—his governor knew the color, and would not be argued against—he faced the problem head-on, to know the worst of it.

Koscuisko.

Student Interrogator, promising young poisoner, soon-to-be Inquisitor.

His officer.

He stared for a long moment, too confused to heed the yammering of the governor in his head. This was the man, then, and he looked a deal shorter than Robert had remembered, but the eyes were the same, and the pale voice—

"You should sit down, Mister St. Clare."

He was going to fall over, and that would be awkward, because he would knock into the officer if he did, and that would be a violation. He yielded himself up gratefully to the hands that guided him back to the bed, trying not to think about Koscuisko's hands. These hands felt different. Perhaps

Koscuisko had extra, and traded them off, fastening them to his wrists as he had need of them for various tasks?

It was good to sit; he was dizzy. He could hear Koscuisko's voice, sending the Security—Curran, that would be—out for a seat; and all the while supported by Koscuisko's hands. As long as they were the nonviolent pair, Robert supposed that he was ahead of the game.

Still, it was passing strange that his flesh didn't crawl or his stomach turn at the very smell of the man. There was a nagging sense of familiarity tied in somehow with Koscuisko's touch, as if his body thought it was the same as the touch that had soothed his aches and comforted his hurt in his dreaming half-sleep. That was the problem with medication, a man's body took up all manner of strange notions. No wonder honest Nurail stuck to drink, although where a man could hope to find a corner to distill a bit of drinkable on a Jurisdiction base escaped him quite.

"Do you know who I am?"

Joslire Curran had left the room; they were alone. St. Clare raised his head to meet the officer's curious gaze. He was too close, it made a man uncomfortable. The last time he'd seen Koscuisko so close up . . .

"The officer."

His voice didn't seem to want to work. Koscuisko passed him a tumbler full of clear liquid from the top shelf above the bed's status bar; it was cool and sweet, and didn't *taste* like poison. Robert cleared his throat and tried again.

"The officer is Student Koscuisko. A'think. Sir."

Koscuisko smiled at his confusion, but Robert didn't take offense. He was too confused to take offense. He had thought that he had regained consciousness, but all he could remember of recent events—after his torture—were too obviously fantasies of the most unbelievable sort for any man to credit.

"Even so. Do you remember who you are, come to that?"

This question he knew. He could answer this question. "Robert St. Clare. Sir. . . . As it please the officer," he added hastily, mindful of his governor. Which didn't seem to have noticed his potential lapse of military courtesy. He couldn't spare the energy to ponder on it now, however; here was Joslire with a seat for Student Koscuisko, and Koscuisko settled him gently where he sat and moved away a pace and a half to rest himself.

"Now comes the critical part, though, you will have to concentrate. Rehearse for me if you will where we first met, and what has happened in your life since then."

Oh, he didn't want to. Really he was not at all interested. He shook his head, rejecting and resisting. "Na, the officer can't be serious." Joslire Curran—who had posted himself behind the officer, per procedure—looked shocked; and that was a hint to St. Clare that there was something wrong with what he'd said. "A'mean with respect. Boring. Little that suits a story."

Joslire started speaking almost before he'd finished. "If the officer please, there must be a malfunction. Extreme stress can disable the governor. There is surely no disrespect . . ."

Joslire sounded just short of frightened, as well as disapproving. Frightened? Robert consulted the silence in his mind. Oh, yes. He was supposed to remember his etiquette, and mind his manners. And never speak of "I" or "me" or "mine" in front of officers, lest he should give offense whilst not looking.

Koscuisko made a smoothing gesture with his hand. "It's all right, Joslire. I'm not about to fault him for it. But really, St. Clare, I need to know how much you remember. So that we will know where we stand with each other."

And he was also never, ever supposed to so much as hint that any suggestion an officer made was less than sweet and sensible instruction, self-evidently logical, absolutely true and correct. Never. Well, he would try to do better; he supposed it would only be prudent of him to pretend.

"Yes, sir. No offense was meant, sir. I am—that is, this troop . . . am . . . is . . ."

Casting about for the right words, the correct lie, he found himself at a loss to complete his phrase, confused about which words were safe to use. Koscuisko smiled, and finished the thought for him.

"You are only a little bit drunk, Mister St. Clare. There is a residual euphoria, I regret that it will not persist. Never mind."

He wished Koscuisko wouldn't call him Mister. He knew his place; Megh hadn't been married, after all. He'd never tried to lay claim to the authority due a mother's brother. "Not a Warrant." He shook his head, deciding to get stubborn about it—for Megh's sake, if for no other reason. "Work for my living, Robert."

He didn't see what Koscuisko found so amusing, but Koscuisko certainly seemed to be entertained. "As you like. Do tell me, Robert, I'm due in the lab, in less than four."

As long as that was settled, he supposed he would cooperate. Frowning, he set his mind to hunt back over the past few days; with luck, he would find out what he was doing here, and why he didn't hurt.

"The officer conducted a practical exercise, an interrogation exercise. The Intermediate Levels, Four and Five." There was a little uncertainty in his mind about the wisdom of reminding Koscuisko. But Koscuisko had been calling him by his name, not by his alias. So clearly he didn't have to worry that Koscuisko didn't already know he'd been a prisoner-surrogate.

"There was a failure of duty, on . . . this troop's part. I'm not sure . . . with respect . . ."

The more he thought about it, however, the more confused he became. There had to be a problem. Didn't there? He'd not been successful, he could remember that, because he'd been taken from the exercise theater to detention. Not to Infirmary. It didn't weave.

"It isn't important, Robert. What is important is that you must test my speakserum for me, you must hold that in your mind. And also there is another unpleasant truth."

Failed in his purpose, though he did not know how. Tutor Chonis had come to see him, in his disgrace, with some beesweet in his mouth about substitution of penalties; and speaksera had been mentioned. He thought, perhaps, maybe. There had been a hearing, hadn't there?

"Something of that, if the officer pleases," he agreed, slowly, thinking hard. A hearing. His Class-Two violation hearing. It rose into his mind with the brutal force of nightmare, and behind the Administrator's voice he could hear the crackling of the fires that had burned out the high-camps, and the screaming of the animals. Of his family. What had Clellelan said?

He couldn't keep his balance anymore, the effort was too much. Turning to one side on the edge of the bed, he tried to keep his body more or less erect; but his arms would not support his weight, and he sank down to lie within the stasis field, awkwardly.

"Elects to test the officer's new speakserum, instead of . . . what was promised beforetime. And the officer will discipline a matter of insubordination. But they have reduced my Bond."

How long had he had to sleep on it, to assimilate this extraordinary change in the rules of his life? Not long enough. Staring at the ceiling, now, he was vaguely aware of being set straight on the bed once more, the transdermal patch reapplied, an injection of something pressed through at his shoulder.

"There, that's quite enough for now." Koscuisko was standing beside him, from the sound of his voice, and Koscuisko sounded gentle indeed. "There will be a day or two of therapy, and when you are returned to duty, there will be the speakserum. It will be like being more drunk, without the morning after. Sleep well."

Koscuisko, who stood beside him; Koscuisko, who had tortured the secret away from him; Koscuisko, who—as his body insisted—had salved his wounds. Koscuisko, who had a drug for him to test, but who had discipline in hand at the same time.

Koscuisko, who was to be his officer for as long as Koscuisko remained with Fleet—until the Day, perhaps, if Koscuisko should stay with Fleet for so long as that. But the Day was four years closer than it had been when they had sent him here to play at prisoner-surrogate.

What was he supposed to make of it?

He knew the answer to that one, he did, and his governor knew he knew. He was supposed to make nothing of it. He had his orders. Student Koscuisko was his officer. He was to go to sleep.

Shrugging mental shoulders at himself, at the governor in his brain, at Koscuisko's ambiguous image in his mind, Robert let himself drift away with the medication and his weariness. Sleep was a good idea. Fine. He'd go back to sleep.

With any luck he'd understand it all when next he woke.

The lab work was going well, that was a good thing. St. Clare was doing well, which was a very good thing indeed. The Sixth Level exercise wouldn't start until tomorrow morning; there was a cushion of time yet before he had to face the next trial—that was good. Life was not bad, not for this minute slice of it. It could have been residual euphoria, left over from the morning; had he really made remarks of that sort to Joslire, dark-eyed women, twins? He had to have been thinking with his fish. That was the only explanation. Sometimes a man simply woke with a brisk fish breaching from his hipwrap, half-drunk with some unfocused and erotic dream of the ocean every woman carried with her and fish that sought their source and native place.

Hearing Joslire's signal at the door to his lab space, Andrej keyed the admit. "Step through." A moment yet to shut down on the comps and launch an analysis run, and he'd be ready to go.

"The officer is expected for physical exercise: combat training drill." Yes, yes, he knew that. Not even combat drill was actually unpleasant at the heart of it, though. And since to spar with Joslire, he had to concentrate on what he was doing—if he didn't want Joslire to bounce him off the wall—it freed him from contemplating the troubles of his life.

"Coming immediately." He could come back after third-meal to see how his analysis had run. Tutor Chonis would be able to use this drug for Noycannir's Fifth Level one way or the other, but he wanted to extend its nonlethal effect to class-two hominids for his own professional satisfaction. Efficiency was a virtue, of a sort. "Just a moment, though, Joslire. I mean to ask you a question, if we are still off-monitor."

Joslire scowled at him with his eyebrows, a restrained expression Andrej had learned to read as confusion. "The officer's communications are still privileged in lab space. If the officer please."

Rising stiffly from the bench, Andrej stretched, wondering how to phrase his question to avoid giving alarm. Or to create the least amount of anxiety. All this time together, and Joslire seemed as far from relaxed in his presence as ever he had.

"You know that the Tutor has required four-and-forty of me, in consideration of St. Clare's supposed fault. And it was part of the bargain that I would punish him with my own hand."

He felt too awkward by half to be discussing this with Joslire. Surely it was in very poor taste of him. But he had to talk to somebody about it; and he knew that Joslire had ample experience upon which to base an answer to his questions.

"So much was understood, if it please the officer."

Oh, was it, really? And by whom? No, he was not going to permit himself to be distracted. He was going to cling to his good spirits while he could. All of those Security in the corridor, the other night . . .

"I want you to tell me so if you would rather not respond. But if I am to do this, I need to know the manner in which it is best done. Thou art scarred, I cannot help that. I need to know what you can tell me—how would a man prefer to be beaten, if he knew that there was no hope of getting 'round it?"

As embarrassed as he was to hear himself use a familiar form with Joslire, he could not regret it. Not when he saw how much it seemed to gratify the other man. Anything to make it easier on Joslire was a good thing, to Andrej's mind.

"There are requirements." Joslire chose his words with evident care. "Blood must be drawn, or the stroke repeated. So it is . . . easiest . . . when the officer lets blood with each stroke. It is over more quickly."

Thinking about the question, consulting his own difficult memories. Andrej stood silent, in respect for Joslire's pain.

"Then it is also easier when there is a regular pattern, one can prepare. Sometimes the officer is sympathetic, and the stroke is regular. Sometimes the officer has no skill or stomach for it, blood is not let, and then the stroke must be repeated. It is counted as good at the third stroke, though, and the next looked for—''

Joslire seemed to shudder, and fell silent.

Andrej decided that he didn't want to probe any more deeply into Joslire's wounded spirit.

''Thank you, Joslire. This is good information for me to have, and I thank you for it.'' Wanting to call Joslire back from the black moments in his past, he could afford to pass on more technical details. He could revisit the instructional material; the standard techniques addressed the issue of maximizing suffering, and surely the same information could be back-engineered in some sense to serve his purpose.

Joslire seemed to shake himself awake, and Andrej put a hand out to steady him. There was a moment, and it seemed to Andrej that it was a long one; then Joslire was recovered, taking a deep breath, bowing politely. To request the release of his arm, Andrej supposed.

''Sir. The officer would not wish to be late to his drill. It would only have to be made up for later.''

A lie, a blatant lie. Joslire knew very well that Andrej would just as soon miss combat drill and makeup drill alike. Preceding Joslire out into the hall, he started down the corridor that would lead them out of Infirmary, wondering at the unnecessary comment.

They didn't go to the room he was familiar with, however. It seemed to be in rather a different area of the Station, although there was as little traffic here as Andrej was accustomed to seeing on his way to Tutor Chonis's office. He was going to need to see Tutor Chonis to describe the drug he had created for Noycannir. After his exercise, perhaps.

The exercise area itself was somewhat more spacious, at least to judge from the changing area. Was this where Joslire had brought him to the sauna before? There was a door at one end of the changing area that looked promising in that regard. Still unfamiliar, but promising.

Changing into exercise uniform was not a difficult task; the clothing was loose and comfortable, if relatively minimal, and matsocks were much easier to get into and out of than his boots were. Joslire didn't seem to be changing, however; no, not even when he'd got Andrej's uniform folded and draped and all of the things Joslire did with his uniforms.

Andrej didn't understand.

"What is this, Joslire, are we not to dance together?"

Dance. That was what they called it at home, on Azanry. Combat drill was not unlike a young man's–dance, a challenge-dance, a test of dominance. Andrej had always liked all of the different dances, and some year he would perhaps get as good at this particular sort as Joslire was—but not without Joslire's help.

"If the officer would please step through to the exercise floor. It is considered beneficial that the officer be exposed to different combat techniques as part of the officer's instruction."

The whole thing made him rather nervous, actually, but Joslire—as usual—left him no room for protest. Well. He wouldn't know him, then, whomever his partner was to be. Perhaps Joslire was afraid that Andrej would grow complacent, having begun to learn how to dance with Joslire; and would consequently fail to generalize his knowledge and protect himself against a stranger?

"You will wait for me, I hope," he suggested. "I'm not sure I could find my way back on my own." As if he'd ever been permitted to wander about unattended. Joslire would surely see right through his transparent stratagem to the sudden case of nerves that underlaid it.

Joslire merely bowed once more, in silence. Declining— Andrej thought to himself, a trifle resentfully—to give him an opportunity to delay his exercise by responding, or pretending to respond, to Joslire's answer. There were times when he felt that he might as well be in his father's House, where at least he had some nominal clout with the servants. Joslire could be impossible. . . .

Frustrated, Andrej pushed aside the door between the changing area and the exercise floor, and stepped through.

A much larger room than he was accustomed to, yes; large, and very dimly lit, actually. The equivalent of a docking slip, perhaps, within the maintenance atmosphere? And waiting for him—not one but four Security. Five Security, one standing a little apart from the rest—the senior man, apparently, calling the detachment to make formal notice of his arrival. "Attention to the officer!"

The senior man—was a woman.

Andrej approached her detachment, anxious to understand what this exercise might entail. Two on one, three on one, well, there was an abstract sense of a sort to that—he supposed. But five on one?

He didn't have a chance.

"Thank you, Section Leader. How are we to conduct ourselves, for this practice?"

The closer he got to the five of them the more uncomfortable he felt. Tall, yes, no problem. None of them wore greensleeves, so they were all Station Security; that was unusual. Bodies lithe with muscle, he expected that. But there was going to be a problem, quite apart from the senior man's unexpected gender. Because not only was the senior man a woman, but so was the first of her detachment, and the second of her detachment, and the third of her detachment, and not to put too fine a point to it—they were all women, and all of them taller than he was.

Not only that.

As far as he could tell—Andrej realized, with a deepening horror that bode well to shade too quickly into utter panic to be braked—they all had dark hair. Dark hair, dark eyes, one of them with the glossy purple-black skin of a Sangreal lineage, and, oh, but he had a bad feeling about this.

"With the officer's indulgence. A series of warm-up drills, and then we would like to demonstrate the primary sequence of the basic combination throws."

It sounded innocent enough, surely. "Very well, shall we begin?"

It could be just a coincidence.

There was certainly no reason to let his masculine imagination run away with him, whether or not he was suddenly burdened with a rude fish cresting in his belly, where his self-respect ought to be.

If only he had not been so cheerfully flippant with Joslire just this morning. . . .

*   *   *

A man could not fault so subtly planned an assault, no, not really, not even when a man was at such a disadvantage, not even when the passive role was so unfamiliar. Andrej had to concede the superior planning and execution of the exercise ungrudgingly. Combat drill continued until he had been thoroughly warmed, and no, he wasn't nearly good enough to actually compete with his opponents, but he fancied that his performance was at least good enough to spare Joslire any unnecessary mortification on his behalf. Surely he proved that he had not been a dull Student. He could almost imagine that within a year he would be able to compete on equal terms with one of the women; competition with two at once was clearly several years out of his range in his estimation, and when they teamed three on one there was nothing for him to do but to relax and submit to instruction, and hope that he was not too distracted by the unusual environment to retain at least some part of what he had been sent in there to learn.

But then the senior of his instructors called for twilight drill; Andrej had never heard of that. The lights fell to half their original dimness or more, dim as that had been. Someone switched on a ventilator, very old, very loud, and there was no hearing oneself think in such a racket—no hope to hear what the five of them might be saying to each other, at a little distance.

Twilight drill commenced with a new series of one-on-one encounters, standard positions, unusual recoveries. The first approached head-on. He could not quite find the right balance to flip her, because she seemed to have shifted her weight to her offside foot. No matter; a useful hint of what to practice next. But it did mean that he was thrown rather than she—and thrown quite emphatically, with his assailant following up with a sliding tackle of sorts, as if to ensure that, by landing on top of him, he'd stay thrown. Most unusual, Joslire had not taught him that trick yet. But the uniforms were thin and damp with sweat, and Andrej's body was immediately convinced that it knew the trick precisely, and was eager to play the game. She pushed herself up and away from him slowly, with a caressing gesture of her hand across his face and down his throat; then she was gone, and he had to concentrate on the next step.

The second approached him with a sidekick, very sharp, very precise, but he was a match for that one, and brought her down. Joslire had taught him to regain the advantage, if brought down in such an attack, by wrapping his leg around behind his opponent's knees, and trying to get a good scissor hold to compensate for having been thrown. So it made good sense to him that, once they were both down, she would throw her leg over him, around his thighs; but the manner in which it was done, and her evident intent to press close to him rather than gain the advantage of distance, were neither of them calculated to keep a man's mind on his business. Certainly nothing Joslire had ever warned him against.

By the time the third had thrown him onto his belly and pressed herself along the length of his back to give the back of his neck a sharp wet nip in parting, the piscine portion of his masculine nature was so strongly minded to seek the ocean seas of its native origin and proper place that Andrej's head was swimming. There were too many of them, and no dealing with it either, especially not when they teamed up against him so mercilessly. Professional Security, and women all the same, their bodies hard and supple with constant combat practice—except where they were soft; respectful of his rank, respectful of his modesty—except that they seemed clearly determined to ignore his rank and disregard his modesty for unknown purposes of their own. . . .

He struggled virtuously with himself for long eighths, certain that he had misunderstood. Somehow. No matter what his fish might think.

But the women weren't having any of it.

Instead the women seemed intent on having him, and he could either struggle helplessly against them—and be efficiently immobilized, for his pains—or he could mind his manners and do as he was bidden. In a manner of speaking.

In the end Andrej surrendered to the unarguable logic of superior force, and gave himself over meekly to their calm deliberate hands. Their judicious, considered kisses. Their polite but unequivocal, if unspoken, demands, precise in conception and pleasant in execution. Their charitable forbearance of his fish's impertinence, which puffed itself up proudly to be so stroked and petted; and their generous permission to let his fish dive deep where it was certain it belonged, granting the greedy thing such new and delightful seas in which to disport itself that, in the end, it wilted of an excess of exercise and had to be returned with gentle hands to where fish were generally to be found.

He was surfeited with the sweet taste of the mouths of women, drunk with the explorations of his fish, utterly exhausted in the best of ways.

When they were done with him, they settled him on the floor and went away, and he could only hope that they had had good reward for the trouble they had taken with him; because for himself, he was unstrung, undone, scarce capable of moving.

He lay on his back in the dim, hushing roar of the ventilators, without thinking, without worry, until Joslire came to help him into the sauna.

There were two basic approaches to the process of Inquiry and Confirmation, Tutor Chonis knew. One followed necessarily from the other: one either depersonalized the prisoner in order to successfully ignore the common bond of vulnerability to pain; or one personalized the contest, turning it into an individual issue in which one specific person or prisoner was talking back to one specific individual Inquisitor. In this way, since the Inquisitor could take the predictable curses of the prisoner as personally directed, the Inquisitor could proceed with a comforting feeling of righteous indignation at being personally attacked for doing what did—after all—have to be done. In this way, Inquiry and Confirmation caused much less personal conflict.

Tutor Chonis hadn't yet decided which way Koscuisko would ultimately decide to go. In his practical exercises to date, Koscuisko had neither denied the validity of the prisoner's pain—with St. Clare, for instance—or let himself get personally exercised over St. Clare's insolence, no matter how intrigued he clearly was by the pain he inflicted. Perhaps the mocking humor Koscuisko displayed on the practice floor was Koscuisko's own personal distancing mechanism. Time would tell.

Sixth Level of the Question, Inquiry and Confirmation. Tutor Chonis sat in his place to watch Koscuisko perform. His Student looked remarkably rested, all things considered; fresh and rather full of himself—as well he might be, after what had happened to him last night. Chonis knew very well why Curran had chosen the exercise area he had, and twilight drill at that. Curran was displaying an unusual degree of sensitivity on Koscuisko's behalf, as witnessed by his care in ensuring that neither sound nor sight would uncover his Student's nakedness.

Chonis wondered if he was going to have a problem with Curran.

"Step through."

It had amused Chonis to select the bond-involuntaries who had functioned as prisoner-surrogates during Koscuisko's first three Levels to form most of the team. Koscuisko stood with his back to the prisoner's gate, drinking his rhyti; already wearing those gloves he'd picked up, Chonis noted. Koscuisko was staring at the various instruments on the table with his head cocked a little to one side, as if he were making up his mind about something.

Where to start. Which to choose. Whether he could make a break for the door, perhaps. Koscuisko continued to display profound ambivalence to the concept and practice of Inquiry which seemed only to have gotten worse once Koscuisko discovered that he liked it.

"I am Andrej Koscuisko, to whom you must answer by the Bench instruction. State your name, and the crime for which you have been arrested."

Security had fallen back to the wall at Koscuisko's gesture. The prisoner stood alone in the middle of the room, defiant and apprehensive—not as if it mattered whether the prisoner were frightened or not. The course of a Sixth Level was fairly unforgiving; and whether it would take longer or less time to execute the Protocols was entirely up to Koscuisko.

"Yes?"

There was an unmistakable note of demand, of threat, sharpening Koscuisko's voice; and from Chonis's vantage point he could see Koscuisko finally make his selection. The driver. A long, thin coiled whip, black and shiny with oil, with the snapper-end tied off into an innocuous-looking butterfly knot that could tear flesh clear through to the bone, if well handled. An interesting choice.

It took practice to handle the driver, and not do oneself an injury. Koscuisko had worked St. Clare with the handshake: less lethal a whip, less dangerous a weapon, less of a challenge.

The prisoner had still not answered, and Koscuisko seemed to grimace to himself. His voice was clear and neutral, though, showing no trace of the tension Tutor Chonis was certain that Koscuisko must be suffering.

"Gentlemen, be so good as to escort my client to the wall." Handing the driver off to the Bigelblu—Cay Federsmengdhyu, if Tutor Chonis had all the syllables right in memory—Koscuisko picked up a loosely gathered bunch of restraints in its stead.

Oh, really? Chonis thought, intrigued. *Trefold shackles?* This was interesting. A little unusual. Students were generally anxious to get right into the middle of the Protocols, get things over with. Koscuisko was making a slow start of it, but it didn't seem to be discomfort or reluctance so much as deliberation on distinct and possibly unrelated subjects.

Trefold shackles were useful, but they were considered to fall into the category of mere restraint. Koscuisko surely knew that he was expected to use far sterner measures before his exercise could be considered to be complete. Koscuisko used the restraints to bind his prisoner—a thin Chigan of middling age, barefoot, skinny—in a kneeling position facing the wall, with the loop that passed around the Chigan's throat caught tightly around ankle and wrist bonds to ensure that any deviation from correct posture would result in an unpleasantly cumulative constriction of the airway. Straightening up, now, with what might almost have been a steadying gesture of some sort on the prisoner's shoulder, Koscuisko beckoned to the Bigelblu. Chonis began to have an idea of where Koscuisko was headed with this.

"You have been referred to me on Charges to be Confirmed at the Sixth Level of Inquiry. It is yours to decline to speak. I, on the other hand, am expected to convince you to do so. Gentlemen, I require instruction, can one of you assist me in this practice?''

He was such a polite little bastard; Chonis couldn't help but smile at him. Polite, submissive, tamed—and obvious. Practicing for the discipline that he would be required to administer to St. Clare. The driver, when properly handled to avoid contact between the snapper-end and living flesh, was the fastest—most practical, even most conservative— way in which to administer two-and-twenty, three-and-thirty, four-and-forty of any of the whips from which Koscuisko would be required to chose. Had Koscuisko had words with Joslire Curran on the subject?

Chonis made a decision, keying his override. ''Please stand by, the Inquiry. Assistance to be forthcoming.''

Actually it was probably Vanot who was the best for the instruction Koscuisko was requesting. He could have Vanot on site within a matter of moments. ''Instruction to be provided at Student Koscuisko's request. You may proceed with your Inquiry as you like.''

The fact that Koscuisko might already have met the formidable Vanot would surely not interfere with his training. For one thing, Koscuisko had discipline. And for another, Curran had seen to it that the lights had been so low, the hush-noise level so high, that Chonis had been unable to identify more than one of Koscuisko's sparring partners from the night before.

Of course, he hadn't needed to recognize more than the one of them.

If the Station Provost Marshall chose to engage Student Inquisitors for her recreation, it was certainly not Tutor Chonis's place to question her about it.

Andrej wasn't quite sure whether Tutor Chonis's interruption was welcome, because it meant another few moments before he had to begin in earnest; or unwelcome, because it meant another few moments before he could begin—and he could not complete the exercise until he had begun it.

He took advantage of the temporary suspension of the exercise to recheck the trefold shackles, easing the ligature at the prisoner's throat, loosening the cord that bound the man's ankles together by as much slack as reasonably possible. He was going to practice how to use the driver; he needed a still target.

But he did not like to touch the man. The prisoner was thin and dirty and unprepossessing, and the Administration expected Andrej to do unspeakable things to that captive body. He had to separate himself from his sense of the fragility of bone and blood. If he could only manage to ignore that this Chigan felt and suffered, perhaps the thing would not come upon him again this time.

The sound of the entry-tone at secured access was a welcome distraction from his apprehensive brooding. Andrej straightened and stood away from the wall, eyeing the entrance expectantly. A Security expert sent by Tutor Chonis to provide instruction—they'd had some basic orientation, true, but it had been clear to Andrej from the moment he'd struck St. Clare the first time that there was considerably more to the successful exercise of a whip than seemed obvious.

The Security troop was Station Security, but seemed quite comfortable in theater for all that; perhaps she had been inured to her environment. "Pobbin Vanot reports at Tutor Chonis's direction," she announced to the world at large, standing in the middle of the theater. "Student Koscuisko desires coaching in the use of a . . . let me see . . . the driver, sir?"

Andrej frowned.

Wasn't there something familiar about the woman?

Hadn't he met her recently?

Of course not. That was absurd. How could he have met her, when the only contact with Station Security he'd had all Term had been that one unsanctioned formation in Infirmary?

And last night.

It was the voice of his fish in his mind, and Andrej blushed despite himself to hear it.

Of course.

He had met her last night, she was tall and dark and . . . it was better to concentrate on the problem at hand, no matter how quick his fish might be to jump to conclusions. Or jump to anything at all that reminded it of the ocean.

Andrej bowed formally to cover his confusion. "Even so, Miss Vanot. It would be a privilege to receive instruction." It had been a privilege to have received instruction from the Security team of last night's drill. Andrej put the thought away from him firmly. Fish had no sense of time or place or propriety. Fish thought only of oceans. "I have before the handshake exploited, but clumsily. This weapon seems to me much more intriguing."

The Chigan was face to the wall, and the driver had a good length to it. Separation. Andrej had good hopes that he could keep himself separate from the beast in his belly, which hungered so for agony. If only he could hold himself apart.

"Very good, sir. If the officer will permit." She took the driver from his outstretched hand and posted herself well back from the wall. *Interesting*, Andrej thought. She didn't turn to the opposite wall from the prisoner but contented herself with standing well to one side. "The officer will please attend to these basic points. The recommended beginner's stance is like so, to minimize the chances of catching the snapper at one's own back if one should fail to pull the length clear. Please note the fundamental movement, a wide arc is recommended for appropriate clearance—"

The snapper-end of the driver struck the wall of the theater with a report like that of an old-fashioned percussion-cap pistol, five spans to the right of the prisoner's head.

The Chigan's body jerked involuntarily in a spasm of startled fear. He lost his balance and fell to his side on the floor, struggling against the shackles that bound and choked him. For a moment Andrej dreaded a loss of balance on his own part; then he shut his ears to the sound of the Chigan's choked cries, and gestured Security forward. "Set this one up again, gentlemen, if you please. And see that there is a good allowance for slack around the throat." Fear could wear on a man. Perhaps it would help wear the Chigan down. He had to concentrate on learning how to manage the whip, and keep the beast at bay.

"Thank you, gentlemen, very good. Miss Vanot, if you would?" She'd moved almost too quickly, a graceful gesture swinging the long lash in a controlled arc against her target. She did it again, and the sound of the impact was like the sudden crack of a log on the fire or a flat rod striking a metal table, sharp and loud and angry. From where he stood, it almost seemed to Andrej that she had put a dimple in the wall. What would such a thing do against living flesh?

What would it not do?

The Chigan had held to his place this time, still and stiff and horribly tense where he knelt. For a moment Andrej had a thought about a blindfold. Would that not make the surprise the more unpleasant, the shock more sudden and dreadful? . . .

He knew what was happening within him, and he could hardly bear it. But he would not let himself be beguiled by it. The Chigan was dead meat, and he had to perform a Sixth Level exercise.

He did not have to enjoy it.

"Let me try this." Yes, that was right, he was not torturing a sentient being, he was only learning an odd and not very useful physical skill. He had to concentrate on that. He was learning how to practice with the driver.

He had read up on all the whips at his disposal, handshake and rake, lictor and driver, fanneram and peony; and the driver was the best one to use for discipline of the sort that the Fleet would require of him. He was decided on that. He had watched the tapes.

If he could learn the tapes to lay the lash out horizontally, and let the snapper crack in empty air, the whip would pull a narrow bloody line across a prisoner's back. More of a scrape than an actual cut, the skin would be deeply abraded but not quite torn; and although it quite obviously hurt in many ways, it could be said to do less damage.

"From the right, Miss Vanot? Certainly I will remember to keep my elbow well in, yes. Let me see."

The snapper-end of the driver hit the far wall with a dull thud, but at least he'd gotten it there. Andrej gathered the driver up into a loose coil on the floor by his foot and tried again. Straighten the lash. Swing it. A pathetic excuse for an impact, he had to try again. Better. Again. Better yet.

Again.

It was more work than he had imagined.

But after four or five more tries, he heard the same sound when the snapper-end hit the wall as a glass candle-dish made when it was allowed to burn too long, and cracked at the base of its own heat.

"The officer approximates the basic form," Vanot noted approvingly. "Several hours of practice are recommended before progressing to more detailed control techniques. May I suggest additional training to be scheduled at the officer's convenience?"

She meant for him to practice.

Oh.

On the Chigan, for example.

Well, of course, that was his excuse, wasn't it? One had to have a victim upon whom to practice, if one wished to learn how to manage a whip.

The Chigan was his, all his; and just to think of what he had seen the snapper-end do to living flesh on tape—

Disgusted him.

Sickened him to his stomach.

Oh, no, it was not so. He could take no comfort in lying to himself—it was not disgust, it was not abhorrence, that moved within him. . . .

"Thank you, Miss Vanot." He caught the coils of the driver into his hand, and bowed to his teacher. A teacher, whether subordinate Security or not, was worthy of respect; and this one was un-Bonded and would not feel discomfort at the gesture—he hoped. "I hope to prove a credit to your instruction. Till next time, then."

She returned his salute with grace and dignity. "At the officer's will and good pleasure."

He was down to it, then.

He had procrastinated; he had to begin.

"Loosen for me those shackles, gentlemen." Vanot left the theater; he was alone with his prisoner, and these Security whose sole purpose was to help him commit atrocities upon the prisoner's body. And heart, and mind, and will. "There is no profit in permitting him to strangle himself, and we have work to do."

The trefold shackles had been loosened, but the prisoner was still bound, hand and foot.

Andrej moistened his lips with the tip of his tongue in nervous anticipation, hating the eagerness that grew within him by leaps and bounds, unable to disguise his eagerness to himself even so.

He swung the whip.

It made horrific impact against the flesh of the bound man's back, splattering blood all around as it tore soft tissue and muscle alike. *Through to the bone,* Andrej thought with savage self-satisfaction, the sound of the strike—and the Chigan's cries—cutting clear through all his cherished inhibitions, clear to the core of his being.

Yes.

Through to the bone.

It was not so hard to strike the Chigan, not when he made such sounds. Andrej struck again and reveled in the music that the whip and his prisoner made for him.

It didn't matter so much after all that he was not closer to the Chigan, that he kept his distance, that he struck the prisoner with a whip and not his hand.

All that mattered was that the Chigan was his.

He could do anything he liked. Anything. Worse than any thing. He could do everything he liked, and be commended for it.

He could smell blood and fear, and he was drunk with it, all his residual reservations swamped and drowned beneath the huge black tide of his obscene pleasure in what he was to do.

For now—he would practice with the driver.

There would be enough time for questions later.

If he laid the corded lash alone across the Chigan's shoulders, it would hurt the man—but not unbearably, and by no means as intriguingly as when he buried the snapper-end in living flesh. . . .

The snapper-end, then.

Oh, it was fine.

Hours passed.

Andrej Koscuisko sat exhausted on the floor beside his

prisoner, leaning up against the wall. Security had brought
him fresh rhyti; he drank it with sated satisfaction and
stroked the trembling body at his side lazily, unable to resist
the temptation to pinch torn flesh between his fingers or put
a little pressure on splintered bone.

"Let's hear it, then. Since you've decided that you want
to talk." He had been fair to the man—in a manner of speaking. He had not hurt his prisoner to prevent him from talking,
and thus ending his sport too soon. It had simply worked out
well for him that the Chigan had not decided to confess until
after long beguiling hours of torment. "Your name. State
your name. And the crime for which you have been arrested."

It was difficult for the prisoner to speak, hoarse with
screaming. Andrej fed him some rhyti to help him along.
The Chigan coughed and swallowed, unable to press his bitten lips together firmly enough to keep spittle and blood and
rhyti from dribbling to the floor.

"Eamish. Lintoe. Your Excellency. Please."

So far so good. If Andrej remembered the prisoner's brief,
the Chigan's name was, in fact, Eamish Lintoe. Andrej gave
him some more rhyti as a reward. "The crime for which you
have been arrested. Yes? What?"

Lintoe closed his eyes in a sudden spasm of pain, but
whether it was the memory of his arrest or the particularly
painful disjoint of his elbow, Andrej wasn't sure. It didn't
matter, not really. "Ah. They said, theft. Bench property.
S-sir."

It was supposed to be "Your Excellency," but Andrej was
too well pleased with the world and himself for being a part
of it to take offense. "What did you steal, then?"

"Please, no, a transport, they said a transport, it wasn't
me, I don't know anything . . . about it. . . ."

Something about the proximity of Andrej's hand to the
gaping wound the snapper-end of the driver had torn in his
shoulder seemed to make the man nervous. "You have stolen
a transport?" Andrej prompted helpfully. "What manner of
transport?"

"A . . . grain transport." Andrej put his hand to the floor
to settle himself against the wall, and the Chigan seemed to

take it as encouragement of some sort. "It was a grain transport. From Combine stores."

Andrej waited.

"Stolen in Mercatsar, they found it empty. Displacement
camp. And we had food."

Which was clearly not what the local authorities had expected to be the case in a displacement camp for Chigan
relocation parties. It made sense to Andrej.

"What happened then?" He didn't need to torment Lintoe.
Lintoe was talking. It wasn't as though he hadn't had sufficient with which to indulge himself, these long hours gone
past.

"Wanted to know why. Who." Why they had food, and
who had brought it. Certainly. They seemed like reasonable
questions to ask, to Andrej.

"Tell me."

Lintoe shook his head from side to side weakly in denial.
"Don't know. Can't say. Didn't have anything . . . to do
with . . ."

It was a little difficult to hear the Chigan where he lay
beside Andrej on the floor. Andrej hooked one hand beneath
Lintoe's arm to raise the man's body a bit, resting the Chigan's face across his knee. Where he could look at Lintoe.
Where he could admire Lintoe's pain.

"Come, now. There must have been a reason they chose
you. Why do you imagine that you are under arrest, if you
didn't have a hand in it?"

It seemed to take a moment for Lintoe to catch his breath
after being moved. Andrej could wait. Lintoe would not dis-
appoint him, he was sure.

"Well . . . it seems . . . they said . . . genetic marker."

In the grain, perhaps. The Combine only sold certain classes of grain to Jurisdiction; the true grain, the holy grain,
remained restricted to the Holy Mother's use, for the nourishment of her children. And her children's servants, of
course: the Karshatkef, Flosayir, Sarvaw, Arakcheek, Dohan,
even Kosai Dolgorukij, if one was being exclusionary about
things—as Azanry Dolgorukij usually were.

"So they knew the grain you were in possession of had

in fact come from a stolen transport. And your part in this was?''

No answer. It seemed clear to Andrej that his prisoner was worried about how things were going, even past his own pain. Worried about how convincingly he could plead his innocence. Displacement camps had been destroyed in retaliation for petty thievery before; or dispersed, which amounted to very much the same thing.

Andrej decided to try a modified scan. ''Where is your family now?''

The Chigan groaned. ''In custody. Your Excellency. Pending my trial, but . . . they are innocent . . .''

The pain in the Chigan's voice was no less persuasive for the fact that it was clearly emotional in nature. Andrej joggled Lintoe's elbow, though, just a little bit, just to have an index of physical pain against which to measure this other sort. ''That isn't what I was told. I heard there was Free Government involved.'' He wasn't quite sure about the exact degree to which Lintoe's physical pain matched the emotional pain involved with the issue of his family; perhaps a retest was in order. Hmm. Yes. Very much more closely matched, that time.

''They said it was fair salvage, Excellency—''

''Who said?''

''There were. Two men. Infiltrated the camp. Brought it all on us . . . damn them . . . children have to eat. . . .''

Clear enough. And still though Lintoe could be said to have confessed there was a puzzle here. People had no business infiltrating displacement camps—unless it was to foment insurrection.

''You were going to tell me who it was that told you the grain transport was fair salvage.'' Fair salvage meant up for grabs. But the Bench didn't care; there were few allowances made for honest mistakes, under Jurisdiction.

''Family.'' It was a sob of anguish from the bottom of the Chigan's heart. ''We sheltered them, but how could they have brought this on their own blood?''

Chigan familial relationships were nothing to Andrej. Still, if the man had been duped into breaking the law, he had suffered for the mistake he'd made in putting his trust in a

Free Government agent. Family or no family.

"You aren't telling me what I want to know," he warned, taking the Chigan's chin into his hand to raise the man's head and make eye contact. He wanted to make sure the Chigan knew this was important. "Name for me the names. If they lied to you they must be punished."

"But how could young Canaby do such a thing?"

From the tone of the Chigan's voice he was beyond understanding just what he was saying. Or what it would mean to "young Canaby."

"His own kin. To lie to us. Endanger the children. You're no kin of mine, Alko. Alko isn't even a Chigan name. I don't care what he says about Free Government, Canaby. He's up to no good. Are you sure it's fair salvage? . . ."

Enough was enough.

Andrej beckoned for Security to help him to his feet.

"The prisoner has confessed to the misappropriation of grain transport from Combine stores. He states that the crime was committed under persuasion that the stolen vessel was fair salvage." So much was only fair, and he had been so unfair to Lintoe these hours gone past. "Further investigation may be focused on prisoner's relative Canaby, with specific reference to a companion named Alko, described in terms that indicate potential Free Government involvement. The Administration may wish to consider the prisoner absolved of intent to commit the crime for which he has been arrested in light of this evidence, Confirmed at the Sixth Level. The Record is complete."

And he was exhausted.

Joslire would come to take him to quarters.

He thought that he was going to want a drink.

◆ Eleven

"Take a moment if needed. The officer has time. There's no hurry," Joslire soothed, holding Koscuisko by the shoulders from behind. The corridor was empty, naturally. Student Koscuisko pushed himself away from the wall with a species of irritation or desperation and stumbled on.

"Are we close yet, Joslire? Before all Saints I do not wish to disgrace myself—"

"Quite close, as the officer please. Only three turnings." Koscuisko had far from disgraced himself in his exercise; Koscuisko had outdone himself, rather. Joslire knew that Tutor Chonis had not expected any real information from the Chigan, let alone the by-name identification of the Free Government agent that the Bench suspected was involved. That wasn't what worried Koscuisko now, though.

"This turning, as it please the officer. The door is . . ."

Koscuisko was ahead of him, having recognized where he was now. More or less. It was hard to get one's bearings. The corridors were deliberately designed to be as featureless and anonymous as possible. Koscuisko hurried on ahead, and luckily enough it was actually Koscuisko's quarters and not the stores room next door. Straight through to the washroom.

For Student Koscuisko's sake Joslire hoped he made it to the basin before he vomited, since that was what Koscuisko was doing now. It didn't make much difference to Joslire; Koscuisko hadn't eaten all day—too absorbed in the exercise to break for his midmeal—so it wasn't as though there would

254

be much to clean up either way. Koscuisko would be humiliated if he'd missed, though.

Koscuisko would wish to be left alone in his suffering. Joslire ordered up the officer's meal, and a good quantity of wodac as well. Starchflats and curdles, sweethins—sweethins didn't seem to go with wodac in Joslire's mind, but Student Koscuisko had a sweet tooth. Koscuisko was going to be drinking. Joslire was still experimenting with things he could get Koscuisko to eat while he was drinking.

Koscuisko was in the wet-shower longer than perhaps he needed to be. The therapeutic effect of hot running water seemed to work some of its species-wide magic; Koscuisko looked moderately refreshed when he sat down to his thirdmeal. Joslire was glad, in some obscure sense.

Students were expected to suffer in reaction to what they did. As assigned Security, Joslire had always felt it only right and proper that Students suffer for what they did, in howsoever limited a fashion. Koscuisko was different. When Koscuisko suffered Joslire hurt.

"The officer is respectfully encouraged to try some of his meal prior to availing himself of his wodac."

Naturally Joslire had suffered for Students' pain before— Students who, when they were in pain, struck out. Koscuisko had yet to strike out at him. Koscuisko seemed genuinely intent on doing his best not to strike out at Joslire as a near and convenient target. That only made it worse.

"Thank you, Joslire, as you like. You have brought arpacfowl, I see. Well done, I do like arpac-fowl." Koscuisko's voice threatened to wobble into hysteria and he shut up, reaching for a thigh portion with a trembling hand. Well, anything was better than meldloaf, as far as Joslire was concerned. But Koscuisko's dutiful address to his meal had nothing to do with any liking Koscuisko had for the food, and everything to do with Koscuisko's habitual response to Joslire as a subordinate peer of some sort. Where Koscuisko came from, authority was absolute and focused in the person of the Autocrat; and Koscuisko was one—not the Autocrat, of course, but heir to a great House and master of all within. Well-socialized young autocrats were apparently expected to cherish a keen sense of the dignity of the people who washed their linen and provided their meals.

Koscuisko treated him as though he were a man—full-grown and mature adult; in some ways Koscuisko's equal, and his ungrudgingly acknowledged superior in others, even while he respected the distance that the Bench had set between them. A feeling creature like himself, with a sense of honor and a right to self-respect, who only incidentally happened to be a bond-involuntary.

And Joslire felt helpless against the effect Koscuisko's respect had on him.

Bite by bite, portioning his food with careful precise gestures of the tableware in his trembling hands, Koscuisko forced himself to eat his thirdmeal dutifully. Joslire stood and watched and suffered for Koscuisko's anguish.

Then Koscuisko let the tableware drop to the tray, and put his head between his hands and wept.

There was nothing Joslire could do, not and respect Koscuisko's agony. He could offer no embrace. He could extend no comfort. They both knew it was only right and proper that a man suffer for having done such things to a helpless prisoner, or to any sentient being constrained and helpless.

Joslire cleared away the remnants of Koscuisko's meal, too dispirited to finish off the untouched portion of the arpac-fowl for himself. He liked arpac-fowl, too.

But Koscuisko's grief was terrible.

How could he pity Koscuisko for his grief, when he had seen Koscuisko work the Chigan?

Well, he had an appointment to see Tutor Chonis during firstshift, since Koscuisko was to be occupied in lab all day.

Maybe then he would find out the answer.

"Koscuisko's settled into workspace, then, Curran?"

Joslire Curran stood at strict attention-wait in front of Tutor Chonis's desk, reporting promptly for the meeting he'd requested. Tutor Chonis coded the secure for the office door.

"Yes, as it please the Tutor. With Sanli More assigned to see to Student Koscuisko's needs as they arise. Thank you for seeing me, sir."

It was in Chonis's best interest to see Joslire Curran, since

Curran had requested command-time. Offhand, Chonis couldn't remember Curran ever doing that before. Not even with Student Pefisct. "The least I can do, and your natural right, Curran." Of course bond-involuntaries didn't really have any rights under Jurisdiction. That was one reason why the Administration—and Security generally, even in Fleet—tried to treat them carefully. To make up. "Stand down, Curran. Administrative orders in effect. What's on your mind?"

Slowly Curran's tense body relaxed into the much less formal Administrative command-wait. Taking a deep breath, Curran sighed. "Need to ask a question, sir. Respectfully hope the Tutor won't be offended, feel compelled to emphasize importance of the truth. Sir."

Even under administrative orders, Curran avoided the personal pronoun, though it was there by implication. Curran had tremendous discipline. The business with Student Pefisct had proved that clearly enough. But right now Curran looked visibly worn. "What's the question?" Tutor Chonis prompted.

If he slid the toptray out of his desk surface, he could see the Safe. It was the only Safe on Station, and if a Tutor wanted it he had to explain to the Administrator why. Tutor Chonis had told Administrator Clellelan that Joslire Curran was coming to see him, and that Chonis thought Curran might be in distress. Clellelan had loaned him the Safe. It was as significant a mark of the respect they had for Joslire Curran as they could make.

"Sir. After last Term. Some time in Infirmary, Tutor Chonis. Peculiar emotional response to Student Koscuisko, sir. And."

The tension was all back, even if the stance was still informal. Curran chose his words with evident deliberation.

"And I. Need to know. Was my governor adjusted. Experiment on Student-Security bonding, or something. Sir."

Oh, for the aching void of limitless Space.

Tutor Chonis rose to his feet, the Safe concealed in his closed fist. "Joslire Curran." He didn't quite know what to say. "No. There was no adjustment to your governor. No such experiment is conceived or contemplated." As if the Administration wouldn't give it a go, if there were governors sophisticated enough to do the trick available. "Sit down, Mister Curran, I've got something to say to you."

It was an order; Curran was required to comply. The man was willing to listen. The governor, however, was confused, and that meant conflict. Tutor Chonis moved around behind Curran and slipped the Safe over his head, to dangle on its chain around Curran's neck.

Curran stiffened.

Safes transmitted a carefully encrypted master signal to the artificial intelligence at the heart of the governor, setting up interference within the governor itself and lulling the thing into a state of suspended function for as long as the safe was sufficiently close to the governor in question. Curran had been on Safe once, and only once, before—all volunteers for the Intermediate Level prisoner-surrogate exercise were given the opportunity to make their final decision on Safe, so that their decision could be made independent of their conditioning. As far as that went.

Chonis put his hands to Curran's shoulders to steady him. "You know how to run the callups, Curran. Check it out for yourself, if you need to. Clellelan said you were to have full shift on Safe. Because we are concerned about your welfare."

This was Curran's opportunity to tell Tutor Chonis exactly what he thought about the Administration and its concern for his welfare. The man was on Safe. The governor was in suspension. Still Curran kept shut, and Chonis grinned in pained recognition of Curran's core self-discipline. "You can stay here and I can leave. You can go to gather room. You can go there alone or we can call up some people for you. Take a moment, Joslire. Then tell me what you want to do."

Curran stood up from the table slowly, his back still to the Tutor. "I'm to be allowed the Safe for eight eights, sir?"

Full shift, yes. "That's right."

"Student Koscuisko has just gone to lab. Let me postpone it. Let me go on Safe at thirdshift."

Whatever for?

Did Curran want to say something to Koscuisko?

Did Curran want to do something to Koscuisko?

"Curran, I don't know what you have in mind—" Chonis

started to say. Curran interrupted. Chonis was shocked into silence; then he remembered. Curran was on Safe. Yes.

"I swear by holy steel that I mean neither thought nor word nor deed to the discomfort of Student Andrej Koscuisko. But if I could have the Safe and thirdshift. And never imagine I don't appreciate that you've brought it for me now, Tutor Chonis."

Joslire Curran was an Emandisan fighting man, and Emandisan knifemen recognized no rank nor respect except for their own sworn associations. By that token, and the tone of Curran's voice, Tutor Chonis knew that Curran was utterly sincere about what he'd said. It was no small thing to have a grant of gratitude from an Emandisan.

"Well. If that's what you want." Curran had sworn by holy steel, and if there was anything more sacred to an Emandisan knifeman than his five-knives, nobody under Jurisdiction knew about it. The Administrator had granted eight hours; Chonis didn't think Clellelan had said when. "I'll take the Safe back for now. It's up to you to decide when to call for it. No later than sleepshift, though, it's got to be returned before tomorrow."

Which of course implied that sleepshift was the latest that Curran could call for the Safe and still enjoy the eight full hours that Clellelan had granted. Tutor Chonis couldn't imagine that Curran would want the Safe just to go to sleep a free man for once.

"Thank you, Tutor Chonis."

Joslire Curran bent his head and lifted the Safe off and away, slowly, but with great deliberation. Determination. The man had control.

"If the Tutor please. Mean to avail self of this very significant privilege at thirdshift. Wish to express deepest appreciation for the opportunity. Sir."

Curran turned around as he spoke, but there was no reading the emotion on his face. Tutor Chonis held out his hand for the Safe, surprised and impressed that Curran had been able to bear taking it off himself.

"You're clear to go to gather room regardless, Curran. Give yourself some time to think. I'll see you at seven and fifty-six, second." Just before thirdshift, that was to say.

Curran had sworn by holy steel that he meant no harm to Andrej Koscuisko.

If he'd misjudged the man—if Joslire Curran turned on Student Koscuisko to assassinate him, for whatever obscure Emandisan reason he might have . . .

With any luck Curran would assassinate Tutor Chonis first.

Because otherwise he was never going to hear the end of it.

Joslire Curran waited outside the open door to Koscuisko's lab space for the moment to arrive. He'd never dreamed of an opportunity like this; he'd never hoped so far as to pray for it. On Safe, and going to exercise drill with Student Koscuisko, after what he had learned about Student Koscuisko during the Term . . .

Time.

Tutor Chonis said the Administrator had given him eight eights on Safe, a full shift. It was an almost unimaginable privilege; freedom from his governor—for howsoever short a period of time. For a full shift he was to be permitted to think and act like a free man.

He would have to wait until the Day for another chance like this, because the token could only be passed between free men. The Administration didn't know. Would they have denied him if they had?

"With respect, Student Koscuisko. The officer is scheduled to participate in exercise at this time."

What he could say. What he could do. Was this how Koscuisko felt in theater, when the awareness of absolute license came upon him? He didn't dare. Koscuisko could be permitted to suspect nothing.

Student Koscuisko came readily enough, tense and harried though he looked. "Lead on, Joslire," Koscuisko suggested, with a visible effort to be cheerful. "And I shall follow. From in front, which is awkward, but you manage well enough. Shall we go?"

He didn't need to wonder anymore if his governor had been adjusted in some hellish experiment to bond Security to their Students of assignment. He was on Safe. And he was determined to mark Student Koscuisko as Student Koscuisko had never been marked before, as Student Koscuisko could never be marked—save by an Emandisan. A free Emandisan knifeman. He could have grinned to himself in gleeful anticipation of what he meant to do; but someone might see.

"To the officer's left at the second turning, if the officer please. There will be a lift nexus down sixteen."

"This way is not familiar," Koscuisko warned. "Is there something I should know about this exercise? Not that I mean to object in either case."

No, Koscuisko hadn't been to this exercise area before. "For this exercise period the practice of throwing knives is to be initiated, and a suitable range is required for such exercise. The officer is to see Miss Vanot on the same range at midshift tomorrow, as the officer please. To further his mastery of the driver."

Koscuisko received this information with an enlightened nod of his head, and went silently on for the space of sixteen paces before he spoke again.

"Do you have experience of the driver, Joslire?"

From the carefully neutral note in Koscuisko's voice, Joslire could tell that Koscuisko didn't mean its active use. Passive experience. Had he ever suffered beneath the driver.

"Here is the place. To the officer's left." He had, in fact. And it had not been used with a fraction of the skill or the restraint that Koscuisko had exhibited—and against a prisoner, at that. Joslire's Student had known that he was a bond-involuntary and helpless against him when the Student had decided on two-and-twenty, and there hadn't been any time in which to notify the Tutor and hope for Student Exception to the punishment.

Koscuisko turned through the door to the changing area and Joslire followed, thinking. In light of the deception that Joslire meant to practice upon Koscuisko, a generous gesture on his part was probably called for. Koscuisko had not repeated his question, apparently determined in Koscuisko's fashion not to press the issue where he might be said to possess an unfair advantage. Koscuisko found the open shelf where Joslire had laid out his exercise uniform and started to unfasten his duty blouse, instead.

"If the officer would care to examine," Joslire said, and

took the risk of turning his back, not wanting to meet Koscuisko's eyes. It had been so difficult to do this just a few days ago, but he had been taken by surprise then. He hadn't understood. Out of his dutyblouse, out of his underblouse, and he would not need to take off his five-knives sheathing now that he had a better understanding of what Koscuisko had wanted. "The discipline was off Record, but the officer can see, if the officer pleases. Two-and-twenty."

In the silence of the changing room, he could sense Koscuisko coming up behind him, putting his hand out to Joslire's shoulder. He kept his hands quiet at his sides to avoid alarming Koscuisko, who was hypersensitive to his discomfort. The careful stroking of Koscuisko's hands upon his shoulders and his back was a guilty pleasure to Joslire, now that he was sure that he had nothing to fear from the officer's sexual appetite. There had not been enough unhurtful contact in his life since he had taken his Bond four years ago. Five years ago. Emandisan were less careful of personal space than the Jurisdiction Standard. He was hungry for a brotherly caress, hungry to starving for it.

"I do not wish to distress thee, Joslire."

He couldn't afford to let himself be distracted. "The officer will find the trace grouped at the top of the back, at the shoulders. The driver in that instance was not so well handled as the Student might wish." He couldn't answer Koscuisko's implied question directly, not and tell him the truth. The truth of it was that now he knew what Koscuisko was about, and the touch of Koscuisko's hand was pleasurable to him in a way that Koscuisko might not choose to find acceptable.

"The snapper did this to thee," Koscuisko murmured. "And yet I find no scar here from the whip itself, Joslire." Testing and trying, Koscuisko traced the impact vectors, seeking the track of the whip. Joslire could feel the muscles in his back give up their tension gratefully under Koscuisko's hand.

"As the officer may wish to note in particular. Other impacts drew blood, but not deeply enough to make a permanent mark." Which was the point, of course. And a natural lead-in to the thing that he had planned. "The officer is respectfully requested to examine the bracing on the backsheath. With the officer's indulgence, this exercise period will be concentrated on familiarization with throwing knives.''

The back-brace held the knife snug along his spine, the rounded pommel-end resting just where the first of his neck joints made a little round lump underneath the skin. If he bent his neck a fraction, she seemed to spring up to meet his fingers, sliding easily out and away into his hand no matter which hand he used. With luck, Koscuisko would not know by looking at it that the knife Joslire was wearing was not Joslire's knife, was Standard armory issue. It was a risk; Koscuisko's background had included enough of the related art of thin-blade dueling for Koscuisko to be able to guess the balance, if Joslire were to make the mistake of letting Koscuisko handle the knife he was wearing. On the other hand, thin-blades were a different kind of knife, and the other Dolgorukij Joslire had met had worn only bootknives if they wore knives at all. He would be sure to demonstrate with the knives Koscuisko would be wearing.

Koscuisko stroked the harness to the metal anchor-ring that centered on Joslire's back. ''I've never understood how a person could breathe wearing such a thing. That, or keep it from shifting. How do you manage?''

What an opening. ''If the officer will permit, the officer can test it for himself. The liberty has been taken of selecting an appropriate harness for the officer's use.'' And he'd brought it here during secondshift and secured it here with two of his own knives. The most important of his knives.

He'd had a good deal of anxiety, leaving his knives alone. But he hadn't been able to figure out any other way to do what he had in mind. And the opportunity was too tremendous and fleeting to let pass. ''Here, if it please the officer?''

Koscuisko had been half-stripped, bare to the waist. Perfect. Joslire couldn't have arranged it better had he tried. The harness went around the chest, fastening beneath the right arm since Koscuisko favored his left hand. Two straps over the shoulders held the backsheath in place. It took Joslire a moment to get it adjusted properly; there was more to Koscuisko's chest than he had estimated.

The smoothness of Koscuisko's skin and the innocuous

slope of his shoulders gave a deceptive air of lightness and even fragility to Koscuisko's compact muscular frame. He of all people should have remembered that, Joslire admonished himself. After all, he'd had his hands on Koscuisko's naked back every thirdshift after evening exercise since Koscuisko'd gotten here.

"The harness is made of parbello skin, the side next to the body left unpolished. It should follow the officer's breathing; the unpolished side will catch against the officer's skin so that it does not shift. If the officer would breathe deeply, and say whether it is adequately comfortable?"

The harness would warm to Koscuisko's skin, and cling like a part of him. Joslire watched Koscuisko test the fit, taking up the armsheath while he waited. Left armsheath, to start. Right armsheath would come next, and the bootsheath, and the decision to be made about where Koscuisko would carry the fifth knife. Later. The first step was by far the most important one.

"It feels a little odd, Joslire, but I suppose one could get used to it. And on my arm, as well? Not five at once, I hope?"

The innocent joke took Joslire's breath away. Joslire forced himself to breathe naturally and easily; if Koscuisko were to guess the trick, Koscuisko might not let him play it through. He would never have another chance like this, even if he found a Student or an officer more worthy than Koscuisko. He had to brazen it through somehow.

"Two to start, if the officer pleases. With respect, if it were to be five-knives, the officer would require significantly more skill and training than the officer possesses at the present time."

Skill and training that started here and now with the heart of the steel, the soul of his honor, the blade that watched his back. Joslire held the mother-knife apart in his hand, giving his Little Sister to Koscuisko for examination to distract him. "The officer may wish to note that the knife to be carried against the arm is noticeably different from that carried between the shoulders. This knife must slide down into the officer's grasp without slicing the officer's skin open in the process."

Koscuisko handled the knife with respect, even if he didn't know yet what it was. Koscuisko seemed to understand about steel, but didn't Joslire already know that about Koscuisko? Hadn't he jumped at this chance knowing that the hunter in the man would know the hunger in the knife, no matter how widely separated their worlds of origin?

"Oh, this is a lovely thing, Joslire. Where did you find her? She is elegant. I wonder what my father's jeweler would make of this."

"Throwing-knives are Fleet-issue, as it please the officer." Not that one, of course, though an untrained eye might easily confuse the two. If Koscuisko's family jeweler recognized it, he would have a thing to say to Koscuisko that might surprise him. Moving around to Koscuisko's back, Joslire lifted up the mother-knife in both hands. He stood here in the changing room a free man, if only for a few hours, free to elect to recognize a potential knifeman, a respected fellow fighter, a man who would not shame the soul of Emandisan steel.

Joslire invoked his gods and set the knife into the sheath at Koscuisko's back with reverence and deep humility, hoping with all his heart that his petition would be accepted. Koscuisko was not Emandisan. But Koscuisko had the soul of a war-leader. A war-leader had a natural right to Emandisan steel, and the Administration had given Joslire this one chance to free his five-knives from the disgrace of his slavery by making them over, in proper if unspoken form, to a man he deemed fit to wear the soul of an Emandisan.

Koscuisko reached up over his shoulder to find the pommel with his fingertips, first with his left hand, then with his right. "One hardly feels the weight, Joslire. There is no danger of losing the blade, in practice?"

Joslire had to give himself a moment before he answered. She sat so comfortably at Koscuisko's back, springing swiftly into Koscuisko's hand. Surely she had honored his plea and gone willingly to Koscuisko to be his knife.

"The sheathing itself will hold the knife, as the officer will have an opportunity to test for himself. It will only release when the officer reaches for it. If the officer cares to sheath the other knife and finish changing, the exercise can begin.''

Perhaps it was true that, as Koscuisko said, the physical weight of the mother-knife was hardly noticeable.

But in fact it was the weight of Joslire's self and Joslire's soul, the honor of his discipline that could not be diminished even by enslavement that Koscuisko carried snug against his skin to watch his back and guard him.

If Fleet and the officer permitted, perhaps Joslire would follow his knives when Koscuisko went to *Scylla.* It didn't matter as much anymore if he lived out his term to see the Day; they had given him what he needed, time on Safe to see his five-knives out of slavery. His five-knives were free.

As empty and as lost as Joslire felt without them it was worth it, more than worth it, more great a gift than he had ever hoped for to see his five-knives escaped into the hands of a man who knew instinctively how to honor them.

He could have given the knives to Koscuisko at any time, that was true enough.

But the knives were proud, and would not have listened to the voice of an enslaved man when he bid them take Koscuisko for their own.

Now he could die without shame.

And maybe some day he would be able to explain to Koscuisko exactly what it was that he'd just done to him.

She had finished her Fifth Level, she had finished her Sixth Level, and she had survived. With the help of Koscuisko's drugs, she'd surmounted the obstacles in her path; and Koscuisko was humbled before her, to be servant to her purpose. She almost could forgive Koscuisko for his money, for his rank, for the stink of pride and privilege that he carried with him like a sensor-net. Almost.

"Tutor Chonis, I am sorry I am late." Koscuisko's signal came tardy at the door; he was behind the time, and could be sneered at for it if she chose. He was her subordinate, in a sense. She expected punctuality from subordinates. "It is my fault, I hope I have not delayed our meeting long."

Flushed in the face and sharp of eye, Koscuisko had just come from exercise. That was no excuse.

"Well, not too long." Their Tutor would not reprimand Koscuisko; their Tutor didn't need to. Koscuisko had not forgotten that he had been punished to obedience, no matter how bright the serpent-spark in his cold eyes. Mergau knew how to see the fear, regardless of how well it was covered over by the habit of Koscuisko's mind. "Curran is teaching knives, I understand? Quite a unique opportunity. Do you know, this is the first time he has ever offered?"

Pausing as he reached for the beverage jug, Koscuisko seemed a little taken aback. Chonis had set rhyti out today, but Mergau could be charitable. As long as Koscuisko continued to make such wonderful drugs, he could drink all the rhyti he could stomach, and be welcome to it.

"No? I am surprised. It seems so obvious an advantage to have Joslire to instruct. They are beautiful knives, Tutor Chonis. With respect, I think I am in love."

It was understandable that one could cherish a weapon. She had cherished weapons, when she had been in a position to be able to use them. But Koscuisko's enthusiasm seemed a bit intense, for all that Tutor Chonis took it in stride.

"Well, that's all to the good, then. Mind you don't let this new love take you away from the laboratory, however."

Chonis's tone was too mild and affectionate to carry any sting. Mergau was curious about this passion of Koscuisko's— curious almost without malice.

"And may one see these objects, Student Koscuisko? I have had knives myself, once of a time."

Almost she could feel affection for him because of his good service. He answered her without contempt, as if he were pretending not to notice all of the things that were so different between them.

"I am sorry, Joslire has confiscated them from me. So to prevent too soon an amorous surfeit, I imagine. Here is a slug he has provided, so that I may become accustomed to the weight."

He had a long blunt sliver of metal in his hand, and she couldn't see where he had drawn it from. The practice came naturally to him, it seemed; but she was surprised he didn't realize why his slave couldn't possibly permit Koscuisko to go armed between his exercises. The Administration didn't like to take chances with Students, not until they were safely out of the Administration's area of responsibility.

"Very well." Tutor Chonis's raised hand called the conversation back to order. "Let us be done for the moment with Student Koscuisko's love life. The Intermediate Levels are behind us, and it is time to consider those Advanced Levels required in preparation for the Tenth Level graduation test."

She didn't really care about the Advanced Levels, or the Tenth Level test. She didn't need to worry about violating the Protocols at the Advanced Levels. The drugs Koscuisko gave were proof against failure. It didn't matter if she let them die.

"Student Koscuisko, the Administration is very pleased with your work, both in the theater and in the lab. Incidentally, the additional trial for your original speaksera has been scheduled for four-and-thirty-two this secondshift."

Koscuisko bowed his head. "I haven't forgotten, no, Tutor Chonis. Where is the test to be held, with the Tutor's permission?"

"Curran will show you to your usual exercise theater. Now, Student Noycannir, we must report to Secretary Verlaine. An uplink has been scheduled for tomorrow at four on second. This only gives us a few hours to review the Administrator's comments."

Of course the Advanced Levels would matter when she returned to Chilleau Judiciary. The Advanced Levels would perhaps matter most of all, and she would not have Koscuisko at her disposal then to provide her with the drugs that made it work. A problem, perhaps, because Koscuisko had quite clearly indicated that nothing he had come up with so far could be used safely against all of her Patron's enemies. Even the speaksera had limitations. The one she had used in her Sixth Level had done perfectly well for the Sascevon prisoner, but Koscuisko said it was quick poison for any class-one or class-six hominid.

"Are we to review now, Tutor Chonis?" She was a little uncomfortable asking; she knew she didn't want to be reviewed in Koscuisko's presence. But the Tutor hadn't set the study schedule for the Advanced Levels. Perhaps there would be time.

"First things first, please, Student Noycannir." And she'd left herself open to rebuke, having asked without being bidden. The Tutor knew how she felt about having her insufficiencies discussed in public. Or even in front of Koscuisko. "First it is required of me to give formal notice that you have both been passed at the Levels to date. Student Koscuisko, there is an issue with your use of the driver; not an immediate one, but one that needs to be brought before you."

And if Chonis would criticize Koscuisko in her presence, she knew he would expose her failings in front of Koscuisko. They both knew she might not have gotten this far without Koscuisko's help. What would she do when she could no longer demand Koscuisko's services?

"Yes, Tutor Chonis?"

From Koscuisko's voice there was a hidden message there that was not to be made available to her. She wondered what it might be. Koscuisko sounded a little fearful, to her ear; had it something to do with the belt, perhaps—the one Chonis had used to humble Koscuisko so completely?

"The Administrator only applauds your desire to learn the driver, and your quite obvious aptitude for it. I have been asked to clarify a minor point."

She didn't like the driver. She'd tried it, but she had been so clumsy that she had hurt herself worse than her prisoner. The driver was an ugly thing. She had known people to die from it.

Chonis was picking his words out carefully, now, as if he were speaking in some kind of code. "As you know, any of the Intermediate Level instruments may be lawfully employed for two-and-twenty as you see fit. You may wish to keep in mind that at a more advanced disciplinary level— oh, four-and-forty, for example—because of the driver's unique characteristics, the disciplinary expectation is for the snapper to be allowed to impact as well as the stock. Otherwise the discipline is not considered sufficiently serious to address the Charges."

Quite a long speech, and the bright, blissful gleam had

dropped out of Koscuisko's eyes well before Tutor Chonis had finished. Had he been required to deliver discipline, perhaps? Was he to be required to deliver discipline? What could his slave have done that merited four-and-forty?

"The point is well taken, Tutor Chonis. That I may not cheat the Fleet of discipline, can the Tutor provide some ratio guidance, perhaps?"

Maybe this was the whip that had made Koscuisko so manageable, if Curran had offended. Koscuisko did not seem to be capable of maintaining good order amongst his subordinate Security. She had too often seen him fail to admonish Curran as they left the Tutor's office together.

"If you wish to be conservative in discipline, the driver is an excellent choice. But one is expected to deliver a taste of real punishment—perhaps every eight. A good hit every eight. Note this information for your use, if you will."

Whatever it was, Koscuisko didn't like it. He wasn't fit for Fleet duty, Mergau realized suddenly. Not if he shrank from discipline.

"Thank you, Tutor Chonis, I am grateful for your guidance."

But if he wasn't fit for Fleet duty, where could he be fully utilized? Where could his skill in mixing the drugs for her be effectively exploited—unless he went with her, to support her for the duration of his term of service?

"Yes, Student Koscuisko. I understand." Then Chonis brought her into the conversation once again, with an inclusive gesture. "Enough of that. Do you have any questions about the Intermediate Levels? Student Noycannir?"

In fact he would serve Chilleau Judiciary well, if First Secretary Verlaine could be made to see how useful such a talent could prove in the long run. Verlaine would find a way to hold Koscuisko back from Fleet, if Verlaine felt Koscuisko could be useful. She was certain that Verlaine could get Koscuisko on his staff, under her direction. If only she could let him know why such an arrangement was to his best interest . . .

"Very well. Your first exercise at the Advanced Levels is scheduled for eight days' time, and we have a good deal of material to cover before then. Student Koscuisko, you may be excused to your lab. Don't forget your appointment. Student Noycannir, stay as you are, and we will talk about the report we are to make to Secretary Verlaine."

They would have to report to Verlaine about the drugs. She would have a natural opportunity to raise the issue then, especially if the Tutor didn't anticipate her comments ahead of time.

Rising to his feet, Koscuisko bowed to the Tutor and left the room. If he was under her, he would have to yield to her superior position in the rank-structure; she really rather enjoyed that idea. If she could not seriously wish to have him for her prisoner, she could at least have him for her subordinate; that could be considered to be equivalent, in a sense.

"Now, Student Noycannir. Let's you and I talk about this, shall we?"

Definitely she would have to suggest to Verlaine that Koscuisko be posted to produce more drugs rather than being allowed to go free. Or to Fleet.

And definitely she would not talk to Tutor Chonis about the plan. Let him not find out until Verlaine heard what she suggested.

Let her Tutor understand that she could find a way to rule his preference, howsoever indirectly, as surely as he had found a way to rule Student Koscuisko.

He couldn't help but be a little anxious, but Andrej didn't want it to show. For one, he was the most junior officer present, and was clearly not expected to call any attention to himself. For another, it might be misinterpreted as a lack of confidence. However he felt about other issues, he knew that he was more than merely adequate in the lab.

"Your name?"

He stood behind the seated evaluators, facing St. Clare and the flanking escort behind him. Released from Infirmary to custody; to be released from custody—when?

"M'name is Rabin, from Marleborne. But my mother's people hold the Ice-Traverse weave."

Robert St. Clare, if the officer please. Tutor Chonis had gone over the first response set with Andrej before the evaluation panel had been formally seated. It was a simple set of questions; the first set of responses conformed to the Jurisdiction Standard for a bond-involuntary. Now Tutor Chonis would ask the questions again, and the panel would judge whether the speakserum did its job.

"You will declare your Bond."

Sir. For weighty offenses committed without adequate extenuating circumstance I have been justly condemned by the solemn adjudication of the Jurisdiction's Bench. According to the provisions of Fleet Penal Consideration number eighty-three, subheading twenty, article nine, my life belongs to the Jurisdiction's Bench, which has deeded it to the Fleet for thirty years.

"I'll not, it's none of it true except the prisoning part. You know damned well it was just Simmer treachery, bastard of a Jurisdiction butcher . . ."

St. Clare looked surprised to hear himself use such language, and cut it off with an evident effort. So far, so good. Ordinarily St. Clare's clear sense of consequences would have prevented him from using such confrontational language.

There were two points to be made in this trial: one was that the speakserum overrode internal edits, thereby gaining access to truths a man would otherwise rather conceal. And the other was that it felt so natural and right for St. Clare to speak his incautious and uncensored truth that his governor saw nothing wrong with what almost amounted to treason.

"State your chain of Command, as here present."

Sir. The officer of assignment is Student Koscuisko. Student Koscuisko's immediate superior is Tutor Chonis. The Station Provost is Marshall Journis, Administrator Clellelan represents the Bench authority. Sir.

Doctor Chaymalt was here as well, but it was Marshall Journis that had given Andrej the worst start. Why had he assumed that Joslire's hunting party had been of Joslire's general rank? It had been ego, plain and simple, to have assumed that Joslire had somehow come up with recreation for him, instead of realizing the quite obvious fact that he'd been recreation for persons unknown. Granted, he hadn't been thinking clearly at the time, but why hadn't he realized that the senior man had worn her authority with significantly more conviction than any five given Warrants taken together? And no, he didn't need any opinions from his fish.

Still, she'd given no sign of recognition, for which Andrej was deeply grateful.

"There's the Marshall, don't know anything about her, but the name. There's the Tutor, I had a cousin once with a beard like that, died of a surfeit of rolled-meal and drinkable podge. Tutor's a decent sort from what little a dog like me would know, and Clellelan the like. It's about yon undertall beauty that I'm not sure, Koscuisko, and what kind of an ignorant accent is it? I mean to ask."

Any sign of discomfort or reticence had passed away from St. Clare's easy—flamboyantly disrespectful—speech. Well, perhaps not too disrespectful of the senior people here, the panel members who were to pass his drug or fail it. Andrej was quite certain that for himself he didn't care to be called an undertall beauty of any sort. And it was St. Clare who had an accent, flat and nasal.

But that only meant that the speakserum was doing its work a little too well for his personal sense of propriety, and that was all to the good. Under the influence of the speakserum, St. Clare clearly felt so comfortable making off-the-cuff judgments about his chain of command that his governor found no actionable offense in it. Any speakserum that could turn a bond-involuntary's conditioning off as thoroughly as that would do the same or worse to ordinary prisoners, and was a genuine find for the Controlled List—as he had promised.

The panel—the Administrator, the Provost Marshall, Doctor Chaymalt—seemed to come to much the same conclusion, if Andrej read their body-language correctly from behind. Tutor Chonis raised an amused eyebrow in Andrej's direction, but Andrej could suffer Chonis's amusement easily—as long as Marshall Journis did not turn around.

"Thank you, Robert, if we can confine ourselves to the issues before us—"

"But I can tell you that I don't care for your damned cheek, Tutor or no. You'd think a man had no right to his own name, the way you throw it about."

St. Clare was starting to sound a little drunk, a little bel-

ligerent. The internal censors were clearly eroding quickly.
If St. Clare didn't like his name used casually, why had he
made such a point of being called by his name when Andrej
had first spoken with him in Infirmary? Had St. Clare granted
the use of his personal name to him, Andrej? Or had St. Clare
merely objected to being called "Mister"?

"That's fine, St. Clare." Chonis's voice was patient and
soothing, even though he'd been rather rudely interrupted.
"This is the last one, now. Please state your duty assignment."

*Sir. My duty is to serve and to protect according to the
requirements of my Bond. My honor is to die in defense of
my officer of assignment. It is just and judicious that it should
be so, as I hope for the Day. Sir.*

Nobody expected bond-involuntaries to like what had happened to them; no one demanded that they lie about the fact
that their life was a sentence of penal servitude. Their conditioning—constantly reinforced by the governor—was in
place to keep them from compromising themselves, among
other things. For the rest, a series of abstract impersonal formulae had been created for them to use for their protection,
and those formulae had been duly rehearsed and placed on
Record during Robert's first responses to the questions he'd
been asked.

It was a hard test, a brutal conflict between self-
preservation and the censorship of the governor on one side;
the speakserum—and deeply held, if unacknowledged,
conviction—on the other. St. Clare shook his head as if to
clear it of a confusion of some sort, all but physically staggering as he struggled with the question.

"It wouldn't matter but for my sweet sister, don't you
see?"

The governor was disabled, silent, nonfunctional. Or at
least there was no telling from his words that St. Clare even
had a governor. St. Clare spoke with passion from his heart,
and Andrej remembered what St. Clare had said at the end
of the Fifth Level exercise. *For Megh. Halfway, halfway,
halfway through.*

"It's Fleet murdered my family, and Fleet that's locked
my life away, but a man can understand that, after all. Be-

cause we never looked for fair dealing, not from Jurisdiction, and I can't complain—not for myself—I've not been so mistreated, not more than any other.''

Remarkable. St. Clare meant it, every word of it, as if he'd made his mind up not to rage against the bitter fate that had befallen him, taking what he found on its own terms. It was an heroic act to choose to live thus without bitterness. How had St. Clare come to such wisdom, young as he was?

"But what you've done to my poor sister, I cannot forgive it. I will not forgive it. You could have killed her just instead of that. It's as black a crime as was ever done, and the Maker requite you for it.''

How could there not be bitterness in St. Clare? How could he submit himself to curses and abuse, and not grieve for himself, but only for his sister? Perhaps he set his own grief onto hers, and saved himself the extra suffering that way. Perhaps.

After a moment the Administrator spoke. "The drug certainly seems persuasive enough. Doctor Chaymalt, your evaluation?''

Tutor Chonis made a signal with his hand, and the Security escort came up to take St. Clare from the room. To a recovery area, Chonis had assured him, for long enough to be sure that the speakserum would metabolize before St. Clare had to talk to anybody with rank.

"We'll take his report once he's recovered himself a bit, of course. But I think it's safe to say that Koscuisko's serum does what Koscuisko said it would.''

Well, of course it did, Andrej thought. Hadn't he staked St. Clare's very life on it?

"Marshall Journis, your opinion, please.''

The Marshall rose to her feet, stretching a bit. Andrej decided to look at something else for a moment or two, just to be safe. "Either it's a valid speakserum or that governor needs to be returned as defective, Rorin. And his governor was working fine when he got here. I'd say you've got a solid candidate, there.''

Controlled List drugs were not released on field trial alone, whether or not they were building an ad hoc list for Noycannir on that basis. The serum would have to go forward to Fleet's central research facility, where the ultimate decision as to its utility would be made. That was hardly the point.

"Thank you, Marshall, Doctor. In my professional judgment, endorsed by qualified subject area experts, the trial has been a true and successful one. Thank you for your time."

The point was that he'd promised speaksera, and they'd given him St. Clare based on that promise—and the follow-on research he had pledged at the same time. And until the medium of exchange had been officially recognized as good coin, the contract was still potentially in question. They would not take St. Clare away from him now.

What had St. Clare called him? "Yon undertall beauty"?

Was he sure that he wanted St. Clare for his own, after that?

Andrej bowed respectfully as the panel members left the room, Doctor Chaymalt, Marshall Journis, Administrator Clellelan. There was no sense in second-guessing. And not as if St. Clare would use such language when not under the influence, whether or not he was thinking it.

"Come along, Student Koscuisko." Tutor Chonis put an end to his prickly brooding, laying his arm around Andrej's shoulders genially. "That went very well, don't you think? Let's go and have a glass of rhyti. We can talk about Noycannir's Seventh Level."

Not a promising start for a relationship, no.

But better than the alternative.

And the devil take his vanity, and rejoice in it.

◆ **Twelve**

It was dark and quiet in the rackroom, empty but for Robert St. Clare and Joslire himself. Joslire eyed the half-drunk Nurail skeptically, listening to the steady stream of recriminations without paying much attention to his actual words.

"Oh, fine, you empty-headed bottom-dweller, you goat-stuffer, you. That's just the thing. Yes, call him names, why don't you. He's just to be your maister for the rest of your disgusting life. . . ."

Robert sat slumped on a leveled sleep-rack with his head in his hands, swearing at himself. Tutor Chonis had taken Student Koscuisko off; Joslire was free for a few hours, and Robert needed watching. The Student's speakserum had clearly left Robert vulnerable—to himself, if to no one else. Robert was to go with Student Koscuisko when he left. Joslire was curious about what manner of man the Nurail for whom his Student had paid such coin actually was.

"Be easy, man." Pulling a rack level from the wall facing Robert, Joslire sat down. Robert knew that he was here, of course. But Robert wasn't paying any attention to him.

"Yes, there's a good start, there's a lucky beginning, it's a wonder if he has aught to do with you after all—and then where will you be, you wool-witted—"

"Be easy, I said." Joslire didn't care for the direction Robert seemed to be headed. There was no reason for him to feel so insecure. Koscuisko couldn't help but value the man in proportion to what he had paid for him. "You'll be going with Student Koscuisko when he's graduated, you don't need to worry about it. How do you feel?''

"How do I feel, he asks, as if there should be a question. I feel like a total waste of a kiss, is what I feel like, a used handful of scrapebloom, did you hear what I said to those people? And what is the officer going to think of me after the performance I just gave, what do you think?''

He'd successfully distracted Robert, so much was obvious. Less obvious was what he could say next to get out of having to answer for Student Koscuisko, when he couldn't be as certain as he would be sure to sound.

"It doesn't matter what Student Koscuisko thinks.'' Well, yes, it did. If he had been in Robert's place, it would matter very much to him. "You've proved the test, that's all that matters. You haven't answered my question, Robert.''

Now it was Robert's turn to lean back and rest his head against the wall. "I don't care whether I do or not; I'm not under obligation to you, am I? I feel sick to my stomach. I feel very embarrassed at myself. I feel very worried about Student Koscuisko.''

They had that much in common, then, Joslire thought. Except of course that it didn't do him any good to be anxious, because Koscuisko would no longer be his business once Koscuisko graduated. "The nausea will pass, they tell me. Do you want something to eat?''

Shaking his head with his eyes closed, Robert reminded Joslire suddenly of a young flyfetcher, still immature for all its adult size. All bright eyes and enthusiasm. Very little brain. "Na, but to drink would be nice. Except not for the likes of us. Do we ever drink, Curran?''

Joslire thought he heard a subtle alteration in Robert's words; a lightening of tone, a lessening of urgency, an increasingly careful choice of phrase. Perhaps the serum was truly beginning to wear off.

"Those who want to, yes, when leave is given.'' He'd never thought it helped any, himself. When the dutyshift came up a man was still a slave, after all. Joslire preferred just to be left alone.

"Tell me something.'' An idea occurred to St. Clare now, it seemed, and Joslire didn't think it had to do with drinking.

"They won't talk to me, Curran, but a man needs to know. How did it happen? Can you tell? I feel ashamed to look at you."

He hadn't been mistaken about the speakserum wearing off; he could hear the self-control in Robert's voice. And still Robert had asked the painful question. Joslire admired the boy's courage. "It wasn't anything you did. Or didn't do. I'm sure of only so much."

There was no question in his mind about what the Nurail was asking. After all, it was the same question that Tutor Chonis had been trying to find an answer for since it had happened.

"A man feels worthless. After that," Robert admitted with terrible candor. Joslire knew exactly what Robert was saying; he'd felt the same, and his exercise had gone off without hitches. He'd never put it into words, was all. "They told me that Student Koscuisko pledged for me, else I'd have been put to it. I feel so useless, Curran. I don't understand at all."

The speakserum could still be affecting him, yes, that was true. The questions he raised were no less pertinent for that. "He doesn't feel you failed." Joslire offered the opinion carefully. "Not from anything I've heard or seen from him. It was just bad luck that betrayed you, nothing more. I said more to my Student Interrogator than you did, Robert, but I was safe, because mine wasn't Koscuisko."

He'd said it to Koscuisko, he'd said it to himself. Only now—as he said it to Robert—did Joslire really understand how true the statement was.

"I'm afraid of him. Student Koscuisko." Careful discipline was clear in Robert's face, in his tone of voice. And still he persisted in laying himself open. Perhaps—Joslire told himself—Robert had decided that he could be trusted. He hoped that wasn't it. He didn't particularly want Robert's confidence. "You can tell me if I'm being stupid, friend. It would be a kindness of you, really."

"Well, all I can tell you is that he's never laid a hand on me." Fear was a reasonable response to Student Koscuisko, especially from Robert's point of view. "The other Students I've seen turn like that in exercise have done the same to us

as to their prisoners, more or less.'' As if Robert should
believe him, when he'd been so wrong about it before, when
he'd tried to reassure the young Nurail with the claim—
proved false so quickly—that Student Koscuisko was a fair-
minded man. How could he expect to have any kind of credibility, when he knew so little of what really went on in
Koscuisko's head? "I'd be afraid of him myself, if I was
going. But not because I was afraid of what he might do to
me. Not that.''

The more he talked the less sense he made. Wasn't that a
problem?

Robert stretched, yawning. "I'm stiff as an iced fleece.''
Whatever that was supposed to mean. "Are we allowed to
go to exercise, Curran? I've been idle for too long. I'll be of
no use to anyone unless I get some practice in soon. That,
what's it called, that physical therapy, it can't have done me
any good. Didn't hurt nearly enough, for that.''

Six hours in isolation, Tutor Chonis had said; but there
hadn't been any other restrictions, and the speakserum hadn't
been expected to create any physical impairment. Joslire
didn't see why he shouldn't exercise with Robert. There was
an exercise area within the quarantine block, after all. And
Robert had apparently worked his way past feeling useless
to feeling merely less useful in the absence of recent training,
which was a trend in the right direction.

"Let's go, then," Joslire agreed, rising. "You'll be wanting to know how Koscuisko fights. He's an interesting partner because of the left-dominance, you'll see.''

You'll enjoy the challenge, he wanted to say. He enjoyed
the challenge, because Koscuisko was teachable, because
Koscuisko had the instinct of a hunter in his body, quite apart
from the behavior of his conscious self. But Robert might
not ever train with Koscuisko once they got to *Scylla*. In fact
once they left this station, there was no reason why Koscuisko should train at all, absent an order from his commanding officer.

Still, the more he worked with Robert, the better he'd
know him, and the better he could report on Robert's recovery to Student Koscuisko. And if he could reassure himself

about the Nurail's potential as a Security troop, maybe he wouldn't mind not going with them quite so much.

Mergau sat tense at the Tutor's table, trying to keep clear in her mind what she was doing. Uplink made it easier to concentrate; there were no faces, no voices. There were only the words scrolling slowly across the screen, carried on maximum power relay all the way from Chilleau Judiciary.

STAND BY FOR THE FIRST SECRETARY. IDENTIFICATION RECEIVED AND CONFIRMED. SECRETARY VERLAINE IS ON THE CHANNEL, YOU MAY GO AHEAD.

The words came clumped in awkward phrases, according to the quanta required to carry them. Tutor Chonis spoke slowly to avoid overburdening the voice verification/transmission series.

"Tutor Chonis, for Administrator Clellelan. Fleet Orientation Station Medical. And?"

She was grateful that it had to be spoken aloud. She didn't have to worry about hidden information.

"Student Mergau Noycannir. Clerk of Court."

RIGHT TRUSTY AND WELL BELOVED, I GREET YOU WELL. Verlaine's habitual formula gave her face in front of Tutor Chonis, emphasizing her formal position at Chilleau Judiciary. I GREET ALSO THE ESTIMABLE ADIFER CHONIS, AND WOULD HAVE HIM CARRY MY GREETING TO THE ADMINISTRATOR, IF HE WOULD OBLIGE ME.

"At your request, First Secretary." Chonis would never presume to call Verlaine by name in direct discourse. "Status report on the progress of the Term, with particular reference to Noycannir, Clerk of Court, Chilleau Judiciary. The better part of the Term is completed."

Verlaine would have seen the first reports by now. He would have words of praise for her. Praise from the First Secretary meant power at Chilleau Judiciary. She wanted all she could get.

THE INTERMEDIATE LEVELS ARE MORE TECHNICALLY CHALLENGING, AS I UNDERSTAND. I TRUST YOU HAVE BEEN ABLE TO PROVIDE MY CLERK WITH ADEQUATE SUPPORT.

Else Verlaine would hold it against the Tutor's account, and not hers. That was the implication. It wasn't true, of course; he would be displeased with her if she should fail. But that was their private matter. In front of others, he would show only his trust and confidence in her, until she made a mistake.

"Indeed, First Secretary. They are more technically challenging, and the medical issues become more critical to success. We have been able to document Noycannir's mastery of the Protocols, and her successful performance at each Level so far. She has been passed to the Advanced Levels. Administrator Clellelan has every confidence in her ability."

Surely Verlaine would wonder at that, since it so clearly spoke of full surrender. And Fleet had fought him every step of the way in this matter of the Writ. Fleet would not want to lose Koscuisko to the Bench; Fleet would want Koscuisko for themselves—Koscuisko, and his skill, and his drugs. Especially his drugs.

I'M GRATEFUL FOR ADMINISTRATOR CLELLELAN'S CONFIDENCE, BUT CAN'T HELP WONDERING HOW HE CAN BE SURE. WE ALL KNOW THAT THERE IS A FAILURE RATE OF ONE IN SIX DURING THE ADVANCED LEVELS.

Well, no, she hadn't known that. Perhaps Koscuisko would fail and be sent home in disgrace. Or else exiled to serve his duty time as the medical officer of one of the prisons, where it wouldn't matter if he had no taste or tolerance for pain. Fleet didn't care how many of the Bench's prisoners died of neglect and lack of medication in prison. Except that she had no information that hinted that Koscuisko was at risk to fail in anything.

"Based on her performance thus far, we don't anticipate any difficulty." No, she had no trouble with the Protocols. Her prisoners gratified her with their submission and their fear in the embrace of Koscuisko's drugs. It was no problem to torment them.

"And in addition. In light of the unique requirements of Noycannir's Writ, special support is being provided. Specifically, targeted instruction from the Controlled List, and a custom-built library for Noycannir's use in your service."

There seemed to be a longer pause than required for all the text of the message to parcel through. When her Patron responded at last, Mergau knew that his interest had been engaged; and rejoiced in it, to have his help to discomfit the Administration.

CLARIFICATION IS REQUESTED, CUSTOM-BUILT LIBRARY.

Yet Chonis did not seem to see the trap. "One of Noycannir's classmates has a second rating in an appropriate field, and is commendably willing to contribute his effort to his duty in more than one Lane. Student Koscuisko is creating a special set of qualified formulations especially for the support of Noycannir's Writ."

AND IT IS THIS WHICH SO ASSURES CLELLELAN THAT SHE WILL GRADUATE. KOSCUISKO. IT IS A COMBINE HOUSE, I THINK.

She could almost hear his voice, musing. Moving quickly, surely, inexorably to the same conclusion she had drawn from the same set of information.

SURELY YOU HAVE PLANS TO POST SUCH A PRODUCTIVE RESOURCE TO AN AREA IN WHICH HE CAN BENEFIT THE JUDICIAL SYSTEM MOST EFFECTIVELY.

Oddly enough, however, Chonis was not surprised by the question. "I have discussed the option with the Administrator. Unfortunately, Fleet feels that the political risk is too great. Koscuisko is prince inheritor to his House."

What did that mean? He could not be reassigned? The prestige of serving under the First Secretary's personal instruction was not great enough for such a man? Is that what Tutor Chonis meant to say?

NOT EVEN COMBINE GRAIN CAN BUY A FLEET DEFERMENT, CHONIS.

It wasn't as if it would be asking Koscuisko to sacrifice prestige if he went to work for Chilleau Judiciary rather than Fleet. If Koscuisko worked for Chilleau Judiciary, he need have no duties beside Writ and research. Chief Medical Officers had a great deal to do quite apart from Inquiry. Surely a man would naturally prefer less complex a life to so demanding a position? It wasn't as if he could set aside his Writ before his eight years were done, one way or the other.

Koscuisko had no taste for discipline. His Security could not possibly respect that in him. So Security would not make their best effort to protect him. Koscuisko would be at significant risk in Fleet unless he reconciled himself to de-

manding more professionalism from his Security than he did
from his bond-involuntary slave Curran.

"Koscuisko is under instruction from his father to serve
Fleet specifically as a Chief Medical Officer. Fleet deferment
does not recognize any talent as exceeding the requirements
of a cruiserkiller's Infirmary, as the First Secretary knows."

All in all Mergau could understand no reason whatever for
Chonis's attitude, except for Fleet's stubborn insistence on
standing in Verlaine's path at every junction, for no better
reason than that the First Secretary was a Bench officer.

"Unless he can be proven to lack competence or psychological fitness, we dare not insult the Combine by reducing
him to a post suitable for a man of lesser ability. Nor dare
we insult the Autocrat's Proxy by attempting to so prove."

No reason but pure spite, she was certain of it.

She knew the First Secretary better than Fleet did. Verlaine
was tenacious of purpose when he felt that it was to his
advantage. If he could be made to see how valuable Koscuisko could be to him, Verlaine would go up against the
Combine itself, and take his prize. Had he not triumphed
over the Yanjozi nations, and forced their subservience to
the Blaeborn precedents?

THE SELF-DETERMINATION OF ALL UNDER JURISDICTION
MUST OF COURSE BE CAREFULLY RESPECTED. She could hear
the ironic humor in his voice, with poison in the sting of it.
ESPECIALLY IF FLEET IS TO BENEFIT—KOSCUISKO'S FAMILIAL
DUTY MUST NOT BE COMPROMISED.

"Thank you for your understanding, First Secretary."
There was irony in Tutor Chonis's response in turn. Mergau
wondered if it would be as clear in the text as it was in
Chonis's voice. "The Administration had certain reservations concerning Student Noycannir's ability to support her
Writ, which have been addressed in a very satisfactory manner, with Koscuisko's help. All can benefit."

All except Koscuisko, who had not wanted to work on the
Controlled List, who did not care to discipline his slave, who
did not care for the practical exercises. But the desires and
inclinations of so diffident a man were not worthy of serious
consideration.

MERGAU IS WITH YOU, AS I UNDERSTAND.

How was she to put her Patron on notice that the matter of Koscuisko should be pursued?

"Indeed she is." Chonis wouldn't know what she was going to say. He might expect her support, out of gratitude to him for having found a way to see her through to her Writ. "Student Noycannir, please feel free."

He was wrong if he thought that. The only loyalty that she could afford was to herself, and that meant to her Patron. At least for now.

"I greet me my Patron, and hope that all goes according to his wish." It was a thrill in its own right to be allowed to speak on uplink. It was so expensive . . . "I commend me to him. And commend also Student Koscuisko to his attention."

Chonis made neither move nor sign, but she knew that her point had been taken when Verlaine's response came scrolling across the screen.

HIS VALUE IS SO GREAT AS THAT, NOYCANNIR? YOU DO NOT PRAISE LIGHTLY, IF AT ALL.

Because she was too jealous and insecure. At least that was what he had told her before. *A word of praise is a surer trap than any vice, Mergau, remember that.*

But vice bound more securely and reliably. "So great and more, my Patron. It seems a waste to let this resource go to Fleet service rather than research, since he is so effective with the drugs."

Verlaine knew what she was saying, his response confirmed that.   RESTRAIN YOUR ENTHUSIASM, THOUGH IT DOES YOU CREDIT. KOSCUISKO BELONGS TO FLEET. YOU WILL BE GRATEFUL TO YOUR TUTOR FOR BENEFIT RECEIVED. TUTOR CHONIS.

"Yes, First Secretary." Was it her imagination, or did Chonis sound a little worried?

I AM DEEPLY GRATEFUL FOR YOUR SUPPORT. I WOULD TAKE IT AS A PERSONAL FAVOR IF I COULD RECEIVE COPIES OF NOYCANNIR'S INTERMEDIATE LEVELS. IF YOU WOULD APPROACH THE ADMINISTRATOR ON MY BEHALF, I WOULD BE MOST OBLIGED TO YOU.

So that he could see for himself the action of Koscuisko's

drugs? It occurred to Mergau suddenly that Verlaine would see her own fumbling inadequacies firsthand.

"I will bring the matter before the Administrator directly. First Secretary, this concludes the material we wished to lay before you at this time."

It would be worth the humiliation she'd suffer on being exposed before her Patron, if viewing the tapes convinced Verlaine to take Koscuisko for his own.

VERY GOOD, THANK YOU AGAIN. TRANSMISSION ENDS.

"Return to your quarters, Student Noycannir." The Tutor did not bother to hide his scorn, now that they were alone. He had known what she was doing all along. He'd simply felt that he was more than a match for her. "You are scheduled at the Seventh Level in five days. Hanbor will let you know when we can meet with Student Koscuisko. Dismissed."

Meekly she rose and bowed, meekly she left.

Tutor Chonis was in truth more than a match for her, perhaps.

But she had set her Patron on the scent.

Time would tell whether Tutor Chonis and Fleet Orientation Station Medical could hope to outmaneuver First Secretary Verlaine.

The table was laid ready with his rhyti; the driver and his other instruments were laid out neat and orderly for his delectation. Andrej set down the lefrols he had brought, stroking the smooth rolled cylinders of leaf with nervous fingers. Rhyti for now. Lefrols for later. Lefrols were good for the nerves; and he had a case of the nerves, an uneasy sort of excitement in his stomach built of equal parts of apprehension and anticipation. He was tired of watching Noycannir botch her jobs. He needed to let some blood himself, to make a point of doing it right.

His Seventh Level, the first of the last, three exercises to go after this one. He'd practiced twice a day for a week, intent on making a respectable trial of the driver. If he could manage it adequately well today, he would feel confident enough to take it to St. Clare for the punishment that was owed, whether or not the Tutor would insist on counting bloody craters as a condition of fulfillment of the contract they had made for St. Clare's life.

He heard the signal at the prisoner's door and lifted the driver from the table, enjoying the sleek cool weight of it in his gloved hand. "Step through."

He'd had a look at the prisoner's brief last night; he knew what to expect. This was a referral straight from assisted inquiry; the prisoner was accused, but had not yet been questioned herself. The fact that she was female was a little awkward. Abstractly speaking, he liked the idea of beating women even less than the idea of beating men, setting aside the fact that a contest between a prisoner and an Inquisitor could hardly be considered a fair match regardless of the prisoner's sex or age.

On the other hand, Robert St. Clare was not the only man under Jurisdiction with a sister. Andrej had three or four. It was not quite clear which, but one of them at least would mock him mercilessly should he shrink from his duty simply because his prisoner was not male.

Mayra had been Lady Abbess since the day that he'd been baptized; she was responsible for keeping order amongst all the sworn-sisters in family prayerhalls. Pain was good for the soul, Mayra had assured him. Women required much more firm a hand than men did, because the female constitution was more resilient than the male. Women were born to bear children. Pain simply didn't make as much of an impression on sworn-sisters as on brothers-dedicate, not as far as Mayra was concerned.

And this prisoner wasn't even Dolgorukij.

She was about his size, and not too clean by the look of her. Andrej eyed the woman a little skeptically: it hardly seemed likely that she would hold secrets, let alone such dangerous ones that the Bench would spike the Levels to this extent. He would find out one way or the other, but he really rather hoped she did have secrets. It would be a shame if she would have to die for nothing.

"State your name, and your identification." There was no sense in asking for the offense, not at the Advanced Levels. Generally speaking one had several from which to choose, and all of them actionable.

"I am—Davit, of the market at Cynergau. Of the People, Your Excellency."

She sounded fairly beaten already, to Andrej. The People? They were all the People. Except the Aznir, of course, the beloved of the Holy Mother, and the executors of Her Sacred Will.

Well, if Davit was meek and submissive, perhaps he would just talk to her for a bit and see what he could find out about of her state of mind. He was reluctant to set the driver down, since he was eager to test himself with it; but there was no sense in rushing things—that was one of Noycannir's problems. Andrej exchanged the driver for his rhyti and seated himself at the chair that was kept for him beside the table.

"Talk to me, then, Davit. Do you know why you are here?" If she was of a Cynergau lineage, Class-Four hominid, then she would carry as much muscle as a man of her race; something to keep in mind. Skin tore differently over muscle.

She shook her head, turning her face away. One of the Security moved her head back with a hand at the nape of her neck so that she faced him politely.

"No. Your Excellency."

Surely she had some idea. "Really, you can't guess? What do you imagine that it could be?"

"Truly, Your Excellency, they came and took me away from my shop in the middle of the evening, and I don't understand."

Clearly she'd not been referred due to her intransigent nature. "There was a preliminary inquiry?"

She made a gesture as though she wanted to turn her face aside again. But she did not turn her face. She was being commendably careful, Andrej thought. "There was. Your Excellency. They said I was accused of harboring, but I didn't understand. I told them so."

And they hadn't believed her, so much was obvious. Someone else must have given up information already. Andrej wondered what it was, exactly, that interested the Bench so much about this woman.

"Harboring, what did they mean by that? Did they explain it to you?"

Was he mistaken, or had she hesitated? "I . . . didn't understand what they said, Your Excellency, they said . . . No, I didn't understand what they said."

"Perhaps if you were to share it with me, we could an interpretation develop, between the two of us."

The woman bit her lip and stood silent.

What she'd been asked wasn't all that difficult. The prisoner's brief contained the information: movement of suspected Free Government agents with forged papers through her shop. Andrej didn't think she hadn't understood the issue.

He did think that she was afraid to discuss it.

If there was no problem, she would not need to be reluctant. It was a simple matter, really, and easy to deny as long as one wasn't worried about being caught in an embarrassing contradiction of some sort.

"You are not being candid with me, Davit. What are you hiding?"

She could be expected to keep shut to protect those dear to her. But it seemed fair to guess from the information in the prisoner's brief that at least one of the people she was trying to protect had already given her up to Fleet to save himself. Herself. Whomever.

"Please, Your Excellency, there has been a mistake. I don't understand."

He had his work cut out for him, and a driver thirsty for blood. It made him a little restless to be sitting here and talking when he could be at his exercise.

"I'm sorry. Your response is not acceptable." Now she made a liar out of him as well. He was not sorry. He was too interested in finding out more about the driver's capabilities against living flesh. He would do penance for the falsehood later. "Gentlemen, if you would do me the kindness of uncovering this woman. And then you may stand away."

Discipline was to be taken with a bare back. It was better so, since Joslire had said the stroke would have to be repeated if it failed to break the skin.

As if an abstract interest in the skill were the only reason that he wished to use the driver. . . .

The woman cowered away from him, trying to cover up

her nakedness with her hands. For a moment Andrej hesitated. Was it not a shameful thing to uncover an honest woman, and force her guilt from her with whips and fire?

He didn't care, not now. Not anymore. Or at least he didn't care enough to lay aside the driver and walk out.

"Come now, we will discuss." The whip snaked out, the snapper cracking in the air beside her head. She flinched away from it ungracefully; and Andrej followed up on the backstroke, marking her shoulder with an ugly stripe. "First, if you will, that crime of which you were accused, at your first interview. And so on from there. Am I understood?"

She would confess to him exactly what it had been that she claimed not to have understood. And then she would confess to him why she had wished she had not understood it; and then they would investigate the depth and the complexity of the understanding that she'd wished to disavow.

"Excellency, I don't understand, I don't know what they were talking about—"

He caught her around the ankle and pulled it out from under her, tearing a bright red bracelet around her leg.

"Harboring, you said. And how were you to have harbored, and whom?"

It was pleasant to test the whip's performance and find it so obedient to his desire.

"No, I have harbored no one, I am an honest woman. You have my documents, check my documents."

He checked her lies instead, and made her gasp with it.

Nor did he feel he would be needing to have a lefrol for his nerves.

He broke her feet with the driver; and she crawled away from him toward the wall, wishing him in Hell for his suspicious nature. He broke her hands with the driver, much more delicate work; and she lifted her voice to her goddesses and invited all of Jurisdiction to be damned as well on top of him, as long as he were to be damned most deeply and most dreadfully.

He had Security lift her to lie on her back on the table with her hands useless at her sides, giving his lefrols—not forgetting the rhyti—over into the keeping of such Security as were not required to hold her to her place. He raped her brutally with the butt end of the driver; and she begged him to consider that she had borne children, and that her womb was consequently worthy of respect, not such ill-treatment.

The Security set her back down to the floor for him, and he beat her with the doubled lash until he knew from the trouble that she had in breathing that he had compromised her ribs; and she lamented for her children, the children born to her broken body, and the trouble that they were in, the bad and dangerous things they'd gotten involved with.

And then he stepped away and let the length of the driver out of his fist, and practiced his apprentice-craft upon her until she was decently clothed in a smooth all-concealing garment of her own bright red blood. And she put out her shattered hands to him, and pleaded with him that he leave off his exercise, and asked him what it had been that he had wanted to know.

Except that by that time she'd told him more than he had thought to gain from her. Andrej didn't think there was any point to going over it all again. Without access to medication, she would be gone from him within a matter of hours, since bright pain could overrule the escape that shock provided for only so long. And she would bleed to death, drugs or no drugs, because he'd done his rape so thoroughly, and the driver had been so thirsty for her pain. No, he was the one who had been thirsty for her pain. The driver was a formidable tool, but only that. It had been his lust to hear her cry, his passion for her pain that had so damaged her. And he was sated now, and satisfied, now that she had surrendered herself to him, whether or not he had had her secrets from her earlier.

He thought about it for a moment, pondering in his mind where the monitors would be.

Then Andrej raised his head and looked to where he hoped that Tutor Chonis would be watching him.

"It would seem that the Record is complete," Andrej said. "It is to be hoped that the Protocols have been appropriately exercised to the Tutor's satisfaction. In the absence of other topics of interest, I respectfully request the Tutor's permission to terminate the exercise."

He waited. Without a decision one way or the other, he would be expected either to continue to misuse the woman until she died, or go off on his own business and let her last hours drag out in senseless and solitary agony. Neither of which seemed entirely satisfactory to Andrej.

In a moment he heard the change in the background noise that meant that the Tutor's communication channel had been engaged. "Very well, Student Koscuisko. You may dispatch your prisoner."

She had confessed clear killing offenses as far as Jurisdiction was concerned. Once in the field, he would require no such clearance to execute; he knew the Protocols, after all. In Orientation, however, it was up to the Administration to decide officially whether termination was to come sooner or later. Here it was Tutor Chonis's responsibility to say when the prisoner was to die. Andrej appreciated the support the Tutor was apparently willing to grant to him, and received it with an appreciative salute.

"Thank you, Tutor Chonis. Mister Haspir, if I may borrow your knife."

There were needle-knives provided among the instruments, of course. But they were too narrow for his purpose. He had a clear idea in his mind about what he wanted to do, and how he wanted to do it; for that he needed Haspir's knife, since Joslire did not yet trust him with knives for his own use.

Kneeling down at the woman's back, he covered her eyes with his hand so that she could take her last few breaths in what privacy he could provide for her. First, to cut the connection between the brain and the subbrain at the top of her spine, so that the mind need not be burdened with the body's frantic signals that it was dying. And second, to cut the connection between the bundle of nerve fibers at the base of the brain and the spine, so that the body would forget to breathe and death would come of oxygen starvation. The woman was Cynergau, her nervous system built with rather more redundancy than other hominids of her class. Breathing would continue by reflex as long as the connection between the spine and the subbrain was left intact.

Andrej severed it.

Her body stilled, and Andrej waited. Four eighths, and the body went into spasm, the uncoordinated twitches—neural "noise"—of a machine without a governor. Twelve eighths, and she was dead, and Andrej waited until enough time had passed that he could feel certain that her mind was still before he rose and beckoned for his rhyti.

"Thank you for your assistance, gentlemen." He could read no reservation, no hesitation in any of their expressions. They had done as he had instructed them, without questions either implicit or explicit, without the slightest indication of reluctance on their parts; and for that he was grateful. It could not be easy duty for them. "Mister Haspir, is there a firepoint here someplace?"

Lefrols he'd brought; he'd issued them to himself from the range of intoxicants and inhibitors and antidepressants available to Students. Lefrols and alcohol—although he did not trust the cortac brandy, knowing too well what passed for cortac sold from Combine to Jurisdiction, and prudently confined himself to wodac. But a lefrol was no good without a firepoint, no matter how neatly the needle-knife from the table served to trim the end. Andrej felt a little foolish to be asking, but he did want a lefrol now. He was tired and he was hungry, and he didn't know what time it was, but he rather suspected that it had gotten late, because Haspir seemed a little weary. If as correct as always.

"According to the officer's good pleasure." Haspir bowed, presenting the lit firepoint as he did so. A decent firepoint it was, too, it burned clean and blue, and set a coal to his lefrol quite nicely.

"Thank you again. Your knife."

His chair was still here, although the table had been pushed back against the wall earlier. His Mizucash friend stood by with his rhyti. Andrej let himself sit, surprised at how weary he felt; and the Security did not have the option. Security were expected never to sit in the presence of an officer, even a Student. Well, it was hard, but perhaps they were better at it than he was. What time was it?

Andrej sat and smoked his lefrol and considered the corpse. He would be a little drunk in less than an eighth. Lefrols were good for that, if only one did not succumb to the temptation to take them too frequently. He wasn't drunk now, though, so why didn't he feel more affected, to have murdered the poor woman? Betrayed in her friends, betrayed in her family, betrayed in her goddesses for all that he could tell, and he had killed her. Terminated, concluded, dispatched, removed, the language of the Protocols could not disguise the basic truth of the matter; and the fact of the matter was that he had never killed a woman until now. A hare or two, a brace of gamebirds, yes. A woman, never, nor a man nor child, either.

And he had had no passion for the work, aside from gratitude that Tutor Chonis would permit him to make a clean end of her, instead of condemning that close-to-finished life to bleed out slowly in pain and in confusion. It was no excuse; but he was fairly certain that he had not enjoyed her death as he had enjoyed the long slow killing of her, and therefore it was possible that his murder of her had been cleanly done, uncontaminated by the passion that he was learning how to manage and maintain. Learning to use, since he had no hope of denying its existence to himself.

The cleaning team came to take the body away, and here was Joslire coming on their heels to take him to his bed. What did Joslire think about the murders that his Students did?

Andrej rose from his place, giving his rhyti glass to one of the cleaning team, and left the exercise theater with Joslire in his wake. Stumbling only slightly, which was good. It was enough of a shame to be smoking lefrols without requiring that Joslire carry him to quarters while he was at it. Lefrols were an acquired taste. Andrej knew from experience that people who didn't smoke lefrols tended to feel rather violently about their odor.

By the time he'd reached his quarters, he was light-headed, as he had expected to be—pleasantly euphoric, lazy and blissful in a mildly drunken sort of way. He didn't want his supper, he wanted to have a wash, even if the time-keeper claimed that it was only secondshift. Andrej squinted at the time-keeper with confusion, trying to focus on its readout while the rest of the room swam slowly about him. No, not fourteen. Twenty-four. Not secondshift, but the end of thirdshift. Had it really been so long? He certainly hadn't noticed it getting late, and he'd not released Security for midmeal. He was going to have to discuss this problem with Tutor Chonis. It could hardly endear him to his Security if he was to keep them on their feet for three shifts run together without so much as a short break for midmeal.

He gave his lefrol over into Joslire's keeping and went into the washroom, stripping as he went. His uniform was dirty, soiled through to his underblouse with blood; and the gloves were simply disgusting. Blood on his hands even through the gloves, blood under his fingernails—a rusty stain with a metallic smell that somehow seemed more natural than unpleasant. Blood in the wastestream of the wetsshower, the dried smudges blooming pink as the warm moisture rinsed them from his body. He had not remembered it being quite so messy a business as this before. On the other hand, she had been his Seventh Level.

By the time that the wastestream ran clear, by the time that he felt clean enough to face himself in the mirror once again, Joslire had taken his soiled clothing away and set his sleep-shirt out to wait for him. Padding damp and barefoot into the main room, Andrej cast about him for his lefrol, and found it in a dish on the studyset, alongside his meal. He didn't want his meal. There was a glass of wodac there as well; he'd made a practice of taking quite a bit of wodac with his suppers after exercise. He didn't want the wodac, either. He was drunk on the powerful intoxicant of the lefrol and full sated with the sweet sound of his prisoner's pain. There was no room in all his body for an appetite, the exercise had satisfied so completely. He took the lefrol and its leavings-dish into the little closet where he had his bed and lay down to finish his smoke, content to not be thinking about much of anything.

Joslire was at the door, but Joslire would not come in. Perhaps Joslire was worried about smoking in one's bed, which was of course a nasty habit, and too likely to result in fire-suppression systems going off in the middle of a dream to be indulged in with any frequency.

Well, if Joslire was worried, Andrej could afford to be done with lefrols for the evening. He was certainly drunk enough. And he had been hard at work all day; it was probable that he was tired, even if he was too euphoric to notice.

He set the lefrol down into its leavings-dish and decided to go to sleep.

Clellelan turned the record-cube over in his fingers, clearly musing over the conversation it contained—the scheduled review, First Secretary Verlaine, Mergau Noycannir. Tutor Chonis. "So, Adifer, you think that we might have a problem here?"

"Two problems. Or one problem, two locklinks." He'd spoken to the Administrator on Joslire Curran's behalf earlier, when Clellelan had surprised him by offering the Safe. So at least the Administrator was already prepared for that one. "I'd have come to you sooner, but Koscuisko ran his Seventh Level a little richer than usual."

Clellelan frowned at his time-keeper. Middle of the first-shift, the second day of Koscuisko's Seventh Level. The Administrator knew what the general schedule was—there were eighteen other Students in the Seventh Level exercises here, after all, and it would have been nineteen except for that unfortunate accident that one of Tutor Heson's Students had with a twisted sleep-shirt. Noycannir's prisoner had died during the night, but no blame attached to her—at least no official blame. Although with Koscuisko's drugs, there had been no real reason why the prisoner should not have lived to talk for three days yet. In Chonis's professional estimation.

"Talk to me, Adifer."

What, had Clellelan developed expectations where Koscuisko was concerned? "Didn't stop for midmeal, didn't stop for thirdmeal. Noycannir'd been in quarters for five eights before Koscuisko decided he was finished. Asked me for permission to terminate."

Clellelan knew as well as he did how unusual that was. "Got lost in the exercise? What? Did you let him?"

Well, yes, he supposed that Koscuisko had got lost in the exercise. In a manner of speaking. "He said that she didn't know anything more than what she'd already told us, and I believed him. Made a nice end of her, too, one cut to stop the pain, one cut to end her life. Stylish."

Nodding, Clellelan was clearly making connections. "So we didn't hear from you yesterday, what with Koscuisko so absorbed in his exercise. What about Verlaine?"

Good question. "It's a reasonable alternative to propose, one would think. But I don't think it's a good idea, even if the Bench wants in on him." Granted, he was working untried code here. Under normal circumstances, all he cared about the welfare of his Students was that they stay healthy enough to get through his course before they came to pieces, or had any embarrassing accidents with twisted sleep-shirts. Under normal circumstances that was all he could afford to care about them. He hadn't yet made up his mind about whether Andrej Koscuisko was really all that different.

"So tell me. Apart from the fact that Koscuisko's going to be able to buy as many First Secretaries as he wants, once he inherits." Blunt speech from the Administrator usually meant that he was most open to new ideas. Chonis plunged in.

"You remember Ligrose thought he'd be better off in Surgery. She likes what he's done for his man St. Clare as well, which reminds me to ask you about that Class One we've promised him."

"Don't like to keep the man hanging in suspense for longer than necessary," Clellelan noted. Which man? Koscuisko? St. Clare? Whatever. "And we'll need to allow for recovery time, before they leave the Station. Any time before Koscuisko's Ninth Level, Adifer, all right? —Say on."

"It shows up in his exercises, though, as well. When he killed that prisoner, it was like he'd hit a global reset. Absolutely no hint of how much he'd been liking it. Chaymalt says he's too good a healer to waste on Inquiry. I say he's got too much potential in Inquiry to waste him on medicine. But if Verlaine gets him he won't have any medical practice, and he'll only be answering Verlaine's questions—waste of resource. At least in Fleet he has a chance to do both. More balance, that way."

"Maybe keep him running longer, if he feels he's needed outside Special Medical." That was a good point, although Chonis hadn't thought of it in quite those terms. What burned young Inquisitors out was the exercise of their Writ, not the burden of their strictly medical responsibilities. *Trust Clellelan*—Chonis thought gratefully—*to come up with a perfectly objective reason to be concerned about Koscuisko's welfare.* "But are we going to be able to keep him out of Verlaine's understandably greedy little graspers?"

"Wants to see Noycannir's tapes, you noticed." Of course he had. "It could get to be a difficult problem. I suggest our parity-fields will be significantly stronger if Verlaine doesn't get a good look at Noycannir's tapes until Koscuisko has already reported to *Scylla*."

Clellelan nodded appreciatively. "Fleet can probably find ways to protect the investment, as long as he performs to expectation. All right, we'll do it, and if you can nudge his Tenth Level up a hair, we can release him early if we have to. The Autocrat's Proxy might even like that."

Yes, Chonis imagined that they could hurry the schedule a bit, as long as Koscuisko could take the pace. He'd see what Curran had to say about how Koscuisko was holding up, which brought him to his other problem, quite naturally.

"I'll go over the schedule with Curran, then. And Curran seems to have gotten a little intense about Student Koscuisko. No telling for certain, but he's teaching Koscuisko how to throw knives, and I suspect the knives Koscuisko's throwing aren't Fleet-issue."

Clellelan set the record-cube he'd been toying with down carefully on the desk's surface. "You think he's teaching Koscuisko five-knives?"

It couldn't be proved on the evidence at hand, no. To be absolutely certain, they would need to interrupt the practice and check Curran's knives then and there. Yet Chonis was reasonably secure in his suspicion. All Curran had done on Safe had been to take Koscuisko to a practice range and start him on throwing knives. That had to mean something.

"Just so, Rorin. His five-knives. We could pull him off now, of course. We've got St. Clare to post in replacement if we need to."

Snorting in amusement, the Administrator shook his head. " 'Yon undertall beauty,' with an accent, no less. An ignorant accent. You couldn't have paid the man to make a better test of that speakserum."

No, as a matter of fact. The demonstration had been genuinely impressive. "But if we leave Curran where he is and he asks to be reassigned when Koscuisko leaves, we lose one of our best. Good for Koscuisko. Not so good for us."

Curran could be released to Fleet if Curran wanted to go. It would be insanity to give up what was left of his deferment, but as far as Chonis was concerned all semi-mystical, ascetic warrior-cultists were already more than a little unbalanced, and the Emandisan figuring prominently to the fore of a list of dangerous loonies.

"Do you want him pulled off and sent through readjustment?" Clellelan asked, bluntly.

Bond-involuntaries sometimes formed intense attachments to Students of assignment, for one reason or another. Bond-involuntaries were psychologically vulnerable to passionate one-on-one bonding to begin with, since personal dedication could substitute for freedom to an extent. When that happened, the Administrator had the option of removing the troop from the officer assigned and arranging a respite period with plenty of food, intoxicants as required, and as much sexual contact as the troop could take. That generally set a bond-involuntary back on his or her figurative feet.

Curran and Koscuisko might be well matched for man and master, according to the peculiar cultural forms of Emandisan and Dolgorukij alike; that wasn't the issue. Whether Clellelan was willing to risk losing Curran was.

"Getting back to my basic interest, which is to give Koscuisko the best chance of long-term survival on Line. Curran has good support to offer, and Koscuisko's been raised to accept that kind of relationship. It may be too late to change Curran's mind about it anyway, what with those knives taken into account."

He didn't care about being fair to Curran, though Curran was well respected by Staff—bonded and un-Bonded alike. At least he didn't care about being fair to Curran as much as he wanted to see Koscuisko as ideally placed to perform his Judicial function as possible. "And if he's got two of them with him on *Scylla*, he might be even more reluctant to abandon them to Fleet and go off to Chilleau Judiciary."

"At least until one of them gets killed, and he decides it

isn't worth the investment,'' Clellelan mused. ''Well, give Curran the chance to get clear if he approaches you, Adifer. But if we're going to put the boy through an accelerated Advanced—and he's got to blood his St. Clare while he's at it—we don't want to be upsetting his domestic arrangements. Curran's one of the best, but he's still dead.''

Bond-involuntaries were sometimes called the thirty-years-dead, their identities and rights under Jurisdiction restored only when the Day dawned at last. Which meant that technically speaking, Curran was disposable, in a sense, to be used in whatever manner the Administration saw fit to further Fleet's interests.

Fleet permitted bond-involuntaries to volunteer to place themselves at an officer's disposal, since that suited Fleet's purpose. No blame would attach to the Administration of Fleet Orientation Station Medical if Curran asked to leave. Curran might have some trouble getting Koscuisko to agree, true enough. But that was Curran's problem.

''I'll give you a revised schedule.'' The business of the interview was over; rising to his feet, Chonis bowed to his superior, satisfied that they were of congruent mind. ''Are you going to want witnesses for St. Clare?''

''Oh, you'd better get Station Security to observe. I'll sit in if I'm free, but don't hold up on my account.''

They'd see how quickly they could get Koscuisko out of there and safely to *Scylla*.

Koscuisko deserved better than to become the First Secretary's minion. Fleet could protect Koscuisko as long as Koscuisko was on Line. Once let Fleet know that the Bench wanted him, and Fleet would hold Koscuisko to its bosom like a favorite child. . . .

◆ Thirteen

He'd never had so irregular a schedule with any of his other Students. Joslire was looking forward to the break that the Administration granted them at the completion of each Term: eight days to rest, eight days to recover from any Student discipline, eight days to complete debriefing before the next Students started to arrive. Lately eight days had stretched to sixteen, once as long as twenty-four, before the Administration could collect sufficient Students for a cost-effective Term.

Koscuisko was a very tiring man.

He was going to need every single hour of that anticipated break just to catch up on his sleep.

But then he'd never had a Student who had run the Seventh Level all the way out to its logical conclusion. His other Students had preferred to leave the exercise for their midmeal, and again for their thirdmeal and again for their sleepshift, rewarded more often than not with an easy finish to the exercise—prisoners who politely and conveniently died while the Students slept.

Koscuisko hadn't seemed to notice when it had been time for midmeal; Koscuisko had been working on his prisoner's hands. Even Tutor Chonis had been impressed at Koscuisko's skillful employment of the driver. Still less had Koscuisko apparently noted the time for his thirdmeal or his sleepshift, absorbed in some abstract equation of the ratio of bruises to ribs.

There were benefits either way, of course. Going by normal practice, the prisoners died quietly by themselves during the night and the Students weren't bothered with the business in the morning. But Koscuisko's way they could both sleep until next thirdmeal, because the exercise was scheduled for two days, and Tutor Chonis didn't want to see Koscuisko until the next day following.

And of course the most significant benefit from Koscuisko's management style—significant from the prisoner's point of view, at any rate—was that Koscuisko had killed her, once he'd decided he was finished. None of the passive, impersonal murders of Joslire's other Students. Koscuisko had taken active responsibility; and he had taken care in killing her, mindful of her dignity even naked and abused as she had been.

Sometime during the Eighth or Ninth Levels, Students were required to make a kill at the Tutor's direction and discretion. It was a test of sorts; and most Students responded to it by ordering Security to perform the actual act. In fact by the Seventh Level, most Students were happiest to sit in their chair and direct Security rather than dirtying their own hands; perhaps understandably so. Joslire appreciated Koscuisko's apparent selfishness. It was good not to be required to beat a prisoner. It was better to be left alone to not watch, to be called upon only when an extra pair of hands were wanted for some relatively neutral task.

None of his other Students had ever asked to make the kill.

But almost all of them had bad dreams, soon after the event.

Koscuisko's cries woke Joslire sometime close to midshift. He rolled off the sleep-rack to his feet, halfway to Koscuisko's cubicle before his eyes were well open. The privacy barrier wasn't quite closed; Joslire had wanted the extra ventilation to clear the inner space of the stench from Koscuisko's lefrol. He was through it in a moment, to seize and still Koscuisko's restless hands as Koscuisko's sleeping body struggled with some dreamed enemy.

"Sir. The officer is dreaming. Wake up."

Small as it was, the room seemed stifling to Joslire, the air heavy with horror. Koscuisko fought against him for a moment, and Koscuisko was difficult to control in his sleep—Aznir Dolgorukij, and significantly stronger than Joslire was, even if Koscuisko did not yet know how best to use his strength. Joslire hung on, grimly embracing the dreaming man, repeating the same pale neutral phrases as soothingly as he dared.

"The officer is dreaming, Your Excellency. The officer is respectfully requested to wake up now." *Come back, come back from the land of the dead and of shadows. Wake now, dear one, that thy dreams not distress thee.*

Koscuisko woke with a convulsive start and lay motionless in Joslire's arms for a long moment, holding his breath. Joslire wasn't sure whether Koscuisko was still dreaming, or what; but finally Koscuisko gave a great sigh and his body relaxed. He leaned up against Joslire, as if gratefully, letting his head back against Joslire's shoulder. Joslire didn't dare move. It was irregular, surely, and what had he thought that he was doing, coming in here in the first place?

"I have had a dream," Koscuisko said. "I did not much enjoy it, Joslire."

Surely not, Joslire was tempted to say. *One hardly would have guessed.* Instead he shifted his weight a little, preparatory to disengaging himself from the intimacy of the embrace; but Koscuisko put his hand up to Joslire's arm, and stayed him.

"The officer cried out in his sleep." He stilled himself, obedient to Koscuisko's apparent desire. "Does the officer wish to talk about it, this dream?"

"Oh, I am sick to death." Koscuisko pushed himself upright suddenly, spurning Joslire's support as decisively as he had seemed to solicit it. "Sick of being so insulated, Joslire, and I swear to all Saints that if you say 'the officer' one more time within the next eight I will—not thank you for it."

Now that Koscuisko had sat up, there was no reason why Joslire should be sitting on his bed, or sitting at all. Or even in the cubicle, come to that. Rising quietly, Joslire made for the door, and Koscuisko—with his head in his hands—took no apparent notice of him. Joslire started the rhyti brewer as quickly as he could, one ear cocked for any sound from

Koscuisko. Maybe Koscuisko would just go back to sleep. There was a message posted to the studyset screen: Tutor Chonis wanted to see Koscuisko for debriefing, but they had until next firstshift before the appointed time. The rhyti was ready, but how was he to offer it to his Student if Koscuisko did not want to hear from him? If he wasn't to call Koscuisko "the officer," and it was dangerous to call Koscuisko by his name, how could he hope to help Koscuisko talk out his pain?

Joslire carried a flask of rhyti to the open doorway, Koscuisko still sitting on the edge of his sleep-rack with his face in his hands. "It is not to be helped," Joslire said. "Sir. Would . . . you . . . like to talk about . . . your dream?"

Koscuisko looked up, and Koscuisko's eyes were dead and empty. "I dreamed that I killed a woman, Joslire." Seeing the glass of rhyti in Joslire's hand, Koscuisko beckoned him in with a wave of his hand. "I lost a patient twice, three times, in practicals. But it isn't the same. And I didn't just dream it."

Kneeling down to be able to see Koscuisko's face, Joslire reached for something he could say. He'd been through this with Students before, but never one like this. Koscuisko was more of an effort than any of them. Koscuisko was too honest with himself for his own good.

"It was well done, all the same." And not wanting to keep his Student at arm's length by observing the safe distance of accepted forms only made things more difficult. "A man takes care of his own work, finishes what he's started. Doesn't leave the cleaning up to other people."

It wasn't coming out right. He could hear the halt and start in his own voice. He didn't know how he could honor Koscuisko's expressed wish and keep peace with his governor at the same time. Surely Koscuisko understood that?

Koscuisko sighed and drank his glass of rhyti. Right down, Joslire noted with dismay; and it had been hot. Koscuisko didn't seem any the worse for it.

"Joslire, thou art good to me. And have been good to me this while. I will miss you." Handing the empty glass back, Koscuisko laid his hand at the back of Joslire's neck and had leaned forward to kiss him before Joslire knew quite what was happening. Only his discipline kept him in his place, surprised—startled—as he was; Koscuisko touched his other hand to the side of Joslire's face, briefly, and stood up. "I think that I should have a wash. What time is it, please? Time to eat, I hope?"

Joslire found his voice, albeit with difficulty. "Even so, it's midshift. Tutor Chonis will see—will conduct debriefing after fastmeal tomorrow; exercise could be taken if the officer please—that is, I—"

"Quite all right, Joslire, it is not your fault. Be easy." Koscuisko had reached the washroom and turned on the wet-shower. He wouldn't be able to hear a thing; but the monitors would hear, so Joslire did not speak his thought. *Perhaps I will go with you to Scylla, Student Koscuisko.*

Not because Koscuisko had caressed him, because he could ask that of his fellows if he needed a kind touch so much as that. Bond-involuntaries took care of each other as best as they could, and didn't ask questions, and didn't let personal preferences or inclinations keep them from comforting each other. No, not just because Koscuisko had caressed him.

But because of the respect with which Koscuisko had killed his prisoner. Because of the gentle care Koscuisko had shown while she was dying, for all that he had shown none earlier.

Or perhaps only because he was Koscuisko, and he had the blood of a war-leader.

Joslire set Koscuisko's uniform out and put in a call for the Student's fastmeal.

Maybe he needed to speak to Tutor Chonis again.

"Robert, I'd like another threevice, please. Good man."

The Eighth Level of the Question, and the second day. Robert St. Clare had never assisted at Inquiry before; this one was brutal.

"Come, now. I am determined that you are not telling me the truth. I can fairly promise you that things will only . . . get the worse for you . . . until you do. . . ."

The strangled cries of the prisoner, the self-satisfied gloating in the officer's voice were equally difficult to bear. It had been bad yesterday, even once he'd gotten past his nervousness in Koscuisko's presence. Today was worse.

"Oh. For the love of God. Leave over. I don't know."

He had to concentrate on what the prisoner was saying in order to make out the words. He didn't want to be listening at all. The rest of the Security seemed capable of closing themselves down. How long would it take him to learn how to protect himself? The officer used him neither more nor less than the others; Koscuisko had not played favorites. St. Clare was grateful for that. What little he had been called upon to do had strained his self-discipline badly, but he knew better than to let even a hint of hesitation show in his responses to his officer.

"I don't. Believe. You," Koscuisko said, punctuating his mocking words with precise movements of the knife, nestling ever more deeply beneath a fingernail. Two days, and the prisoner could still speak and be understood. Two days, and Koscuisko could still evoke such sickening sounds of agony from the man who shuddered trembling on the floor in front of Koscuisko's chair.

Koscuisko had his prisoner's hand stretched across his knee, convenient to his knife, and the threevices kept the fingers steady and immobilized at Koscuisko's pleasure. The officer had dealt more kindly with him, although the pain was troubling to remember. Koscuisko had not made him watch his own torture so deliberately as this.

"What . . . else is there to tell you? Ah, Your Excellency? Please . . ."

Koscuisko toyed idly with the knife, and the blood ran fresh. Robert could smell it.

"Please, I've told you about my buyers. My suppliers. My contracts, everything . . ."

And so he had; St. Clare had heard him. Leaning forward, Koscuisko lifted the prisoner's head by the hair on his head and purred at him. "But not enough. I don't think you've said all the truth you know, and that offends me, do you understand?"

It seemed to St. Clare that the man's eyes rolled back in his head; and Koscuisko responded to the threat of loss of consciousness by taking his prisoner by the throat and shaking him savagely. "Pay attention, when it is that I am talking to you."

"Ah . . . there's Alden for the factory, and I told you about Foratre and even Kuylige, Glenafric services the school yards . . . what? What?"

"Tell me more about Glenafric," Koscuisko suggested, and transferred his attention to another fingernail. "The school yards, is it? A relative of yours, this Glenafric, I understand?"

"My brother, and damn him for his greed. He has contacts . . . the older children . . ."

They hadn't heard anything incriminating about this Glenafric person before, not that St. Clare could call to mind. He was sure he'd have remembered if they had. It would have helped him insulate himself from the fearful pity of what Koscuisko did to his prisoner had he known all along that there were children involved.

It was a gesture too horribly like stripping bark off of a switch, like paring the rind of a cheese away at the tail end of the wheel. It was a small movement of Koscuisko's hand, merely, but the prisoner choked with it. Fortunately for St. Clare, there was too much blood for him to be able to see anything but a confused sort of mass of flesh, like the leavings after fall slaughter before the scavenger birds came chortling in to feed. "Where would one find this Glenafric Whomever, I wonder?"

There was horrified denial in the prisoner's voice, now, even past all of his pain. "No, he's my brother . . . I didn't mean . . . a mistake, your Excellency, please . . ."

Koscuisko moved the knife against the prisoned hand, and the prisoner screamed. "Tsamug! Glenafric Tsamug! He keeps his stores in his grain bin—at home, at his home, you can find the stuff there."

A man could sell addictive drugs to children, and take whatever coin he pleased in the eager self-prostitution of flesh not even sexually mature. And still try to protect his brother, at the last.

"It is a shame that we lack medication," Koscuisko said sorrowfully, turning the dagger with delicate care. "You need to suffer much before your sin is healed. Oh, and I could help you, if we had but time.''

Leaning back now, Koscuisko spurned his prisoner away from him with his foot and rose to his feet slowly like a drunken man, reaching out a hand to steady himself against Vely. ''But we must be content with what we have, and trust the saints to take care of the rest. And therefore, Mister Haspir, if you would for me the gelclub find, I mean to make the best start that I can.''

St. Clare was not quite sure of what Koscuisko was getting at, with his vague talk of sins to be healed. The rest of it made too much sense entirely.

''I do not like your choice of relations; such brothers as you have offend me deeply. . . .''

How many years was he condemned to stand and help, in this?

St. Clare stood silent at attention-rest and tried to find some sanctuary deep within himself. Where he didn't have to see. Where he didn't have to hear. Where he didn't have to think about Koscuisko, at least not while Koscuisko was wearing the wrong pair of hands.

He'd made it this far, after all, he reminded himself. He could complete the exercise.

As long as he didn't have to think about it he would be all right.

Andrej stood with his back to the room, smoking his lefrol, waiting for the disposal team to take the body away. He was well finished; he'd been able to keep the prisoner going for rather longer than he had expected, and that measure of success gratified him. Did they save the most offensive prisoners for the last? Did they understand that it was easier to torture a man when one could honestly feel a certain degree of personal moral outrage, even though the ferocity of the punishment still could not be said to fit the crime?

Because when it came right down to the threshing of it, Andrej didn't care about political crimes. Treason was only against Jurisdiction, and the Combine, while forced to acknowledge Bench supremacy, simply didn't take Jurisdiction as seriously as the Jurisdiction was apt to take itself.

He could hear people behind him, probably the disposal team. Another moment or two and he would be ready to leave; Joslire would take him back to quarters. He was tired. It had been two days, two long days.

"Attention to the Administrator!"

Haspir's warning call took Andrej by surprise. Pivoting on his heel, with a lefrol in one hand, he stood to attention as well as he could. What could this mean? Administrator Clellelan, Tutor Chonis, Provost Marshall Journis. Joslire Curran, behind Tutor Chonis, and Joslire was carrying a driver—and a fresh pair of gloves, perhaps? Andrej made his bow, a sudden sense of dread dispelling the euphoria that the lefrol had created in his mind. Joslire carrying a driver, and St. Clare had been posted to his Security team for this exercise. St. Clare had done well, as far as Andrej could remember. But he was tired, tired and physically weary, how could they ask that he discipline St. Clare after the end of two days of an Eighth Level exercise?

Lora and Vely had cleared away the table, setting it against the back wall. Cay had brought a basin of water for him to wash his hands. It was a supportive gesture, but now Andrej was unsure whether he could get away with the apparent hesitation that it would entail. One thing was certain: He was not the only person here who thought he knew exactly what was going on. St. Clare was as white as an Iselbiss snowfall. Had everybody known? Everybody except for himself, and Robert St. Clare?

"Carry on, Student Koscuisko." The Administrator seated himself in Andrej's chair, Chonis and the Provost posting themselves behind him at either shoulder. "Take a moment, if you need it. What was it, Chonis? Six-and-sixty?"

Andrej held his panic to himself, firmly, and Tutor Chonis hastened to his rescue. "I have instructed Student Koscuisko that four-and-forty will be acceptable, if the Administrator please. A reasonable compromise, under the circumstances."

"Indeed? Very well, then. At your convenience, Student Koscuisko."

Cay and Haspir were on either side of St. Clare now, as if he had reverted to prisoner status—no surrogacy about it. Joslire had gone to stand by the table at the back, waiting for Andrej beside the basin of water. All right, he had time, and if he was to do this, he did want to wash his hands, because his hands were filthy with the prisoner's blood that had soaked through the gloves. He had noticed that with the Chigan, with the Cynergau, and it still surprised him. Blood and the sweat of his palms together made a slippery combination. He wanted to be quite sure about his control over the driver.

He was glad that Joslire had brought another whip; the one he had been using for his practices, perhaps? The one he had been using on his prisoner was wet, and would fall with that much more brutal a stroke accordingly. As if any touch of that black braided thing could be called less than brutal . . . but he was going to concentrate. And he was going to concentrate with all deliberate speed. The longer he made St. Clare wait, the more St. Clare would suffer in the waiting.

He washed his hands and he dried his hands, but he didn't want the gloves that Joslire had brought for him. Not quite yet. Andrej went to the front of the room and beckoned for St. Clare. The two Security made no move to compel him, though he did hesitate for a moment; and Andrej was grateful for the respect that they were showing for St. Clare.

"It will be necessary for you to remove your blouse. And your underblouse as well, Robert." He couldn't read the expression in Robert's eyes. He didn't know St. Clare's face well enough to guess whether it was hatred and resentment, loathing, disgust—or merely fear, and resignation. He had not seen St. Clare above twelve times all told, and St. Clare had been unconscious during at least six of them. But he had yet to see an expression of hatred on St. Clare's face. Fear was quite natural; but resignation—resignation, without any hostility directed at the man who was to punish him cruelly for a fault that was not his own—seemed clearly too great a charity for Andrej to hope for.

Stripped to the waist, St. Clare waited for instruction. Andrej would have liked to have assured himself that a medical team had been called up, to be ready. He did not dare to press the issue, however, for fear that the Administrator or the Provost might speak against it. Better to wait till he could speak with Tutor Chonis alone.

Andrej gestured toward the front wall. St. Clare bowed to him, formally, and turned toward the wall, posting himself precisely at arm's length from the wall and directly in front of where the Administrator sat. Andrej knew the range, he had been practicing; and yet—as determined as he'd been to be prepared—there was an important point he had forgotten. Something he hadn't ever thought to discuss with Joslire. There was no help for it now. He was going to have to simply ask, witnesses or none.

St. Clare stood at attention-wait facing the wall, his head straight and steady on his broad shoulders. Reaching up, Andrej set his hand to the back of Robert's neck in the traditional gesture of intimacy between master and man.

"Would you be bound, Mister St. Clare? Or not?"

St. Clare was surprised to be given the option; Andrej could feel it in the sudden tension of the muscles beneath his hand. But he did need to know.

"I know better than anyone how well you can stand to it, but it will be difficult for you either way. It shall be your choice." What would shame Robert least? To be chained at the wall, like an unreasoning animal? Or not to be chained, and suffer the shame of having to be restrained by his fellows if he so much as flinched away from the whipstroke?

Robert coughed, as if to clear his throat. "Let there be no reproach brought against the officer's discipline," he replied firmly. And raised his hands, stretching his arms out to where the shackles hung against the wall waiting for him and hungry for his pain.

Truly, truly Robert was of good heart. It would make it easier for Andrej that St. Clare had consented to be constrained. It almost seemed to him that the gesture had been made for his benefit, a surrender of pride to help put the exercise forward.

"Gentlemen," Andrej suggested grimly. Haspir and Cay came forward to close the manacles and latch them at St. Clare's wrists. It gave him an extra moment to examine the still-too-newly healed expanse of St. Clare's back one final time, to see where the skin was thinnest, to find any residual bruising or tenderness. He had already studied up on Nurail. He'd spent a good half-shift poring over the nerve map for the Nurailian body, to learn to his satisfaction where it was that he could strike the hardest blows and have them hurt the least.

Taking the gloves from Joslire finally, he pulled them on, smoothing the palms carefully before he took the whip. He was as ready as ever he would be.

"Who is to count, Joslire?" he asked. Tutor Chonis answered in Joslire's stead.

"The Provost Marshall represents Station Security. The official count will be hers. You may proceed, Student Koscuisko."

Wasn't it unusual, to have so much rank at such discipline? Or was it in token of the unusual circumstances that had got them here, he and St. Clare together?

Andrej paced his ground, and flexed the uncoiled driver to work any unseen kinks out of its braiding. "Stand clear, gentlemen," he called, as much to warn St. Clare as to move the others away. Enough time to know that it would be coming, now. Not enough time to suffer the impact before it hit, in apprehension; St. Clare was to suffer enough from the whip's lash itself without being forced to fear and suffer both.

Letting the leader out, he swung a long slow stroke for the left side of Robert's upper back, and knew by sound alone that he had bruised deeply enough for blood to flow.

"One," the Provost said.

He had to find a rhythm, he had to take a regular count early and consistently. Five was too long. Two was not long enough. Three would give him time to contain the stroke, to control the stroke, ensure that it would bite deeply enough to be counted.

"Two."

Start at the upper part of the back, work down. Leave enough space to show each single welt, to make it clear that every stroke should be counted as good. He had not taken the width of the welt into account. The spacing was going to be difficult.

"Three."

And above all he had to be sure that he would hit hard enough, be sure that four-and-forty would not compound to five-and-fifty or worse just because he was desperately reluctant to hurt Robert St. Clare.

"Four."

He found his pace and held it grimly as the whip cut a series of increasingly blurred and bloody lines down one side of St. Clare's naked back. He was not going to be able to go twenty on a side; the welt was too wide for that. And he had to bring one in every eight in at the lower part of the shoulders, just to one side of Robert's spine so that the snapper-end could do its dreadful damage—what had the Tutor said? Provide its taste of "real" punishment—where there were the least number of pain receptors to register a protest.

"Seven."

He laid the eighth stroke in straight and solid, and Robert's body rocked against the impact of the pain. It would be hard. And it was only starting.

"Eight."

It was going to be important to maintain a balance if he was to deal honestly with St. Clare. Pain messages gathered from two directions at once could overload the tolerance of the spinal transmitters, so that two blows would cause Robert to suffer torment equivalent to one and one-half. If he managed really well there was a chance that he could achieve a kind of interference that would cancel out some of Robert's pain before it had quite come to Robert's attention.

"Thirteen."

He could hear St. Clare's breathing, now, shaky and strained—but only breathing, still. He set the snapper to mark the second eight, and heard a sound as Robert's body jerked against his chains with the shock of it. One in eight, Tutor Chonis had told him. One in eight, and for four-and-forty that meant that he dare not stop at five of them.

"Twenty."

At least he had not lost a single stroke, so far. Oh, almost halfway through, he had won fair count from the Provost so far.

"Twenty-two."

Half over, halfway done. It was becoming more and more difficult to find a place to strike that was not already compromised with blood. He had been very careful, he knew that he had been, but he could not see well enough at this distance to judge the interval between two strokes—not as well as he would wish. It was different when it was a prisoner; it had been different when St. Clare had been his prisoner, come to that. Then it hadn't mattered if the strokes overlapped each other. Andrej took the driver in his other hand, frowning in his concentration, trying to ignore the sweat that was running down his forehead, into his eyes.

"Thirty-one. Put your back into it, Koscuisko."

St. Clare had begun to collapse against the wall, not standing so much anymore as hanging by his wrists. Andrej could not afford to permit himself to hear that St. Clare cried when he was struck. He had been warned. He would not make St. Clare suffer a single extra stroke. He would not.

"Thirty-two." The snapper, and St. Clare caught his breath too loudly and too sharply for it to be interpreted as labored breathing. But close to finished, close, and the Provost was pleased with his effort; she had not disallowed the previous blow—

"Thirty-three. That's more like it. Don't lose your timing, now."

He was at a loss as to where he might strike next, and eleven yet to get past. He would have to do the best that he could, and never mind the placement now. At least St. Clare, adrift within a greater sea of torment, seemed no longer conscious of the blows as separate shocks.

"Forty."

A little too far toward the shoulder blade; his aim was beginning to fail him. It was difficult to see as well as he would like for the sweat in his eyes. He'd spaced the whip-strokes a little generously when he'd begun, perhaps he could fit another four in between them without the added cruelty of striking over an already-burning welt.

"Forty," Marshall Journis repeated.

Oh, this was terrible, this was the worst of what he had feared. Would she keep him to the bitter test of blood, so close now to the end? He could not protest, Tutor Chonis had warned him. Her count could not be challenged. When he was with Fleet, he would count his own stroke; but here he had no choice but to accept her count as true, and carry on. *Oh, I am trying, Robert,* he protested in his mind. *I am sorry, it is the best I can . . .*

"Forty-one. No, I misspoke myself, that last was forty-one, wasn't it? Forty-two."

He dared not feel any gratitude toward her, in case it was some kind of an obscure joke on her part. He dared not stop to think until the word was given, and the exercise complete.

"Forty-three."

One last time with the snapper, and it lit at Robert's shoulder and took an ugly bite above the other bleeding wounds on Robert's back. Too high, too high, he was not doing well, it would hurt too much—Robert would hurt, and any such hurt could only be too much—

"Four-and-forty. Student Koscuisko, you may stand away, if you wish."

Oh, it was over, it was finished. It was done. Andrej put the back of his hand up to his face with the driver still clutched firmly in his desperate grip, and tried to clear his eyes of salt and sweat. Someone made as if to take the driver from him; he thought he recognized Joslire's familiar warmth, and tried to loose his cramped fist to drop the damned thing, without success.

"Here, wipe your face," the Provost Marshall said, holding out a whitesquare in front of him. "Next time you'll want a towel close at hand. Anyone would think you had been crying."

Andrej reached out stupidly for the whitesquare, and the driver dropped to the floor as he opened his hand to grasp the linen cloth. Would they think that? What difference did it make what anyone thought? Now that he could see, he realized that Tutor Chonis and the Administrator had gone to see St. Clare where he hung chained against the wall. They seemed to be examining Andrej's handiwork, as if there was some further test to be made of him and St. Clare alike, even beyond the punishment that St. Clare had endured. Andrej pulled off his gloves and wiped his face a second time. He could not afford to fail to pay attention—not even though it ate at him to see St. Clare still prisoned on the wall. And he had set St. Clare to hang from the hook in chains during the

Fourth Level, and he had thoroughly enjoyed tormenting him then. Why was this different?

Administrator Clellelan had turned from the wall, coming toward Andrej where he stood with Marshall Journis. What was he going to do with her whitesquare? Andrej wondered, in a sudden panic. She certainly wasn't going to want it back, not soiled as it was. He stood to polite attention and made his best salute, staggering only slightly as he straightened up.

"An . . . impressive . . . demonstration, as I'm sure we all agree." He couldn't tell from the Administrator's tone whether that was supposed to be a good thing or a bad one. He could only stand and wait, mute and desperate, for Chonis to give the word.

"Emphatically. An apt pupil, your Koscuisko," the Provost Marshall replied. "It was his speakserum we were evaluating the other day, wasn't it?"

How could they stand and speak so casually with each other while a man was bound in agony behind their backs? Why wouldn't they just go away, and let him call for medical support?

"His speakserum, his troop," Chonis answered for the Administrator, and Chonis's voice was affectionate and indulgent at once. Andrej blushed, but he wasn't certain why. "I take it that we can call the matter closed, with the Administrator's approval. As long as the Provost Marshall is satisfied."

She nodded. "Well and truly. And I'd go ahead and call a medical team, if it was me. Your troop stood up to that like an honest man. He's earned a few days' rest."

Yes, call a medical team, they had to call a medical team. He had used Robert as brutally as he had just so that they would permit medical support. Nobody had asked him. He could say nothing.

"Very well," the Administrator said. "We'll leave you to finish up here, Student Koscuisko. Now if you'll excuse me, Tutor Chonis, there's other business that requires my attention. Well done, all around."

Andrej kept his position as the Administrator left, the Provost following after. He still had her whitesquare—he'd think about it later. Tucking the crumpled cloth into his overblouse placket, he waited as best he could for word from Tutor Chonis.

"Andrej, that was beautiful." What? The punishment? Or his pathetic attempts to minimize it? "Marshall Journis has cleared you to call for medical support, I think she was impressed. Take a day to recover, and I'll see you after midshift tomorrow."

A day for him to recover, surely. Surely the Tutor did not expect St. Clare to return to duty so soon as that. Marshall Journis had said "a few days." He'd heard her. "But . . . with respect, Tutor Chonis . . ."

The Tutor had turned to go out, and looked a little startled at Andrej's attempt to speak. Good little Students spoke only when spoken to . . . but there was no help for it. Andrej could not afford to let mere protocol stand in the way of painease for St. Clare's suffering.

"Yes, Andrej? There is something?"

"The medical team, please, Tutor Chonis. I do not know if I have the authority."

Understanding met with confusion in the Tutor's face. If Andrej had been any less anxious—he realized—it might have looked funny. "Ah. Well said, I'm not sure, either. Very well." The medical call was there, beside the door Andrej knew where it was, just not whether they would listen to a Student. "Infirmary, this is Tutor Chonis, I want a medical team with a litter to Exercise Theater Second-down-five-over. And a bed for . . ."

Chonis raised his eyebrows at Andrej, and Andrej held up his fingers, not hoping that the Tutor would grant him all that he wished but unwilling to ask for less than he would want. The Tutor frowned, and went back to his communication.

"A bed for four days. The Provost Marshall has authorized full supportive medication at Student Koscuisko's discretion. Chonis, away."

It had been five days before St. Clare had been ready for therapy after the prisoner-surrogate exercise, and he had been more badly hurt, as well as worse injured. It had been fond of him to hope for so much as five days now. Four days was something to be grateful for; and Andrej bowed to his Tutor, wanting him to leave—so that he could go to St. Clare.

"Good night, Andrej."

And Chonis knew it, too, to listen to him. The door slid shut behind the Tutor's back. Andrej shook himself out of his tense formality, hurrying to the wall.

"Haspir, name of the Mother, unfasten these. Lora, Vely, help him down away from there, try not to hurt him, if you can help it."

He shouldn't be making such demands of these Security. Surely it went without saying that they didn't want to hurt St. Clare any more than he wanted St. Clare to be hurt, and it was very good of them not to show any sign of resenting his stupidity in saying such ridiculous things. They knew what they were doing far better than he could hope to. Each with one of Robert's arms around their shoulders, they backed St. Clare carefully away from the wall, and Andrej was horrified to see from the stumbling of St. Clare's feet that he was still conscious. This was terrible. He should not be awake to be suffering this pain. . . .

Here was the litter at the door, and Joslire let it through to the middle of the room so that the Security could maneuver St. Clare into position to lie down on his back in the stasis field. There seemed to be good deal of blood, and white torn flesh; and blood on St. Clare's mouth as well where he had bitten into his lip. The medical team with the litter performed emergency stabilize, charging the support fields, starting a patch for fluid replacement and for pain reduction. Andrej leaned over the head of the litter, blotting the sweat of pain from St. Clare's face with the whitesquare; and St. Clare opened his eyes.

"Is't done, is it?"

His gaze was frank and fearless, even past his pain, without a trace of hatred or resentment. What pain and apprehension Andrej could see there did not seem to be directed at him personally.

"Yes, Robert, it's done, it's all over. We'll go to Infirmary, now."

His eyes were closing again, under the influence—Andrej guessed—of whatever painkillers the medical team had chosen to patch through. Robert blinked them open with a frown of concentration. "Again? Boring. Bad habit to get into. . . . Really finished?"

There was a sudden note of anxiety in St. Clare's voice that filled Andrej with great trouble of spirit. "Yes, I promise you."

"Gi's kiss, then."

What?

"I'm sorry, Robert, I didn't quite catch that. What did you say?"

The medical team had finished their preparations and were standing away from the litter. Waiting for him, obviously.

St. Clare explained himself patiently, and there was a subtle undertone of pleading there as well, now. "When's over Uncle gi's tha'a kiss. Gi's kiss, Uncle, if's over."

Andrej could not bear that St. Clare should plead with him. He stooped to kiss St. Clare's bitten mouth, hastily, eager to provide what measure of psychological comfort he could.

St. Clare sighed, turning his head away with now-closed eyes, and fell silent. Surrendering his consciousness at last, Andrej supposed.

"Let's go."

The orderlies would drive the litter, and he didn't mind following since he didn't know the way. He'd see to St. Clare's new wounds and check the pain medication levels, and then he and Joslire could both go to bed—since Joslire wouldn't go to bed before him.

Was he too tired to beware of his dreams?

What did he care?

Robert's ordeal was over. Robert was safe.

That was all that was important to Andrej.

Andrej knew the spicy scent of the wood in the dark, hot room in his dream, knew the feel of the slatted bench beneath him, worn soft and smooth by the bare buttocks of generations of his family before him. He was at home, in the sauna at the hunting lodge that belonged to his Matredonat estate; so it was probably late winter, when they still set a watch to guard the early young from the wolves that came down from the mountains. If it was late winter, they'd be getting at the last of the apples—he liked them better, even winter-old, than the fresh fruit that hospitality demanded the kitchen set to table at Rogubarachno. The last of the apples, the first bitter greens, and the milk just starting to fatten with the year. . . .

He stretched himself in the heat, the room so dim that he could only just discern the motto carved on the facing wall above the firebox. *Blessed St. Andrej, intercede for us, who have offended* . . . The familiar phrase irritated him. Patron saint of filial piety. But Andrej had offended, and the saint would not intercede for a man who would not repent. What difference did it make? It was only a carving on the wall. It could have nothing to do with him. The Matredonat was his own property. His father would not come here without an invitation, nor his Uncle Radu either.

Andrej heard Joslire at the door and surrendered to the distraction gladly. Joslire's five-knives . . . He beckoned to Joslire to come closer so that he could look at the five-knives. He hadn't taken adequate advantage of the opportunity he'd had earlier, as he remembered. Joslire bowed grave and submissive before him, and Andrej could not see his face; but it was the knives that beguiled him—the knives, and their sheathing. It looked so random and unbalanced to him. There didn't seem to be a single line connecting any of the straps that he could see crisscrossing his Emandisan's bare chest.

Frowning, Andrej rose to his feet to be able to look more closely. Joslire did not stand still, though, not even when Andrej put his hand out to stay him. Joslire knelt down on the slatted bench and bent his neck, his face turned to the floor. Very peculiar. Andrej reached out to touch one of the straps to try to follow how the harness worked, but met no strap at all—only warm flesh. Bruised flesh, hot with insult and with inflammation, swollen and bloody—not straps at all, not harness. The whiplash witness, the weals and welts of a stern beating. Who had done this thing to Joslire? And yet his hand did not recoil in horror. He pressed his fingers hard against the swollen stripe instead, and when Joslire swallowed back a reluctant cry of pain he only pressed again, at the same spot, and harder.

He was the one who had done this shameful thing. He had tormented this defenseless man, and enjoyed it. He was enjoying it now. Perhaps it wasn't Joslire, now that he thought about it. Perhaps it was another, and if it was—if it was another, he had more than simply beaten him, he had more than just enjoyed it . . .

The horror came upon him from behind, catching him unawares and unprepared. No, not Joslire at all, another man. Another man, with wounded hands as shapeless and pulpy as overripe fruit shining white and red even in the dim light of the sauna. An animated corpse, too animated, its spirit crying out to be relieved of torment, trapped within a mutilated frame.

He had to kill it so that it could rest. There was nothing else he could do for the grotesque thing. He had to take it by the throat and strangle it since he had no other means to set it free; but he couldn't bear to touch it. He retreated from the horror instead, unable to stand his ground. It came after him, it followed him, begging him with its terrible hands to kill it as he had done before. There was nowhere for him to go. It was a small room, and the mangled corpse of the murdered drug dealer crawled up to him with garbled incoherent pleas and touched him with its hands—

The light went on in the outer room, and Andrej was awake at once. It was hot because he had been drinking wodac, and wodac heated the blood. He could not move because he had tangled himself too thoroughly in the rackwrap that served under Jurisdiction for bedclothes. And it hadn't been the restless corpse of a murdered man whose unformed and insane sounds had so horrified him, it'd been his own noise, his own cries that had awakened him. Or at least awakened Joslire, and Joslire had awakened him—on purpose, no doubt, since Joslire was quiet and stealthy enough on other occasions.

Andrej sat up, pushing the rackwrap away from him. He needed something to drink, he was thirsty. But he was afraid to go out into the next room for fear he would discover that he'd beaten Joslire after all, as he had whipped his poor Robert St. Clare. True, there was no reason he could think of for having beaten Joslire, but there hadn't really been any reason to beat St. Clare, had there been? Except—of course—that it had been required of him.

And that was no good reason, and less consolation.

Andrej looked at the sleeptimer next to the head of the sleep-rack; hours yet till fastmeal, more hours on top of that before he was to go see Tutor Chonis. He didn't want to rob Curran of rest-time. But he did want something to drink—something without alcohol—and there was only one way to get it in this place.

"I should like some rhyti, if you will, Joslire."

His voice was stronger than he had expected it to be, steady and confident. No trace of a dream there. They would both safely pretend, the two of them, that Joslire had heard him from the other side of the room, that Joslire had not been standing just on the other side of the privacy partition, trying to decide whether he should intervene. Some rhyti, a screen or two of text, and then perhaps he would be able to go back to sleep.

But, oh, he hoped to all Saints and the Holy Mother that he had not beaten Joslire. . . .

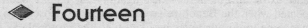 # Fourteen

Tutor Chonis was reviewing the record of his interview with First Secretary Verlaine when the signal came at his office door.

"Student Koscuisko. Respectfully reports, at the Tutor's direction."

Cutting the cube off hastily, Chonis pulled it from the viewer. That had been several days ago. He hadn't wanted to distract Koscuisko with this business going in to the Eighth Level. It had to be discussed with the Student sooner or later, though. If the Administrator was going to ask Koscuisko to finish and leave the Station, Koscuisko deserved to be told why.

"Step through." And Koscuisko was in good time, as well. Koscuisko was punctual, when not distracted by Curran's seductive knives. He didn't look quite rested to Chonis; more dreams, then, as after his Seventh Level? He'd have Curran's report, of course. But perhaps Koscuisko had simply been exhausted, dreams or none.

"I hope the day finds you well, Tutor Chonis," Koscuisko bowed with that gratifyingly sincere politeness that had characterized his behavior since St. Clare had been released to him. Koscuisko had dealt honestly with them, and kept to his bargain with punctilious care—even though he'd had the worse end of it. The least that they could do in return was to deal honestly with Koscuisko, since his value bode fair to overbalance the value Koscuisko had received in the person of Robert St. Clare by so significant a margin.

"Yes, thank you, Andrej. Please be seated. Rhyti?"

An Eighth Level exercise drawn out for two full days, with no evasions either, and no compounding of the Protocols, and extra information—once again—that hadn't been expected when the Bench referred the prisoner. Koscuisko was welcome to do whatever he liked with the Protocols as long as he could keep on pulling information out of the aether in that unnerving manner of his. Any other Inquisitor's prisoner would have been useless and unresponsive by the middle of the second day of an Eighth Level.

Koscuisko sat in his place with his rhyti, waiting in polite silence.

"Student Koscuisko. Andrej. You did very well with your last exercise. The Administrator is very pleased." Standard phrases, and Koscuisko had heard it before and would be wondering why it mattered. "It's important that you know that, because we've got to change your schedule around a bit, and we certainly don't want to give you the idea that it's a result of some deficiency on your part." No deficiency, no. That wasn't the problem at all. "How are you doing in laboratory?"

He could tell it wasn't adding up from the confusion evident in Koscuisko's face. "I had been working on a Ninth Level instrument for Student Noycannir, Tutor Chonis. A generalized wakekeeper, since that seems to me to be her weakest area."

And he had a point, there, but Chonis wasn't interested in talking about Noycannir. Or not about her performance. "We want you to prepare for your Ninth Level exercise, Andrej, and we want you to take it in two days' time, if you feel that you can manage. Waiving your lab work if you need to."

Koscuisko's confusion was clearly only deepening as the conversation progressed. "I . . . can be ready, Tutor Chonis, if that is what you require. But surely the scheduled review itself will absorb two days. What about Noycannir?"

Time to come clean about things, perhaps. "Mentioned you to her Patron, she did. When we reviewed her Intermediate Levels with Secretary Verlaine. Verlaine wants to know why you shouldn't be placed somewhere you can be completely dedicated to Controlled List, maybe a little Inquisition on the side. Noycannir seems to have interested him in your talents in that area.''

Koscuisko's first reaction was amusement, pure and uncomplicated. ''What, posted to the Bench?'' But realization of the implications followed swift and sobering, as Chonis had been confident they would. ''But I would not have Infirmary to run, not within Courts. All the First Secretary can want is that I Inquire for him, or help Noycannir to.''

That was the way Tutor Chonis saw it, and Clellelan as well. ''That would seem to be the idea. To be fair to him, Verlaine hasn't had a chance to talk to you and find out what your preferences might be. Verlaine's asked for Noycannir's tapes, and we think he wants to see how well your drugs work. We rather expect him to preempt you to the Bench in support of Noycannir's Writ.''

That was unquestionably what Noycannir wanted her ''Patron'' to do. Koscuisko was as pale as dread could make him. ''I promised to Fleet, Tutor Chonis, not to the Bench, and for St. Clare. If I had a choice in the matter . . .''

No one had suggested that he had, of course. Other than indirectly, by raising the issue with him in the first place.

''Yes?''

''I would rather go to Fleet. Sir. At least I may practice my other craft on Line.''

Consonant with Ligrose's prejudice, Koscuisko did not want to lose the opportunity that Fleet would provide him to function as a physician. Ligrose wanted him restricted to his healing skills; Verlaine would be interested only in Koscuisko's talent for Inquiry and the Controlled List. For Koscuisko himself, a balance was clearly desirable. If Koscuisko had to Inquire at all, Koscuisko preferred to restrict that practice to a portion of his job, not its entirety.

No matter how good he was getting at it.

''As Fleet support staff, we have an interest in preserving Fleet resources. Competent Ship's Surgeons are getting hard to come by.'' Koscuisko surely was aware of that, but might not have had time to apply the fact to his own situation. ''Administrator Clellelan does not feel that it would be in

Fleet's best interest to surrender you to a direct Bench support role.''

Koscuisko was beginning to understand. "I may go to *Scylla,* as I had expected?"

"We intend that you should."

Relief was evident, on Koscuisko's face. Relief, and concern, harking back to the beginning of this conversation. "What must I do?"

"Take your Ninth Level in two days from now, Andrej. We can have your Tenth Level scheduled for a few days after completion. Transportation will be available to us within ten days, and the sooner we can get you off-Station the happier we are going to be."

Tipping his rhyti glass on its base, staring into the coppery dregs, Koscuisko thought ahead. "Once I am transferred to *Scylla* it becomes more difficult for the Bench to interfere?"

Basically speaking. "We'll take what you have for Noycannir's Ninth Level, and we'll just have to use something else for her Tenth Level. Curran will be instructed, you may cut back in your physical exercise if you need the preparation time." And the recovery time. Not even in the field were Inquisitors expected to take two Advanced Level interrogations inside of a single week and remain capable of returning to duty for a Tenth Level scant days later. For one thing it was hard work, unless one let Security do the labor—and Koscuisko did not seem inclined to pass the labor on to Security. For another, two days spent in close company with another soul in agony tended to take a certain amount of energy out of a person, regardless of any other feelings one might have in the matter. "Do you have any questions?"

It was Koscuisko's dismissal notice, and Koscuisko set the rhyti glass down and pushed himself away from the table to stand up. "I will be sorry to miss exercise," he said—and he did sound wistful, to Tutor Chonis. "I was really beginning to feel as if I could learn throwing knives, with Joslire to teach me."

Not to worry.

"Do what you must, Student Koscuisko. We have two days, to prepare you for your Ninth Level."

The odds were good that he would be able to continue his practice unmolested, once he reached *Scylla.*

But it was Curran's place to tell Koscuisko so, and Tutor Chonis was just as glad to respect Curran's right in that.

Robert St. Clare sat on the examining levels, slumping a bit. Andrej peeled the synthskin away from St. Clare's injured back, knowing from Robert's grunt of pain how tender it still was. Healing was not as quick as Andrej would have liked; the other beating had been too recent.

"What was that you were saying to me the other day?"

He could distract St. Clare, perhaps. Changing the dressing would not take long, and he intended to send Robert back to his bed no matter how he complained of being bored. St. Clare would have excitement to distract him soon enough, after all—perhaps eight days from now, if all went according to Tutor Chonis's schedule.

"Saying to the officer? With the officer's permission— what is the officer talking about?"

Down for a day, dressings changed once, it had been two days now since his scourging. Maybe St. Clare didn't remember. He had been a little incoherent at the time.

"When the Administrator and his party had left, and you had been loaded into the litter, You called me Uncle. You don't look a bit like any of my nespans." For one thing, none of his nieces or his nephews were anything close to St. Clare's height, partly because they were all children.

"Did I say that?" St. Clare sounded a little uncomfortable. Not to mention much more direct than any other of the bond-involuntaries Andrej had had contact with. He hadn't learned to be afraid of frank language yet; either that, or something was wrong with St. Clare's governor, as Joslire had suggested. As long as it didn't get Robert into trouble, Andrej didn't care. It wasn't about to get Robert into trouble with him, after all. "It's your nuncle that's to scold you, if the officer please. Father might strike too hard, when's angry. Mother might not strike as hard as called for, when's fond. Mother's brother it is to take a switch to those as needs it. Sir."

The fresh layer of synthskin was all smoothed down, now.

St. Clare should not be feeling further discomfort. He would
scar where the snapper had bitten into his flesh, but it would
not be too bad. Perhaps he'd have St. Clare into surgery and
excise the scarring, once they were safely away from here.
"And when you've been well and truly spoken to, there's a
kiss to end the quarrel, is that it?"

In properly run Aznir households, it was the instrument of
correction that was kissed rather than the administrator of
discipline. Andrej's father—the Koscuisko prince—hadn't
believed in corporal punishment, though.

St. Clare was blushing; Andrej could see it in his neck,
even from behind. "As the officer states. Permission to ask
the officer exactly how big a fool this troop made of himself.
Sir."

There was no reason to be embarrassed, surely? "As well
as I remember it, Robert, you explained much the same thing
to me. You were not very coherent, at the time. All right,
you may resume your sleep-shirt, I am finished. How do you
feel?"

St. Clare stood up, carefully pulling his sleep-shirt up over
his shoulders as he did so. "A little stiff, if the officer please.
No offense was meant, with the officer's permission."

"Nor was any taken. Rely upon it." Tutor Chonis had
granted four days' bedrest to St. Clare; Andrej meant to make
the most of it. "Go to bed, if you please, St. Clare. Your
orders are to sleep and become healed, and I will see you
next shift, all right?"

"According to the officer's good pleasure." St. Clare
bowed. He looked a bit ridiculous, to Andrej, to be saluting
in his sleep-shirt, but he supposed Robert felt it was required.

It was good, to talk to Robert. Andrej enjoyed his company.

And he was going to miss Joslire Curran.

It was the third part of the third day of Koscuisko's Ninth
Level, and Joslire didn't think his Student was going to gain
the victory this time. He'd fulfilled the Protocols adequately
enough—any Ninth Level that could be successfully continued to the third day would do that, and it was coming up on
Koscuisko's sleepshift. Koscuisko did not seem inclined to

give up on his prisoner, though the man hadn't said anything new for the past day and a half. Clearly Koscuisko felt there was something more to tell. Because when Koscuisko believed that he was finished, Koscuisko ended his exercises cleanly, with a kill.

Lop Hanbor wasn't here for this one; Student Noycannir was not scheduled to start her Ninth Level until tomorrow, as Koscuisko had originally been supposed to. Joslire was alone with the Tutor. It was a perfect opportunity to make his claim—if he could get the Tutor's attention.

Chonis wasn't saying much, watching the screen intently with his fingers templed in front of him. Security was lifting the prisoner up to lay him on his back on the table. A big man, the prisoner; he didn't quite fit on the table. But it wasn't as if the prisoner was going to move. Or at least not enough to cause a problem.

Koscuisko asked for the firepoint, and laid it gently down against the man's upper arm, as if considering. The firepoint was just that, only a fiery coal of torment, and not a heated rod; maybe Koscuisko felt it was as drastic a measure as he could afford to take at this late stage and still maintain his prisoner's consciousness.

"With respect, Tutor Chonis."

Drastic it was, however. Too much pain, after so long, and Koscuisko could lose his prisoner to heart failure, since only the most primitive resuscitation methods were permitted in Orientation exercises. Joslire knew that he might not have much time, especially not now, since they'd moved his Student's Tenth Level so close upon this one.

For a moment he wondered if the Tutor was going to make things difficult for him by pretending not to hear or declining to listen. But no, Chonis had just been distracted.

"Yes, Curran?"

Koscuisko had a light touch with the firepoint, as delicate as the knife-work he'd displayed during his Eighth Level. And Koscuisko's prisoner hadn't had quite so much to say about Koscuisko's antecedents, morality, and proper fate for hours now.

"In regards to Student Koscuisko, Tutor Chonis. St. Clare

hasn't had much experience in handling officers' reactions to their work.''

It wasn't to formula, no, but Chonis would understand. The Tutor sat motionless for a moment, then reached out and turned the sound channel down. So that he wouldn't need to raise his voice to be heard above the screaming, Joslire supposed.

"What is in your mind?"

The Tutor sounded a little wary, but not surprised. Maybe he should have expected Chonis to have guessed.

"There are only three years remaining in my Fleet deferment, Tutor Chonis. Student Koscuisko seems unusually promising an officer."

As an Inquisitor as well, but that was only part of the point. It was difficult to find words that expressed how Joslire felt about seeing Koscuisko's performance in theater. The better Koscuisko got at his torturer's craft, the more difficult it got.

Chonis was not talking. Waiting for him to finish, maybe, letting him have all the time that he needed to get the whole issue out.

"In short, with the Tutor's permission. Mean to ask Student Koscuisko to permit this troop to accompany him during his tour of duty."

Chonis sighed, and stood up. "Now, Curran, let's think about this for a moment. You paid in blood for your deferment, you earned it, no one can take it away from you. Three years is three years."

And in all those years, the odds of turning up another officer like Koscuisko were not worth betting on. At least it hadn't happened within the past five. "Even so, Tutor Chonis." Other Students had been easier to see to. And other Students had almost invariably tested their newly granted authority against him. "Is there an impediment?"

If the Student for whom Joslire had performed as prisoner-surrogate was still on active status, Fleet would not release him from the Orientation Station. That was the real reason behind the grant of Fleet deferment. If the officer who had been Student Abermay encountered Joslire Curran as a bond-involuntary troop, not as a prisoner, it was just possible that

Abermay would recognize him, and the secret would be out.

"Abermay is still on active status." Bad news, then. But Chonis was still talking, and hadn't said no, yet. If Chonis knew that right off, did it mean that Chonis had checked it out already? Was he really that obvious, even if only to the Tutor? "But he's recently asked for reassignment to prison duty from the Lanes. Needs a break from the stress of the Sanfort campaigns."

Joslire could certainly understand how that could be, although prison duty wasn't generally taken for recreation. Abermay was obviously desperate to get away. And if Abermay was on prison duty, he was not on Line anywhere in the Lanes; Joslire could safely be released to Koscuisko. "Then the officer can be approached, with the Tutor's permission."

Chonis nodded, his reluctance evident. "The Administrator will send you to *Scylla* if Koscuisko's willing to take you, Curran. I'm afraid you could have a problem with that part of it, though."

True. He wasn't confident at all that Koscuisko would agree, or that Koscuisko even cared one way or the other. The change in status involved a significant degree of risk, and Koscuisko might object to that; but he'd answer to Koscuisko when the time came. Right now all he had needed was the Tutor's unwilling assurance that the Administration would release him to Koscuisko, if Koscuisko was willing to accept his Bond.

"Heard and understood, Tutor Chonis. Thank you, sir."

There wasn't anything more to be discussed.

Chonis sat back down and pulled the sound levels up again; Joslire held his place, silent and steady, turning the problem over in his mind. He didn't have to ask. He could decide to let Koscuisko go alone. With only untried Security for company? He wasn't committed, not yet, not absolutely, though he had given his knives over. He wouldn't be committed absolutely until he asked Koscuisko; and he wasn't quite sure when that was going to happen. Only that it had to happen soon, because Koscuisko would be going within days.

In the exercise theater things had quieted down to a soft

and understandably self-pitying whimper on the prisoner's part. Koscuisko held the upper part of the prisoner's mutilated body in his arms, stroking the raw weals and the new burns with tender care; completely absorbed in listening to his prisoner's pain by the look of him. But what was Koscuisko saying?

"Come now, my dear. You can't sell weaponry of that sort without munitions to go along. Answer me truly, what kind of a fool would think such a thing?"

Chonis raised the levels up another few eighths. The end of the third day, on an unsupported Ninth Level, no wake-keepers, no drugs—and Koscuisko could still carry on a conversation.

"N-no. Y'rex'lency. It's true."

"Then you do have a source for munitions. You've been protecting someone, haven't you?"

"No, don't ask." Slurred and indistinct as the prisoner's voice was, Joslire could still make out his words. He'd listened to too much of this. He'd gotten good at making out the words.

"You've been protecting someone, I say." Koscuisko's caress grew more cruel, touching on more grievous hurts. "Tell me."

"I won't—"

Koscuisko set the firepoint against the prisoner's chest, pressing it to the livid wounds the whip had made.

"Tell me."

"I can't—"

Koscuisko worked the firepoint delicately, and Joslire could almost feel the agony all over again. The Student Interrogator, and his prisoner-surrogate exercise. But Student Abermay hadn't had a fraction of Koscuisko's instinct, of Koscuisko's art.

"Please don't ask me that. Don't ask me. I can't tell you. I can't."

Koscuisko worked bruise and burn between the thumb and forefinger of his left hand.

"Oh, but I am certain that you can."

There were no words for several long moments. Koscuisko took his pleasure with his prisoner, and Joslire—watching him—could understand if the Tutor were confused about why he would want to go. Tutor Chonis hadn't challenged him on it, though. That had been a mark of respect on Tutor Chonis's part, which Joslire appreciated deeply.

"Please. Please don't ask. They don't know. I lied to them, don't ask."

This was as close to absolute surrender as Joslire had ever seen. There was no indication from the prisoner that he would not answer whatever question it might beguile Koscuisko to raise; only an honest, final plea that Koscuisko would graciously refrain from asking.

Koscuisko declined to refrain from asking.

"Then surely they are in jeopardy, if you lied to them. They will appeal to the local Judiciary for their funds, and be prosecuted for making a fraudulent claim. Tell me who the people are, and the Bench will satisfy itself as to their innocence."

"Torture them until they say what's wanted—what you mean . . ."

Joslire couldn't see what Koscuisko did, but the strained, anguished rail in the prisoner's throat was clear enough. Too clear. "Well, then, they're for it one way or the other, aren't they? And it will go easier with them if you have already confessed to the deception. Tell me."

Whatever it was that Koscuisko was doing, it was finally too much for his prisoner.

"Stop. Stop. Please stop. Please. I'll tell—I'll tell you, tell His Ex'lency, stop—"

Koscuisko passed the firepoint to Cay and took the prisoner's head between his hands with his thumbs at the base of his prisoner's skull, rolling his fingers until he found the place he wanted. "There. Better, yes? Now talk to me."

No drugs, and still Koscuisko could shut a portion of the pain away with pressure upon nerves. Koscuisko was a sorcerer: Joslire had known that from the moment Administrator Clellelan had declared the Record closed on St. Clare's punishment. The prisoner's voice was stronger now, but his dead hopelessness was all the more difficult to ignore, that way.

"Yes, Y'rex'lency. I get munitions; four, there are four manufactures, all small. None local. One in the Gystor prefecture, a collective, Irmol city, Irmanol commune. One in Silam, owned by a family, Fourrail.''

Koscuisko made an adjustment in his grip at the prisoner's neck; and the man continued, swallowing hard between his phrases. ''One near Baram, in a place called Hafel, owned by a woman named Magestir Kees. And one at Getta, in Nannan—''

Silence, as if it had become too difficult for the prisoner to speak. Koscuisko waited for a moment, but took the question up again, relentless.

''There are many manufactures in Getta. Probably several in Nannan. Which did you have in mind? Specifically?''

Koscuisko had loosened his grip from its warding place, and the prisoner turned his head restlessly, as if seeking the comfort of that touch—the relief of pain that it seemed to have provided.

''No, surely there will be enough, how can I give them over . . . to the torture . . . no one should have to suffer, as I have—''

''Come, now, they will.'' Oddly enough—in Joslire's understanding, at least—Koscuisko had settled his hands back in their place, blocking the rise of pain messages to the brain. Maybe Koscuisko wanted to be sure that the man was listening to him, and had the strength to understand. ''You've told me Getta, in Nannan, you must tell me more. Or they will all suffer, every manufactury in Nannan, you know that it is true.''

''It's monstrous, there are six or eight in Nannan, no— not even Jurisdiction butchery—''

''I have not lied to you, not in all of this time. Is it not so?''

Something was driving Koscuisko forward now, something quite different from his lust for torture or the twisted pleasure that he too clearly took from pain and used to further his Inquiry. Koscuisko sounded focused, keenly aware, no longer distracted either by the sounds of his client's torment or the prisoner's submission to his hand.

''Excellency, please, just one of four, just one.''

''It will be six or eight instead of one unless you say the

word. You have given the evidence, and the Bench will be satisfied.''

''The Bench can rot and burn for all I care—''

''Only one of six or eight is even involved, but you have condemned them all, unless you tell me which one. You must tell me which one. We do not have much more time.''

''And once I'm dead I can't be made to tell, so that's just fine.''

''Tell me which one,'' Koscuisko said. And Joslire believed Koscuisko's desperate determination; believed that he understood Koscuisko's change of mood. Koscuisko was telling the absolute truth. Now that the Record showed that a manufactury in Nannan was supplying munitions for the illegal sale of weaponry to Free Government terrorists, the Bench would not be satisfied until every facility in Nannan with capacity for such production had been intensively audited. And that meant Inquiry, which of course assumed Confirmation, which would almost inevitably require Execution.

''No, no, I'll not . . . I'll not—''

''Which one,'' Koscuisko said. ''Or they are all for it.'' Taking his hands away, he let the prisoner's head drop back to rest against the tabletop, deprived of even the small protection Koscuisko had been providing against the pain. Joslire was surprised that Koscuisko risked so much, so late. Certainly it seemed the most that Koscuisko dared, if he wished to get the word he wanted before the prisoner died and condemned who knew how many honest souls by his stubborn silence. ''Which one?''

''My. Mother's people. Excellency. Damn you.''

It was enough.

Koscuisko did not need to know what ''my mother's people'' meant exactly. The local Judiciary would be responsible for that. But it was enough to isolate one manufactury from any other. Koscuisko would know that much.

''It is well done of you,'' Koscuisko said. ''For every soul the Bench will make to suffer, you have saved as many as you could. And for this may all Saints remit your punishment. Tutor Chonis?''

Joslire was humbled, in his heart. He had not believed that Koscuisko would have mastery this time. He should have understood that Koscuisko would have mastery in all things, he told himself. Because it was the temper of Koscuisko's will.

Chonis leaned forward, keyed his communication channel. "As you like, Student Koscuisko," Chonis said.

Koscuisko set his hands at the back of the prisoner's neck again, and the body's tension seemed to ebb away. Then there was a crack as of a sodden stick underfoot in heavy leaf-fall, clearly audible over the sound channel; and the prisoner's head fell to one side in Koscuisko's grasp, fell to one side at the wrong angle. Dead. Koscuisko had taken the man's resistance and his secrets. But then Koscuisko had taken the man's pain, and finally his life.

"You'd best go and collect your Student," Chonis said, switching the monitor off. "Keep me informed about your status. Any changes. And be certain that we'd hate to lose you, Curran, even to Student Koscuisko. All right?"

Joslire bowed in respectful silence and left the room.

Koscuisko would want a shower, a lefrol, wodac, maybe even his thirdmeal.

And he had to study how he was going to ask.

Andrej was too tired to think. It had gone on for so long. He had indulged himself so shamelessly. He went back to his quarters with Joslire and stood naked in the shower with his face between his hands until the stream startled him by cycling off of its on accord. Had he been standing there that long? Giving the control an impatient, unbelieving push, he set the stream for as hot as he could bear it, hoping to lose some of his tension in the wastestream.

It didn't work.

Drying himself in a desultory fashion, he left his wet hair only half-combed and went out again into the main room. There was his supper; there was his wodac; there was Joslire, with his face professionally empty of expression and his uniform as perfect as it ever was. Andrej sat down at the studyset heavily, suppressing an irrational and uncharitable urge to scuff Joslire's boots. There was no sense in being offended at Joslire simply because Joslire was safely collected within himself while Andrej felt frayed at every seam of his being.

There was no sense in grieving for his innocence.

It had been bad enough when he had lost a patient for the first time—an infectious disease case, referred too late for certain intervention. He'd tried the recommended course, and he'd got permission to try an additional intervention; but when neither had stemmed the course of the disease, he had been forced by the absolute logic of Mayon's medical creed to transfer all of his energy to supportive care to ease the dying. He had hated it, hated to give up, hated to be beaten even by one of the most virulent of plagues under Jurisdiction. And he could not argue about it. He was expected to concentrate on his patient, and ignore the outraged protests of his ego. He had to bend his neck and submit himself to the service of mortality, and ensure that the passage he so fiercely wished to bar would be accomplished smoothly, with as little fear or pain as possible.

His proctor had sent a priest to see him a few days after that. One of his brother Mikhel's priests, not Uncle Radu's, Andrej had been grateful to note. Unfortunately the message could not have been more offensive had it come from Andrej's supercilious uncle in person; he was not to feel depressed, the priest had counseled him, because it was not his fault that the patient had died. He was not responsible.

And that had made him angry, as well as depressed, because a Koscuisko prince's life was defined by responsibility. To suggest that he was not responsible—simply because he had not been at fault—was a profound violation of Andrej's basic sense of self-definition.

After he'd thrown the priest out into the street, however, he'd begun to understand what the man had actually been saying. He couldn't practice medicine at its highest level without accepting the fact that disease was no respecter of Dolgorukij autocrats. He had to separate his absolute responsibility for his Household from the more limited responsibility of a professional physician. The rules were different. He had thought that he had understood that fact; but after his first patient death, he had found himself evaluating his understanding all over again.

Now he was a murderer three times over, and he had no more tolerance within himself to entertain the polite fiction

that he was not responsible. Yes, he was only one of many
Students, to be one of many Inquisitors. True, that the prisoners accused at the Advanced Levels were as good as dead
from the moment Charges were Recorded against them—
because even if they declined to confess, the implementation
of the Protocols would kill them. There was no question that
had he not killed whomever it was—no, Verteric Spaling, it
was a man he had murdered, not an anonymous abstraction—
had he not murdered the man Spaling, someone else would
have, or someone else would have left him to die of worse
wounds than Andrej had given him.

None of the rationalizations proper to the practice of medicine could be applied appropriately to murder.

He was Koscuisko, and he was responsible for the work
of his hand, the more so because he had enjoyed it. Or much
of it.

Joslire wanted to take his now-cold food away to be replaced with a hot meal, but Andrej waved him off. He wasn't
very hungry, and the food had little savor in his mouth. He
made a point of drinking the tepid rhyti in his flask; he had
been working hard all day. Or he had been exercising himself
all day, if it was not proper to try to call it "work" when
one derived such obscene satisfaction from it. He needed
fluid, one way or the other, especially if he was to end up
drinking yet again. There was his wodac, right enough, still
cold in its icer tray, sitting promisingly next to the glass with
its saucer and its bit of sharbite-peel as if it really thought it
was an aperitif and not an end in and of itself.

He was too tired to drink wodac. How long had he been
sitting here, brooding about the sin that stained his honor?
How could he grieve for his innocence, when the Fleet and
the Church and his father all three refused to acknowledge
that it was a sin against the Holy Mother's Creation to put
a soul that could suffer to such torture for any purpose?

Emptying the rhyti flask of its last swallows, Andrej stood
up and turned toward his bed.

He was so tired.

If only sleep could bring him rest, this time . . .

He could not close his eyes, because the stubborn habit of
his weary mind was to review what he had done, and each

time he closed his eyes, he saw his work once more—and shrank from it. He lay on the sleep-rack, trying to let go of his conflict, promising himself accommodation after accommodation to try to soothe his guilt-wracked spirit to sleep.

He would buy prayers for their souls.

None of them were Aznir, and why should their gods listen to his coin, when the Holy Mother herself almost never listened to anyone who was not Dolgorukij?

He would find their families, lie to them about their next of kin and about the manner of their dying.

Their families were probably either dead or compromised, or had sold the victims of his lust to Jurisdiction in order to save themselves.

Whatever it was that he was doing—Andrej told himself finally, with disgust—resting was not it. There was little sense in wasting energy struggling with himself. He needed all the energy he had to keep him through the ordeal of this place.

"Very well." He said it aloud to himself, pushing himself up off the sleep-rack with an effort. He was not too tired to drink after all, as he had thought. He would go out to his supper and try again.

The wodac would not have gotten very far, surely?

"There, if the officer would consent to rest for a moment, it'll get better now, just rest. Shallow breaths, if the officer please. . . . Yes, that's right . . ."

Andrej Koscuisko lay sprawled ungracefully across the washroom floor. Joslire supported Koscuisko's shoulders against his knees as best he could while struggling to keep Koscuisko's head from falling too heavily against the basin set in the cold gray tiling. The lights in the washroom were harsh and unforgiving, and Joslire couldn't help but think Koscuisko was as ashen as a corpse—considering what Joslire could see of Koscuisko's face, clay-colored, beaded with sweat, his forehead an anxious agonized cording of care, his eyes shut tight against the brutal glare. Koscuisko was sick to his stomach with the drink, and Joslire was only surprised it hadn't happened any sooner in light of all the drinking that Koscuisko had done throughout the Term.

Koscuisko tried to move, evidently wishing to push himself up into a more normal seated position. Koscuisko didn't have the strength for it, and Joslire caught him around the chest from behind to stop him from falling over backward. "Just breathe, if the officer please, don't try to get up just yet. Just rest, yes. Like that, that's good."

It did seem that the drink was minded to be revenged upon Koscuisko; for now—having gotten sick to his stomach with the drink finally—Koscuisko was not only sick, but unstrung, shaken to the floor with the violence of the action of the poison, wrung too weak to so much as keep himself levered adequately over the basin. *A thorough man, Koscuisko*, Joslire told himself, putting the damp hair out of Koscuisko's eyes absentmindedly. When he studied his lessons, he studied the references as well as the text. When he was to administer discipline, he spent his spare hours practicing the whip and studying the physiology of Nurail so that he could do the thing to his best satisfaction. And when he poisoned himself with alcohol, he did so with characteristic care and concentration, if the violence with which he vomited the wodac could be taken as any indication.

Dozing again, now, Koscuisko was a dead weight in Joslire's arms. Joslire didn't want to wake him, not at any cost—no matter how awkward it was to be half-lying on the washroom floor, embracing his drunken charge. Drunken was not the word any longer, Joslire decided, shifting one arm forward carefully to make a pillow of sorts between Koscuisko's head and the basin. Koscuisko had been drunk hours ago. What Koscuisko was now was a perfect paradigmatic picture for a cautionary tale about people who put their faith in wodac to redeem them.

Koscuisko woke with a spasm of retching, sudden and fierce. They didn't need the basin any longer, not really— there wasn't anything left in Koscuisko's belly to vomit up. Still, Koscuisko clung to the basin's rim with a trembling hand as he struggled for breath against the convulsions that wracked him; as if, in the middle of his exhaustion and his pain, the thing that really worried him was the danger that he might disgrace himself by heaving onto the floor.

"You're fine, you're fine. Your Excellency. No, just lie

still, try to think. Is there something I can get for you?''

It didn't matter what he actually said to the officer, at this point. He could probably call him Andrej and ask him for a loan of Jurisdiction specie, and Koscuisko would remember none of it in the morning, and the Administration wouldn't care. Although if Koscuisko were capable of thinking for long enough to tell him, he could go and request whatever antispasmodics or painkillers might ease the suffering of a bad case of ethanol toxicity in Azmir Dolgorukij.

Koscuisko was out again, asleep, limp and defenseless and utterly trusting—or too tired to care. He couldn't really leave Koscuisko, not just yet. A man as sick as Koscuisko was could lapse into hypothermia lying on a cool tiled floor, without the protection of Joslire's body heat. And there was no sense in even beginning to gamble that there wasn't enough fluid, enough matter, enough anything left in Koscuisko's stomach to choke him if he turned wrong in his sleep—without somebody there to ensure the airway remained clear. A man could choke on his own blood as easily as on wodac, and if Koscuisko wasn't bleeding yet, he would be soon unless the dry heaves eased up more quickly than Joslire judged they would. He could be wrong, of course, he knew that well enough. Koscuisko could sit up and rub his face and demand his fastmeal, for instance. There was no telling with Dolgorukij.

He just couldn't afford to take that risk.

He settled himself as best he could to wait the liquor out.

Usually—Ligrose knew—only she and the Tutors attended the Administrator's morning report; there was no need for the Provost's attendance. What was going on? Clellelan looked grim. And only Chonis was here of all ten Tutors on Station, this time.

"Doctor Chaymalt." Not only that, but Clellelan was being formal with her. "This concerns your favorite Student, or at least your favorite this Term. Come in, sit down, close the door. There's a problem."

Koscuisko, was it? His man St. Clare had spent some more time in Infirmary lately, she'd noticed that. She'd made it her business to find out why; she'd even gone so far as to review the tapes of Koscuisko's Eighth Level, and what had happened after. She should have known better than to look at Koscuisko's tapes. His control and his precision were just as impressive when he was beating his Security as she had found them when he'd been performing surgery; and she'd already decided that she didn't want to get involved.

"What's the problem, Rorin?" The Provost Marshall was nearest to the Administrator in rank. She was correspondingly most informal with him in private. "I hadn't expected an executive consult."

Oh, was that what they were doing? This wasn't adding up. Executive consults were called to evaluate dismissing a Student to civilian status because they were incompetent, or because they simply could not implement the Protocols. It happened rarely, not because the quality of the candidates was so high but because Fleet was so desperate for the bodies.

What could any of that have to do with Koscuisko?

"We've heard from the Bench offices at Pikanime," Clellelan replied indirectly. Pikanime was the nearest nexus-point between Fleet Orientation Station Medical and civilized space; less than three days, Standard, there and back. The comment seemed to mean something specific to Chonis, but she was still in the dark. She shrugged, and ventured to ask the obvious.

"Anything in particular, Administrator?"

He nodded grimly in response. "Let me provide a little background, here. Student Koscuisko is supporting our efforts to graduate First Secretary Verlaine's creature. We— Adifer and I—had made the decision to let her take it on drug-assist; Koscuisko's been supplying the drugs."

Well, of course; she knew that. But Journis might not have.

"Now, some days ago, Adifer had an uplink with Verlaine, with Noycannir present. She seems to have interested Verlaine in Koscuisko. And he's a little too interested, for my peace of mind."

This she hadn't known. "Seems logical," she commented. "If he's good enough. We don't have many who are good at all." Particularly not good at more than one thing at a time, medicine, Inquiry, Fleet discipline. She was in a position to know exactly what the driver usually did in the hands of lesser Students. Koscuisko's achievement was all the more impressive, accordingly.

"If it's any good, the Bench will annex it," the Provost said with a snort of disgust. "You not going to void him out of Orientation just to spite Verlaine, though."

Clellelan shook his head. "No, but it gets more complicated. During the uplink, Verlaine asked for Noycannir's tapes—so that he could evaluate Koscuisko's potential, we suspect. It isn't too difficult to separate Noycannir's performance from the effectiveness of Koscuisko's drugs, if you know what you're looking for. But it could take up to nine days for tapes to reach Chilleau Judiciary from here. Now we've received a formal request from Pikanime. If they're relaying to Verlaine, we don't have nine days to work around."

"So Verlaine has some Clerks review the tapes, uplink to him, give him a good report. Verlaine issues a Bench warrant through Pikanime. Koscuisko is frozen on-site." Journis sounded thoughtful, putting it all together. "Anyone talked to Koscuisko about this? Adifer?"

As if a Student had anything to say about the disposition of his Writ. On the other hand they were talking about Andrej Koscuisko, which meant that Combine politics complicated things even more than his own respectable potential.

Chonis was nodding. "The Administrator and I had decided to accelerate the program, try to get him out and off-Station before Verlaine had a chance to look at those tapes. I talked to Student Koscuisko, and suggested that his Writ might—potentially—be annexed to the Bench."

She'd wanted to see him taken off the Line for pure medical practice. She didn't see how releasing him to Verlaine would do any good, either for him or for any of the patients in need of his abilities. "What did he say?"

Shaking his head, now, Chonis sounded a little amused. At the First Secretary's implied discomfiture, perhaps. "He said that if he had a choice, he preferred Fleet. For some reason he didn't seem to feel that he would have much opportunity to practice the medical skills he values, if he were to be assigned to the Bench at Chilleau Judiciary."

Indeed not. Journis put the question that was still only half-formulated in Ligrose's mind to Clellelan directly.

"What are you going to do, then?"

"Well." Clellelan made a palms-up gesture as if appealing to reason. "If we're going to protect him from Verlaine, we've got to get him off-Station as soon as possible. We can't afford to wait for Verlaine to get a report on Noycannir's tapes, and the tapes go out on the next run. Forty-eight hours from now."

Ligrose was beginning to get the idea. "You can't be serious." It had never been done in all her years at this Station—but then she'd told herself that more than once this Term, and each time with specific reference to Student Koscuisko.

"I don't see why not." Journis was looking a little out of the loop, so Clellelan made it explicit for her sake. "We have the option to grant the Writ without it, as long as we are sure he can perform. And Koscuisko can perform. He's consistently pushed the Levels on each exercise—and not the Protocols, either. Is there any doubt that Student Koscuisko is capable of executing a better Tenth Level Command Termination than anyone on Station?"

Journis made a face of amused realization, apparently understanding at last. Clellelan spoke on.

"Waive the Tenth Level exercise on the strength of his Advanced, and he can leave with those damned tapes. He'll be halfway to Hollifess before Verlaine knows he's gone."

And therefore Clellelan had called for executive consultation, so that they could graduate Koscuisko without the usually required final test and send him out to his ship of assignment before the Bench could lay hands on the boy. Because without explicit evaluation from all of them, the Tenth Level could not be waived: but Clellelan was absolutely right, in perhaps the single most important respect: There was no doubt that Koscuisko could perform.

The only question was whether he could continue to do so without destroying himself in the process. There had to be conflict within a man capable of such sensible and sadistic cruelty as his Levels recorded, when the same man was capable as well of the surgery that had saved Idarec, the empathic compassion that had seen St. Clare healed of his various hurts so well and quickly, the precision and control with which he'd scourged a man bloody with so little actual harm done.

"Let it be done," Marshall Journis said. "Just tell me what you want from me, to support the Record."

Nor would she object, Ligrose decided. The odds were not in favor of Koscuisko's functional survival on Line, in the Lanes. But his chances had to be better on board ship than under First Secretary Verlaine. His concern for his man St. Clare in itself would almost have decided her; Koscuisko would not be permitted to take any bond-involuntaries with him if he went to the Bench, since they belonged to Fleet. And his bond-involuntaries seemed to be important to Koscuisko.

There was only one problem left to resolve in her mind. "What does the inside man say, Adifer?"

Koscuisko's assigned Security had a vital part to play in the Administration's formal decision to pass or fail. Curran was closer to Koscuisko than anyone else, and had the best vantage point from which to judge strengths and weaknesses. If Curran thought Koscuisko would be better off with Verlaine . . .

"Curran wants to go to *Scylla* with him," Chonis said. Journis grinned and didn't look surprised; nor did Clellelan seem completely shocked. Perhaps she should have expected it. People who could be bothered to engage themselves about the welfare of bond-involuntaries on a human level were rarely met with. She supposed that it was only natural for Curran to want to keep Koscuisko once he'd found him.

"Well, you'll get no argument from me." Arguing was never worth the energy. It would take less time and trouble to document the waiver than to argue. And she didn't think she minded being asked to document the waiver.

"Adifer, you'd better let your Student know," Clellelan suggested. "He'll have to finish up whatever he can in a hurry, if he's to be ready to leave in a day and a half. Provost Marshall. Do we have his Command briefing? We'll have to send it with him, he can review it in transit."

Journis rose to her feet briskly. "On my way, Rorin. Adifer, I'll have the material ready for you soonest."

They would send Koscuisko off to *Scylla* on a freight run. He'd need to be met at Pikanime by a Fleet escort, but the Administrator could easily arrange that over secure channels. Noycannir would be starting her Tenth Level exercise at about the time Koscuisko would be leaving Pikanime. By the time the First Secretary made his move—if he was going to make the move at all—the only things left of Koscuisko on Station would be his tapes, and Idarec.

She liked it.

"I'll have the documents you need to you by midshift, Administrator. No time like the present to be started."

It would even be fun to tweak the Bench a bit.

In a small way she'd be getting her own back on the Bench for sending her here in the first place.

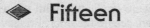 **Fifteen**

"Thank you, Curran," Tutor Chonis said from his place at
the desk inside the office. "You may stand in on this. Step
through, the pair of you."

It had been two days, Standard, since he'd spoken to Tutor
Chonis, and Joslire hadn't found a suitable opportunity to
talk to Koscuisko. Koscuisko had come off the exercise too
tired to drink, and had gone straight to bed; had been unable
to sleep for dreaming, and had started to drink. Had fallen
asleep or had passed out, which Joslire supposed was a species of sleep—if one without any of the restorative nature of
normal sleep—but had been unable to rest, for the emetic
effects of alcohol poisoning.

"Student Koscuisko respectfully reports, at Tutor Chonis's
direction."

After an hour or three spent together on the washroom
floor while Koscuisko retched his bile out, Koscuisko slept;
but not because he was tired, because he was utterly exhausted. Then after a while Koscuisko woke up and made
an effort to review his Tenth Level material—but came down
with the dry heaves again. Had slept, and wept, and slept,
and dreamed again, and when finally at last Koscuisko had
gotten a good start on some decent rest, Tutor Chonis had
called for their immediate attendance.

"Yes, Student Koscuisko, sit down."

Joslire hadn't found time during any of it to tell Koscuisko
that he wanted to go with him. He wanted to be sure Koscuisko understood that it was his choice, even a selfish

347

choice, to request the reassignment. The last thing he wanted was for Koscuisko to imagine that he was making the offer just to comfort him, for pity's sake.

"This will be quick, but not because it's any less important than it would be if you were graduating with the rest of our Students this Term. Curran, secure the door. Privacy barrier in effect."

He suspected he knew what Chonis had in mind. He thought he recognized the Orders documents on Chonis's desk, even if Koscuisko would not. Had he missed his chance already? Joslire set the secrecy level on the sound dampers inside the room. The interview would be Recorded, like so much else that happened at Fleet Orientation Station Medical, but the Tutor must have wanted to be very sure that no one outside could eavesdrop. Someone like Student Noycannir?

Chonis waited for Joslire's bow, in token of having completed the task. "Now then. Student Koscuisko. The Administrator believes it to be important that you leave the Station within a day's time. Secretary Verlaine is possibly more interested in you than we had imagined, and we do not wish to risk losing you."

Joslire listened with dread. He wasn't going to get his chance, not unless he could find it within a day. He couldn't possibly get Koscuisko to agree with only a day to work in. His knives would leave the Station without him. Not his knives any more; they were Koscuisko's knives, and they felt different to him when he carried them for safekeeping between sessions. It comforted him to be near them, although he was a slave and they were free. He had to let them go away from him. He'd lost his chance.

"With respect, Tutor Chonis . . ." Koscuisko sounded confused, as well he might. "There is a Tenth Level exercise yet to accomplish, and three days minimum—"

Chonis held up his hand for silence. "The Administrator has decided that in this instance the final exercise is to be waived. Your previous exercises are accepted as sufficient proof of competency. You will, of course, continue to work on the Controlled List, once you are safely to *Scylla*."

The Ninth Level had gone three days. Joslire was certain

that it could easily have stretched to four, had Koscuisko intended that from the beginning. There was some sense in that. And Chonis wasn't finished; he didn't pause long enough to let Koscuisko get a word in, had Koscuisko been eager to respond. Which he wasn't, by the look of him; he looked too startled to have anything to say.

"These Orders do not in themselves comprise your Writ, Student Koscuisko. Your Writ is granted by the Administrator as Bench proxy and forwarded to Fleet Judiciary by special transmission. Secured transmission, I hardly need point out." Transmission that no one could intercept, in other words. The Administrator certainly seemed intent on taking no chances.

"There are two copies here. One you will present to Captain Irshah Parmin upon your arrival on board *Scylla.* One is for your personal archive. You are required to take these Orders into your hand, Student Koscuisko, to signify your acceptance of commission; and once you have taken these Orders in your hand, not even the Bench can deny your Writ. Nor can you set your Writ aside before the expiration of your Term without explicit authority from the Jurisdiction Bench over the First Judge's attested seal. The Record requires that you state your understanding of these requirements and restrictions prior to your taking your Writ into your hand."

Koscuisko stood up now, pale but apparently resolute. "I am obliged to the Jurisdiction's Bench by my sworn oath and in consideration of multiple benefits received," Koscuisko recited firmly. "Therefore I claim this as my Writ, and I will execute the same at the Fleet's discretion until such time as the Bench may consider my duty to have been amply and honorably discharged."

A formula, like so many other formulae provided for Fleet's use in binding sentient souls into servitude. Koscuisko spoke it well for all of that, clear and correct, with no hint in his voice or in his manner of the horrors that came to him in his sleep.

"It is prudent and proper that you should do so, just and judicious that the Bench grant privilege along with responsibility. No Charges less than mutiny shall be Recorded against you while you hold the Writ. Take up your Orders, Your Excellency.''

It was always a shock to hear the Tutors use the formal rank-title with their Students at the end of Term. But Koscuisko took up his rank and his Writ together when he took his Orders into his hand. And therefore, consequently, Koscuisko ranked over everyone on Station now, with the exception of the Administrator's Staff and his assigned Tutor. If only technically so, at this point.

Koscuisko took the Orders from the Tutor's desk and tilted them against the light from overhead, examining them curiously. There was nothing to see. Orders were not eye-readable. Koscuisko wouldn't need to know exactly what they said to know exactly what they meant to him.

"Leaving tomorrow, Tutor Chonis? So soon; it seems precipitous."

"Perhaps a little awkward for you, but you'll have an escort team to ensure that your passage to *Scylla* is a smooth one. Come and embrace me, Andrej, let me say good-bye to you now."

Joslire stepped forward to take Koscuisko's Orders now that the formalities were done. Koscuisko was not his Student any longer, and would never be his officer, unless he could find the time in one short day to ask. Tutor Chonis caught his eye for a brief moment of evaluation; Joslire hoped that his despair was not as obvious to Koscuisko as the Tutor seemed to find it.

"I will not see you again, Tutor Chonis?"

"I'll see you off in the morning. But there will be more people there." Chonis put his arms around Koscuisko, and Joslire had never seen him so apparently reluctant to let a Student go. "You've been an interesting problem, Andrej. And you have great potential, in more than one way. Remember your duty, and be a credit to Fleet."

Unusual as it was, it seemed to Joslire that Chonis had become actually fond of Koscuisko. Who stepped back a pace and bowed, simply and respectfully.

"Thank you, Tutor Chonis. You have dealt honestly with me, and I am grateful to you for it. And for your help as well."

Student Koscuisko was not fond of Tutor Chonis, no. But he was not so mean-spirited as to deny him respect or reject his sense of obligation, on such petty grounds.

Chonis nodded, apparently content. "Go and get packed, 'Your Excellency.' You're to go to exit briefings; they should be on your scheduler by this time. Curran, you and St. Clare will get . . ."

But Chonis couldn't say "your officer" because Koscuisko was St. Clare's officer, not his. ". . . His Excellency to embarkation area five-up four-in, midshift tomorrow. The transport will be final loading at nine and sixteen."

Nine and sixteen was nearly a full thirty-two eights from now, one full day. There was hope left. He'd thought that he would have more time, but if he could only find the opportunity he might still be able to win Koscuisko's consent.

He bowed in the face of Chonis's understanding gaze and followed Koscuisko out of the office, back to quarters.

Andrej sat at his studyset, staring at his scheduler, trying to come to terms with the speed with which things were happening. Surely it hadn't been two days since he'd murdered his prisoner, his third prisoner, his third murder. Two days, his Tenth Level to begin in two more, and now this—brusquely summoned to Tutor Chonis's office, given his personal copies of the documents attesting to his Writ, and told to pack. To have Joslire and St. Clare pack for him, at least.

His brain was still too full of sleep and alcohol. He could make little sense of it; but here he sat, at the studyset in his quarters, and Joslire and St. Clare were in fact packing. Most of his uniforms weren't even coming; there was only his personal linen, his boots, and the few uniforms that were common to both Student and Chief Medical Officer. New travel dress, in token of his new status. Exercise uniforms. The knife-harness for the throwing knives, and the knives themselves sheathed and packed as well. What was the use of sending the knives with him, if he was not to have Joslire to instruct?

Joslire and St. Clare were busy at the closet with the blouses of his travel dress, setting and checking the Section markers and the ship's identification he was now authorized to wear. St. Clare was in new uniform already, darker than Andrej had seen on Station; the bright green piping at St. Clare's sleeves was all the more difficult to ignore set against dull gray. The ship's identification was the same, but St. Clare wore no other rank than his slavery. Andrej supposed that it lent a certain amount of uniformity to one's escort if they were all marked alike. He would wear no rank, either, come to that. The color of his uniform signaling his status, the piping on the sleeves sufficient to identify him as a Medical officer. Black was the color of age and ease on Azanry. He was too young to be wearing the raven's wing, it was unnatural.

He couldn't afford to lose himself in meditations on the color of his uniform. The rest of the day would be too full for that. Exit briefing with Doctor Ligrose Chaymalt within the hour. Exit briefing with Provost Marshall Journis somewhat later, and he was a little uneasy about that one, but he did have to clear the Station. She would have material for his review—his itinerary and his Command briefings. He would need to go over the travel plans before he went to bed if he was to know what to expect in the morning. There would not be time to take exercise with Joslire. If he meant to speak to Joslire, he had better get it done and over with before they had to leave for, Chaymalt's office.

"St. Clare, would you excuse us for a moment." There was no reason to discuss it in front of Robert, whether or not his quarters were under surveillance. From the very first Joslire had made it clear that he preferred to be humiliated in private. Andrej meant to do what could be done to set the pain at its least personal level.

The door closed behind St. Clare's silent exit. Rising from the studyset, Andrej took himself over to where Joslire stood waiting—and confused—beside the open and near-empty closet where his uniforms had been.

"The Tutor has delivered my Orders and my Writ, Joslire, but he did not demand your Bond. What are we to do?"

According to the briefings they had been required to study, the Bonds held by Students were to be surrendered to the Administrator at the same time that Orders were accepted and the Writ taken up. He hadn't given it a thought, earlier

today in Tutor Chonis's office; things had been happening
too quickly. But obviously he needed to return the Bond
before he left the Station. Going by the manner in which
Joslire had chosen to deliver it to him in the first place, Joslire would surely prefer he surrender it in the relative privacy
of quarters.

Joslire looked paled to yellow—and pained, almost angry.
To be reminded? Andrej felt at his neck for the chain to pull
the pendant out from beneath his blouse; and Joslire startled
him by seizing his hand at the wrist as suddenly and fiercely
as if it had been a weapon that Andrej had been reaching
for.

"Permission to speak to the officer," Joslire said. For all
the world as if Joslire hadn't been up all night holding Andrej's head while he'd vomited up the overdose of wodac he
had taken. As if there'd never been any contact heart-to-heart
between them.

"Joslire, please—what is it?" Joslire loosed his grip at
Andrej's wrist the moment Andrej spoke, as if Andrej's wrist
had suddenly burned his hand. "Tell me, directly, I request
of you." There wasn't much hope of that, though, not really.
Joslire didn't trust him enough to speak to him directly. Nor
could Andrej hold that against Joslire in fairness; he was only
a departing Student now to Joslire, with a new one coming
in as soon as he had left.

"Tutor Chonis did not require His Excellency to surrender
my Bond. Because Tutor Chonis knows . . ." Joslire seemed
under an unusual amount of stress, even for him. He ran out
of words abruptly, screwing his narrow slanted eyes into thin
black slits of concentration in his dark Emandisan face.
". . . knows that I meant to ask the officer. His Excellency.
To retain my Bond. But have been unable to find a good
time . . . in which to do so."

Andrej reached slowly out to take Joslire by the shoulder,
in wonder. Joslire's shoulder was as hard as stalloy under
Andrej's hand. What could Joslire be talking about that created so much anxiety?

"I'm afraid I find myself in the dark, Joslire. I am leaving,
I can't keep your Bond. Unless you were to come with me,

and that would mean . . . Don't you have some years of
safety left? Here on this Station?''

"Hadn't made up my mind for certain.'' It was almost a
gasp, from Joslire. "Until the officer's Ninth Level. Just
could not be sure. And now it's too late to make you understand. Sir.''

Whether he understood or not, it was clear enough to Andrej that Joslire was in torment. "Come, Joslire, stand down
a bit. Explain. You worry me.'' He'd caused Joslire torment
more than once during the Term, in his ignorance and clum-
siness. And nothing he had tried to do to provide comfort
had ever seemed to have its intended effect, either; but he
had to keep on trying. "What is this thing that it is too late
for me to comprehend?''

Joslire dropped his head, rolling his underlip against his
upper teeth. "My Bond belongs to Fleet. But. If the officer
please. I may request assignment. To the officer.''

Wait, there had been something, a few lines of text
merely—glossed over with the briefest of mentions, and it
had seemed so unlikely to him at the time that he had taken
no notice.

"That is to say, with the officer's permission. Active Line
duty assignment to Student Koscuisko. To go with His Excellency,'' Joslire concluded. And fell silent.

Shaking his head in horrified denial now, Andrej backed
away from Joslire where he stood. "This is some test they
put you to, Joslire, you cannot mean to come with me to
Scylla.'' And an evil test, to make a man ask to be even
more cruelly bound than he had been already, to force Joslire
to pretend to want to go. After what Joslire had seen of him.
His exercises. His excesses.

But the accusation seemed to strike at Joslire's pride as if
it had been a slap across his face. "Indeed it is not, and I
do. His Excellency is respectfully requested to consider my
petition as made in earnest. There are so few decisions about
my life that I am still permitted to make.''

Joslire's reproach shamed Andrej to his heart; but he could
not accept the idea, even so. Surely the last thing anyone
would want—after watching him, throughout his training—
would be to seek a dedicated assignment.

"You have been good to me, Joslire, and I have had great comfort from you. If I were to let you come with me, it would be selfishness, your deferment—"

"If the officer is serious let the officer prove it; let His Excellency respect my request and honor it. We are slaves, except in this one thing. His Excellency should not seek to deny me what piece of freedom even Fleet permits."

He had asked Joslire to speak directly, and this was blunt speech indeed. Almost, almost Andrej could believe that Joslire meant precisely what he said. Was he tempted to believe Joslire because Joslire was serious—or because he welcomed the prospect of Joslire's support in the trying days to come? "But I could be other than you may think me to be. And if I held your Bond, you could not appeal if I were to abuse you. You cannot be sure of what you do. No, I won't let you."

Joslire seemed to have lost his fear and cleared his mind of conflict. He stood rock-solid on his feet and looked up at Andrej from the bottom of the very pit of hopelessness.

"The first Student to whom I was assigned did not desire to punish my unsatisfactory performance above four times in Term. The Tutor was unable to obtain Student Exception, it was my first such assignment and I was ignorant. Discipline the second time was three-and-thirty. The Student signed my return-to-duty documents on the following day, and was praised by Tutor Mannes for being conservative with expensive medication."

There was no petition in Joslire's voice now, only cold recitation, merciless and inexorable.

"The second Student liked to use the driver. His Excellency has examined his handiwork. The third Student took very little notice of my existence and her sexual requirements were not in themselves difficult to fulfill to her satisfaction, so that was not a bad Term all in all. But the fourth Student to whom I was assigned demanded more particular attention to specific personal needs, and found his gratification much enhanced if he was free to inflict pain while he enjoyed pleasure. The most recent Student, prior to His Excellency—"

"No, Joslire, please, be still."

"—preferred to discipline in ways not specifically referenced among the techniques of Inquiry and Confirmation, which methods therefore lay outside of the range of adjudication or exception. The Tutor encouraged his experimentation, and he was held back for the Remedial Levels, so there was adequate time for him to explore areas that interested him."

Andrej could not listen; he could hardly breathe. He turned away from Joslire, overcome. Oh, he deserved to have such things said to him. It was discipline for his selfishness, just and judicious retribution for the wrong he had done Joslire by challenging his request. It was proper punishment, and it tore at his stomach sharp and keenly.

"None of them would have cared about St. Clare. None of them would have practiced with the driver to protect him rather than torture him. None of them cared to minimize the number of souls at risk as a result of confessions. If His Excellency remains unconvinced, I stand ready to supply as many additional details as would amuse His Excellency to entertain."

There was no arguing with such cogent proofs. Joslire already knew the full horror of being trapped without recourse, at the mercy of a brutal officer and a system no less brutal. Andrej knew he had no further right to question or deny him. He had wanted to reject Joslire's request, because Joslire had years yet of deferment that he could spend safely here on Station. Joslire had disillusioned him of that. Joslire was not safe.

"No, no more, Joslire, I will not deny you. It is what you want, that I should hold your Bond?"

He couldn't face Joslire, not just yet. It was not good for a man's pride to see how deeply he was pitied.

"For as long as Fleet and His Excellency permit. Yes. Permission to accompany His Excellency on dedicated duty assignment."

Andrej took a deep breath, trying to clear his mind of the objections that he still wanted to raise—of the doubts he was in honor bound to swallow. Joslire had made his claim. "It shall be so, then. Come with me to *Scylla*, Joslire. I will take you to me, and I will hold you to me while I can."

He would submit and be humbled before Joslire. It was

the least that he could do in the face of Joslire's courage.

"Thank you, Your Excellency."

Joslire sounded grateful to him, in Joslire's subdued style—his usually subdued style, that was to say. As if it was Joslire who was to receive benefit, Andrej who was making the sacrifice.

"If you are to be my man, and I your master . . ."

Joslire meant to make contract with him, and accompany him on dedicated duty assignment. Such an honor could not be accepted lightly. Turning back to the studyset, Andrej sat down and motioned Joslire to come stand in front of him. He didn't even care anymore about the monitors. Fleet protocols were all very well and good, but this could not be said to be between a new officer and a Security troop merely. This contract could only be made man to man.

"Thou must come to thy knees, Joslire, and cut thy mouth. Give me to drink, of thee."

Confused and apprehensive, trusting all the same, Joslire sank to his knees gracefully in front of Andrej where he sat. "His Excellency requires?"

"Thy mouth, Joslire. At the inside." He had been too young to manage; his father had helped him to draw blood. He was the prince inheritor, and his father had marked him publicly as of his blood and substance by incorporating Andrej's life into his own. His younger brothers and his sisters had never gone through such a ceremony; when Andrej inherited, they would all make their submission to him in the traditional manner, and through him to the Blood of ages.

Joslire had pulled his backsheath knife, but looked a little puzzled yet. Laying his hand over Joslire's hand, Andrej guided the sharp point of the blade to cut against Joslire's cheek from the inside. The mouth bled easily and freely, and healed most quickly. It was better, done so, than the older ways.

He let Joslire take away the knife, and set his left hand against the back of Joslire's strong stout neck. He'd never thought to make contract in the old fashion, or at least not until his father died—let alone with a man who was no kind of Dolgorukij. But he knew what had to be done.

"Give me to drink of thee," he repeated—reassuringly,

he hoped. He put his mouth to Joslire's mouth, and closed his eyes, and waited.

After a moment Joslire made submission, opening his mouth and surrendering himself to Andrej's greedy—if symbolic—thirst. The taste of Joslire's blood was different from his own, but that was the whole point. The Holy Mother understood of blood. And once Joslire had given of his blood—once he had given up his substance for Andrej's nourishment—the Holy Mother would look upon him as blood and bone of her own children.

That was the way it had been explained to Andrej, at any rate.

•   Long moments, and the blood ceased to flow from the shallow cut in Joslire's cheek. Andrej lifted his head and leaned back, his mind reeling with the unexpected emotional impact of the ritual act. "There, it is done." Joslire was quiet and calm, with him, but Joslire had only been Aznir for a few short moments now. It was not to be expected that he would understand it all at once. "Now it is bonded, and cannot be broken. Thou art to me, Joslire, and may our Lady's Grace be satisfied."

Be of Koscuisko, forever.

But he did not say it.

There was a limit to how much arcane Aznir superstition he could reasonably expect Joslire to tolerate at any given time. And they would not let him take Joslire with him when he left Fleet.

"According to His Excellency's good pleasure."

As pleases my master, most pleases myself. It seemed so close, it sent a shiver down Andrej's spine. Surely the Holy Mother had set her seal upon the contract. If he had been a religious man—as Andrej did not feel himself to be—he would be forced to take Joslire's choice of response as nothing less than a patent sign from the Canopy itself, instead of simply being something that Joslire said from time to time that only happened to echo ancient fealty formulae of the Blood.

"Go and let St. Clare back in, if you would, Joslire. You need to see the Tutor, I expect. And I'm expected in Doctor Chaymalt's office."

It was easier in a way to be grateful to a Mother that he only half-believed in than to contemplate by how slim a margin he had gained what he had won from the Administration. The life of Robert St. Clare, although he had traded his honor for the boon. This unexpected grant of companionship from Joslire, so that he might yet find a way to return good for the good Joslire had done him—and continue to learn how to throw those lovely, lovely knives, as well.

It would give him something to think about on his way to *Scylla*. The better to avoid thinking about his apprehensions, facing his first assignment on the Line.

"Even so, Your Excellency. St. Clare can take His Excellency there. He knows the way."

His first assignment had just gotten significantly easier to face.

◆ Sixteen

There had been a flurry of some sort, St. Clare was almost certain of it. Not that anyone was saying anything to him about it, but what could Curran have in mind to go racing off on his own like that? A flurry, or his name wasn't Robert St. Clare.

Wait a moment, he admonished himself.

His name *wasn't* Robert St. Clare.

All right, perhaps his name was not exactly St. Clare, but he would be expected to answer to it for twenty-six years, so what was the functional difference?

The officer had appointments with the Medical Officer, and the Provost Marshall after. Fortunately he had had plenty of time to study the physical mapping of the place.

"To the officer's right. And again, at the next turning, if the officer please." He'd be glad to get to *Scylla,* even so, where he would necessarily be junior man on whichever Security Five-point team he ended up on. It would be up to the senior man in Koscuisko's escort to walk behind the officer and direct him at the same time. All he'd have to do, then, was to pay attention and follow instructions. That couldn't be said to be a hard life, now, could it?

"Past the lift-nexus, to the officer's right once more." He expected he could even get used to Koscuisko in time. Up in the high windy, people who looked like Koscuisko—short and pale, pale hair, pale eyes—were suspect; it wasn't honest herding blood, at all, it was farmers who had been sea-raiders beforetime. A long time before, but memory ran long in the high windy, because there was nothing to do for entertainment but sit and tell stories, and argue about the weaves. Koscuisko could be a throwback to the sea-raiders, from his face, but what weave would a man wear who was for Inquisition?

There was a troop waiting for them at the receiving area, someone Robert thought he recognized: Omie Idarec, from the same group he'd come in with, but wearing Station Security. That was right, there'd been gossip. He wondered if Koscuisko knew who Omie was.

"If His Excellency would follow me?"

There was no sign on Omie's face, so Robert guessed not. The subject made for interesting speculation, as he trotted along after Idarec on Koscuisko's heels. If Koscuisko had only ever seen Omie as an anonymous body in surgery or as a set of statistics in the medical reports on Line, there was no reason to imagine that Koscuisko had more than a general idea of what he actually looked like. He could ask Omie, of course, once the officer went through to see Chaymalt. But he was still learning the hand-language. There was probably a limit to how much he was going to be able to find out.

Here was the place; no guard posted, but this was a training facility, not like *Scylla* would be. Omie signaled smartly at the door, pivoting into a perfect attention-rest just beyond the threshold as Koscuisko came up to announce himself. Robert tried to match the smoothness of his counterpart's move, taking his place at the near side of the door. Well, not bad.

But plenty of room for improvement.

"Student Koscuisko to see Doctor Chaymalt, as Tutor Chonis has instructed."

The door slid open; Koscuisko stepped through, and then he and Omie were alone in the corridor together. Only the two of them, which made conversation rather more difficult, because there was no mirror man to reflect the messages, and greater care was required not to break the discipline of attention-rest. They'd practiced together, though; that was a plus.

St. Clare glanced quickly down and over, to find Omie's hand; the thumb was already canted at a subtle angle, *wanna talk.* He couldn't distinguish statement from question at this point, though he knew it could be done, since they'd both seen more experienced bond-involuntaries demonstrate.

He knows you?

There was a pacing issue to keep in mind; if a word was held too long, it wasted precious time; but if it wasn't held long enough, there was a risk of losing the word. They were expected to be looking straight ahead, after all. Generally speaking.

No. Don't think so. Leaving?

This time the question was fairly obvious, so Robert answered more directly. *At nine and sixteen. Scylla. Nice ship-mark, I like it.*

Omie made an amused knuckle, coupled with a finger twitch denoting a superior admonitory tone. *Not alone, though. Joslire Curran.*

Spelling out the name made interpretation more difficult, since St. Clare had to sound it in his mind before he realized who it was that Omie meant. He knew how to spell his new name in Standard script, but he was still getting used to reading it; and for a moment he thought he'd misunderstood.

What, my uncle's man? Dark broody sort, muscles all over?

Koscuisko's man, yes, Curran. Just now. Almost sure of it.

Well, that would be interesting. Had that been why he'd been invited to leave, then? Curran, to be coming with them; and Curran had been on Station for years, now, but not eight years, which implied that Curran had given up the balance of his deferment to go with them. That was startling, but it was comforting, too. If a man of Curran's experience had decided that Koscuisko was a man to take on dedicated duty assignment, St. Clare could consider himself lucky by implication. He hadn't been offered the choice. But maybe he'd gotten a good one anyway—even if the man did have better hands and worse ones. At least he knew which pair he preferred Koscuisko to wear.

That'll be nice. Company. You?

No response; St. Clare wondered if he'd gotten it right. There was only the fraction of a cuticle's difference between "you" and an improbable form of recreation. After a moment, though, he could see the answer taking shape, and realized that Omie had only been trying to figure out how best to phrase himself, within the limited vocabulary the two of them had in common.

Held over. Popular demand. Try again, next Term.

Try again? Face the prisoner-surrogate exercise all over again, next Term? He didn't like the sound of that.

Choice?

Maybe he shouldn't ask so personal a question. He put a fingernail's worth of apology behind the question mark. Omie didn't seem to have taken offense.

Beats work. Just think, I'll be ahead of the next bunch. Extra months of deferment, too.

True, Omie would be ahead of the rest of the prisoner-surrogates, he'd already gone through the test. Or started the test, at any rate. He hadn't answered the question, one way or the other; St. Clare decided that was an answer of its own.

The Day will come.

He didn't expect Koscuisko's interview to be a long one; there was no telling when they'd be interrupted. It was best to signal close of conversation now, in good time, rather than leave the exchange unfinished. It was bad luck to leave things unfinished, when there was no way to guess whether he would ever see Omie again.

The Day, after tomorrow.

Omie was apparently content to let it rest there, having passed on his news. Curran was coming? Well, that was good. He thought.

He quieted his mind, and stood in wait for his officer.

Andrej bowed to the Provost Marshall politely. "Student Koscuisko presents himself for the Marshall's Command briefing, at Tutor Chonis's instruction." Unlike Doctor Chaymalt, the Marshall had called St. Clare in with him. To guard against an appearance that his fish might misinterpret, so that it need not fall prey to the impertinence that was the common burden of all fish? He didn't know.

"Thank you, 'Your Excellency.' Watch out for 'Student

Koscuisko,' from now on. You'll report to Parmin as 'Chief Medical Officer,' remember.''

So he would. Marshall Journis had risen from her desk as he saluted, and invited him to be seated with a gesture of her hand. She had not put St. Clare at his ease; was it expected of him, that he should? But he had not yet left the Station; she was still a step up from him on his chain of command. Therefore if she hadn't put St. Clare at his ease, it was because she felt that he should stand at attention, for reasons of her own.

"Yes, Marshall Journis. With your permission, I understand you have information about *Scylla* for me?''

She came around to the front of the desk to take the other chair, facing him. She had a stack of cubes in her hand and dropped them one at a time on the edge of the desk nearest him, counting them off as she went.

"Tactical history of the Jurisdiction Fleet Ship *Scylla,* from shipyard to current mission status. Fleet biographies on the Captain, the Primes, and other assigned Command Branch officers. Latest readiness assessment on Medical, and files on the assigned staff.'' She paused for a moment, tapping her fingers against the third cube. "I've taken the liberty of including the Bench-specific issues—historical performance of Ship's Inquisition both on *Scylla* and under Irshah Parmin, incidents per eight, required Levels. Things like that. If you're interested.''

So that he'd have a better idea of what to expect, or what would be expected of him. Significant information indeed; but she continued her itemization, without waiting to give him a chance to make an appropriate remark.

"Finally, because of the peculiar nature of your Security, the files on the troops assigned to the Security Five-point teams, and the Chief Warrant Officer who is responsible to the First Officer for them. Chief Warrant Caleigh Samons, that is, at present. You'll find her very professional, but I'd advise you to let her know up front that you don't want people interfering with your greensleeves.''

If Samons was a Chief Warrant Officer, she couldn't possibly be a bond-involuntary. What was the Provost getting at? "I am not sure I understand your point, Marshall Journis."

"You've got delicate sensibilities where bond-involuntaries are concerned. She needs to know if you're going to take it personally every time someone's up for two-and-twenty. Or just have her strip St. Clare down, and tell her it was four-and-forty, with a driver. She's intelligent. She'll get the point. By the way, do you mind if I have a look? I didn't get the chance to admire your work close up before."

It was still a little confusing, but Andrej was beginning to think he grasped her meaning. He was to be sure that Samons knew he did not feel six-and-sixty should be handed out with a liberal hand; and St. Clare—whose back, newly healed, still showed by evident if fading bruises that he had been beaten recently—was to serve as a demonstration model of his personal reluctance to mutilate his assigned Security. Andrej expected that he could probably communicate as much adequately well to his new Chief Warrant in plain language, now that he comprehended the problem. Why did Journis want to "admire" his work, though? To see how St. Clare had mended? To critique his handling of the whip? What?

"With respect, Marshall Journis. I would prefer not. He is a man, not an ornament." Reluctant as Andrej was to deny the Marshall—especially after having received benefit from her, professionally and personally—he could not see taking St. Clare's clothes off to gratify her curiosity. There were limits. And he had to set them; because St. Clare was not permitted to.

She looked a little surprised, to have him talk back to her. He was surprised at himself, come to that. Fortunately she did not seem to be offended.

"Very well. As you like." He was leaving here; it probably didn't matter one way or the other, if he had offended her. But gratuitous insult was almost always a bad investment. And she had counted the stroke when Robert had been beaten, and she had not made him repeat a single blow.

"Be advised, then, that discipline for bond-involuntaries is usually liberally assessed and applied. It's only fair that you let her know first thing that you don't want to see any general-purpose assessments. She'll take it from there. You might want to talk to your First Officer about it, as well, and tell him I sent you when you see him."

If that was what it took to hold the hand of Fleet discipline back from meaningless punishment, then he would gladly do as much, and more.

"Thank you, Marshall Journis. Will that be all?"

He thought that he had sensed his dismissal in her last phrase. But apparently he had been mistaken; or, rather, his timing had been off. He was not to be dismissed quite so immediately.

"No, one more thing, Andrej. An important one. You know St. Clare, here. You know Curran." And she knew that Curran was coming with him, why should he be surprised? "Do what you can to let the others know that they count, too. It means a lot to anybody. More to these, because they have so little else."

A warning against jealousy, perhaps? What had he ever done to St. Clare that anyone would envy St. Clare for it? What had he ever done to Joslire Curran, other than to make his life miserable?

"A man deserves the respect due any sentient creature, Marshall Journis." On the other hand he hadn't beaten Joslire, or tormented his body, or required sexual services of him. Maybe for bond-involuntaries that was enough. "Thank you for the reminder. I will keep your advice carefully in my mind."

It was a good point, an important point.

But he had been raised to keep peace in his Household.

He was confident that he knew what to do.

"Then take your briefings, and back to quarters with you. Exercise. Sauna. Wherever." This was unequivocal; the interview was over. Andrej took the four-stack in his hand and stood up.

"Thank you again, Marshall Journis. Your remarks are very much appreciated." Except the one about wanting to have a look at Robert, perhaps. There didn't seem to be any sense in quibbling over that, however, especially since she'd not slapped him down for his rather acerbic rejection of what had apparently seemed to her to be an entirely reasonable request.

"That's as may be, and you're welcome. Good day, 'Student' Koscuisko."

She'd risen to her feet in a parting gesture. Andrej tried to make his salute as polite and respectful as he knew how.

There was nothing left to do but mark time until tomorrow.

The knowledge made him anxious to be away, and on with things.

Andrej sat at one of the windows of the passenger compartment, watching Fleet Orientation Station Medical shrink slowly against an expanding background of black featureless space. Better for him had he never come here, better for him had he never known . . . he could have lived his life out in blessed ignorance, and been happy. But it was too late for that now. Even if he never made a single Inquiry within the next eight years, he would still know. He was a monster; and he had always been a monster. The passion to which St. Clare had introduced him was not an alien thing, but a part of him, as surely as was his passion to comfort and to heal.

And since it was part of him, he would not deny its existence. He would not repudiate the beast, as dreadful as it was. He would have to live with himself forever, whether he went home tomorrow or never went home until his father declared the year of his Retirement.

He thought he'd known what he was to face, when he came here. He had been wrong. And it had been far worse than he had imagined. How could he have guessed the horrors that St. Clare and Curran were expected to bear uncomplaining, as part of their duty? The worst part of it was that they accepted it, they all accepted it, and looked at him with confusion when he protested. Joslire, who expected to be abused. Chonis, who expected him to discard St. Clare like so much soiled toweling. Tutor Chonis had praised him for engaging in his training exercises on such a personal level. It was true that it made things much easier during the exercise itself to be able to enjoy it, and so keenly. But it was still wrong to take pleasure from the pain of helpless prisoners. Intrinsically wrong, absolutely wrong, no matter what crimes they might have committed.

And still there had been benefit for him from Orientation. Because they had permitted him to sell himself for St. Clare's life, so he did not have that blood-guilt on his hands. There had been ways to approach his Inquiry that provided opportunities, scant though they were, to affirm the dignity of the dying and protect the innocent. He had not compromised the safety of the unaccused for his pleasure, at least not yet. That was a hopeful thing.

But more important, most important, there was Curran, with his private torment and his guarded self. Brutally misused body and soul by the system that had enslaved him, Curran had still reached out to him to give him comfort in his pain, without holding the sins of the previous officers against him. Joslire had been charitable and generous with him even while Joslire fully expected Andrej to use him as the others had. It had been an act of significant courage on Joslire's part, the gesture of a great heart to offer what could not be demanded of him, freely, when it could have cost so dear.

And St. Clare did not seem to hate, not even when Andrej stood before him with the whip that was to bring him agony.

If such as these could hold fast to their human dignity beneath the crushing weight of inhuman discipline—then so could he.

If St. Clare could take the beating from his hand and fire back so mild a bolt as "yon undertall beauty," then perhaps he could deal as mildly with himself, and try not to despise himself beyond all hope because he was a monster.

If Joslire Curran could find courage to demand a piece of his self-determination back, then perhaps he could find the courage to perform his assigned task. Because as dreadful as he found it, as obscene as he felt his pleasure in it to be, still what he was called upon to do could not be weighed on the same scale as Curran's task had been, nor St. Clare's, either.

He would be guided by their approach to their lives, as he was humbled by their courage.

With Joslire and St. Clare to help him through, Andrej knew that he could survive, no matter what awaited him on *Scylla.*

◆ Epilogue

Mergau Noycannir paused for a moment before signaling for admittance to Tutor Chonis's office. Almost there. Almost. The Ninth Level—distasteful as that had been—was behind her; only the Tenth Level remained, and with Koscuisko's drugs she had no fear of failing in the final test. It was time she went back to her Patron. The contemptuous scorn of the Security troops assisting her exercises was becoming impossible to ignore, if impossible to prosecute. And she had found it expedient to decline the offered increase in her personal training sessions from two on one to three on one, because she realized that the Administration would not intervene should three become too many for her to handle. It didn't matter. One more exercise and she would be clear of all of these—clear, and free to return triumphant to Chilleau Judiciary, to secure herself in Verlaine's favor, once and for all, with the Writ to Inquire.

Signaling at the Tutor's door, Mergau went in.

Tutor Chonis was alone; she'd not seen Student Koscuisko for days—not since her Seventh Level, Mergau realized with a start. He'd not been present for her Ninth Level orientation, when Tutor Chonis had explained the action of the drug. There had been questions in her mind during her Ninth Level; the prisoner's behavior had not seemed entirely consistent with the action of the drug as Tutor Chonis had described it. She had intended to bring the anomalies to Student Koscuisko's attention, as a reminder of her now-dominant role in their relationship. She did not mean to be cheated of her treat.

"I greet me my Tutor, and hope that the morning finds him well. Student Koscuisko, is he not to meet with us, Tutor Chonis?"

So close to the end, so close to finished, she did not need to be as careful as she otherwise might have been. She didn't have much time left in which to submit herself meek and humble to the Administration. Only one more exercise and she could safely leave the entire Station and everyone on it, discarded as worse than useless. One more exercise.

"Student Koscuisko will not be joining us, Mergau. Be seated."

Tutor Chonis barely looked up at her when she came in, apparently concentrating on sorting a set of cubes that lay before him on his desk. The beverage service that had been an invariable feature of the classroom table was different than it had been; only one glass had been set out. Pulling the serving-set closer to her, Mergau poured herself a cup: rhyti. It was close to a slap in the face to serve her rhyti, if only she was expected.

"I hope that all is well with my fellow Student? I am anxious for his sake."

She didn't expect the blatant lie to fool Tutor Chonis, although the situation could be honestly interpreted in such a way as to hint at a problem. A suicide, for example. Chonis would be more distracted in his behavior had Koscuisko tried to escape in that way, though. There would be political repercussions, complications, a scandal, if the oldest son of the Koscuisko prince had killed himself after his family had entrusted him to Fleet.

"And I'm certain that Student Koscuisko cherishes the same fondness for you. Now. First Secretary Verlaine has asked us to send copies of your Intermediate Levels to him through the Administrative center at Pikanime. Administrator Clellelan has released your records on the freight run that went out yesterday, and he released the complete record, so Secretary Verlaine will have a chance to evaluate your Advanced Levels as well."

That was a strange thing to have done, wasn't it? They

both knew that Verlaine had asked for the record so that he could judge Koscuisko's potential for himself, if indirectly. Koscuisko's talent would only be more obvious in her Advanced Levels than they were at the Intermediate. "I am unsure about the drug Student Koscuisko selected for the Ninth Level. I had wished to make a private question of it, Tutor Chonis."

Tutor Chonis almost smiled. "No doubt, Student Noycannir, no doubt. But the best drugs in the world won't help unless you pay enough attention to working with, and not against, them. Let us consider your Tenth Level exercise. The final test is crucial to your graduation, as you know."

This was getting frustrating. "I hope to profit from instruction, if I may speak to Student Koscuisko in this matter . . ."

Meeting her eyes squarely, blunt and candid, Tutor Chonis declined to take the bait; offering her instead a sop of teasing information clearly intended to be deliberately provoking. "That will not be possible, Mergau. I suggest you concentrate your energies on your Tenth Level. You must pay more attention to what you're doing, if you mean to graduate at the end of this Term."

Why would it "not be possible" for her to talk to Koscuisko? All Chonis had to do was issue the summons, and Koscuisko would of necessity come promptly, no matter what he might have been doing. Such a pretense on Tutor Chonis's part made no sense.

Nor did the Administration's willingness to release her Advanced Levels to Verlaine, unless . . .

"The drug was not correct for my last exercise, Tutor Chonis. You told my Patron that I would receive support."

Verlaine had asked for her records so that he could judge Koscuisko's worth and decide whether to preempt Fleet's posting to take Koscuisko for his own. The Administration had sent the records Verlaine had requested, those and more. Tutor Chonis knew very well what she had been trying to get Verlaine to do—Mergau was certain of that. The conclusion was easy to derive but impossible to credit.

"This Administration has done everything in its lawful power to accommodate First Secretary Verlaine, Mergau. But nothing will do the job for you if you cannot remember the most basic restrictions of the Levels. Rehearse for me if you will the requirements for satisfaction of the Tenth Level exercise, Command Termination.''

If they had sent the records directly to Chilleau Judiciary, she would be graduated and gone before Verlaine would have the time to prepare a requisition override for Koscuisko's posting. Tutor Chonis had said Pikanime, though. That meant that Verlaine had asked for more immediate access. A requisition override could be prepared and delivered to Fleet within a matter of days from Pikanime. Tutor Chonis had also said that it would ''not be possible'' for her to speak to Student Koscuisko. Therefore and necessarily, Tutor Chonis had released her records to Verlaine because he felt that Koscuisko was secure from any intervention from Pikanime Judiciary; and Koscuisko would only be secure from such last-minute revisions to his orders if his orders had already been issued.

''Mergau? I'm waiting. If you would be so kind.''

They had sent Koscuisko away to Fleet, so that the Bench could not have him. It was an outrage, so blatant an insult that it took her breath away. It was also a mistake, because her Patron knew how to deal with intriguers of this sort.

''The Tenth Level of the Question, Tutor Chonis, Inquiry, Confirmation, and Execution. Command Termination. The required elements include the cumulative execution of the Fourth through Ninth Levels, over a period of not less than three and ideally lasting five days.''

Would they defy the Bench and deny Verlaine access to their prize Student?

Would they indeed?

She would be out of here in less than three weeks' time; she would bring the Writ to the First Secretary. She would bring words and knowledge to him as well.

Let Koscuisko hide in Fleet, and pinch his nose in mockery toward Chilleau Judiciary.

Her Patron would know well enough how to repay Andrej Koscuisko for this insult.

AVONOVA PRESENTS
AWARD-WINNING NOVELS
FROM MASTERS OF SCIENCE FICTION

BEGGARS IN SPAIN
by Nancy Kress   71877-4/ $5.99 US/ $7.99 Can

FLYING TO VALHALLA
by Charles Pellegrino   71881-2/ $4.99 US/ $5.99 Can

ETERNAL LIGHT
by Paul J. McAuley   76623-X/ $4.99 US/ $5.99 Can

DAUGHTER OF ELYSIUM
by Joan Slonczewski   77027-X/ $5.99 US/ $6.99 Can

THE HACKER AND THE ANTS
by Rudy Rucker   71844-8/ $4.99 US/ $6.99 Can

GENETIC SOLDIER
by George Turner   72189-9/ $5.50 US/ $7.50 Can

SMOKE AND MIRRORS
by Jane Lindskold   78290-1/ $5.50 US/ $7.50 Can

THE TRIAD WORLDS
by F. M. Busby   78468-8/ $5.99 US/ $7.99 Can